M000073475

SENSE AND SENSIBILITY

JANE AUSTEN

SENSE AND SENSIBILITY

With an Introduction and
Contemporary Criticism

Edited by ELEANOR BOURG NICHOLSON

Series Editor JOSEPH PEARCE

IGNATIUS PRESS   SAN FRANCISCO

Cover art:
Portrait of Anne and Maria Russell
by John Russell
1804 (coloured chalks and pastel)
© Yale Center for British Art, Paul Mellon Fund, USA/Bridgeman Images

Cover design by John Herreid

© 2014 by Ignatius Press, San Francisco
ISBN 978-1-58617-838-3
Library of Congress Control Number 2014936823
Printed in India ⊗

Tradition is the extension of Democracy through time; it is the proxy of the dead and the enfranchisement of the unborn.

Tradition may be defined as the extension of the franchise. Tradition means giving votes to the most obscure of all classes, our ancestors. It is the democracy of the dead. Tradition refuses to submit to the small and arrogant oligarchy of those who merely happen to be walking about. All democrats object to men being disqualified by the accident of birth; tradition objects to their being disqualified by the accident of death. Democracy tells us not to neglect a good man's opinion, even if he is our groom; tradition asks us not to neglect a good man's opinion, even if he is our father. I, at any rate, cannot separate the two ideas of democracy and tradition.

— G. K. Chesterton

Ignatius Critical Editions—Tradition-Oriented Criticism for a new generation

CONTENTS

INTRODUCTION

"A genteel, well-written novel is as agreeable a lounge as a genteel comedy, from which both amusement and instruction may be derived."[1] Such are the words with which the author of an unsigned review introduces a contemporary assessment of Jane Austen's first published novel, *Sense and Sensibility* (1811). This "fair praise" may well sound scant to a twenty-first-century reader. The reviewer adds: "The story may be thought trifling by the readers of novels, who are insatiable after *something new*."[2] The defense is not likely to console the discontented modern: we are told that the "excellent lesson" and "useful moral" outweigh the fact that there is nothing distinctly original to be found in Miss Austen's execution.[3]

Of course, this desire for newness is not merely an early nineteenth-century handicap. Innovation is often prized over skill; novelty can superficially appeal without really bringing satisfaction. From the vantage point of our current historical moment, the problem is evident in television and movie adaptations of Miss Austen's novels. They are frequently "modernized", which almost always translates to an oversexed debasement of the novel so that, short of character names and basic plot points, the novel is no longer identifiable with its source, and, severed from that source, makes little actual sense. Made "new", the novels become a pale ghost of themselves, if not an out-and-out caricature.

[1] Unsigned review, in *Critical Review*, 4th series, vol. 1, no. 2 (February 1812), as quoted in Jane Austen, *Sense and Sensibility*, ed. Claudia L. Johnson, Norton Critical Editions (New York: W. W. Norton & Company, 2001), p. 313.
[2] Ibid., p. 314.
[3] Ibid.

Even setting all of this aside, the fact remains that, even among devout readers of Miss Austen's oeuvre, few will step forward and note *Sense and Sensibility* as a personal favorite. While young ladies swoon at the thought of *Pride and Prejudice*'s Mr. Darcy or *Persuasion*'s Captain Wentworth, and while arch wits relate personally to *Emma*'s heroine, and devotees of the Gothic novel appreciate the brilliance of *Northanger Abbey*, *Sense and Sensibility* is sometimes forgotten. The novel does not even appear to inspire the same frenzied "controversy" that has hampered modern appreciation of *Mansfield Park*. How then are we to see this first successful foray into publication? Do we only read it out of literary critical or biographical curiosity?

The answer to the latter question is, of course, resoundingly in the negative. *Sense and Sensibility*, like all of the novels of Jane Austen, must be valued in particular on three points: first, as a display of the author's singular mastery of the English language, shown in the clarity and sophistication of her syntax, and its relative accessibility even to a less patient modern reader (who might well balk at the heavier, though similarly exquisite prose of some Victorian novelists);[4] second, for her colorful and realistic characters, which shine with the author's appreciation of what it is to be human; and third (relating closely to the second), as a vessel of her wise understanding of that toward which all human life must tend. To encounter any of the books of Jane Austen is to meet with the comprehensive mind of a deeply convicted Christian. Further, *Sense and Sensibility* can claim a special power in challenging, and making new, the expectations of those "readers of novels". This will be clearly shown as we consider first the author and then her first published work.

---

[4] It is appropriate here to undercut the negative assertion, levied by some critics, that because Miss Austen edited her work (and followed editorial suggestions from her publisher), her usage of the language is less than masterful. All such critics should be set to diagram every sentence of one of her novels, and if the exercise does not develop a greater respect for her work, it should at least improve the grammar and sentence structure of the unwilling student.

Biography[5]

Jane Austen was the seventh of the eight children of the Anglican clergyman Rev. William George Austen (1731–1805) and his wife, Cassandra (1739–1827). She had six brothers: James (1765–1819), a clergyman; George (1766–1838), born deaf, dumb, and subject to severe epileptic fits (he lived with a surrogate family and has occasionally been forgotten in lists of the Austen children); Edward (1767–1852), adopted by his fourth cousin, Mr. Thomas Knight, of Godmersham Park in Kent and Chawton House in Hampshire (Edward eventually inherited the estate, in recognition of which he took the surname of Knight); Henry Thomas (1771–1850), first a banker, and then a clergyman; and, finally, Francis William (Frank) (1774–1865) and Charles John (1779–1852), both sailors and later admirals in the Royal Navy. She had one sister, her dearest friend, two years older than herself and, like herself, unmarried: Elizabeth Cassandra (1773–1845).

A similar tone to that adopted by the unknown reviewer of *Sense and Sensibility* might be discerned in the comment of Austen's brother Henry: "A life of usefulness, literature, and religion was not by any means a life of event."[6] Born on

[5] Primary information concerning Jane Austen's life is notoriously sparse, drawn only from several brief sources: the 1869 *Memoir of Jane Austen*, written by her nephew James Edward Austen-Leigh (the edition here referenced is James Edward Austen-Leigh, *A Memoir of Jane Austen*, ed. R. W. Chapman [1926; repr., Oxford: Oxford University Press, 1967]); the biographical note by her brother Henry attached to the posthumously published novels *Northanger Abbey* and *Persuasion*; a collection of letters, not extensive since many of them were destroyed by Cassandra and by subsequent members of the family (Cassandra's careful elimination of letters was recorded by their niece Caroline Austen, daughter of James Austen); a portrait sketched by Cassandra; and reminiscences by Caroline Mary Craven Austen (daughter of Jane Austen's eldest brother, James, and younger sister of James Edward Austen-Leigh), whose recollections were quoted extensively in her brother's 1869 *Memoir* and in the 1913 *Life and Letters* and presented nearly in full in Mary Augusta Austen-Leigh's 1920 *Personal Aspects of Jane Austen*.

[6] Henry Thomas Austen, "Biographical Notice of the Author", in *Northanger Abbey and Persuasion*, by Jane Austen (London: John Murray, 1817), p. 3. This bibliographic note is included in R. W. Chapman's Oxford edition of *Mansfield Park* (Oxford: Oxford University Press, 1923 and subsequent reprints), pp. 3–9.

December 16, 1775, Jane Austen lived the early part of her life in Steventon, in the county of Hampshire, where her father served as rector. With her sister, Cassandra, Jane was at school briefly in Oxford and Southampton. This period away from home was trying for the girls, particularly when they were both afflicted by typhus—Jane nearly fatally. From 1786, when the girls returned home from boarding school, Austen's education was supervised at home by her father and brothers.

Her life throughout early and mature adulthood was, as Henry notes, largely uneventful, suited to the life of a small country community. Though lacking both family and finances to make them socially important, as the daughters of a clergyman, the girls were nevertheless elevated to take part in the life of the upper middle class of the district. They were closely acquainted to the other end of the social spectrum, of course, and would assist their father in serving the poorest of his flock. It was a life full of everyday business: the management of the household, letter writing (particularly to her young nieces), music, sewing, religious observances, parish visiting, occasional trips from home (like many of her sex and her social position, she would visit relatives to assist during childbirth and death), and some quiet entertainments—social engagements, dancing (of which Austen was purportedly a devotee), and even some private theatricals, mostly comedies. As her juvenilia particularly demonstrates, the small home and social environment did not stifle her wit and imagination; on the contrary, it was precisely in this circle that her genius developed. Her writing originated as a source of amusement to herself and her family.

Like Cassandra, Jane Austen never married. During the brief time that the family lived in Bath (after the Reverend Austen's retirement from his ministry in 1800), Austen received her first and only proposal of marriage. At first she accepted the proposal from Harris Bigg-Wither—reportedly an unprepossessing man, but a long-standing acquaintance—but she withdrew her acceptance on the following morning. This romantic interlude in her life, along with a short-lived flirtation with Thomas

Lefroy, later a politician and judge, has provoked a maelstrom of hypotheses from biographers and moviemakers alike. The scarcity of detail or dramatic incident in the life of the author sometimes provokes high fantastical speculation.

But Austen's life was very clearly grounded in reality, not in fantasy. In 1805, the swift decline and death of George Austen left his widow and two daughters with some financial uncertainty. For a time they remained in Bath, then moved to Southampton, all the while spending a great deal of time visiting family members. In 1809, they moved to a small house in Chawton that was part of Edward Knight's inheritance from his adopted father. It was at Chawton that Miss Austen produced the greater part of her finished writing, and where she first experienced the disease that would eventually cause her death at the age of forty-one.

The effects of Austen's final illness were first visible in 1816. In May 1817 the increasing severity of her illness prompted her medically advised removal to Winchester for constant medical attention. This illness has been diagnosed both as Addison's disease and as Hodgkin's lymphoma. Both are severely debilitating diseases, and their application to her illness and death is primarily owing to the significant deterioration described by her family in the months leading up to her death. Even more fascinating than these theoretical medical diagnoses is the description of her death left by her brother Henry:

> She supported, during two months, all the varying pain, irksomeness, and tedium, attendant on decaying nature, with more than resignation, with a truly elastic cheerfulness. She retained her faculties, her memory, her fancy, her temper, and her affections, warm, clear, and unimpaired, to the last. Neither her love of God, nor of her fellow creatures flagged for a moment. She made a point of receiving the sacrament before excessive bodily weakness might have rendered her perception unequal to her wishes. She wrote whilst she could hold a pen, and with a pencil when a pen was become too laborious. The day preceding her death she composed some stanzas replete with fancy and vigour. Her last voluntary speech conveyed

thanks to her medical attendant; and to the final question asked of her, purporting to know her wants, she replied, "I want nothing but death."[7]

On July 18, 1817, Miss Austen died in the arms of her beloved sister, Cassandra. She was buried in Winchester Cathedral, "which," as her brother Henry wrote, "in the whole catalogue of its mighty dead, does not contain the ashes of a brighter genius or a sincerer Christian."[8] Though her authorial talents were not directly recorded there, the epitaph penned by her brother James and affixed to her tomb celebrated the "benevolence of her heart, the sweetness of her temper, and the extraordinary endowments of her mind", movingly demonstrating the fact that it was her family who first and most comprehensively valued Austen, both as a woman and as a writer. Little wonder that Proverbs 31:26 appears upon a memorial plaque to the author in Winchester Cathedral: "She opened her mouth with wisdom and in her tongue is the law of kindness."[9]

The Works

Austen's first writings of note, commenced between the ages of fourteen and sixteen (1789–1791), included "Love and Friendship" (a novel), "History of England", "Lesley Castle" (a story), and "A Collection of Letters" (an epistolary tale). Between 1793 and 1796, she wrote *Lady Susan* and "Elinor and Marianne" (an early version of *Sense and Sensibility*). "First Impressions", an early version of *Pride and Prejudice*, followed in 1797. In the years that followed, she revisited "Elinor and Marianne" and wrote *Susan* (an early version of *Northanger Abbey*). She completed six novels during her lifetime: *Sense*

---

[7] Ibid., pp. 4–5.

[8] Ibid., p. 5.

[9] The plaque was placed there in 1872 after the publication of James Edward Austen-Leigh's *Memoir* of his aunt. The remainder says as follows: "JANE AUSTEN known to many by her writings, endeared to her family by the varied charms of her Character and ennobled by Christian faith and piety, was born at Steventon in the County of Hants Dec. XVI MDCCLXXV, and buried in this Cathedral July XXIV MDCCCXVII."

and Sensibility (published in 1811),[10] *Pride and Prejudice* (1813), *Mansfield Park* (1814), *Emma* (1816), and *Northanger Abbey and Persuasion* (published posthumously and jointly in 1818).[11] In addition to the above, she left behind her two unfinished novels: *The Watsons* (1804) and *Sanditon* (1817).

Austen's work united realism and comedy, deep feeling and wry satire. She drew on many literary inspirations—the prose style of the great essayists Joseph Addison (1672–1719) and Richard Steele (1672–1729); the genius of poet Alexander Pope (1688–1744), about whom Austen playfully wrote, "There has been one infallible Pope in the world";[12] and the incomparable Dr. Samuel Johnson (1709–1784). She also drew on the novelistic legacy of high eighteenth-century novelists, including Daniel Defoe (ca.1659–1731), Henry Fielding (1707–1754), Lawrence Sterne (1713–1768), Samuel Richardson (1689–1761), Fanny Burney (1752–1840), and Maria Edgeworth (1767–1849); the Gothic tradition as exemplified in the melodramatic Ann Radcliffe (1764–1823), whom Austen roundly satirized, particularly in *Northanger Abbey*, and Horace Walpole (1717–1797); and the poetic inspiration of George Crabbe (1754–1832) and William Cowper (1731–1800). She drew as well on spiritual and religious works, principally the Bible, and from her own experience of life as the daughter of a clergyman. Her literary sensibilities have caused her to be spoken of in connection with a number of writers, from those who inspired her own work to those who followed in her footsteps. Not only is she often discussed alongside the Victorians, but she is frequently mistaken *for* a Victorian. In fact, however, she died nearly two years before the future Queen Victoria (1819–1901) was born.

[10] Austen's joy in the publication of the novel is shown in a letter to her sister: "I am never too busy to think of S & S. I can no more forget it, than a mother can forget her sucking child." Jane Austen, letter to her sister, Cassandra Austen, April 25, 1811, in *Jane Austen's Letters*, 4th ed., ed. Deidre Le Faye (Oxford: Oxford University Press, 2011), p. 190.

[11] They were actually published and released to the public in December 1817, though the publication information was printed to reflect the 1818 date.

[12] Written in a letter dated October 20, 1813.

Austen was valued and celebrated by a number of prestigious Victorian authors, including the theological writer and Anglican Archbishop Richard Whateley (1787–1863), Henry James (1843–1916), George Henry Lewes (1817–1878), and Anthony Trollope (1815–1882). The morality of her works was resoundingly respected, but she did not vie with any of the monumental mid-century novelists for marketable popularity. The 1869 publication of James Edward Austen-Leigh's *Memoir* of his aunt, and the subsequent republication of her novels in popular editions, inspired an increase both in scholarly attention and widespread readership.

The true rise of scholarly interest in Austen came after the turn of the century, with an essay by Oxford Shakespearean scholar A.C. Bradley (1851–1935). A dramatic increase followed in 1923 when R.W. Chapman edited the collected works. For some time, criticism focused primarily on the author's style. Indeed, her merging of parody, realism, irony, and, in a special way, her deployment of free indirect speech are worthy of comment. After the 1940s, revisionism took fire and a posse of professors declared that Austen's work was seething with subversive agendas and themes. This critical flavor has continued on into the present day, fueled by the imagination, funds, and propagandic tendencies of the film industry.

Like its fellows, *Sense and Sensibility* has spawned more than one film adaptation, with varying degrees of success. It has, however, not always been afforded the same attention as the other novels. It has even at times been dismissed as somehow underdeveloped or lacking in comparison to her later, more mature works. Indeed, the novel addresses some harsher themes than in the other novels (for example, though most Austen heroines are to some degree financially constrained, the Dashwood girls are the most financially dependent). It also bears the heaviest (by comparison, at least) authorial tone. Is there still some validity in the mild attitude of that reviewer? Are we to be satisfied in saying that the novel is "agreeable" and teaches a good lesson?

Sense and Sensibility

In *Jane Austen: A Family Record*, the story is recounted that a niece of the author came across *Sense and Sensibility* in a circulation library and dismissed it, saying, "Oh that must be rubbish I am sure from the title."[13]

Although far from "rubbish", *Sense and Sensibility* is dramatically situated in readers' minds by virtue of its title. The novel chronicles the most intense period of the social existence (i.e., leading up to marriage) of two sisters: Elinor and Marianne Dashwood. They are described very early in the novel:

> Elinor, this eldest daughter whose advice was so effectual, possessed a strength of understanding, and coolness of judgment, which qualified her, though only nineteen, to be the counsellor of her mother.... She had an excellent heart;—her disposition was affectionate, and her feelings were strong; but she knew how to govern them....
>
> Marianne's abilities were, in many respects, quite equal to Elinor's. She was sensible and clever; but eager in every thing; her sorrows, her joys, could have no moderation. She was generous, amiable, interesting: she was every thing but prudent.[14]

Thus personified, Sense and Sensibility are prepared to face their shared fortunes and misfortunes. Upon their father's death and the passing of his estate to their stepbrother and his family, the Dashwood girls (along with their mother and younger sister, Margaret) are left with very little money. Finding life with the snobbish, grasping Fanny Dashwood (their stepbrother's wife) unsupportable, they quit their beloved home, Norland, to live in a small cottage in Devon, under the patronage of Mrs. Dashwood's cousin, Sir John Middleton.

In their small, comparatively isolated new home, the Dashwoods acquire a new social set, including Sir John and Lady

[13] William Austen-Leigh and Richard Arthur Austen-Leigh, *Jane Austen: A Family Record*, ed. Deirdre Le Faye, rev. ed. (London: British Library, 1989), p. 171.

[14] Jane Austen, *Sense and Sensibility*, ed. Eleanor Bourg Nicholson, Ignatius Critical Editions (San Francisco: Ignatius Press, 2014), pp. 6–7. Subsequent quotations from this edition will be cited in the text.

Middleton (he, good-natured, friendly, and utterly lacking in self-awareness, and she of vain and simple manner, though not cruel or petty); Lady Middleton's incorrigible matchmaking mother, the widowed Mrs. Jennings, "who talked a great deal, seemed very happy, and rather vulgar"; and their close friend Colonel Brandon, who was dismissed by Marianne because he has the misfortune to be "on the wrong side of five and thirty", though he is not so abandoned by the narrator: "though his face was not handsome his countenance was sensible, and his address was particularly gentlemanlike" (see p. 34). Brandon is immediately and deeply attracted to Marianne's beauty and exuberance, and not overly dismayed by her sometime rudeness. He even tells Elinor that "there is something so amiable in the prejudices of a young mind, that one is sorry to see them give way to the reception of more general opinions" (see p. 56). (Elinor, of course, does not agree, seeing the dangers of her sister's imprudence.)

Marianne encounters the dashing young Mr. Willoughby and falls desperately in love. In contrast to this precipitate romance, Elinor quietly suffers in her love for Edward Ferrars, brother to her much-loathed sister-in-law, Fanny. Willoughby departs suddenly (leaving Marianne desolate). Soon after, circumstances arise to cause even greater pain to Elinor, and the two sisters suffer keenly (though dealing with this suffering very differently) in their individual romances. Many dramatic elements arise in characteristically indirect Austen fashion: a divorce (told in a third- or fourth-hand account), a seduction (likewise mediated), a duel (so quietly indicated that it might be missed in a moment of readerly inattention), and a breach of almost-promise (about which no one but the victim and her close circle cares).

Throughout, the questions, begged by the title itself, remain. Little wonder that the author of the BabyLit series of children's board books would choose *Sense and Sensibility* for an "Opposites Primer".[15] Are sense (represented by Elinor) and

---

[15] Jennifer Adams, *Sense and Sensibility: A BabyLit Opposites Primer* (Layton, Utah: Gibbs Smith, 2013).

sensibility (Marianne) diametrically opposed? Is one right and the other wrong? (*Pride and Prejudice*, in contrast, does not usually prompt this sort of conflict.) A promising answer is to be found in two vastly different film adaptations of the novel. In its opening credits, the 1981 TV miniseries displays the two sisters seated on a seesaw, teetering gently back and forth to establish equilibrium. In contrast, the 2007 televised adaptation begins with a graphic depiction of the seduction of a character who is mentioned but never seen in the novel. Elinor's sense is reduced to nonthreatening, nonpreachy dullness, and Marianne shines as the preeminent heroine in her unquestioned self-realization.

In a backward way, this shows that the operative word of the title must be "and"—not "or". There is an equilibrium to be achieved. Characters span the entire spectrum between the two—with Fanny Dashwood and her mother so profoundly "sensible" of societal and financial pressures that they are cold, petty, and rude, and Marianne and Willoughby so devoted to feeling that they (and particularly he) offend on innumerable levels of social and moral decency. Neither sense nor sensibility is the ultimate keystone of the work; rather, both are integral parts of each heroine's individual quest for the self-knowledge that is vital to moral growth. Marriage is, indeed, the ultimate prize to be sought by an Austen heroine, and the novelist's goal. But the unspoken vision for the author must hearken back to the commendation by her brother Henry (quoted above), in not imagining "a brighter genius or a sincerer Christian" among the hallowed tombs at Winchester.

With the quiet respectability of her class, Austen does not "go in" for overzealous or emotional declarations of faith. Nevertheless, the character arc of every Austen heroine (and most if not all of her heroes as well) only makes sense in the context of an unspoken but coherent appreciation of Christian morality. In this light, the ancient Greek aphorism "know thyself" provides the answer. Marianne, like Elinor, must come to know both her faults and her virtues. Elinor's comparative calmness throughout the novel is not owing to a lack of feeling. We are told from the start, "She had an excellent heart;—her

XX Sense and Sensibility

disposition was affectionate, and her feelings were strong; but she knew how to govern them". Marianne, on the other hand, "was generous, amiable, interesting: she was every thing but prudent" (see p. 7). When she gains this lacking practical wisdom, which requires self-restraint and the correction of her faults, she will grow in other virtues as well. Sense and sensibility thus need not be in opposition.

Because such maturation is so critical in understanding Jane Austen, the philosopher Alisdair MacIntyre (following Gilbert Ryle) is quite correct in celebrating her as one of the last "adherents of the older tradition of the virtues", and even directly as "an Aristotelian".[16] Though it is unlikely she labored nightly in secret at a personal translation of Saint Thomas Aquinas' *Summa Theologiae* or bore in her pocket a worn, dog-eared copy of Aristotle's *Nichomachean Ethics*, she demonstrates so acute an understanding of what it is that makes man happy that she might be suspected of either. Self-knowledge, self-discipline, and moderation—these are the hallmarks of an Austen heroine, and, indeed, of any Christian soul who has passed through the quiet fire of maturation. From this, a comfortable and healthy future community will flow (represented in the off-screen offspring of the virtuous married heroine).

In fact, this turns the entire expectation of "newness" on its head; there may be nothing *new* in *Sense and Sensibility*, but Austen conveys the fact that that which is most new, most interesting, and most packed with dramatic potentiality is to be found in the authentic work of good men and women to grow in virtue and be free of vice. That is why the 1995 Ang Lee adaptation, with the screenplay by Emma Thompson, is a notable exception to the unimpressive performance of modern moviemakers in adapting Austen novels. Beyond some

---

[16] Alisdair MacIntyre, *After Virtue: A Study in Moral Theory*, 3rd ed. (Notre Dame, Ind.: University of Notre Dame Press, 1981), pp. 238, 240. Ryle's excellent and groundbreaking 1966 article, "Jane Austen and the Moralists" (*The Oxford Review*, no. 1), compellingly argues for her Aristotelianism, but unfortunately casts it in a secular light, which seems dismissive of the many indications of her religious upbringing and conviction.

quibbles, it is faithful to the novel and even its spirit. Because the film discloses that critical moral understanding, we can forgive and even value some aspects of the modern perspective: for instance, we can appreciate the vivid visual presentation of setting, and some extraliterary touches to show the difference between life at their life and social standing at Norland and their new home at Barton Cottage.

The shock value of the more devastating sins of the novel notwithstanding, the greatest interest and pathos is to be found in the quiet, uneventful, day-to-day life of our heroines. The wealthy, high-flying characters are actually petty and dull— though, as Austen comments, "there was no peculiar disgrace in this, for it was very much the case with the chief of their visitors, who almost all laboured under one or other of these disqualifications for being agreeable—Want of sense, either natural or improved—Want of elegance—want of spirits—or want of temper" (see p. 227). Their power to entertain comes from Austen's masterful use of irony, highlighting what they are, with the clear understanding of what they *ought* to be. As Marianne herself comments to her sister at a particularly beautiful moment in the novel, her standard of judging her own behavior is to "compare it with what it ought to have been; I compare it with yours" (see p. 333). But, importantly, growth does not require that Marianne become Elinor. On the contrary, even as she develops "a scheme of such rational employment and virtuous self-controul" (see p. 331), it still smacks of her characteristic eagerness (prompting a smile from her sister). Marianne is still Marianne. Elinor is still Elinor. Through suffering and growth, they are even more perfectly themselves.

Pace the dramatic expectations of some modern readers (and viewers), that is why the ultimate joy of the novel, found in its conclusion, is understated. That is why the most dramatic moments of Austen's work (including the critical moment of her triumphant proposal scenes)[17] are described

---

[17] Interestingly, the Dashwoods are the only Austen heroines who do *not* receive more than one proposal.

rather than presented as dialogue. Virtue proceeds from the gradual development of good habits; it is not necessarily *denouematic*. Such is the happy conundrum of Jane Austen; while some have lamented the limited scope of the world she describes, she describes nothing more and nothing less than reality. And she sees reality with a sense of humor and affectionate kindness that could only be born of a gracious Christian spirit. It is wisdom, not limitation, that has produced the "brush so fine" with which she labors upon "a little bit of ivory, two inches wide".[18] Such wisdom appreciates that, even if there is nothing new to say, we may yet express truths and present a story more deeply and impressively real than those who came before us. We therefore invite the reader to prepare to appreciate this exquisitely unnovel first published work of Jane Austen, and exercise both sense and sensibility in encountering the supreme wisdom of one of the greatest writers of the English language, and one of the wisest ladies ever to flourish (if one can flourish with silent decorousness) a modest quill.[19]

Textual Note

Perhaps more than all of her other novels, Miss Austen's *Sense and Sensibility* has a significant textual history. The novel was first developed as "Elinor and Marianne", an epistolary novel begun as early as 1785. Austen substantially rewrote her work two years later, transforming it into a third-person narrative. It is likely that she revisited the novel several times over the next

---

[18] Austen wrote this "playful defense" against "a mock charge of having pilfered the manuscripts of a young relation":

> What should I do, my dearest E. with your manly, vigorous sketches, so full of life and spirit? How could I possibly join them on to a little bit of ivory, two inches wide, on which I work with a brush so fine as to produce little effect after much labour?

This quotation was included in a postscript to Henry's "Biographical Notice of the Author", p. 8.

[19] Or any other writing implement, for that matter.

decade.[20] In 1811, Thomas Egerton published the first edition (known as A)—at Austen's expense, though she published anonymously. In November 1813, Egerton printed a second edition (known as B). Since B contains Austen's revisions, it is (with one exception in the form of a 1995 Penguin edition) the basis for all subsequent editions of the novel. This edition for the most part follows the work of Dr. R. W. Chapman (considered definitive) and his collation of the various editions (1923, with subsequent revisions during the following two decades). As far as possible, usages of punctuation and spelling have been conveyed as they were in the original editions; and, when necessary, usages that might seem irregular to the modern reader, as well as substantial differences between A and B, are glossed in a footnote.

[20] For more details regarding the composition history of the novel, see B.C. Southam, *Jane Austen's Literary MSS* (Oxford: Clarendon, 1964), pp. 55–57.

VOLUME I

Chapter I

The family of Dashwood had been long settled in Sussex. Their estate was large, and their residence was at Norland Park, in the centre of their property, where, for many generations, they had lived in so respectable a manner, as to engage the general good opinion of their surrounding acquaintance. The late owner[1] of this estate was a single man, who lived to a very advanced age, and who for many years of his life, had a constant companion and housekeeper in his sister. But her death, which happened ten years before his own, produced a great alteration in his home; for to supply her loss, he invited and received into his house the family of his nephew Mr. Henry Dashwood, the legal inheritor of the Norland estate, and the person to whom he intended to bequeath it.[2] In the society of his nephew and niece, and their children, the old Gentleman's days were comfortably spent. His attachment to them all increased. The constant attention of Mr. and Mrs. Henry Dashwood to his wishes, which proceeded not merely from interest, but from goodness of heart, gave him every degree of solid comfort which his age could receive, and the cheerfulness of the children added a relish to his existence.

By a former marriage, Mr. Henry Dashwood had one son: by his present lady, three daughters. The son, a steady respectable young man, was amply provided for by the fortune of his mother, which had been large, and half of which devolved[3] on him on his coming of age. By his own marriage, likewise, which happened soon afterwards, he added to his

[1] *late owner*: Edition A gives this as "The last owner but one". See textual note, pp. xxii–xxiii.
[2] *legal . . . bequeath it*: Traditionally, an estate would be passed through the male line. The bequest here is probably nominal, since the property would pass legally to Mr. Dashwood in any case.
[3] *devolved on*: passed down to.

wealth.[4] To him therefore the succession[5] to the Norland
estate was not so really important as to his sisters; for their fortune, independent of what might arise to them from their
father's inheriting that property, could be but small. Their
mother had nothing, and their father only seven thousand
pounds[6] in his own disposal; for the remaining moiety[7] of his
first wife's fortune was also secured to her child, and he had
only a life interest[8] in it.

The old Gentleman died; his will was read, and like almost
every other will, gave as much disappointment as pleasure. He
was neither so unjust, nor so ungrateful, as to leave his estate
from[9] his nephew;—but he left it to him on such terms as
destroyed half the value of the bequest. Mr. Dashwood had
wished for it more for the sake of his wife and daughters than
for himself or his son:—but to his son, and his son's son, a child
of four years old, it was secured, in such a way, as to leave to
himself no power of providing for those who were most dear
to him, and who most needed a provision, by any charge on
the estate,[10] or by any sale of its valuable woods. The whole
was tied up for the benefit of this child, who, in occasional
visits with his father and mother at Norland, had so far gained
on the affections of his uncle, by such attractions as are by
no means unusual in children of two or three years old; an

[4] Edition A additionally states: "His wife had something considerable at present, and something still more to expect hereafter from her mother, her only
surviving parent, who had much to give." This was removed from Edition B
(hereafter B), perhaps because Miss Austen felt the point had been made clearly
enough already.

[5] *succession*: i.e., legal acquisition.

[6] *seven thousand pounds*: Following the work of Edward Copeland, we can calculate this to be roughly equivalent to $560,000. For more information, see "The
Economic Realities of Jane Eyre", *Approaches to Teaching Jane Austen's* Pride
and Prejudice, ed. Marcia McClintock Folsom (New York: Modern Language
Association, 1993).

[7] *moiety*: literally a half, but, generally, any portion.

[8] *life interest*: legal control, but only during his lifetime.

[9] *from*: away from.

[10] *by ... estate*: Edition A gives "by any division of the estate". The change
may reflect the advice received by Miss Austen from Henry Austen (her favorite
brother) as to the likely settlement of a property such as Norland. A division of
the estate would be unlikely.

imperfect articulation, an earnest desire of having his own way, many cunning tricks, and a great deal of noise, as to outweigh all the value of all the attention which, for years, he had received from his niece and her daughters. He meant not to be unkind however, and, as a mark of his affection for the three girls, he left them a thousand pounds a-piece.

Mr. Dashwood's disappointment was, at first, severe; but his temper was cheerful and sanguine,[11] and he might reasonably hope to live many years, and by living economically, lay by a considerable sum from the produce of an estate already large, and capable of almost immediate improvement. But the fortune, which had been so tardy in coming, was his only one twelvemonth. He survived his uncle no longer; and ten thousand pounds, including the late legacies, was all that remained for his widow and daughters.

His son was sent for, as soon as his danger was known, and to him Mr. Dashwood recommended, with all the strength and urgency which illness could command, the interest of his mother-in-law[12] and sisters.

Mr. John Dashwood had not the strong feelings of the rest of the family; but he was affected by a recommendation of such a nature at such a time, and he promised to do every thing in his power to make them comfortable. His father was rendered easy by such an assurance, and Mr. John Dashwood had then leisure to consider how much there might prudently be in his power to do for them.

He was not an ill-disposed young man, unless to be rather cold hearted, and rather selfish, is to be ill-disposed: but he was, in general, well respected; for he conducted himself with propriety in the discharge of his ordinary duties. Had he married a more amiable woman, he might have been made still more respectable than he was:—he might even have been made amiable himself; for he was very young when he married, and very fond of his wife. But Mrs. John Dashwood was a strong caricature of himself;—more narrow-minded and selfish.

---

[11] *sanguine*: pleasant, optimistic (from the classical understanding of the four humors, having a predominance of blood in the bodily humors).

[12] *mother-in-law*: stepmother.

When he gave his promise to his father, he meditated within himself to increase the fortunes of his sisters by the present of a thousand pounds a-piece. He then really thought himself equal to it. The prospect of four thousand a-year, in addition to his present income, besides the remaining half of his own mother's fortune, warmed his heart and made him feel capable of generosity.—"Yes, he would give them three thousand pounds: it would be liberal and handsome! It would be enough to make them completely easy. Three thousand pounds! he could spare so considerable a sum with little inconvenience."—He thought of it all day long, and for many days successively, and he did not repent.

No sooner was his father's funeral over, than Mrs. John Dashwood, without sending any notice of her intention to her mother-in-law, arrived with her child and their attendants. No one could dispute her right to come; the house was her husband's from the moment of his father's decease; but the indelicacy of her conduct was so much the greater, and to a woman in Mrs. Dashwood's situation, with only common feelings, must have been highly unpleasing;—but in *her* mind there was a sense of honour so keen, a generosity so romantic,[13] that any offence of the kind, by whomsoever given or received, was to her a source of immoveable disgust. Mrs. John Dashwood had never been a favourite with any of her husband's family; but she had had no opportunity, till the present, of shewing them with how little attention to the comfort of other people she could act when occasion required it.

So acutely did Mrs. Dashwood feel this ungracious behaviour, and so earnestly did she despise her daughter-in-law for it, that, on the arrival of the latter, she would have quitted the house for ever, had not the entreaty of her eldest girl induced her first to reflect on the propriety of going, and her own tender love for all her three children determined her afterwards to stay, and for their sakes avoid a breach with their brother.

Elinor, this eldest daughter whose advice was so effectual, possessed a strength of understanding, and coolness of judgment,

---

[13] *romantic*: informed by a strong and imaginative heart.

which qualified her, though only nineteen, to be the counsellor of her mother, and enabled her frequently to counteract, to the advantage of them all, that eagerness of mind in Mrs. Dashwood which must generally have led to imprudence. She had an excellent heart;—her disposition was affectionate, and her feelings were strong; but she knew how to govern them: it was a knowledge which her mother had yet to learn, and which one of her sisters had resolved never to be taught.

Marianne's abilities were, in many respects, quite equal to Elinor's. She was sensible and clever; but eager in every thing; her sorrows, her joys, could have no moderation. She was generous, amiable, interesting: she was every thing but prudent. The resemblance between her and her mother was strikingly great.

Elinor saw, with concern, the excess of her sister's sensibility; but by Mrs. Dashwood it was valued and cherished. They encouraged each other now in the violence of their affliction. The agony of grief which overpowered them at first, was voluntarily renewed, was sought for, was created again and again. They gave themselves up wholly to their sorrow, seeking increase of wretchedness in every reflection that could afford it, and resolved against ever admitting consolation in future. Elinor, too, was deeply afflicted; but still she could struggle, she could exert herself. She could consult with her brother, could receive her sister-in-law on her arrival, and treat her with proper attention; and could strive to rouse her mother to similar exertion, and encourage her to similar forbearance.

Margaret, the other sister, was a good-humoured well-disposed girl; but as she had already imbibed a good deal of Marianne's romance, without having much of her sense,[14] she did not, at thirteen, bid fair to equal her sisters at a more advanced period of life.

---

[14] *her sense*: R.W. Chapman (British scholar and editor of Jane Austen's works) puzzles over this; "her" seems to refer to Marianne's sense, though the term is associated primarily with Elinor rather than Marianne. Its reference point is debatable.

Chapter II

Mrs. John Dashwood now installed herself mistress of Norland; and her mother and sisters-in-law were degraded to the condition of visitors. As such, however, they were treated by her with quiet civility; and by her husband with as much kindness as he could feel towards any body beyond himself, his wife, and their child. He really pressed them, with some earnestness, to consider Norland as their home; and, as no plan appeared so eligible to Mrs. Dashwood as remaining there till she could accommodate herself with a house in the neighbourhood, his invitation was accepted.

A continuance in a place where every thing reminded her of former delight, was exactly what suited her mind. In seasons of cheerfulness, no temper could be more cheerful than hers, or possess, in a greater degree, that sanguine expectation of happiness which is happiness itself. But in sorrow she must be equally carried away by her fancy, and as far beyond consolation as in pleasure she was beyond alloy.[1]

Mrs. John Dashwood did not at all approve of what her husband intended to do for his sisters. To take three thousand pounds from the fortune of their dear little boy, would be impoverishing him to the most dreadful degree. She begged him to think again on the subject. How could he answer it to himself to rob his child, and his only child too, of so large a sum? And what possible claim could the Miss Dashwoods, who were related to him only by half blood, which she considered as no relationship at all, have on his generosity to so large an amount. It was very well known that no affection was ever supposed to exist between the children of any man by different marriages; and why was he to ruin himself, and their poor little Harry, by giving away all his money to his half sisters?

[1] *alloy*: having her emotions rendered more mild (the term is from metallurgy, referring to the mixture of metals that usually lessens the value).

"It was my father's last request to me," replied her husband, "that I should assist his widow and daughters."

"He did not know what he was talking of, I dare say; ten to one but he was light-headed at the time. Had he been in his right senses, he could not have thought of such a thing as begging you to give away half your fortune from your own child."

"He did not stipulate for any particular sum, my dear Fanny; he only requested me, in general terms, to assist them, and make their situation more comfortable than it was in his power to do. Perhaps it would have been as well if he had left it wholly to myself. He could hardly suppose I should neglect them. But as he required the promise, I could not do less than give it: at least I thought so at the time. The promise, therefore, was given, and must be performed. Something must be done for them whenever they leave Norland and settle in a new home."

"Well, then, *let* something be done for them; but *that* something need not be three thousand pounds.[2] Consider," she added, "that when the money is once parted with, it never can return. Your sisters will marry, and it will be gone for ever. If, indeed, it could ever be restored to our poor little boy—"

"Why, to be sure," said her husband, very gravely, "that would make a great difference. The time may come when Harry will regret that so large a sum was parted with. If he should have a numerous family, for instance, it would be a very convenient addition."

"To be sure it would."

"Perhaps, then, it would be better for all parties if the sum were diminished one half.—Five hundred pounds would be a prodigious increase to their fortunes!"

"Oh! beyond any thing great! What brother on earth would do half so much for his sisters, even if *really* his sisters! And as it is—only half blood!—But you have such a generous spirit!"

"I would not wish to do any thing mean," he replied. "One had rather, on such occasions, do too much than too little. No

[2] *three thousand pounds*: roughly equivalent to $240,000.

one, at least, can think I have not done enough for them: even themselves, they can hardly expect more."

"There is no knowing what *they* may expect," said the lady, "but we are not to think of their expectations: the question is, what you can afford to do."

"Certainly—and I think I may afford to give them five hundred pounds a-piece. As it is, without any addition of mine, they will each have above three thousand pounds on their mother's death—a very comfortable fortune for any young woman."

"To be sure it is: and, indeed, it strikes me that they can want no addition at all. They will have ten thousand pounds[3] divided amongst them. If they marry, they will be sure of doing well, and if they do not, they may all live very comfortably together on the interest of ten thousand pounds."

"That is very true, and, therefore, I do not know whether, upon the whole, it would not be more advisable to do something for their mother while she lives rather than for them— something of the annuity[4] kind I mean.—My sisters would feel the good effects of it as well as herself. A hundred a year would make them all perfectly comfortable."

His wife hesitated a little, however, in giving her consent to this plan.

"To be sure," said she, "it is better than parting with fifteen hundred pounds at once. But then if Mrs. Dashwood should live fifteen years, we shall be completely taken in."

"Fifteen years! my dear Fanny; her life cannot be worth half that purchase."[5]

---

[3] *ten thousand pounds*: (the seven thousand pound inheritance plus the three thousand pound gift—which he won't give them) roughly equivalent to $800,000 (*if* he gives them the gift of five hundred pounds each of course). It is important to note that this is not an annual or recurring income; they would live off of this indefinitely, and without means of growth beyond the interest. It would be used to pay rent, buy food, and support their servants. If the Dashwood girls do not marry into financial security, they cannot expect to remain stable in their social sphere.

[4] *annuity*: fixed sum of money paid to someone each year, typically for the rest of his life.

[5] *half that purchase*: Mrs. Dashwood is forty; cf. Marianne's assertion that Colonel Brandon will live "twenty years longer" (see p. 37), which reflects her romantic ideals and is not demonstrative of a clear appreciation for life expectancy at that time.

"Certainly not; but if you observe, people always live for ever when there is any annuity to be paid them; and she is very stout and healthy, and hardly forty. An annuity is a very serious business; it comes over and over every year, and there is no getting rid of it. You are not aware of what you are doing. I have known a great deal of the trouble of annuities; for my mother was clogged with the payment of three to old superannuated[6] servants by my father's will, and it is amazing how disagreeable she found it. Twice every year these annuities were to be paid; and then there was the trouble of getting it to them; and then one of them was said to have died, and afterwards it turned out to be no such thing. My mother was quite sick of it. Her income was not her own, she said, with such perpetual claims on it; and it was the more unkind in my father, because, otherwise, the money would have been entirely at my mother's disposal, without any restriction whatever. It has given me such an abhorrence of annuities, that I am sure I would not pin myself down to the payment of one for all the world."

"It is certainly an unpleasant thing," replied Mr. Dashwood, "to have those kind of yearly drains on one's income. One's fortune, as your mother justly says, is *not* one's own. To be tied down to the regular payment of such a sum, on every rent day, is by no means desirable: it takes away one's independence."

"Undoubtedly; and after all you have no thanks for it. They think themselves secure, you do no more than what is expected, and it raises no gratitude at all. If I were you, whatever I did should be done at my own discretion entirely. I would not bind myself to allow them any thing yearly. It may be very inconvenient some years to spare a hundred, or even fifty pounds from our own expences."

"I believe you are right, my love; it will be better that there should be no annuity in the case; whatever I may give them occasionally will be of far greater assistance than a yearly allowance, because they would only enlarge their style of living if they felt sure of a larger income, and would not be sixpence the richer for it at the end of the year. It will certainly be much

[6] *superannuated*: elderly.

the best way. A present of fifty pounds, now and then, will prevent their ever being distressed for money, and will, I think, be amply discharging my promise to my father."

"To be sure it will. Indeed, to say the truth, I am convinced within myself that your father had no idea of your giving them any money at all. The assistance he thought of, I dare say, was only such as might be reasonably expected of you; for instance, such as looking out for a comfortable small house for them, helping them to move their things, and sending them presents of fish and game, and so forth, whenever they are in season. I'll lay my life that he meant nothing farther; indeed, it would be very strange and unreasonable if he did. Do but consider, my dear Mr. Dashwood, how excessively comfortable your mother-in-law and her daughters may live on the interest of seven thousand pounds, besides the thousand pounds belonging to each of the girls, which brings them in fifty pounds a-year a-piece, and, of course, they will pay their mother for their board out of it. Altogether, they will have five hundred a-year amongst them, and what on earth can four women want for more than that?—They will live so cheap! Their housekeeping will be nothing at all. They will have no carriage, no horses, and hardly any servants; they will keep no company, and can have no expences of any kind! Only conceive how comfortable they will be! Five hundred a-year! I am sure I cannot imagine how they will spend half of it; and as to your giving them more, it is quite absurd to think of it. They will be much more able to give *you* something."

"Upon my word," said Mr. Dashwood, "I believe you are perfectly right. My father certainly could mean nothing more by his request to me than what you say. I clearly understand it now, and I will strictly fulfil my engagement by such acts of assistance and kindness to them as you have described. When my mother removes into another house my services shall be readily given to accommodate her as far as I can. Some little present of furniture too may be acceptable then."

"Certainly," returned Mrs. John Dashwood. "But, however, *one* thing must be considered. When your father and mother moved to Norland, though the furniture of Stanhill was sold, all the china, plate, and linen was saved, and is now left to your mother. Her house will therefore be almost completely fitted up as soon as she takes it."

"That is a material consideration undoubtedly. A valuable legacy indeed! And yet some of the plate would have been a very pleasant addition to our own stock here."

"Yes; and the set of breakfast china is twice as handsome as what belongs to this house. A great deal too handsome, in my opinion, for any place *they* can ever afford to live in. But, however, so it is. Your father thought only of *them*. And I must say this: that you owe no particular gratitude to him, nor attention to his wishes, for we very well know that if he could, he would have left almost every thing in the world to *them*."

This argument was irresistible. It gave to his intentions whatever of decision was wanting before; and he finally resolved, that it would be absolutely unnecessary, if not highly indecorous, to do more for the widow and children of his father, than such kind of neighbourly acts as his own wife pointed out.

Chapter III

Mrs. Dashwood remained at Norland several months; not from any disinclination to move when the sight of every well known spot ceased to raise the violent emotion which it produced for a while; for when her spirits began to revive, and her mind became capable of some other exertion than that of heightening its affliction by melancholy remembrances, she was impatient to be gone, and indefatigable in her inquiries for a suitable dwelling in the neighbourhood of Norland; for to remove far from that beloved spot was impossible. But she could hear of no situation that at once answered her notions of comfort and ease, and suited the prudence of her eldest daughter, whose steadier judgment rejected several houses as too large for their income, which her mother would have approved.

Mrs. Dashwood had been informed by her husband of the solemn promise on the part of his son in their favour, which gave comfort to his last earthly reflections. She doubted the sincerity of this assurance no more than he had doubted it himself, and she thought of it for her daughters' sake with satisfaction, though as for herself she was persuaded that a much smaller provision than seven thousand pounds, would support her in affluence. For their brother's sake too, for the sake of his own heart she rejoiced; and she reproached herself for being unjust to his merit before, in believing him incapable of generosity. His attentive behaviour to herself and his sisters convinced her that their welfare was dear to him, and, for a long time, she firmly relied on the liberality of his intentions.

The contempt which she had, very early in their acquaintance, felt for her daughter-in-law, was very much increased by the farther knowledge of her character, which half a year's residence in her family afforded; and perhaps in spite of every consideration of politeness or maternal affection on the side of the former, the two ladies might have found it impossible to have lived together so long, had not a particular circumstance occurred to give still greater eligibility, according to the opinions of Mrs. Dashwood, to her daughters' continuance at Norland.

This circumstance was a growing attachment between her eldest girl and the brother of Mrs. John Dashwood, a gentlemanlike and pleasing young man, who was introduced to their acquaintance soon after his sister's establishment at Norland, and who had since spent the greatest part of his time there.

Some mothers might have encouraged the intimacy from motives of interest, for Edward Ferrars was the eldest son of a man who had died very rich; and some might have repressed it from motives of prudence, for, except a trifling sum, the whole of his fortune depended on the will of his mother. But Mrs. Dashwood was alike uninfluenced by either consideration. It was enough for her that he appeared to be amiable, that he loved her daughter, and that Elinor returned the partiality. It was contrary to every doctrine of her's that difference of fortune should keep any couple asunder who were attracted by resemblance of disposition; and that Elinor's merit should not be acknowledged by every one who knew her, was to her comprehension impossible.

Edward Ferrars was not recommended to their good opinion by any peculiar graces of person or address. He was not handsome, and his manners required intimacy to make them pleasing. He was too diffident[1] to do justice to himself; but when his natural shyness was overcome, his behaviour gave every indication of an open affectionate heart. His understanding was good, and his education had given it solid improvement. But he was neither fitted by abilities nor disposition to answer the wishes of his mother and sister, who longed to see him distinguished—as—they hardly knew what. They wanted him to make a fine figure in the world in some manner or other. His mother wished to interest him in political

---

[1] *diffident*: modest or shy (usually from lack of self-confidence).

concerns, to get him into parliament, or to see him connected with some of the great men of the day. Mrs. John Dashwood wished it likewise; but in the mean while, till one of these superior blessings could be attained, it would have quieted her ambition to see him driving a barouche.[2] But Edward had no turn for great men or barouches. All his wishes centered in domestic comfort and the quiet of private life. Fortunately he had a younger brother who was more promising.

Edward had been staying several weeks in the house before he engaged much of Mrs. Dashwood's attention; for she was, at that time, in such affliction as rendered her careless of surrounding objects. She saw only that he was quiet and unobtrusive, and she liked him for it. He did not disturb the wretchedness of her mind by ill-timed conversation. She was first called to observe and approve him farther, by a reflection which Elinor chanced one day to make on the difference between him and his sister. It was a contrast which recommended him most forcibly to her mother.

"It is enough," said she; "to say that he is unlike Fanny is enough. It implies every thing amiable. I love him already."

"I think you will like him," said Elinor, "when you know more of him."

"Like him!" replied her mother with a smile. "I can feel no sentiment of approbation inferior to love."

"You may esteem him."

"I have never yet known what it was to separate esteem and love."

Mrs. Dashwood now took pains to get acquainted with him. Her manners were attaching[3] and soon banished his reserve. She speedily comprehended all his merits; the persuasion of his regard for Elinor perhaps assisted her penetration; but she really felt assured of his worth: and even that quietness of manner which militated against all her established ideas of

---

[2] *barouche*: four-wheeled horse-drawn carriage with a collapsible hood over the rear half.

[3] *attaching*: engaging, winning.

what a young man's address ought to be, was no longer uninteresting when she knew his heart to be warm and his temper
affectionate.

No sooner did she perceive any symptom of love in his
behaviour to Elinor, than she considered their serious attachment as certain, and looked forward to their marriage as rapidly
approaching.

"In a few months, my dear Marianne," said she, "Elinor will
in all probability be settled for life. We shall miss her; but *she*
will be happy."

"Oh! mama, how shall we do without her?"

"My love, it will be scarcely a separation. We shall live within
a few miles of each other, and shall meet every day of our lives.
You will gain a brother, a real, affectionate brother. I have the
highest opinion in the world of Edward's heart. But you look
grave, Marianne; do you disapprove your sister's choice?"

"Perhaps," said Marianne, "I may consider it with some
surprise. Edward is very amiable, and I love him tenderly.
But yet—he is not the kind of young man—there is a something wanting[4]—his figure is not striking; it has none of that
grace which I should expect in the man who could seriously
attach[5] my sister. His eyes want all that spirit, that fire, which
at once announce virtue and intelligence. And besides all this,
I am afraid, mama, he has no real taste. Music seems scarcely
to attract him, and though he admires Elinor's drawings very
much, it is not the admiration of a person who can understand
their worth. It is evident, in spite of his frequent attention to
her while she draws, that in fact he knows nothing of the matter. He admires as a lover, not as a connoisseur. To satisfy me,
those characters must be united. I could not be happy with a
man whose taste did not in every point coincide with my own.
He must enter into all my feelings; the same books, the same
music must charm us both. Oh! mama, how spiritless, how
tame was Edward's manner in reading to us last night! I felt

[4] *wanting*: needed, lacking.
[5] *attach*: i.e., attach the affections of.

for my sister most severely. Yet she bore it with so much composure; she seemed scarcely to notice it. I could hardly keep my seat. To hear those beautiful lines which have frequently almost driven me wild, pronounced with such impenetrable calmness, such dreadful indifference!"—

"He would certainly have done more justice to simple and elegant prose. I thought so at the time; but you *would* give him Cowper."[6]

"Nay, mama, if he is not to be animated by Cowper!—but we must allow for difference of taste. Elinor has not my feelings, and therefore she may overlook it, and be happy with him. But it would have broke *my* heart had I loved him, to hear him read with so little sensibility. Mama, the more I know of the world, the more am I convinced that I shall never see a man whom I can really love. I require so much! He must have all Edward's virtues, and his person and manners must ornament his goodness with every possible charm."

"Remember, my love, that you are not seventeen. It is yet too early in life to despair of such an happiness. Why should you be less fortunate than your mother? In one circumstance only, my Marianne, may your destiny be different from hers!"

[6] *Cowper*: William Cowper (1731–1800), English poet and hymnodist, particularly known for his emotive love of nature.

Chapter IV

"What a pity it is, Elinor," said Marianne, "that Edward should have no taste for drawing."

"No taste for drawing," replied Elinor; "why should you think so? He does not draw himself, indeed, but he has great pleasure in seeing the performances of other people, and I assure you he is by no means deficient in natural taste, though he has not had opportunities of improving it. Had he ever been in the way of learning, I think he would have drawn very well. He distrusts his own judgment in such matters so much, that he is always unwilling to give his opinion on any picture; but he has an innate propriety and simplicity of taste, which in general direct him perfectly right."

Marianne was afraid of offending, and said no more on the subject; but the kind of approbation which Elinor described as excited in him by the drawings of other people, was very far from that rapturous delight, which, in her opinion, could alone be called taste. Yet, though smiling within herself at the mistake, she honoured her sister for that blind partiality to Edward which produced it.

"I hope, Marianne," continued Elinor, "you do not consider him as deficient in general taste. Indeed, I think I may say that you cannot, for your behaviour to him is perfectly cordial, and if *that* were your opinion, I am sure you could never be civil to him."

Marianne hardly knew what to say. She would not wound the feelings of her sister on any account, and yet to say what she did not believe was impossible. At length she replied:

"Do not be offended, Elinor, if my praise of him is not in every thing equal to your sense of his merits. I have not had so many opportunities of estimating the minuter propensities of his mind, his inclinations and tastes as you have; but I have the highest opinion in the world of his goodness and sense. I think him every thing that is worthy and amiable."

"I am sure," replied Elinor with a smile, "that his dearest friends could not be dissatisfied with such commendation as that. I do not perceive how you could express yourself more warmly."

Marianne was rejoiced to find her sister so easily pleased.

"Of his sense and his goodness," continued Elinor, "no one can, I think, be in doubt, who has seen him often enough to engage him in unreserved conversation. The excellence of his understanding and his principles can be concealed only by that shyness which too often keeps him silent. You know enough of him to do justice to his solid worth. But of his minuter propensities as you call them, you have from peculiar circumstances been kept more ignorant than myself. He and I have been at times thrown a good deal together, while you have been wholly engrossed on the most affectionate principle by my mother. I have seen a great deal of him, have studied his sentiments and heard his opinion on subjects of literature and taste; and, upon the whole, I venture to pronounce that his mind is well-informed, his enjoyment of books exceedingly great, his imagination lively, his observation just and correct, and his taste delicate and pure. His abilities in every respect improve as much upon acquaintance as his manners and person. At first sight, his address is certainly not striking; and his person can hardly be called handsome, till the expression of his eyes, which are uncommonly good, and the general sweetness of his countenance, is perceived. At present, I know him so well, that I think him really handsome; or, at least, almost so. What say you, Marianne?"

"I shall very soon think him handsome, Elinor, if I do not now. When you tell me to love him as a brother, I shall no more see imperfection in his face, than I now do in his heart."

Elinor started at this declaration, and was sorry for the warmth she had been betrayed into, in speaking of him. She felt that Edward stood very high in her opinion. She believed the regard to be mutual; but she required greater certainty of it to make Marianne's conviction of their attachment agreeable to her. She knew that what Marianne and her mother conjectured one moment, they believed the next—that with them, to wish was to hope, and to hope was to expect. She tried to explain the real state of the case to her sister.

"I do not attempt to deny," said she, "that I think very highly of him—that I greatly esteem, that I like him."

Marianne here burst forth with indignation—

"Esteem him! Like him! Cold-hearted Elinor! Oh! worse than cold-hearted! Ashamed of being otherwise. Use those words again and I will leave the room this moment."

Elinor could not help laughing. "Excuse me," said she, "and be assured that I meant no offence to you, by speaking, in so quiet a way, of my own feelings. Believe them to be stronger than I have declared; believe them, in short, to be such as his merit, and the suspicion—the hope of his affection for me may warrant, without imprudence or folly. But farther than this you must *not* believe. I am by no means assured of his regard for me. There are moments when the extent of it seems doubtful; and till his sentiments are fully known, you cannot wonder at my wishing to avoid any encouragement of my own partiality, by believing or calling it more than it is. In my heart I feel little— scarcely any doubt of his preference. But there are other points to be considered besides his inclination. He is very far from being independent. What his mother really is we cannot know; but, from Fanny's occasional mention of her conduct and opinions, we have never been disposed to think her amiable; and I am very much mistaken if Edward is not himself aware that there would be many difficulties in his way, if he were wish to marry a woman who had not either a great fortune or high rank."

Marianne was astonished to find how much the imagination of her mother and herself had outstripped the truth.

"And you really are not engaged to him!" said she. "Yet it certainly soon will happen. But two advantages will proceed from this delay. *I* shall not lose you so soon, and Edward will have greater opportunity of improving that natural taste for

your favourite pursuit which must be so indispensably necessary to your future felicity. Oh! if he should be so far stimulated
by your genius as to learn to draw himself, how delightful it
would be!"

Elinor had given her real opinion to her sister. She could
not consider her partiality for Edward in so prosperous a state
as Marianne had believed it. There was, at times, a want of
spirits about him which, if it did not denote indifference, spoke
a something almost as unpromising. A doubt of her regard, supposing him to feel it, need not give him more than inquietude.
It would not be likely to produce that dejection of mind which
frequently attended him. A more reasonable cause might be
found in the dependent situation which forbad the indulgence
of his affection. She knew that his mother neither behaved to
him so as to make his home comfortable at present, nor to give
him any assurance that he might form a home for himself, without strictly attending to her views for his aggrandizement. With
such a knowledge as this, it was impossible for Elinor to feel easy
on the subject. She was far from depending on that result of his
preference of her, which her mother and sister still considered
as certain. Nay, the longer they were together the more doubtful seemed the nature of his regard; and sometimes, for a few
painful minutes, she believed it to be no more than friendship.

But, whatever might really be its limits, it was enough, when
perceived by his sister, to make her uneasy; and at the same
time, (which was still more common,) to make her uncivil.
She took the first opportunity of affronting her mother-in-law
on the occasion, talking to her so expressively of her brother's
great expectations, of Mrs. Ferrars's resolution that both her
sons should marry well, and of the danger attending any young
woman who attempted to *draw him in*; that Mrs. Dashwood
could neither pretend to be unconscious, nor endeavour to be
calm. She gave her an answer which marked her contempt,
and instantly left the room, resolving that, whatever might
be the inconvenience or expense of so sudden a removal, her
beloved Elinor should not be exposed another week to such
insinuations.

In this state of her spirits, a letter was delivered to her from the post, which contained a proposal particularly well timed. It was the offer of a small house, on very easy terms, belonging to a relation of her own, a gentleman of consequence and property in Devonshire. The letter was from this gentleman himself, and written in the true spirit of friendly accommodation. He understood that she was in need of a dwelling, and though the house he now offered her was merely a cottage, he assured her that every thing should be done to it which she might think necessary, if the situation pleased her. He earnestly pressed her, after giving the particulars of the house and garden, to come with her daughters to Barton Park, the place of his own residence, from whence she might judge, herself, whether Barton Cottage, for the houses were in the same parish, could, by any alteration, be made comfortable to her. He seemed really anxious to accommodate them, and the whole of his letter was written in so friendly a style as could not fail of giving pleasure to his cousin;[1] more especially at a moment when she was suffering under the cold and unfeeling behaviour of her nearer connections. She needed no time for deliberation or inquiry. Her resolution was formed as she read. The situation of Barton, in a county so far distant from Sussex as Devonshire,[2] which, but a few hours before, would have been a sufficient objection to outweigh every possible advantage belonging to the place, was now its first recommendation. To quit the neighbourhood of Norland was no longer an evil; it was an object of desire; it was a blessing, in comparison of the misery of continuing her daughter-in-law's guest: and to remove for ever from that beloved place would be less painful than to inhabit or visit it while such a woman was its mistress. She instantly wrote Sir John Middleton her acknowledgement of his kindness, and her acceptance of his proposal; and then

[1] *cousin*: kinsman (not necessarily a cousin of clearly fixed degree).

[2] *Sussex . . . Devonshire*: While not literally polar opposites, Sussex (a county of South East England) and Devon (a county of South West England) were indeed profoundly distant from each other. The latter's distance from London gives particular emphasis to its unfashionability (by London standards).

hastened to shew both letters to her daughters, that she might be secure of their approbation before her answer were sent.

Elinor had always thought it would be more prudent for them to settle at some distance from Norland than immediately amongst their present acquaintance. On *that* head, therefore, it was not for her to oppose her mother's intention of removing into Devonshire. The house, too, as described by Sir John, was on so simple a scale, and the rent so uncommonly moderate, as to leave her no right of objection on either point; and, therefore, though it was not a plan which brought any charm to her fancy, though it was a removal from the vicinity of Norland beyond her wishes, she made no attempt to dissuade her mother from sending her letter of acquiescence.

Chapter V

No sooner was her answer dispatched, than Mrs. Dashwood indulged herself in the pleasure of announcing to her son-in-law and his wife that she was provided with an house, and should incommode them no longer than till every thing were ready for her inhabiting it. They heard her with surprise. Mrs. John Dashwood said nothing; but her husband civilly hoped that she would not be settled far from Norland. She had great satisfaction in replying that she was going into Devonshire.— Edward turned hastily towards her, on hearing this, and, in a voice of surprise and concern, which required no explanation to her, repeated, "Devonshire! Are you, indeed, going there? So far from hence! And to what part of it?" She explained the situation. It was within four miles northward of Exeter.[1]

"It is but a cottage," she continued, "but I hope to see many of my friends in it. A room or two can easily be added; and if my friends find no difficulty in travelling so far to see me, I am sure I will find none in accommodating them."

She concluded with a very kind invitation to Mr. and Mrs. John Dashwood to visit her at Barton; and to Edward she gave one with still greater affection. Though her late conversation with her daughter-in-law had made her resolve on remaining at Norland no longer than was unavoidable, it had not produced the smallest effect on her in that point to which it principally tended. To separate Edward and Elinor was as far from being her object as ever; and she wished to shew Mrs. John Dashwood by this pointed invitation to her brother, how totally she disregarded her disapprobation of the match.

Mr. John Dashwood told his mother again and again how exceedingly sorry he was that she had taken an house at such a distance from Norland as to prevent his being of any service

[1] *Exeter*: county seat of Devon.

to her in removing her furniture. He really felt conscientiously vexed on the occasion; for the very exertion to which he had limited the performance of his promise to his father was by this arrangement rendered impracticable.—The furniture was all sent round by water.[2] It chiefly consisted of household linen, plate, china, and books, with an handsome pianoforté of Marianne's. Mrs. John Dashwood saw the packages depart with a sigh: she could not help feeling it hard that as Mrs. Dashwood's income would be so trifling in comparison with their own, she should have any handsome article of furniture.

Mrs. Dashwood took the house for a twelvemonth; it was ready furnished, and she might have immediate possession. No difficulty arose on either side in the agreement; and she waited only for the disposal of her effects at Norland, and to determine her future household, before she set off for the west; and this, as she was exceedingly rapid in the performance of every thing that interested her, was soon done.—The horses which were left her by her husband, had been sold soon after his death, and an opportunity now offering of disposing of her carriage, she agreed to sell that likewise at the earnest advice of her eldest daughter.[3] For the comfort of her children, had she consulted only her own wishes, she would have kept it; but the discretion of Elinor prevailed. *Her* wisdom too limited the number of their servants to three; two maids and a man, with whom they were speedily provided from amongst those who had formed their establishment at Norland.

The man and one of the maids were sent off immediately into Devonshire, to prepare the house for their mistress's arrival; for as Lady Middleton was entirely unknown to Mrs. Dashwood, she preferred going directly to the cottage to being a visitor at Barton Park; and she relied so undoubtingly on Sir

---

[2] *sent ... water*: Transportation of their belongings via the English Channel along England's southern border would be a rapid and presumably economic choice.

[3] *The horses ... daughter*: It was an expensive business to keep horses (cf. Elinor's persuasion of Marianne on pp. 58–59), though it was also a sign of higher social status to have a carriage at one's own disposal.

John's description of the house, as to feel no curiosity to examine it herself till she entered it as her own. Her eagerness to be gone from Norland was preserved from diminution by the evident satisfaction of her daughter-in-law in the prospect of her removal; a satisfaction which was but feebly attempted to be concealed under a cold invitation to her to defer her departure. Now was the time when her son-in-law's promise to his father might with particular propriety be fulfilled. Since he had neglected to do it on first coming to the estate, their quitting his house might be looked on as the most suitable period for its accomplishment. But Mrs. Dashwood began shortly to give over every hope of the kind, and to be convinced, from the general drift of his discourse, that his assistance extended no farther than their maintenance for six months at Norland. He so frequently talked of the increasing expenses of housekeeping, and of the perpetual demands upon his purse, which a man of any consequence in the world was beyond calculation exposed to, that he seemed rather to stand in need of more money himself than to have any design of giving money away.

In a very few weeks from the day which brought Sir John Middleton's first letter to Norland, every thing was so far settled in their future abode as to enable Mrs. Dashwood and her daughters to begin their journey.

Many were the tears shed by them in their last adieus to a place so much beloved. "Dear, dear Norland!" said Marianne, as she wandered alone before the house, on the last evening of their being there; "when shall I cease to regret you!—when learn to feel a home elsewhere!—Oh! happy house, could you know what I suffer in now viewing you from this spot, from whence perhaps I may view you no more!—And you, ye well-known trees!—but you will continue the same.—No leaf will decay because we are removed, nor any branch become motionless although we can observe you no longer!—No; you will continue the same; unconscious of the pleasure or the regret you occasion, and insensible of any change in those who walk under your shade!—But who will remain to enjoy you?"

Chapter VI

The first part of their journey was performed in too melancholy a disposition to be otherwise than tedious and unpleasant. But as they drew towards the end of it, their interest in the appearance of a country which they were to inhabit overcame their dejection, and a view of Barton Valley as they entered it gave them cheerfulness. It was a pleasant fertile spot, well wooded, and rich in pasture. After winding along it for more than a mile, they reached their own house. A small green court was the whole of its demesne[1] in front; and a neat wicket gate admitted them into it.

As a house, Barton Cottage, though small, was comfortable and compact; but as a cottage it was defective,[2] for the building was regular, the roof was tiled, the window shutters were not painted green, nor were the walls covered with honeysuckles. A narrow passage led directly through the house into the garden behind. On each side of the entrance was a sitting room, about sixteen feet square; and beyond them were the offices[3] and the stairs. Four bed-rooms and two garrets formed the rest of the house. It had not been built many years and was in good repair. In comparison of Norland, it was poor and small indeed!—but the tears which recollection called forth as they entered the house were soon dried away. They were cheered by the joy of the servants on their arrival, and each for the sake of the others resolved to appear happy. It was very early in September; the season was fine, and from first seeing the place under the advantage of good weather, they received an impression in its

[1] *demesne*: land, domain.

[2] *defective*: In the eighteenth century, a quaint cottage was a sentimentalized habitation, representative of rustic simplicity (in contrast to the depravity and opulence of the city). The ways in which Barton Cottage fails to live up to the idealized cottage clearly show of what that ideal consisted.

[3] *offices*: kitchen, pantry, scullery, etc. (the "working" rooms of the house).

favour which was of material service in recommending it to their lasting approbation.

The situation of the house was good. High hills rose immediately behind, and at no great distance on each side; some of which were open downs,[4] the others cultivated and woody. The village of Barton was chiefly on one of these hills, and formed a pleasant view from the cottage windows. The prospect in front was more extensive; it commanded the whole of the valley, and reached into the country beyond. The hills which surrounded the cottage terminated the valley in that direction; under another name, and in another course, it branched out again between two of the steepest of them.

With the size and furniture of the house Mrs. Dashwood was upon the whole well satisfied; for though her former style of life rendered many additions to the latter indispensable, yet to add and improve was a delight to her; and she had at this time ready money enough to supply all that was wanted of greater elegance to the apartments. "As for the house itself, to be sure," said she, "it is too small for our family, but we will make ourselves tolerably comfortable for the present as it is too late in the year for improvements. Perhaps in the spring, if I have plenty of money, as I dare say I shall, we may think about building. These parlours are both too small for such parties of our friends as I hope to see often collected here; and I have some thoughts of throwing the passage into one of them with perhaps a part of the other, and so leave the remainder of that other for an entrance; this, with a new drawing-room which may be easily added, and a bed-chamber and garret above, will make it a very snug little cottage. I could wish the stairs were handsome. But one must not expect every thing; though I suppose it would be no difficult matter to widen them. I shall see how much I am before-hand with the world in the spring, and we will plan our improvements accordingly."

In the mean time, till all these alterations could be made from the savings of an income of five hundred a-year by a

---

[4] *downs*: hills.

woman who never saved in her life, they were wise enough to be contented with the house as it was; and each of them was busy in arranging their particular concerns, and endeavouring, by placing around them their books and other possessions, to form themselves a home. Marianne's pianoforté was unpacked and properly disposed of; and Elinor's drawings were affixed to the walls of their sitting room.

In such employments as these they were interrupted soon after breakfast the next day by the entrance of their landlord, who called to welcome them to Barton, and to offer them every accommodation from his own house and garden in which their's might at present be deficient. Sir John Middleton was a good looking man about forty. He had formerly visited at Stanhill, but it was too long ago for his young cousins to remember him. His countenance was thoroughly good-humoured; and his manners were as friendly as the style of his letter. Their arrival seemed to afford him real satisfaction, and their comfort to be an object of real solicitude[5] to him. He said much of his earnest desire of their living in the most sociable terms with his family, and pressed them so cordially to dine at Barton Park every day till they were better settled at home, that, though his entreaties were carried to a point of perseverance beyond civility, they could not give offence. His kindness was not confined to words; for within an hour after he left them, a large basket full of garden stuff[6] and fruit arrived from the park, which was followed before the end of the day by a present of game.[7] He insisted moreover on conveying all their letters to and from the post for them, and would not be denied the satisfaction of sending them his newspaper every day.[8]

Lady Middleton had sent a very civil message by him, denoting her intention of waiting on Mrs. Dashwood as soon as she

[5] *solicitude*: anxiety, concern.
[6] *garden stuff*: i.e., vegetables.
[7] *game*: game birds and other meats (presumably hunted by the local gentry).
[8] *newspaper every day*: According to Chapman, this may be a reference to *Trueman's Exeter Flying Post* or *Plymouth and Cornish Advertiser*, or it may be a reference to *Woolmer's Exeter and Plymouth Gazette* (later called *The Devon and Exeter Daily Gazette*).

could be assured that her visit would be no inconvenience; and as this message was answered by an invitation equally polite, her ladyship was introduced to them the next day.

They were of course very anxious to see a person on whom so much of their comfort at Barton must depend; and the elegance of her appearance was favourable to their wishes. Lady Middleton was not more than six or seven and twenty; her face was handsome, her figure tall and striking, and her address graceful. Her manners had all the elegance which her husband's wanted. But they would have been improved by some share of his frankness and warmth; and her visit was long enough to detract something from their first admiration, by shewing that though perfectly well-bred, she was reserved, cold, and had nothing to say for herself beyond the most common-place inquiry or remark.

Conversation however was not wanted, for Sir John was very chatty, and Lady Middleton had taken the wise precaution of bringing with her their eldest child, a fine little boy about six years old, by which means there was one subject always to be recurred to by the ladies in case of extremity, for they had to inquire his name and age, admire his beauty, and ask him questions which his mother answered for him, while he hung about her and held down his head, to the great surprise of her ladyship, who wondered at his being so shy before company as he could make noise enough at home. On every formal visit a child ought to be of the party, by way of provision for discourse. In the present case it took up ten minutes to determine whether the boy were most like his father or mother, and in what particular he resembled either, for of course every body differed, and every body was astonished at the opinion of the others.

An opportunity was soon to be given to the Dashwoods of debating on the rest of the children, as Sir John would not leave the house without securing their promise of dining at the park the next day.

Chapter VII

Barton Park was about half a mile from the cottage. The ladies had passed near it in their way along the valley, but it was screened from their view at home by the projection of an hill. The house was large and handsome; and the Middletons lived in a style of equal hospitality and elegance. The former was for Sir John's gratification, the latter for that of his lady. They were scarcely ever without some friends staying with them in the house, and they kept more company of every kind than any other family in the neighbourhood. It was necessary to the happiness of both; for however dissimilar in temper and outward behaviour, they strongly resembled each other in that total want of talent and taste which confined their employments, unconnected with such as society produced, within a very narrow compass. Sir John was a sportsman,[1] Lady Middleton a mother. He hunted and shot, and she humoured her children; and these were their only resources. Lady Middleton had the advantage of being able to spoil her children all the year round, while Sir John's independent employments were in existence only half the time. Continual engagements at home and abroad, however, supplied all the deficiencies of nature and education; supported the good spirits of Sir John, and gave exercise to the good-breeding of his wife.

Lady Middleton piqued[2] herself upon the elegance of her table, and of all her domestic arrangements; and from this kind of vanity was her greatest enjoyment in any of their parties. But Sir John's satisfaction in society was much more real; he delighted in collecting about him more young people than his house would hold, and the noisier they were the better was he pleased. He was a blessing to all the juvenile part of the

[1] *sportsman*: hunter.
[2] *piqued*: prided.

neighbourhood, for in summer he was for ever forming parties to eat cold ham and chicken out of doors, and in winter his private balls were numerous enough for any young lady who was not suffering under the insatiable appetite of fifteen.

The arrival of a new family in the country was always a matter of joy to him, and in every point of view he was charmed with the inhabitants he had now procured for his cottage at Barton. The Miss Dashwoods were young, pretty, and unaffected. It was enough to secure his good opinion; for to be unaffected was all that a pretty girl could want to make her mind as captivating as her person. The friendliness of his disposition made him happy in accommodating those, whose situation might be considered, in comparison with the past, as unfortunate. In shewing kindness to his cousins therefore he had the real satisfaction of a good heart; and in settling a family of females only in his cottage, he had all the satisfaction of a sportsman; for a sportsman, though he esteems only those of his sex who are sportsmen likewise, is not often desirous of encouraging their taste by admitting them to a residence within his own manor.

Mrs. Dashwood and her daughters were met at the door of the house by Sir John, who welcomed them to Barton Park with unaffected sincerity; and as he attended them to the drawing room repeated to the young ladies the concern which the same subject had drawn from him the day before, at being unable to get any smart young men to meet them. They would see, he said, only one gentleman there besides himself; a particular friend who was staying at the park, but who was neither very young nor very gay. He hoped they would all excuse the smallness of the party, and could assure them it should never happen so again. He had been to several families that morning in hopes of procuring some addition to their number, but it was moonlight[3] and every body was full of engagements. Luckily

---

[3] *moonlight:* To reduce the expense of candles, summer parties were scheduled according to the full moon—consequently, most in their circle have already made evening engagements.

Lady Middleton's mother had arrived at Barton within the last hour, and as she was a very cheerful agreeable woman, he hoped the young ladies would not find it so very dull as they might imagine. The young ladies as well as their mother, were perfectly satisfied with having two entire strangers of the party, and wished for no more.

Mrs. Jennings, Lady Middleton's mother, was a good-humoured, merry, fat, elderly woman, who talked a great deal, seemed very happy, and rather vulgar. She was full of jokes and laughter, and before dinner was over had said many witty things on the subject of lovers and husbands; hoped they had not left their hearts behind them in Sussex, and pretended to see them blush whether they did or not. Marianne was vexed at it for her sister's sake, and turned her eyes towards Elinor to see how she bore these attacks, with an earnestness which gave Elinor far more pain than could arise from such common-place raillery[4] as Mrs. Jennings's.

Colonel Brandon, the friend of Sir John, seemed no more adapted by resemblance of manner to be his friend, than Lady Middleton was to be his wife, or Mrs. Jennings to be Lady Middleton's mother. He was silent and grave. His appearance however was not unpleasing, in spite of his being in the opinion of Marianne and Margaret an absolute old bachelor, for he was on the wrong side of five and thirty; but though his face was not handsome his countenance was sensible, and his address was particularly gentlemanlike.

There was nothing in any of the party which could recommend them as companions to the Dashwoods; but the cold insipidity of Lady Middleton was so particularly repulsive, that in comparison of it the gravity of Colonel Brandon, and even the boisterous mirth of Sir John and his mother-in-law was interesting. Lady Middleton seemed to be roused to enjoyment only by the entrance of her four noisy children after dinner, who pulled her about, tore her clothes, and put an end to every kind of discourse except what related to themselves.

[4] *raillery*: good-humored teasing.

In the evening, as Marianne was discovered to be musical, she was invited to play. The instrument was unlocked, every body prepared to be charmed, and Marianne, who sang very well, at their request went through the chief of the songs which Lady Middleton had brought into the family on her marriage, and which perhaps had lain ever since in the same position on the pianoforté, for her ladyship had celebrated that event by giving up music, although by her mother's account she had played extremely well, and by her own was very fond of it.

Marianne's performance was highly applauded. Sir John was loud in his admiration at the end of every song, and as loud in his conversation with the others while every song lasted. Lady Middleton frequently called him to order, wondered how any one's attention could be diverted from music for a moment, and asked Marianne to sing a particular song which Marianne had just finished. Colonel Brandon alone, of all the party, heard her without being in raptures. He paid her only the compliment of attention; and she felt a respect for him on the occasion, which the others had reasonably forfeited by their shameless want of taste. His pleasure in music, though it amounted not to that extatic[5] delight which alone could sympathize with her own, was estimable when contrasted against the horrible insensibility of the others; and she was reasonable enough to allow that a man of five and thirty might well have outlived all acuteness of feeling and every exquisite power of enjoyment. She was perfectly disposed to make every allowance for the colonel's advanced state of life which humanity required.

[5] *extatic*: ecstatic.

Chapter VIII

Mrs. Jennings was a widow, with an ample jointure.[1] She had only two daughters, both of whom she had lived to see respectably married, and she had now therefore nothing to do but to marry all the rest of the world. In the promotion of this object she was zealously active, as far as her ability reached; and missed no opportunity of projecting weddings among all the young people of her acquaintance. She was remarkably quick in the discovery of attachments, and had enjoyed the advantage of raising the blushes and the vanity of many a young lady by insinuations of her power over such a young man; and this kind of discernment enabled her soon after her arrival at Barton decisively to pronounce that Colonel Brandon was very much in love with Marianne Dashwood. She rather suspected it to be so, on the very first evening of their being together, from his listening so attentively while she sang to them; and when the visit was returned by the Middletons' dining at the cottage, the fact was ascertained by his listening to her again. It must be so. She was perfectly convinced of it. It would be an excellent match, for *he* was rich and *she* was handsome. Mrs. Jennings had been anxious to see Colonel Brandon well married, ever since her connection with Sir John first brought him to her knowledge; and she was always anxious to get a good husband for every pretty girl.

The immediate advantage to herself was by no means inconsiderable, for it supplied her with endless jokes against them both. At the park she laughed at the colonel, and in the cottage at Marianne. To the former her raillery was probably, as far as it regarded only himself, perfectly indifferent; but to the latter it was at first incomprehensible; and when its object

---

[1] *jointure*: estate settled on a widow for the period during which she survives her husband.

was understood, she hardly knew whether most to laugh at its absurdity, or censure its impertinence, for she considered it as an unfeeling reflection on the colonel's advanced years, and on his forlorn condition as an old bachelor.

Mrs. Dashwood, who could not think a man five years younger than herself, so exceedingly ancient as he appeared to the youthful fancy of her daughter, ventured to clear Mrs. Jennings from the probability of wishing to throw ridicule on his age.

"But at least, mama, you cannot deny the absurdity of the accusation, though you may not think it intentionally ill-natured. Colonel Brandon is certainly younger than Mrs. Jennings, but he is old enough to be *my* father; and if he were ever animated enough to be in love, must have long outlived every sensation of the kind. It is too ridiculous! When is a man to be safe from such wit, if age and infirmity will not protect him?"

"Infirmity!" said Elinor, "do you call Colonel Brandon infirm? I can easily suppose that his age may appear much greater to you than to my mother; but you can hardly deceive yourself as to his having the use of his limbs!"

"Did not you hear him complain of the rheumatism?[2] and is not that the commonest infirmity of declining life?"

"My dearest child," said her mother laughing, "at this rate you must be in continual terror of *my* decay; and it must seem to you a miracle that my life has been extended to the advanced age of forty."

"Mama, you are not doing me justice. I know very well that Colonel Brandon is not old enough to make his friends yet apprehensive of losing him in the course of nature. He may live twenty years longer. But thirty-five has nothing to do with matrimony."

"Perhaps," said Elinor, "thirty-five and seventeen had better not have any thing to do with matrimony together. But if there

---

[2] *rheumatism:* general term for stiffness and pain in the muscles and swelling and pain in the joints.

should by any chance happen to be a woman who is single at seven and twenty, I should not think Colonel Brandon's being thirty-five any objection to his marrying *her*."

"A woman of seven and twenty," said Marianne, after pausing a moment, "can never hope to feel or inspire affection again, and if her home be uncomfortable, or her fortune small, I can suppose that she might bring herself to submit to the offices of a nurse, for the sake of the provision and security of a wife. In his marrying such a woman therefore there would be nothing unsuitable. It would be a compact of convenience, and the world would be satisfied. In my eyes it would be no marriage at all, but that would be nothing. To me it would seem only a commercial exchange, in which each wished to be benefited at the expense of the other."

"It would be impossible, I know," replied Elinor, "to convince you that a woman of seven and twenty could feel for a man of thirty-five any thing near enough to love, to make him a desirable companion to her. But I must object to your dooming Colonel Brandon and his wife to the constant confinement of a sick chamber, merely because he chanced to complain yesterday (a very cold damp day) of a slight rheumatic feel in one of his shoulders."

"But he talked of flannel waistcoats," said Marianne; "and with me a flannel waistcoat is invariably connected with aches, cramps, rheumatisms, and every species of ailment that can afflict the old and the feeble."

"Had he been only in a violent fever, you would not have despised him half so much. Confess, Marianne, is not there something interesting to you in the flushed cheek, hollow eye, and quick pulse of a fever?"

Soon after this, upon Elinor's leaving the room, "Mama," said Marianne, "I have an alarm on the subject of illness, which I cannot conceal from you. I am sure Edward Ferrars is not well. We have now been here almost a fortnight, and yet he does not come. Nothing but real indisposition could occasion this extraordinary delay. What else can detain him at Norland?"

"Had you any idea of his coming so soon?" said Mrs. Dashwood. "I had none. On the contrary, if I have felt any anxiety at all on the subject, it has been in recollecting that he sometimes shewed a want of pleasure and readiness in accepting my invitation, when I talked of his coming to Barton. Does Elinor expect him already?"

"I have never mentioned it to her, but of course she must."

"I rather think you are mistaken, for when I was talking to her yesterday of getting a new grate for the spare bedchamber, she observed that there was no immediate hurry for it, as it was not likely that the room would be wanted for some time."

"How strange this is! what can be the meaning of it! But the whole of their behaviour to each other has been unaccountable! How cold, how composed were their last adieus! How languid their conversation the last evening of their being together! In Edward's farewell there was no distinction between Elinor and me: it was the good wishes of an affectionate brother to both. Twice did I leave them purposely together in the course of the last morning, and each time did he most unaccountably follow me out of the room. And Elinor, in quitting Norland and Edward, cried not as I did. Even now her self-command is invariable. When is she dejected or melancholy? When does she try to avoid society, or appear restless and dissatisfied in it?"

Chapter IX

The Dashwoods were now settled at Barton with tolerable comfort to themselves. The house and the garden, with all the objects surrounding them, were now become familiar, and the ordinary pursuits which had given to Norland half its charms, were engaged in again with far greater enjoyment than Norland had been able to afford, since the loss of their father. Sir John Middleton, who called on them every day for the first fortnight, and who was not in the habit of seeing much occupation at home, could not conceal his amazement on finding them always employed.

Their visitors, except those from Barton Park, were not many; for, in spite of Sir John's urgent entreaties that they would mix more in the neighbourhood, and repeated assurances of his carriage being always at their service, the independence of Mrs. Dashwood's spirit overcame the wish of society for her children; and she was resolute in declining to visit any family beyond the distance of a walk. There were but few who could be so classed; and it was not all of them that were attainable. About a mile and a half from the cottage, along the narrow winding valley of Allenham, which issued from that of Barton, as formerly described, the girls had, in one of their earliest walks, discovered an ancient respectable looking mansion, which, by reminding them a little of Norland, interested their imagination and made them wish to be better acquainted with it. But they learnt, on inquiry, that its possessor, an elderly lady of very good character, was unfortunately too infirm to mix with the world, and never stirred from home.

The whole country about them abounded in beautiful walks. The high downs which invited them from almost every window of the cottage to seek the exquisite enjoyment of air on their summits, were an happy alternative when the dirt of the valleys beneath shut up their superior beauties; and towards one of these hills did Marianne and Margaret one memorable morning direct their steps, attracted by the partial sunshine of a showery sky, and unable longer to bear the confinement which the settled rain of the two preceding days had occasioned. The weather was not tempting enough to draw the two others from their pencil and their book, in spite of Marianne's declaration that the day would be lastingly fair, and that every threatening cloud would be drawn off from their hills; and the two girls set off together.

They gaily ascended the downs, rejoicing in their own penetration at every glimpse of blue sky; and when they caught in their faces the animating gales of an high south-westerly wind, they pitied the fears which had prevented their mother and Elinor from sharing such delightful sensations.

"Is there a felicity in the world," said Marianne, "superior to this?—Margaret, we will walk here at least two hours."

Margaret agreed, and they pursued their way against the wind, resisting it with laughing delight for about twenty minutes longer, when suddenly the clouds united over their heads, and a driving rain set full in their face.—Chagrined and surprised, they were obliged, though unwillingly, to turn back, for no shelter was nearer than their own house. One consolation however remained for them, to which the exigence of the moment gave more than usual propriety; it was that of running with all possible speed down the steep side of the hill which led immediately to their garden gate.

They set off. Marianne had at first the advantage, but a false step brought her suddenly to the ground, and Margaret, unable to stop herself to assist her, was involuntarily hurried along, and reached the bottom in safety.

A gentleman carrying a gun, with two pointers playing round him, was passing up the hill and within a few yards of Marianne, when her accident happened. He put down his gun and ran to her assistance. She had raised herself from the ground, but her foot had been twisted in the fall, and she was scarcely able to stand. The gentleman offered his services, and perceiving that her modesty declined what her situation rendered necessary, took her up in his arms without farther delay, and carried her down the hill. Then passing through the garden, the gate of which had been left open by Margaret, he bore her directly into the house, whither Margaret was just arrived, and quitted not his hold till he had seated her in a chair in the parlour.

Elinor and her mother rose up in amazement at their entrance, and while the eyes of both were fixed on him with an evident wonder and a secret admiration which equally sprung from his appearance, he apologized for his intrusion by relating its cause, in a manner so frank and so graceful, that his person, which was uncommonly handsome, received additional charms from his voice and expression. Had he been even old, ugly, and vulgar, the gratitude and kindness of Mrs. Dashwood would have been secured by any act of attention to her child; but the influence of youth, beauty, and elegance, gave an interest to the action which came home to her feelings.

She thanked him again and again; and with a sweetness of address which always attended her, invited him to be seated. But this he declined, as he was dirty and wet. Mrs. Dashwood then begged to know to whom she was obliged. His name, he replied, was Willoughby and his present home was at Allenham, from whence he hoped she would allow him the honour of calling to-morrow to inquire after Miss Dashwood. The honour was readily granted, and he then departed, to make himself still more interesting, in the midst of an heavy rain.

His manly beauty and more than common gracefulness were instantly the theme of general admiration, and the laugh which his gallantry raised against Marianne, received particular spirit from his exterior attractions.—Marianne herself had seen less of his person than the rest, for the confusion which crimsoned over her face, on his lifting her up, had robbed her of the power of regarding him after their entering the house. But she had seen enough of him to join in all the admiration of the others, and with an energy which always adorned her praise. His person and air were equal to what her fancy had ever drawn for the hero of a favourite story; and in his carrying her into the house with so little previous formality, there was a rapidity of thought which particularly recommended the action to her. Every circumstance belonging to him was interesting. His name was good, his residence was in their favourite village, and she soon found out that of all manly dresses a shooting-jacket was the most becoming. Her imagination was busy, her reflections were pleasant, and the pain of a sprained ancle was disregarded.

Sir John called on them as soon as the next interval of fair weather that morning allowed him to get out of doors; and Marianne's accident being related to him, he was eagerly asked whether he knew any gentleman of the name of Willoughby at Allenham.

"Willoughby!" cried Sir John; "what, is *he* in the country? That is good news however; I will ride over to-morrow, and ask him to dinner on Thursday."

"You know him then," said Mrs. Dashwood.

"Know him! to be sure I do. Why, he is down here every year."

"And what sort of a young man is he?"

"As good a kind of fellow as ever lived, I assure you. A very decent shot, and there is not a bolder rider in England."

"And is *that* all you can say for him?" cried Marianne, indignantly. "But what are his manners on more intimate acquaintance? What his pursuits, his talents and genius?"

Sir John was rather puzzled.

"Upon my soul," said he, "I do not know much about him as to all *that*. But he is a pleasant, good humoured fellow, and has got the nicest little black bitch of a pointer[1] I ever saw. Was she out with him to-day?"

But Marianne could no more satisfy him as to the colour of Mr. Willoughby's pointer, than he could describe to her the shades of his mind.

"But who is he?" said Elinor. "Where does he come from? Has he a house at Allenham?"

---

[1] *black . . . pointer:* female hunting dog.

On this point Sir John could give more certain intelligence; and he told them that Mr. Willoughby had no property of his own in the country; that he resided there only while he was visiting the old lady at Allenham Court, to whom he was related, and whose possessions he was to inherit; adding, "Yes, yes, he is very well worth catching, I can tell you, Miss Dashwood; he has a pretty little estate of his own in Somersetshire[2] besides; and if I were you, I would not give him up to my younger sister in spite of all this tumbling down hills. Miss Marianne must not expect to have all the men to herself. Brandon will be jealous, if she does not take care."

"I do not believe," said Mrs. Dashwood, with a good humoured smile, "that Mr. Willoughby will be incommoded by the attempts of either of *my* daughters towards what you call *catching him*. It is not an employment to which they have been brought up. Men are very safe with us, let them be ever so rich. I am glad to find, however, from what you say, that he is a respectable young man, and one whose acquaintance will not be ineligible."

"He is as good a sort of fellow, I believe, as ever lived," repeated Sir John. "I remember last Christmas, at a little hop[3] at the park, he danced from eight o'clock till four, without once sitting down."

"Did he indeed?" cried Marianne, with sparkling eyes, "and with elegance, with spirit?"

"Yes; and he was up again at eight to ride to covert."[4]

"That is what I like; that is what a young man ought to be. Whatever be his pursuits, his eagerness in them should know no moderation, and leave him no sense of fatigue."

"Aye, aye, I see how it will be," said Sir John, "I see how it will be. You will be setting your cap[5] at him now, and never think of poor Brandon."

---

[2] *Somersetshire*: Somerset, county northeast of Devon.

[3] *hop*: informal dance.

[4] *covert*: thicket where game can hide (thus he would be riding to hunt where the game will be found).

[5] *setting your cap*: idiomatic expression for attempting to capture a man's attentions.

"That is an expression, Sir John," said Marianne, warmly, "which I particularly dislike. I abhor every common-place phrase by which wit is intended; and 'setting one's cap at a man,' or 'making a conquest,' are the most odious of all. Their tendency is gross and illiberal; and if their construction could ever be deemed clever, time has long ago destroyed all its ingenuity."

Sir John did not much understand this reproof; but he laughed as heartily as if he did, and then replied,

"Aye, you will make conquests enough, I dare say, one way or other. Poor Brandon! he is quite smitten already, and he is very well worth setting your cap at, I can tell you, in spite of all this tumbling about and spraining of ancles."

Chapter X

Marianne's preserver, as Margaret, with more elegance than precision, stiled Willoughby, called at the cottage early the next morning to make his personal inquiries. He was received by Mrs. Dashwood with more than politeness; with a kindness which Sir John's account of him and her own gratitude prompted; and every thing that passed during the visit, tended to assure him of the sense, elegance, mutual affection, and domestic comfort of the family to whom accident had now introduced him. Of their personal charms he had not required a second interview to be convinced.

Miss Dashwood had a delicate complexion, regular features, and a remarkably pretty figure. Marianne was still handsomer. Her form, though not so correct as her sister's, in having the advantage of height, was more striking; and her face was so lovely, that when in the common cant of praise she was called a beautiful girl, truth was less violently outraged than usually happens. Her skin was very brown, but from its transparency, her complexion was uncommonly brilliant; her features were all good; her smile was sweet and attractive, and in her eyes, which were very dark, there was a life, a spirit, an eagerness which could hardly be seen without delight. From Willoughby their expression was at first held back, by the embarrassment which the remembrance of his assistance created. But when this passed away, when her spirits became collected, when she saw that to the perfect good-breeding of the gentleman, he united frankness and vivacity, and above all, when she heard him declare that of music and dancing he was passionately fond, she gave him such a look of approbation as secured the largest share of his discourse to herself for the rest of his stay.

It was only necessary to mention any favourite amusement to engage her to talk. She could not be silent when such points were introduced, and she had neither shyness nor reserve in their discussion. They speedily discovered that their enjoyment of dancing and music was mutual, and that it arose from a general conformity of judgment in all that related to either. Encouraged by this to a further examination of his opinions, she proceeded to question him on the subject of books; her favourite authors were brought forward and dwelt upon with so rapturous a delight, that any young man of five and twenty must have been insensible indeed, not to become an immediate convert to the excellence of such works, however disregarded before. Their taste was strikingly alike. The same books, the same passages were idolized by each—or if any difference appeared, any objection arose, it lasted no longer than till the force of her arguments and the brightness of her eyes could be displayed. He acquiesced in all her decisions, caught all her enthusiasm; and long before his visit concluded, they conversed with the familiarity of a long-established acquaintance.

"Well, Marianne," said Elinor, as soon as he had left them, "for *one* morning I think you have done pretty well. You have already ascertained Mr. Willoughby's opinion in almost every matter of importance. You know what he thinks of Cowper and Scott;[1] you are certain of his estimating their beauties as he ought, and you have received every assurance of his admiring Pope[2] no more than is proper. But how is your acquaintance to be long supported, under such extraordinary dispatch of every subject for discourse? You will soon have exhausted

---

[1] *Scott:* Sir Walter Scott (1771–1832), monumental novelist of the period, known for his works of historical fiction. With Cowper, Scott represents the contemporary "Romantic" movement in English literature.

[2] *Pope:* Alexander Pope (1688–1744), influential eighteenth-century poet (often satirical) and translator of Homer, one of the principal authors of the "Augustan" period of English literature, which modeled itself on the high style and arch wit of the classical Augustan period of literature (during the reign of Caesar Augustus, 27 B.C.–A.D. 14).

each favourite topic. Another meeting will suffice to explain his sentiments on picturesque beauty,[3] and second marriages, and then you can have nothing farther to ask."—

"Elinor," cried Marianne, "is this fair? is this just? are my ideas so scanty? But I see what you mean. I have been too much at my ease, too happy, too frank. I have erred against every common-place notion of decorum; I have been open and sincere where I ought to have been reserved, spiritless, dull, and deceitful:—had I talked only of the weather and the roads, and had I spoken only once in ten minutes, this reproach would have been spared."

"My love," said her mother, "you must not be offended with Elinor—she was only in jest. I should scold her myself, if she were capable of wishing to check the delight of your conversation with our new friend."—Marianne was softened in a moment.

Willoughby, on his side, gave every proof of his pleasure in their acquaintance,[4] which an evident wish of improving it could offer. He came to them every day. To inquire after Marianne was at first his excuse; but the encouragement of his reception, to which every day gave greater kindness, made such an excuse unnecessary before it had ceased to be possible, by Marianne's perfect recovery. She was confined for some days to the house; but never had any confinement been less irksome. Willoughby was a young man of good abilities, quick imagination, lively spirits, and open, affectionate manners. He was exactly formed to engage Marianne's heart, for with all this, he joined not only a captivating person, but a natural ardour of mind which was now roused and increased by the example of her own, and which recommended him to her affection beyond every thing else.

[3] *picturesque beauty*: The word bore particular artistic connotations during the period, drawn from eighteenth-century sensibilities by which irregularity and even decay were valued as interesting and piquant. Cf. Marianne, Elinor, and Edward's conversation on pp. 95–96, which outlines many of the principles of the picturesque.

[4] *their acquaintance*: Edition A gives this as "her acquaintance".

His society became gradually her most exquisite enjoyment. They read, they talked, they sang together; his musical talents were considerable; and he read with all the sensibility and spirit which Edward had unfortunately wanted.

In Mrs. Dashwood's estimation, he was as faultless as in Marianne's; and Elinor saw nothing to censure in him but a propensity, in which he strongly resembled and peculiarly delighted her sister, of saying too much what he thought on every occasion, without attention to persons or circumstances. In hastily forming and giving his opinion of other people, in sacrificing general politeness to the enjoyment of undivided attention where his heart was engaged, and in slighting too easily the forms of worldly propriety, he displayed a want of caution which Elinor could not approve, in spite of all that he and Marianne could say in its support.

Marianne began now to perceive that the desperation which had seized her at sixteen and a half, of ever seeing a man who could satisfy her ideas of perfection, had been rash and unjustifiable. Willoughby was all that her fancy had delineated in that unhappy hour and in every brighter period, as capable of attaching her and his behaviour declared his wishes to be in that respect as earnest, as his abilities were strong.

Her mother too, in whose mind not one speculative thought of their marriage had been raised, by his prospect of riches, was led before the end of a week to hope and expect it; and secretly to congratulate herself on having gained two such sons-in-law as Edward and Willoughby.

Colonel Brandon's partiality for Marianne, which had so early been discovered[5] by his friends, now first became perceptible to Elinor, when it ceased to be noticed by them. Their attention and wit were drawn off to his more fortunate rival; and the raillery which the other had incurred before any partiality arose, was removed when his feelings began really to call for the ridicule so justly annexed to sensibility. Elinor was obliged, though unwillingly, to believe that the sentiments

[5] *discovered*: revealed.

which Mrs. Jennings had assigned him for her own satisfaction, were now actually excited by her sister; and that however a general resemblance of disposition between the parties might forward the affection of Mr. Willoughby, an equally striking opposition of character was no hindrance to the regard of Colonel Brandon. She saw it with concern; for what could a silent man of five and thirty hope, when opposed by a very lively one of five and twenty? and as she could not even wish him successful, she heartily wished him indifferent. She liked him—in spite of his gravity and reserve, she beheld in him an object of interest. His manners, though serious, were mild; and his reserve appeared rather the result of some oppression of spirits, than of any natural gloominess of temper. Sir John had dropt hints of past injuries and disappointments, which justified her belief of his being an unfortunate man, and she regarded him with respect and compassion.

Perhaps she pitied and esteemed him the more because he was slighted by Willoughby and Marianne, who, prejudiced against him for being neither lively nor young, seemed resolved to undervalue his merits.

"Brandon is just the kind of man," said Willoughby one day, when they were talking of him together, "whom every body speaks well of, and nobody cares about; whom all are delighted to see, and nobody remembers to talk to."

"That is exactly what I think of him," cried Marianne.

"Do not boast of it, however," said Elinor, "for it is injustice in both of you. He is highly esteemed by all the family at the park, and I never see him myself without taking pains to converse with him."

"That he is patronized by *you*," replied Willoughby, "is certainly in his favour; but as for the esteem of the others, it is a reproach in itself. Who would submit to the indignity of being approved by such women as Lady Middleton and Mrs. Jennings, that could command the indifference of any body else?"

"But perhaps the abuse of such people as yourself and Marianne, will make amends for the regard of Lady Middleton and her mother. If their praise is censure, your censure may be praise, for they are not more undiscerning, than you are prejudiced and unjust."

"In defence of your protegé you can even be saucy."

"My protegé, as you call him, is a sensible man; and sense will always have attractions for me. Yes, Marianne, even in a man between thirty and forty. He has seen a great deal of the world; has been abroad; has read, and has a thinking mind. I have found him capable of giving me much information on various subjects, and he has always answered my inquiries with the readiness of good-breeding and good nature."

"That is to say," cried Marianne contemptuously, "he has told you that in the East Indies[6] the climate is hot, and the mosquitoes are troublesome."

"He *would* have told me so, I doubt not, had I made any such inquiries, but they happened to be points on which I had been previously informed."

"Perhaps," said Willoughby, "his observations may have extended to the existence of nabobs, gold mohrs, and palanquins."[7]

"I may venture to say that *his* observations have stretched much farther than *your* candour. But why should you dislike him?"

"I do not dislike him. I consider him, on the contrary, as a very respectable man, who has every body's good word and nobody's notice; who has more money than he can spend, more time than he knows how to employ, and two new coats every year."

"Add to which," cried Marianne, "that he has neither genius, taste, nor spirit. That his understanding has no brilliancy, his feelings no ardour, and his voice no expression."

"You decide on his imperfections so much in the mass," replied Elinor, "and so much on the strength of your own

[6] *East Indies*: South Asia and Southeast Asia.

[7] *nabobs, gold mohrs, and palanquins*: A nabob is a person of great wealth or prominence (originally in India); gold mohrs are coins used in India; and palanquins are covered litters for one passenger to be carried by four or six bearers.

imagination, that the commendation *I* am able to give of him is comparatively cold and insipid. I can only pronounce him to be a sensible man, well-bred, well-informed, of gentle address, and I believe possessing an amiable heart."

"Miss Dashwood," cried Willoughby, "you are now using me unkindly. You are endeavouring to disarm me by reason, and to convince me against my will. But it will not do. You shall find me as stubborn as you can be artful. I have three unanswerable reasons for disliking Colonel Brandon: he has threatened me with rain when I wanted it to be fine; he has found fault with the hanging of my curricle,[8] and I cannot persuade him to buy my brown mare. If it will be any satisfaction to you, however, to be told, that I believe his character to be in other respects irreproachable, I am ready to confess it. And in return for an acknowledgement, which must give me some pain, you cannot deny me the privilege of disliking him as much as ever."

[8] *curricle*: light, open, two-wheeled carriage pulled by two horses side by side.

Chapter XI

Little had Mrs. Dashwood or her daughters imagined, when they first came into Devonshire, that so many engagements would arise to occupy their time as shortly presented themselves, or that they should have such frequent invitations and such constant visitors as to leave them little leisure for serious employment. Yet such was the case. When Marianne was recovered, the schemes of amusement at home and abroad, which Sir John had been previously forming, were put in execution. The private balls at the park then began; and parties on the water were made and accomplished as often as a showery October would allow. In every meeting of the kind Willoughby was included; and the ease and familiarity which naturally attended these parties were exactly calculated to give increasing intimacy to his acquaintance with the Dashwoods, to afford him opportunity of witnessing the excellencies of Marianne, of marking his animated admiration of her, and of receiving, in her behaviour to himself, the most pointed assurance of her affection.

Elinor could not be surprised at their attachment. She only wished that it were less openly shewn; and once or twice did venture to suggest the propriety of some self-command to Marianne. But Marianne abhorred all concealment where no real disgrace could attend unreserve; and to aim at the restraint of sentiments which were not in themselves illaudable, appeared to her not merely an unnecessary effort, but a disgraceful subjection of reason to common-place and mistaken notions. Willoughby thought the same; and their behaviour, at all times, was an illustration of their opinions.

When he was present she had no eyes for any one else. Every thing he did, was right. Every thing he said was clever. If their evenings at the park were concluded with cards, he cheated himself and all the rest of the party to get her a good hand. If dancing formed the amusement of the night, they were partners for half the time; and when obliged to separate for a couple of dances, were careful to stand together and scarcely spoke a word to any body else. Such conduct made them of course most exceedingly laughed at; but ridicule could not shame, and seemed hardly to provoke them.

Mrs. Dashwood entered into all their feelings with a warmth which left her no inclination for checking this excessive display of them.[1] To her it was but the natural consequence of a strong affection in a young and ardent mind.

This was the season of happiness to Marianne. Her heart was devoted to Willoughby, and the fond attachment to Norland, which she brought with her from Sussex, was more likely to be softened than she had thought it possible before, by the charms which his society bestowed on her present home.

Elinor's happiness was not so great. Her heart was not so much at ease, nor her satisfaction in their amusements so pure. They afforded her no companion that could make amends for what she had left behind, nor that could teach her to think of Norland with less regret than ever. Neither Lady Middleton nor Mrs. Jennings could supply to her the conversation she missed; although the latter was an everlasting talker, and from the first had regarded her with a kindness which ensured her a large share of her discourse. She had already repeated her own history to Elinor three or four times; and had Elinor's memory been equal to her means of improvement,[2] she might have known very early in their acquaintance, all the particulars of Mr. Jennings's last illness, and what he said to his wife a few minutes before he died. Lady Middleton was more agreeable than her mother, only in being more silent. Elinor needed little observation to perceive that her reserve was a mere calmness of manner with which sense had nothing to do. Towards

---

[1] *them*: i.e., their feelings.
[2] *means of improvement*: i.e., Mrs. Jennings's repetition (which could serve as an exercise for expanding Elinor's powers of memory).

her husband and mother she was the same as to them; and intimacy was therefore neither to be looked for nor desired. She had nothing to say one day that she had not said the day before. Her insipidity was invariable, for even her spirits were always the same; and though she did not oppose the parties arranged by her husband, provided every thing were conducted in style and her two eldest children attended her, she never appeared to receive more enjoyment from them, than she might have experienced in sitting at home;—and so little did her presence add to the pleasure of the others, by any share in their conversation, that they were sometimes only reminded of her being amongst them by her solicitude about her troublesome boys.

In Colonel Brandon alone, of all her new acquaintance, did Elinor find a person who could in any degree claim the respect of abilities, excite the interest of friendship, or give pleasure as a companion. Willoughby was out of the question. Her admiration and regard, even her sisterly regard, was all his own; but he was a lover; his attentions were wholly Marianne's, and a far less agreeable man might have been more generally pleasing. Colonel Brandon, unfortunately for himself, had no such encouragement to think only of Marianne, and in conversing with Elinor he found the greatest consolation for the total indifference of her sister.

Elinor's compassion for him increased, as she had reason to suspect that the misery of disappointed love had already been known by him. This suspicion was given by some words which accidentally dropt from him one evening at the park, when they were sitting down together by mutual consent, while the others were dancing. His eyes were fixed on Marianne, and, after a silence of some minutes, he said with a faint smile, "Your sister, I understand, does not approve of second attachments."

"No," replied Elinor, "her opinions are all romantic."

"Or rather, as I believe, she considers them impossible to exist."

"I believe she does. But how she contrives it without reflecting on the character of her own father, who had himself two wives, I know not. A few years however will settle her opinions on the reasonable basis of common sense and observation; and then they may be more easy to define and to justify than they now are, by any body but herself."

"This will probably be the case," he replied; "and yet there is something so amiable in the prejudices of a young mind, that one is sorry to see them give way to the reception of more general opinions."

"I cannot agree with you there," said Elinor. "There are inconveniences attending such feelings as Marianne's, which all the charms of enthusiasm and ignorance of the world cannot atone for. Her systems have all the unfortunate tendency of setting propriety at nought; and a better acquaintance with the world is what I look forward to as her greatest possible advantage."

After a short pause he resumed the conversation by saying—

"Does your sister make no distinction in her objections against a second attachment? or is it equally criminal in every body? Are those who have been disappointed in their first choice, whether from the inconstancy of its object, or the perverseness of circumstances, to be equally indifferent during the rest of their lives?"

"Upon my word, I am not acquainted with the minutia of her principles. I only know that I never yet heard her admit any instance of a second attachment's being pardonable."

"This," said he, "cannot hold; but a change, a total change of sentiments—No, no, do not desire it,—for when the romantic refinements of a young mind are obliged to give way, how frequently are they succeeded by such opinions as are but too common, and too dangerous! I speak from experience. I once knew a lady who in temper and mind greatly resembled your sister, who thought and judged like her, but who from an inforced change—from a series of unfortunate circumstances"—Here he stopt suddenly; appeared to think that he had said too much, and by his countenance gave rise to conjectures, which might not otherwise have entered Elinor's head. The lady would probably have passed without suspicion, had he not convinced Miss Dashwood that what concerned her ought not to escape his lips. As it was, it required but a slight effort of fancy to connect his emotion with the tender recollection of past regard. Elinor attempted no more. But Marianne, in her place, would not have done so little. The whole story would have been speedily formed under her active imagination; and every thing established in the most melancholy order of disastrous love.

Chapter XII

As Elinor and Marianne were walking together the next morning the latter communicated a piece of news to her sister, which
in spite of all that she knew before of Marianne's imprudence
and want of thought, surprised her by its extravagant testimony of both. Marianne told her, with the greatest delight,
that Willoughby had given her a horse, one that he had bred
himself on his estate in Somersetshire, and which was exactly
calculated to carry a woman. Without considering that it was
not in her mother's plan to keep any horse, that if she were to
alter her resolution in favour of this gift, she must buy another
for the servant, and keep a servant to ride it, and after all, build
a stable to receive them, she had accepted the present without
hesitation, and told her sister of it in raptures.

"He intends to send his groom into Somersetshire immediately for it," she added, "and when it arrives, we will ride every
day. You shall share its use with me. Imagine to yourself, my
dear Elinor, the delight of a gallop on some of these downs."

Most unwilling was she to awaken from such a dream of
felicity, to comprehend all the unhappy truths which attended
the affair; and for some time she refused to submit to them. As
to an additional servant, the expence would be a trifle; mama
she was sure would never object to it; and any horse would do
for *him*; he might always get one at the park; as to a stable, the
merest shed would be sufficient. Elinor then ventured to doubt
the propriety of her receiving such a present from a man so
little, or at least so lately known to her. This was too much.

"You are mistaken, Elinor," said she warmly, "in supposing
I know very little of Willoughby. I have not known him long
indeed, but I am much better acquainted with him, than I am
with any other creature in the world, except yourself and mama.
It is not time or opportunity that is to determine intimacy;—it
is disposition alone. Seven years would be insufficient to make

some people acquainted with each other, and seven days are more than enough for others. I should hold myself guilty of greater impropriety in accepting a horse from my brother, than from Willoughby. Of John I know very little, though we have lived together for years; but of Willoughby my judgment has long been formed."

Elinor thought it wisest to touch that point no more. She knew her sister's temper. Opposition on so tender a subject would only attach her the more to her own opinion. But by an appeal to her affection for her mother, by representing the inconveniences which that indulgent mother must draw on herself, if (as would probably be the case) she consented to this increase of establishment,[1] Marianne was shortly subdued; and she promised not to tempt her mother to such imprudent kindness by mentioning the offer, and to tell Willoughby when she saw him next, that it must be declined.

She was faithful to her word; and when Willoughby called at the cottage, the same day, Elinor heard her express her disappointment to him in a low voice, on being obliged to forego the acceptance of his present. The reasons for this alteration were at the same time related, and they were such as to make further entreaty on his side impossible. His concern however was very apparent; and after expressing it with earnestness, he added in the same low voice—"But, Marianne, the horse is still yours, though you cannot use it now. I shall keep it only till you can claim it. When you leave Barton to form your own establishment in a more lasting home, Queen Mab[2] shall receive you."

This was all overheard by Miss Dashwood; and in the whole of the sentence, in his manner of pronouncing it, and in his addressing her sister by her christian name alone,[3] she

---

[1] *establishment*: rate and level on which they conduct their domestic economy (i.e., with servants, livery, etc.).

[2] *Queen Mab*: fairy who is also mentioned in Shakespeare's *Romeo and Juliet* (1.4.53–95)—considered a powerful agent in wish-fulfilling dreams.

[3] *by her christian name alone*: As the second daughter, she would have been known as "Miss Marianne"; the liberty would only be permitted by someone on a truly intimate basis with her (e.g., an affianced lover or a relative).

instantly saw an intimacy so decided, a meaning so direct, as marked a perfect agreement between them. From that moment she doubted not of their being engaged to each other; and the belief of it created no other surprise, than that she, or any of their friends, should be left by tempers so frank, to discover it by accident.

Margaret related something to her the next day, which placed this matter in a still clearer light. Willoughby had spent the preceding evening with them, and Margaret, by being left some time in the parlour with only him and Marianne, had had opportunity for observations, which, with a most important face, she communicated to her eldest sister, when they were next by themselves.

"Oh! Elinor," she cried, "I have such a secret to tell you about Marianne. I am sure she will be married to Mr. Willoughby very soon."

"You have said so," replied Elinor, "almost every day since they first met on High-church Down; and they had not known each other a week, I believe, before you were certain that Marianne wore his picture round her neck; but it turned out to be only the miniature of our great uncle."

"But indeed this is quite another thing. I am sure they will be married very soon, for he has got a lock of her hair."

"Take care, Margaret. It may be only the hair of some great uncle of *his*."

"But indeed, Elinor, it is Marianne's. I am almost sure it is, for I saw him cut it off. Last night after tea, when you and mama went out of the room, they were whispering and talking together as fast as could be, and he seemed to be begging something of her, and presently he took up her scissars and cut off a long lock of her hair, for it was all tumbled down her back; and he kissed it, and folded it up in a piece of white paper, and put it into his pocket-book."

From such particulars, stated on such authority, Elinor could not withhold her credit: nor was she disposed to it, for the circumstance was in perfect unison with what she had heard and seen herself.

Margaret's sagacity was not always displayed in a way so satisfactory to her sister. When Mrs. Jennings attacked her one evening at the park, to give the name of the young man who was Elinor's particular favourite, which had been long a matter of great curiosity to her, Margaret answered by looking at her sister, and saying, "I must not tell, may I, Elinor?"

This of course made every body laugh; and Elinor tried to laugh too. But the effort was painful. She was convinced that Margaret had fixed on a person, whose name she could not bear with composure to become a standing joke with Mrs. Jennings.

Marianne felt for her most sincerely; but she did more harm than good to the cause, by turning very red, and saying in an angry manner to Margaret,

"Remember that whatever your conjectures may be, you have no right to repeat them."

"I never had any conjectures about it," replied Margaret; "it was you who told me of it yourself."

This increased the mirth of the company, and Margaret was eagerly pressed to say something more.

"Oh! pray, Miss Margaret, let us know all about it," said Mrs. Jennings. "What is the gentleman's name?"

"I must not tell, ma'am. But I know very well what it is; and I know where he is too."

"Yes, yes, we can guess where he is; at his own house at Norland to be sure. He is the curate of the parish I dare say."

"No, *that* he is not. He is of no profession at all."

"Margaret," said Marianne with great warmth, "you know that all this is an invention of your own, and that there is no such person in existence."

"Well then he is lately dead, Marianne, for I am sure there was such a man once, and his name begins with an F."

Most grateful did Elinor feel to Lady Middleton for observing at this moment, "that it rained very hard," though she believed the interruption to proceed less from any attention to her, than from her ladyship's great dislike of all such inelegant subjects of raillery as delighted her husband and mother. The idea however started by her, was immediately pursued by Colonel

Brandon, who was on every occasion mindful of the feelings of others; and much was said on the subject of rain by both of them. Willoughby opened the pianoforté, and asked Marianne to sit down to it; and thus amidst the various endeavours of different people to quit the topic, it fell to the ground. But not so easily did Elinor recover from the alarm into which it had thrown her.

A party was formed this evening for going on the following day to see a very fine place about twelve miles from Barton, belonging to a brother-in-law of Colonel Brandon, without whose interest it could not be seen, as the proprietor, who was then abroad, had left strict orders on that head. The grounds were declared to be highly beautiful, and Sir John, who was particularly warm in their praise, might be allowed to be a tolerable judge, for he had formed parties to visit them, at least, twice every summer for the last ten years. They contained a noble piece of water; a sail on which was to form a great part of the morning's amusement; cold provisions were to be taken, open carriages only to be employed, and every thing conducted in the usual style of a complete party of pleasure.

To some few of the company, it appeared rather a bold undertaking, considering the time of year, and that it had rained every day for the last fortnight;—and Mrs. Dashwood, who had already a cold, was persuaded by Elinor to stay at home.

Chapter XIII

Their intended excursion to Whitwell turned out very differently from what Elinor had expected. She was prepared to be wet through, fatigued, and frightened; but the event was still more unfortunate, for they did not go at all.

By ten o'clock the whole party were assembled at the park, where they were to breakfast. The morning was rather favourable, though it had rained all night, as the clouds were then dispersing across the sky, and the sun frequently appeared.—They were all in high spirits and good humour, eager to be happy, and determined to submit to the greatest inconveniences and hardships rather than be otherwise.

While they were at breakfast the letters were brought in. Among the rest there was one for Colonel Brandon;—he took it, looked at the direction,[1] changed colour, and immediately left the room.

"What is the matter with Brandon?" said Sir John.

Nobody could tell.

"I hope he has had no bad news," said Lady Middleton. "It must be something extraordinary that could make Colonel Brandon leave my breakfast table so suddenly."

In about five minutes he returned.

"No bad news, Colonel, I hope;" said Mrs. Jennings, as soon as he entered the room.

"None at all, ma'am, I thank you."

"Was it from Avignon?[2] I hope it is not to say that your sister is worse."

"No, ma'am. It came from town, and is merely a letter of business."

[1] *direction*: address.
[2] *Avignon*: southeastern French commune.

"But how came the hand to discompose you so much, if it was only a letter of business? Come, come, this won't do, Colonel; so let us hear the truth of it."

"My dear Madam," said Lady Middleton, "recollect what you are saying."

"Perhaps it is to tell you that your cousin Fanny is married?" said Mrs. Jennings, without attending to her daughter's reproof.

"No, indeed, it is not."

"Well, then, I know who it is from, Colonel. And I hope she is well."

"Whom do you mean, ma'am?" said he, colouring a little.

"Oh! you know who I mean."

"I am particularly sorry, ma'am," said he, addressing Lady Middleton, "that I should receive this letter today, for it is on business which requires my immediate attendance in town."

"In town!" cried Mrs. Jennings. "What can you have to do in town at this time of year?"

"My own loss is great," he continued, "in being obliged to leave so agreeable a party; but I am the more concerned, as I fear my presence is necessary to gain your admittance at Whitwell."

What a blow upon them all was this!

"But if you write a note to the housekeeper, Mr. Brandon," said Marianne eagerly, "will it not be sufficient?"

He shook his head.

"We must go," said Sir John.—"It shall not be put off when we are so near it. You cannot go to town till to-morrow, Brandon, that is all."

"I wish it could be so easily settled. But it is not in my power to delay my journey for one day!"

"If you would but let us know what your business is," said Mrs. Jennings, "we might see whether it could be put off or not."

"You would not be six hours later," said Willoughby, "if you were to defer your journey till our return."

"I cannot afford to lose *one* hour."—

Elinor then heard Willoughby say in a low voice to Marianne, "There are some people who cannot bear a party of pleasure.

Brandon is one of them. He was afraid of catching cold I dare say, and invented this trick for getting out of it. I would lay fifty guineas the letter was of his own writing."

"I have no doubt of it," replied Marianne.

"There is no persuading you to change your mind, Brandon, I know of old," said Sir John, "when once you are determined on any thing. But, however, I hope you will think better of it. Consider, here are the two Miss Careys come over from Newton, the three Miss Dashwoods walked up from the cottage, and Mr. Willoughby got up two hours before his usual time, on purpose to go to Whitwell."

Colonel Brandon again repeated his sorrow at being the cause of disappointing the party; but at the same time declared it to be unavoidable.

"Well then, when will you come back again?"

"I hope we shall see you at Barton," added her ladyship, "as soon as you can conveniently leave town; and we must put off the party to Whitwell till you return."

"You are very obliging. But it is so uncertain, when I may have it in my power to return, that I dare not engage for it at all."

"Oh! he must and shall come back," cried Sir John. "If he is not here by the end of the week, I shall go after him."

"Aye, so do, Sir John," cried Mrs. Jennings, "and then perhaps you may find out what his business is."

"I do not want to pry into other men's concerns. I suppose it is something he is ashamed of."

Colonel Brandon's horses were announced.

"You do not go to town on horseback, do you?" added Sir John.

"No. Only to Honiton.[3] I shall then go post."[4]

"Well, as you are resolved to go, I wish you a good journey. But you had better change your mind."

[3] *Honiton*: market town of East Devon.

[4] *go post*: travel in a post chaise—a light, horse-drawn, open carriage (employing one or two horses) for up to two people, hired from postal stations and changed at each post (a means of speed here).

"I assure you it is not in my power."

He then took leave of the whole party.

"Is there no chance of my seeing you and your sisters in town this winter, Miss Dashwood?"

"I am afraid, none at all."

"Then I must bid you farewell for longer time than I should wish to do."

To Marianne, he merely bowed and said nothing.

"Come, Colonel," said Mrs. Jennings, "before you go, do let us know what you are going about."

He wished her a good morning, and attended by Sir John, left the room.

The complaints and lamentations which politeness had hitherto restrained, now burst forth universally; and they all agreed again and again how provoking it was to be so disappointed.

"I can guess what his business is, however," said Mrs. Jennings exultingly.

"Can you, ma'am?" said almost every body.

"Yes; it is about Miss Williams. I am sure."

"And who is Miss Williams?" asked Marianne.

"What! do not you know who Miss Williams is? I am sure you must have heard of her before. She is a relation of the Colonel's, my dear; a very near relation. We will not say how near, for fear of shocking the young ladies." Then lowering her voice a little, she said to Elinor, "She is his natural[5] daughter."

"Indeed!"

"Oh! yes; and as like him as she can stare. I dare say the Colonel will leave her all his fortune."

When Sir John returned, he joined most heartily in the general regret on so unfortunate an event; concluding however by observing, that as they were all got together, they must do something by way of being happy; and after some consultation

---

[5] *natural*: i.e., illegitimate (since he is unmarried). Edition A adds: "Lady Middleton's delicacy was shocked; and in order to banish so improper a subject as the mention of a natural daughter, she actually took the trouble of saying something herself about the weather."

it was agreed, that although happiness could only be enjoyed at Whitwell, they might procure a tolerable composure of mind by driving about the country. The carriages were then ordered; Willoughby's was first, and Marianne never looked happier than when she got into it. He drove through the park very fast, and they were soon out of sight; and nothing more of them was seen till their return, which did not happen till after the return of all the rest. They both seemed delighted with their drive, but said only in general terms that they had kept in the lanes, while the others went on the downs.

It was settled that there should be a dance in the evening, and that every body should be extremely merry all day long. Some more of the Careys came to dinner, and they had the pleasure of sitting down nearly twenty to table, which Sir John observed with great contentment. Willoughby took his usual place between the two elder Miss Dashwoods. Mrs. Jennings sat on Elinor's right hand; and they had not been long seated, before she leant behind her and Willoughby, and said to Marianne; loud enough for them both to hear, "I have found you out in spite of all your tricks. I know where you spent the morning."

Marianne coloured, and replied very hastily, "Where, pray?"—

"Did not you know," said Willoughby, "that we had been out in my curricle?"

"Yes, yes, Mr. Impudence, I know that very well, and I was determined to find out *where* you had been to.—I hope you like your house, Miss Marianne. It is a very large one I know, and when I come to see you, I hope you will have new-furnished it, for it wanted it very much, when I was there six years ago."

Marianne turned away in great confusion. Mrs. Jennings laughed heartily; and Elinor found that in her resolution to know where they had been, she had actually made her own woman enquire of Mr. Willoughby's groom, and that she had by that method been informed that they had gone to Allenham, and spent a considerable time there in walking about the garden and going all over the house.

Elinor could hardly believe this to be true, as it seemed very unlikely that Willoughby should propose, or Marianne consent, to enter the house while Mrs. Smith was in it, with whom Marianne had not the smallest acquaintance.

As soon as they left the dining-room, Elinor enquired of her about it; and great was her surprise when she found that every circumstance related by Mrs. Jennings was perfectly true. Marianne was quite angry with her for doubting it.

"Why should you imagine, Elinor, that we did not go there, or that we did not see the house? Is not it what you have often wished to do yourself?"

"Yes, Marianne, but I would not go while Mrs. Smith was there, and with no other companion than Mr. Willoughby."

"Mr. Willoughby however is the only person who can have a right to shew that house; and as we went in an open carriage, it was impossible to have any other companion. I never spent a pleasanter morning in my life."

"I am afraid," replied Elinor, "that the pleasantness of an employment does not always evince[6] its propriety."

"On the contrary, nothing can be a stronger proof of it, Elinor; for if there had been any real impropriety in what I did, I should have been sensible of it at the time, for we always know when we are acting wrong, and with such a conviction I could have had no pleasure."

"But, my dear Marianne, as it has already exposed you to some very impertinent remarks, do you not now begin to doubt the discretion of your own conduct?"

"If the impertinent remarks of Mrs. Jennings are to be the proof of impropriety in conduct, we are all offending every moment of all our lives. I value not her censure any more than I should do her commendation. I am not sensible of having done any thing wrong in walking over Mrs. Smith's grounds, or in seeing her house. They will one day be Mr. Willoughby's, and ..."

"If they were one day to be your own, Marianne, you would not be justified in what you have done."

---

[6] *evince*: reveal, indicate.

She blushed at this hint; but it was even visibly gratifying to her; and after a ten minutes' interval of earnest thought, she came to her sister again, and said with great good humour, "Perhaps, Elinor, it *was* rather ill-judged in me to go to Allenham; but Mr. Willoughby wanted particularly to shew me the place; and it is a charming house I assure you.—There is one remarkably pretty sitting room up stairs; of a nice comfortable size for constant use, and with modern furniture it would be delightful. It is a corner room, and has windows on two sides. On one side you look across the bowling-green,[7] behind the house, to a beautiful hanging wood,[8] and on the other you have a view of the church and village, and, beyond them, of those fine bold hills that we have so often admired. I did not see it to advantage, for nothing could be more forlorn than the furniture,—but if it were newly fitted up—a couple of hundred pounds, Willoughby says, would make it one of the pleasantest summer-rooms in England."

Could Elinor have listened to her without interruption from the others, she would have described every room in the house with equal delight.

[7] *bowling-green*: flat, closely mowed lawn for bowling (a lawn game).
[8] *hanging wood*: forest on a slope.

Chapter XIV

The sudden termination of Colonel Brandon's visit at the park, with his steadiness in concealing its cause, filled the mind and raised the wonder of Mrs. Jennings for two or three days; she was a great wonderer, as every one must be who takes a very lively interest in all the comings and goings of all their acquaintance. She wondered with little intermission what could be the reason of it; was sure there must be some bad news, and thought over every kind of distress that could have befallen him, with a fixed determination that he should not escape them all.

"Something very melancholy must be the matter, I am sure," said she. "I could see it in his face. Poor man! I am afraid his circumstances may be bad. The estate at Delaford was never reckoned more than two thousand a year, and his brother left every thing sadly involved.[1] I do think he must have been sent for about money matters, for what else can it be? I wonder whether it is so. I would give any thing to know the truth of it. Perhaps it is about Miss Williams—and, by the bye, I dare say it is, because he looked so conscious when I mentioned her. May be she is ill in town; nothing in the world more likely, for I have a notion she is always rather sickly. I would lay any wager it is about Miss Williams. It is not so very likely he should be distressed in his circumstances *now*, for he is a very prudent man, and to be sure must have cleared the estate by this time. I wonder what it can be! May be his sister is worse at Avignon, and has sent for him over. His setting off in such a hurry seems very like it. Well, I wish him out of all his trouble with all my heart, and a good wife into the bargain."

So wondered, so talked Mrs. Jennings. Her opinion varying with every fresh conjecture, and all seeming equally probable

[1] *involved*: probably mortgaged or otherwise encumbered financially and legally.

as they arose. Elinor, though she felt really interested in the welfare of Colonel Brandon, could not bestow all the wonder on his going so suddenly away, which Mrs. Jennings was desirous of her feeling; for besides that the circumstance did not in her opinion justify such lasting amazement or variety of speculation, her wonder was otherwise disposed of. It was engrossed by the extraordinary silence of her sister and Willoughby on the subject, which they must know to be peculiarly interesting to them all. As this silence continued, every day made it appear more strange and more incompatible with the disposition of both. Why they should not openly acknowledge to her mother and herself, what their constant behaviour to each other declared to have taken place, Elinor could not imagine.

She could easily conceive that marriage might not be immediately in their power; for though Willoughby was independent, there was no reason to believe him rich. His estate had been rated by Sir John at about six or seven hundred a year; but he lived at an expense to which that income could hardly be equal, and he had himself often complained of his poverty. But for this strange kind of secrecy maintained by them relative to their engagement, which in fact concealed nothing at all, she could not account; and it was so wholly contradictory to their general opinions and practice, that a doubt sometimes entered her mind of their being really engaged, and this doubt was enough to prevent her making any inquiry of Marianne.

Nothing could be more expressive of attachment to them all, than Willoughby's behaviour. To Marianne it had all the distinguishing tenderness which a lover's heart could give, and to the rest of the family it was the affectionate attention of a son and a brother. The cottage seemed to be considered and loved by him as his home; many more of his hours were spent there than at Allenham; and if no general engagement collected them at the park, the exercise which called him out in the morning was almost certain of ending there, where the rest of the day was spent by himself at the side of Marianne, and by his favourite pointer at her feet.

One evening in particular, about a week after Colonel Brandon had left the country, his heart seemed more than usually open to every feeling of attachment to the objects around him; and on Mrs. Dashwood's happening to mention her design of improving the cottage in the spring, he warmly opposed every alteration of a place which affection had established as perfect with him.

"What!" he exclaimed—"Improve this dear cottage! No. *That* I will never consent to. Not a stone must be added to its walls, not an inch to its size, if my feelings are regarded."

"Do not be alarmed," said Miss Dashwood, "nothing of the kind will be done; for my mother will never have money enough to attempt it."

"I am heartily glad of it," he cried. "May she always be poor, if she can employ her riches no better."

"Thank you, Willoughby. But you may be assured that I would not sacrifice one sentiment of local attachment of yours, or of any one whom I loved, for all the improvements in the world. Depend upon it that whatever unemployed sum may remain, when I make up my accounts in the spring, I would even rather lay it uselessly by than dispose of it in a manner so painful to you. But are you really so attached to this place as to see no defect in it?"

"I am," said he. "To me it is faultless. Nay, more, I consider it as the only form of building in which happiness is attainable, and were I rich enough, I would instantly pull Combe down, and build it up again in the exact plan of this cottage."

"With dark narrow stairs, and a kitchen that smokes, I suppose," said Elinor.

"Yes," cried he in the same eager tone, "with all and every thing belonging to it;—in no one convenience or *in*convenience about it, should the least variation be perceptible. Then, and then only, under such a roof, I might perhaps be as happy at Combe as I have been at Barton."

"I flatter myself," replied Elinor, "that even under the disadvantage of better rooms and a broader staircase, you will hereafter find your own house as faultless as you now do this."

"There certainly are circumstances," said Willoughby, "which might greatly endear it to me; but this place will always have one claim on my affection, which no other can possibly share."

Mrs. Dashwood looked with pleasure at Marianne, whose fine eyes were fixed so expressively on Willoughby, as plainly denoted how well she understood him.

"How often did I wish," added he, "when I was at Allenham this time twelvemonth, that Barton cottage were inhabited! I never passed within view of it without admiring its situation, and grieving that no one should live in it. How little did I then think that the very first news I should hear from Mrs. Smith, when I next came into the country, would be that Barton cottage was taken: and I felt an immediate satisfaction and interest in the event, which nothing but a kind of prescience of what happiness I should experience from it, can account for. Must it not have been so, Marianne?" speaking to her in a lowered voice. Then continuing his former tone, he said, "And yet this house you would spoil, Mrs. Dashwood? You would rob it of its simplicity by imaginary improvement! and this dear parlour, in which our acquaintance first began, and in which so many happy hours have been since spent by us together, you would degrade to the condition of a common entrance,[2] and every body would be eager to pass through the room which has hitherto contained within itself, more real accommodation and comfort than any other apartment of the handsomest dimensions in the world could possibly afford."

Mrs. Dashwood again assured him that no alteration of the kind should be attempted.

"You are a good woman," he warmly replied. "Your promise makes me easy. Extend it a little farther, and it will make me happy. Tell me that not only your house will remain the same, but that I shall ever find you and yours as unchanged as your dwelling; and that you will always consider me with the

---

[2] *common entrance:* In a larger or more fashionably designed house, an entry hall would be necessary.

kindness which has made every thing belonging to you so dear to me."

The promise was readily given, and Willoughby's behaviour during the whole of the evening declared at once his affection and happiness.

"Shall we see you to-morrow to dinner?" said Mrs. Dashwood when he was leaving them. "I do not ask you to come in the morning, for we must walk to the park, to call on Lady Middleton."

He engaged to be with them by four o'clock.

Chapter XV

Mrs. Dashwood's visit to Lady Middleton took place the next day, and two of her daughters went with her; but Marianne excused herself from being of the party under some trifling pretext of employment; and her mother, who concluded that a promise had been made by Willoughby the night before of calling on her while they were absent, was perfectly satisfied with her remaining at home.

On their return from the park they found Willoughby's curricle and servant in waiting at the cottage, and Mrs. Dashwood was convinced that her conjecture had been just. So far it was all as she had foreseen; but on entering the house she beheld what no foresight had taught her to expect. They were no sooner in the passage than Marianne came hastily out of the parlour apparently in violent affliction, with her handkerchief at her eyes; and without noticing them ran up stairs. Surprised and alarmed they proceeded directly into the room she had just quitted, where they found only Willoughby, who was leaning against the mantle-piece with his back towards them. He turned round on their coming in, and his countenance shewed that he strongly partook of the emotion which overpowered Marianne.

"Is any thing the matter with her?" cried Mrs. Dashwood as she entered—"is she ill?"

"I hope not," he replied, trying to look cheerful; and with a forced smile presently added, "It is I who may rather expect to be ill—for I am now suffering under a very heavy disappointment!"

"Disappointment!"

"Yes, for I am unable to keep my engagement with you. Mrs. Smith has this morning exercised the privilege of riches upon a poor dependant cousin, by sending me on business to London.

I have just received my dispatches, and taken my farewel of Allenham; and by way of exhilaration I am now come to take my farewel of you."

"To London!—and are you going this morning?"

"Almost this moment."

"This is very unfortunate. But Mrs. Smith must be obliged;—and her business will not detain you from us long I hope."

He coloured as he replied, "You are very kind, but I have no idea of returning into Devonshire immediately. My visits to Mrs. Smith are never repeated within the twelvemonth."

"And is Mrs. Smith your only friend? Is Allenham the only house in the neighbourhood to which you will be welcome? For shame, Willoughby. Can you wait for an invitation here?"

His colour increased; and with his eyes fixed on the ground he only replied, "You are too good."

Mrs. Dashwood looked at Elinor with surprise. Elinor felt equal amazement. For a few moments every one was silent. Mrs. Dashwood first spoke.

"I have only to add, my dear Willoughby, that at Barton cottage you will always be welcome; for I will not press you to return here immediately, because you only can judge how far *that* might be pleasing to Mrs. Smith; and on this head I shall be no more disposed to question your judgment than to doubt your inclination."

"My engagements at present," replied Willoughby confusedly, "are of such a nature—that—I dare not flatter myself"—

He stopt. Mrs. Dashwood was too much astonished to speak, and another pause succeeded. This was broken by Willoughby, who said with a faint smile, "It is folly to linger in this manner. I will not torment myself any longer by remaining among friends whose society it is impossible for me now to enjoy."

He then hastily took leave of them all and left the room. They saw him step into his carriage, and in a minute it was out of sight.

Mrs. Dashwood felt too much for speech, and instantly quitted the parlour to give way in solitude to the concern and alarm which this sudden departure occasioned.

Elinor's uneasiness was at least equal to her mother's. She thought of what had just passed with anxiety and distrust. Willoughby's behaviour in taking leave of them, his embarrassment, and affectation of cheerfulness and, above all, his unwillingness to accept her mother's invitation, a backwardness so unlike a lover, so unlike himself, greatly disturbed her. One moment she feared that no serious design had ever been formed on his side; and the next that some unfortunate quarrel had taken place between him and her sister;—the distress in which Marianne had quitted the room was such as a serious quarrel could most reasonably account for, though when she considered what Marianne's love for him was, a quarrel seemed almost impossible.

But whatever might be the particulars of their separation, her sister's affliction was indubitable; and she thought with the tenderest compassion of that violent sorrow which Marianne was in all probability not merely giving way to as a relief, but feeding and encouraging as a duty.

In about half an hour her mother returned, and though her eyes were red, her countenance was not uncheerful.

"Our dear Willoughby is now some miles from Barton, Elinor," said she, as she sat down to work,[1] "and with how heavy a heart does he travel?"

"It is all very strange. So suddenly to be gone! It seems but the work of a moment. And last night he was with us so happy, so cheerful, so affectionate? And now after only ten minutes' notice—Gone too without intending to return!—Something more than what he owned to us must have happened. He did not speak, he did not behave like himself. *You* must have seen the difference as well as I. What can it be? Can they have quarrelled? Why else should he have shewn such unwillingness to accept your invitation here?"—

"It was not inclination that he wanted, Elinor; I could plainly see *that*. He had not the power of accepting it. I have thought it all over I assure you, and I can perfectly account

---

[1] *to work*: i.e., to do needlework.

for every thing that at first seemed strange to me as well as to you."

"Can you indeed?"

"Yes. I have explained it to myself in the most satisfactory way;—but you, Elinor, who love to doubt where you can—It will not satisfy *you*, I know; but you shall not talk *me* out of my trust in it. I am persuaded that Mrs. Smith suspects his regard for Marianne, disapproves of it, (perhaps because she has other views for him,) and on that account is eager to get him away;—and that the business which she sends him off to transact, is invented as an excuse to dismiss him. This is what I believe to have happened. He is moreover aware that she *does* disapprove the connection, he dares not therefore at present confess to her his engagement with Marianne, and he feels himself obliged, from his dependent situation, to give into her schemes, and absent himself from Devonshire for a while. You will tell me, I know, that this may, or may *not* have happened; but I will listen to no cavil,[2] unless you can point out any other method of understanding the affair as satisfactory as this. And now, Elinor, what have you to say?"

"Nothing, for you have anticipated my answer."

"Then you would have told me, that it might or might not have happened. Oh! Elinor, how incomprehensible are your feelings! You had rather take evil upon credit than good. You had rather look out for misery for Marianne and guilt for poor Willoughby, than an apology[3] for the latter. You are resolved to think him blameable, because he took leave of us with less affection than his usual behaviour has shewn. And is no allowance to be made for inadvertence, or for spirits depressed by recent disappointment? Are no probabilities to be accepted, merely because they are not certainties? Is nothing due to the man whom we have all so much reason to love, and no reason in the world to think ill of? To the possibility of motives

[2] *cavil*: petty objection.
[3] *apology*: defense.

unanswerable in themselves, though unavoidably secret for a while? And, after all, what is it you suspect him of?"

"I can hardly tell you myself.—But suspicion of something unpleasant is the inevitable consequence of such an alteration as we have just witnessed in him. There is great truth, however, in what you have now urged of the allowances which ought to be made for him, and it is my wish to be candid in my judgment of every body. Willoughby may undoubtedly have very sufficient reasons for his conduct, and I will hope that he has. But it would have been more like Willoughby to acknowledge them at once. Secrecy may be advisable; but still I cannot help wondering at its being practised by him."

"Do not blame him, however, for departing from his character, where the deviation is necessary. But you really do admit the justice of what I have said in his defence?—I am happy—and he is acquitted."

"Not entirely. It may be proper to conceal their engagement (if they *are* engaged) from Mrs. Smith—and if that is the case, it must be highly expedient for Willoughby to be but little in Devonshire at present. But this is no excuse for their concealing it from us."

"Concealing it from us! my dear child, do you accuse Willoughby and Marianne of concealment? This is strange indeed, when your eyes have been reproaching them every day for incautiousness."

"I want no proof of their affection," said Elinor; "but of their engagement I do."

"I am perfectly satisfied of both."

"Yet not a syllable has been said to you on the subject, by either of them."

"I have not wanted syllables where actions have spoken so plainly. Has not his behaviour to Marianne and to all of us, for at least the last fortnight, declared that he loved and considered her as his future wife, and that he felt for us the attachment of the nearest relation? Have we not perfectly understood each other? Has not my consent been daily asked by his looks, his manner, his attentive and affectionate respect? My Elinor, is it possible to doubt their engagement? How could such a thought occur to you? How is it to be supposed that Willoughby, persuaded as he must be of your sister's love, should leave her, and leave her perhaps for months, without telling her of his affection;—that they should part without a mutual exchange of confidence?"

"I confess," replied Elinor, "that every circumstance except *one* in favour of their engagement; but that *one* is the total silence of both on the subject, and with me it almost outweighs every other."

"How strange this is! You must think wretchedly indeed of Willoughby, if after all that has openly passed between them, you can doubt the nature of the terms on which they are together. Has he been acting a part in his behaviour to your sister all this time? Do you suppose him really indifferent to her?"

"No, I cannot think that. He must and does love her I am sure."

"But with a strange kind of tenderness, if he can leave her with such indifference, such carelessness of the future, as you attribute to him."

"You must remember, my dear mother, that I have never considered this matter as certain. I have had my doubts, I confess; but they are fainter than they were, and they may soon be entirely done away. If we find they correspond,[4] every fear of mine will be removed."

"A mighty concession indeed! If you were to see them at the altar, you would suppose they were going to be married. Ungracious girl! But *I* require no such proof. Nothing in my opinion has ever passed to justify doubt; no secrecy has been attempted; all has been uniformly open and unreserved. You cannot doubt your sister's wishes. It must be Willoughby therefore whom you suspect. But why? Is he not a man of honour and feeling? Has there been any inconsistency on his side to create alarm? can he be deceitful?"

---

[4] *they correspond*: Correspondence between an unmarried young woman and an eligible bachelor would only be socially acceptable if they were engaged.

"I hope not, I believe not," cried Elinor. "I love Willoughby, sincerely love him; and suspicion of his integrity cannot be more painful to yourself than to me. It has been involuntary, and I will not encourage it. I was startled, I confess, by the alteration in his manners this morning;—he did not speak like himself, and did not return your kindness with any cordiality. But all this may be explained by such a situation of his affairs as you have supposed. He had just parted from my sister, had seen her leave him in the greatest affliction; and if he felt obliged, from a fear of offending Mrs. Smith, to resist the temptation of returning here soon, and yet aware that by declining your invitation, by saying that he was going away for some time, he should seem to act an ungenerous, a suspicious part by our family, he might well be embarrassed and disturbed. In such a case, a plain and open avowal of his difficulties would have been more to his honour I think, as well as more consistent with his general character;—but I will not raise objections against any one's conduct on so illiberal a foundation, as a difference in judgment from myself, or a deviation from what I may think right and consistent."

"You speak very properly. Willoughby certainly does not deserve to be suspected. Though *we* have not known him long, he is no stranger in this part of the world; and who has ever spoken to his disadvantage? Had he been in a situation to act independently and marry immediately, it might have been odd that he should leave us without acknowledging every thing to me at once: but this is not the case. It is an engagement in some respects not prosperously begun, for their marriage must be at a very uncertain distance; and even secrecy, as far as it can be observed, may now be very advisable."

They were interrupted by the entrance of Margaret; and Elinor was then at liberty to think over the representations of her mother, to acknowledge the probability of many, and hope for the justice of all.

They saw nothing of Marianne till dinner time, when she entered the room and took her place at the table without saying a word. Her eyes were red and swollen; and it seemed as if her tears were even then restrained with difficulty. She avoided the looks of them all, could neither eat nor speak, and after some time, on her mother's silently pressing her hand with tender compassion, her small degree of fortitude was quite overcome, she burst into tears and left the room.

This violent oppression of spirits continued the whole evening. She was without any power, because she was without any desire of command over herself. The slightest mention of any thing relative to Willoughby overpowered her in an instant; and though her family were most anxiously attentive to her comfort, it was impossible for them, if they spoke at all, to keep clear of every subject which her feelings connected with him.

Chapter XVI

Marianne would have thought herself very inexcusable had she been able to sleep at all the first night after parting from Willoughby. She would have been ashamed to look her family in the face the next morning, had she not risen from her bed in more need of repose than when she lay down in it. But the feelings which made such composure a disgrace, left her in no danger of incurring it. She was awake the whole night, and she wept the greatest part of it. She got up with an headache, was unable to talk, and unwilling to take any nourishment; giving pain every moment to her mother and sisters, and forbidding all attempt at consolation from either. Her sensibility was potent enough!

When breakfast was over she walked out by herself, and wandered about the village of Allenham, indulging the recollection of past enjoyment and crying over the present reverse[1] for the chief of the morning.

The evening passed off in the equal indulgence of feeling. She played over every favourite song that she had been used to play to Willoughby, every air in which their voices had been oftenest joined, and sat at the instrument gazing on every line of music that he had written out for her, till her heart was so heavy that no farther sadness could be gained; and this nourishment of grief was every day applied. She spent whole hours at the pianoforté alternately singing and crying; her voice often totally suspended by her tears. In books too, as well as in music, she courted the misery which a contrast between the past and present was certain of giving. She read nothing but what they had been used to read together.

Such violence of affliction indeed could not be supported for ever; it sunk within a few days into a calmer melancholy; but

[1] *reverse*: reversal (of fortune).

83

these employments, to which she daily recurred, her solitary walks and silent meditations, still produced occasional effusions of sorrow as lively as ever.

No letter from Willoughby came; and none seemed expected by Marianne. Her mother was surprised, and Elinor again became uneasy. But Mrs. Dashwood could find explanations whenever she wanted them, which at least satisfied herself.

"Remember, Elinor," said she, "how very often Sir John fetches our letters himself from the post, and carries them to it. We have already agreed that secrecy may be necessary, and we must acknowledge that it could not be maintained if their correspondence were to pass through Sir John's hands."

Elinor could not deny the truth of this, and she tried to find in it a motive sufficient for their silence. But there was one method so direct, so simple, and in her opinion so eligible of knowing the real state of the affair, and of instantly removing all mystery, that she could not help suggesting it to her mother.

"Why do you not ask Marianne at once," said she, "whether she is or is not engaged to Willoughby? From you, her mother, and so kind, so indulgent a mother, the question could not give offence. It would be the natural result of your affection for her. She used to be all unreserve, and to you more especially."

"I would not ask such a question for the world. Supposing it possible that they are not engaged, what distress would not such an inquiry inflict! At any rate it would be most ungenerous. I should never deserve her confidence again, after forcing from her a confession of what is meant at present to be unacknowledged to any one. I know Marianne's heart: I know that she dearly loves me, and that I shall not be the last to whom the affair is made known, when circumstances make the revealment[2] of it eligible. I would not attempt to force the confidence of any one; of a child much less; because a sense of duty would prevent the denial which her wishes might direct."

Elinor thought this generosity overstrained, considering her sister's youth, and urged the matter farther, but in vain;

---

[2] *revealment*: revelation.

common sense, common care, common prudence, were all sunk in Mrs. Dashwood's romantic delicacy.

It was several days before Willoughby's name was mentioned before Marianne by any of her family; Sir John and Mrs. Jennings, indeed, were not so nice; their witticisms added pain to many a painful hour;—but one evening, Mrs. Dashwood, accidentally taking up a volume of Shakespeare,[3] exclaimed,

"We have never finished Hamlet,[4] Marianne; our dear Willoughby went away before we could get through it. We will put it by, that when he comes again ... But it may be months, perhaps, before *that* happens."

"Months!" cried Marianne, with strong surprise. "No—nor many weeks."

Mrs. Dashwood was sorry for what she had said; but it gave Elinor pleasure, as it produced a reply from Marianne so expressive of confidence in Willoughby and knowledge of his intentions.

One morning, about a week after his leaving the country, Marianne was prevailed on to join her sisters in their usual walk, instead of wandering away by herself. Hitherto she had carefully avoided every companion in her rambles. If her sisters intended to walk on the downs, she directly stole away towards the lanes; if they talked of the valley, she was as speedy in climbing the hills, and could never be found when the others set off. But at length she was secured by the exertions of Elinor, who greatly disapproved such continual seclusion. They walked along the road through the valley, and chiefly in silence, for Marianne's *mind* could not be controuled, and Elinor, satisfied with gaining one point, would not then attempt more. Beyond the entrance of the valley, where the country, though still rich, was less wild and more open, a long stretch of the road which they had travelled on first coming to Barton, lay before them; and on reaching that point, they stopped to look around them,

---

[3] *Shakespeare*: William Shakespeare (ca. 1564–1616), the most influential English poet and playwright.

[4] *Hamlet*: perhaps Shakespeare's most famous tragedy.

and examine a prospect which formed the distance of their view from the cottage, from a spot which they had never happened to reach in any of their walks before.

Amongst the objects in the scene, they soon discovered an animated one; it was a man on horseback riding towards them. In a few minutes they could distinguish him to be a gentleman; and in a moment afterwards Marianne rapturously exclaimed,

"It is he; it is indeed;—I know it is!"—And was hastening to meet him, when Elinor cried out,

"Indeed, Marianne, I think you are mistaken. It is not Willoughby. The person is not tall enough for him, and has not his air."

"He has, he has," cried Marianne, "I am sure he has. His air, his coat, his horse. I knew how soon he would come."

She walked eagerly on as she spoke; and Elinor, to screen Marianne from particularity,[5] as she felt almost certain of its not being Willoughby, quickened her pace and kept up with her. They were soon within thirty yards of the gentleman. Marianne looked again; her heart sunk within her; and abruptly turning round, she was hurrying back, when the voices of both her sisters were raised to detain her, a third, almost as well known as Willoughby's, joined them in begging her to stop, and she turned round with surprise to see and welcome Edward Ferrars.

He was the only person in the world who could at that moment be forgiven for not being Willoughby; the only one who could have gained a smile from her; but she dispersed her tears to smile on *him*, and in her sister's happiness forgot for a time her own disappointment.

He dismounted, and giving his horse to his servant, walked back with them to Barton, whither he was purposely coming to visit them.

He was welcomed by them all with great cordiality, but especially by Marianne, who shewed more warmth of regard in her reception of him than even Elinor herself. To Marianne, indeed, the meeting between Edward and her sister was but a

[5] *from particularity*: either from being noted by others particularly or from showing undue particularity in greeting this guest.

continuation of that unaccountable coldness which she had often observed at Norland in their mutual behaviour. On Edward's side, more particularly, there was a deficiency of all that a lover ought to look and say on such an occasion. He was confused, seemed scarcely sensible of pleasure in seeing them, looked neither rapturous nor gay, said little but what was forced from him by questions, and distinguished Elinor by no mark of affection. Marianne saw and listened with increasing surprise. She began almost to feel a dislike of Edward; and it ended, as every feeling must end with her, by carrying back her thoughts to Willoughby, whose manners formed a contrast sufficiently striking to those of his brother elect.[6]

After a short silence which succeeded the first surprise and inquiries of meeting, Marianne asked Edward if he came directly from London. No, he had been in Devonshire a fortnight.

"A fortnight!" she repeated, surprised at his being so long in the same country with Elinor without seeing her before.

He looked rather distressed as he added, that he had been staying with some friends near Plymouth.[7]

"Have you been lately in Sussex?" said Elinor.

"I was at Norland about a month ago."

"And how does dear, dear Norland look?" cried Marianne.

"Dear, dear Norland," said Elinor, "probably looks much as it always does at this time of year. The woods and walks thickly covered with dead leaves."

"Oh!" cried Marianne, "with what transporting sensations have I formerly seen them fall? How have I delighted, as I walked, to see them driven in showers about me by the wind! What feelings have they, the season, the air altogether inspired! Now there is no one to regard them. They are seen only as a nuisance, swept hastily off, and driven as much as possible from the sight."

"It is not every one," said Elinor, "who has your passion for dead leaves."

---

[6] *brother elect*: brother-in-law by her popular election—though not yet instated in that position (i.e., not married to Elinor or even betrothed).

[7] *Plymouth*: large coastal town in Devon.

"No; my feelings are not often shared, not often understood. But *sometimes* they are."—As she said this, she sunk into a reverie for a few moments;—but rousing herself again, "Now, Edward," said she, calling his attention to the prospect, "here is Barton valley. Look up it, and be tranquil if you can. Look at those hills! Did you ever see their equals? To the left is Barton park, amongst those woods and plantations.[8] You may see one end of the house. And there, beneath that farthest hill, which rises with such grandeur, is our cottage."

"It is a beautiful country," he replied; "but these bottoms[9] must be dirty in winter."

"How can you think of dirt, with such objects before you?"

"Because," replied he, smiling, "among the rest of the objects before me, I see a very dirty lane."

"How strange!" said Marianne to herself as she walked on.

"Have you an agreeable neighbourhood here? Are the Middletons pleasant people?"

"No, not at all," answered Marianne, "we could not be more unfortunately situated."

"Marianne," cried her sister, "how can you say so? How can you be so unjust? They are a very respectable family, Mr. Ferrars; and towards us have behaved in the friendliest manner. Have you forgot, Marianne, how many pleasant days we have owed to them?"

"No," said Marianne in a low voice, "nor how many painful moments."

Elinor took no notice of this, and directing her attention to their visitor, endeavoured to support something like discourse with him by talking of their present residence, its conveniences, &c. extorting from him occasional questions and remarks. His coldness and reserve mortified her severely; she was vexed and half angry; but resolving to regulate her behaviour to him by the past rather than the present, she avoided every appearance of resentment or displeasure, and treated him as she thought he ought to be treated from the family connection.

[8] *plantations*: areas used for planting trees.
[9] *bottoms*: valleys.

Chapter XVII

Mrs. Dashwood was surprised only for a moment at seeing him; for his coming to Barton was, in her opinion, of all things the most natural. Her joy and expressions of regard long outlived her wonder. He received the kindest welcome from her; and shyness, coldness, reserve could not stand against such a reception. They had begun to fail him before he entered the house, and they were quite overcome by the captivating manners of Mrs. Dashwood. Indeed a man could not very well be in love with either of her daughters, without extending the passion to her; and Elinor had the satisfaction of seeing him soon become more like himself. His affections seemed to reanimate towards them all, and his interest in their welfare again became perceptible. He was not in spirits however; he praised their house, admired its prospect, was attentive, and kind; but still he was not in spirits. The whole family perceived it, and Mrs. Dashwood, attributing it to some want of liberality in his mother, sat down to table indignant against all selfish parents.

"What are Mrs. Ferrars's views for you at present, Edward?" said she, when dinner was over and they had drawn round the fire; "are you still to be a great orator in spite of yourself?"

"No. I hope my mother is now convinced that I have no more talents than inclination for a public life!"

"But how is your fame to be established? for famous you must be to satisfy all your family; and with no inclination for expense, no affection for strangers, no profession, and no assurance, you may find it a difficult matter."

"I shall not attempt it. I have no wish to be distinguished; and I have every reason to hope I never shall. Thank Heaven! I cannot be forced into genius and eloquence."

"You have no ambition, I well know. Your wishes are all moderate."

"As moderate as those of the rest of the world, I believe. I wish as well as every body else to be perfectly happy; but like every body else it must be in my own way. Greatness will not make me so."

"Strange if it would!" cried Marianne. "What have wealth or grandeur to do with happiness?"

"Grandeur has but little," said Elinor, "but wealth has much to do with it."

"Elinor, for shame!" said Marianne; "money can only give happiness where there is nothing else to give it. Beyond a competence,[1] it can afford no real satisfaction, as far as mere self is concerned."

"Perhaps," said Elinor, smiling, "we may come to the same point. *Your* competence and *my* wealth are very much alike, I dare say; and without them, as the world goes now, we shall both agree that every kind of external comfort must be wanting. Your ideas are only more noble than mine. Come, what is your competence?"

"About eighteen hundred or two thousand a-year; not more than *that*."

Elinor laughed. "*Two* thousand a-year! *One* is my wealth! I guessed how it would end."

"And yet two thousand a-year is a very moderate income," said Marianne. "A family[2] cannot well be maintained on a smaller. I am sure I am not extravagant in my demands. A proper establishment of servants, a carriage, perhaps two, and hunters,[3] cannot be supported on less."

Elinor smiled again, to hear her sister describing so accurately their future expenses at Combe Magna.

"Hunters!" repeated Edward—"But why must you have hunters? Every body does not hunt."

Marianne coloured as she replied, "But most people do."

"I wish," said Margaret, striking out a novel thought, "that somebody would give us all a large fortune apiece!"

---

[1] *competence*: income large enough to support a family.

[2] *family*: A family also included servants and other dependents.

[3] *hunters*: large horses, purchased by gentlemen for hunting.

"Oh that they would!" cried Marianne, her eyes sparkling with animation, and her cheeks glowing with the delight of such imaginary happiness.

"We are all unanimous in that wish, I suppose," said Elinor, "in spite of the insufficiency of wealth."

"Oh dear!" cried Margaret, "how happy I should be! I wonder what I should do with it!"

Marianne looked as if she had no doubt on that point.

"I should be puzzled to spend a large fortune myself," said Mrs. Dashwood, "if my children were all to be rich without my help."

"You must begin your improvements on this house," observed Elinor, "and your difficulties will soon vanish."

"What magnificent orders would travel from this family to London," said Edward, "in such an event! What a happy day for booksellers, music-sellers, and print-shops! You, Miss Dashwood, would give a general commission for every new print of merit to be sent you—and as for Marianne, I know her greatness of soul, there would not be music enough in London to content her. And books!—Thomson,[4] Cowper, Scott—she would buy them all over and over again; she would buy up every copy, I believe, to prevent their falling into unworthy hands; and she would have every book that tells her how to admire an old twisted tree. Should not you, Marianne? Forgive me, if I am very saucy. But I was willing to shew you that I had not forgot our old disputes."

"I love to be reminded of the past, Edward—whether it be melancholy or gay, I love to recall it—and you will never offend me by talking of former times. You are very right in supposing how my money would be spent—some of it, at least—my loose cash would certainly be employed in improving my collection of music and books."

"And the bulk of your fortune would be laid out in annuities on the authors or their heirs."

"No, Edward, I should have something else to do with it."

[4] *Thomson*: Scottish poet James Thomson (1700–1748), famous for his 1730s proto-Romantic work *The Seasons*.

"Perhaps then you would bestow it as a reward on that person who wrote the ablest defence of your favorite maxim, that no one can ever be in love more than once in their life—for your opinion on that point is unchanged, I presume?"

"Undoubtedly. At my time of life opinions are tolerably fixed. It is not likely that I should now see or hear anything to change them."

"Marianne is as stedfast as ever, you see," said Elinor, "she is not at all altered."

"She is only grown a little more grave than she was."

"Nay, Edward," said Marianne, "*you* need not reproach me. You are not very gay yourself."

"Why should you think so!" replied he, with a sigh. "But gaiety never was a part of *my* character."

"Nor do I think it a part of Marianne's," said Elinor; "I should hardly call her a lively girl—she is very earnest, very eager in all she does—sometimes talks a great deal and always with animation—but she is not often really merry."

"I believe you are right," he replied, "and yet I have always set her down as a lively girl."

"I have frequently detected myself in such kind of mistakes," said Elinor, "in a total misapprehension of character in some point or other: fancying people so much more gay or grave, or ingenious or stupid than they really are, and I can hardly tell why, or in what the deception originated. Sometimes one is guided by what they say of themselves, and very frequently by what other people say of them, without giving oneself time to deliberate and judge."

"But I thought it was right, Elinor," said Marianne, "to be guided wholly by the opinion of other people. I thought our judgments were given us merely to be subservient to those of our neighbours. This has always been your doctrine, I am sure."

"No, Marianne, never. My doctrine has never aimed at the subjection of the understanding. All I have ever attempted to influence has been the behaviour. You must not confound my meaning. I am guilty, I confess, of having often wished you to treat our acquaintance in general with greater attention; but when have I advised you to adopt their sentiments or conform to their judgment in serious matters?"

"You have not been able then to bring your sister over to your plan of general civility," said Edward to Elinor. "Do you gain no ground?"

"Quite the contrary," replied Elinor, looking expressively at Marianne.

"My judgment," he returned, "is all on your side of the question; but I am afraid my practice is much more on your sister's. I never wish to offend, but I am so foolishly shy, that I often seem negligent, when I am only kept back by my natural aukwardness. I have frequently thought that I must have been intended by nature to be fond of low company, I am so little at my ease among strangers of gentility!"

"Marianne has not shyness to excuse any inattention of hers," said Elinor.

"She knows her own worth too well for false shame," replied Edward. "Shyness is only the effect of a sense of inferiority in some way or other. If I could persuade myself that my manners were perfectly easy and graceful, I should not be shy."

"But you would still be reserved," said Marianne, "and that is worse."

Edward stared—"Reserved! Am I reserved, Marianne?"

"Yes, very."

"I do not understand you," replied he, colouring. "Reserved!— how, in what manner? What am I to tell you? What can you suppose?"

Elinor looked surprised at his emotion, but trying to laugh off the subject, she said to him, "Do not you know my sister well enough to understand what she means? Do not you know she calls every one reserved who does not talk as fast, and admire what she admires as rapturously as herself?"

Edward made no answer. His gravity and thoughtfulness returned on him in their fullest extent—and he sat for some time silent and dull.

Chapter XVIII

Elinor saw, with great uneasiness, the low spirits of her friend. His visit afforded her but a very partial satisfaction, while his own enjoyment in it appeared so imperfect. It was evident that he was unhappy; she wished it were equally evident that he still distinguished her by the same affection which once she had felt no doubt of inspiring; but hitherto the continuance of his preference seemed very uncertain; and the reservedness of his manner towards her contradicted one moment what a more animated look had intimated the preceding one.

He joined her and Marianne in the breakfast-room the next morning before the others were down; and Marianne, who was always eager to promote their happiness as far as she could, soon left them to themselves. But before she was half way up stairs she heard the parlour door open, and, turning round, was astonished to see Edward himself come out.

"I am going into the village to see my horses," said he, "as you are not yet ready for breakfast; I shall be back again presently."

❧ ❧ ❧

Edward returned to them with fresh admiration of the surrounding country; in his walk to the village, he had seen many parts of the valley to advantage; and the village itself, in a much higher situation than the cottage, afforded; a general view of the whole, which had exceedingly pleased him. This was a subject which ensured Marianne's attention, and she was beginning to describe her own admiration of these scenes, and to question him more minutely on the objects that had particularly struck him, when Edward interrupted her by saying, "You must not inquire too far, Marianne—remember I have no knowledge in the picturesque, and I shall offend you by my ignorance and want of taste if we come to particulars. I shall call hills steep, which ought to be bold; surfaces strange and uncouth, which ought to be irregular and rugged; and distant objects out of sight, which ought only to be indistinct through the soft medium of a hazy atmosphere. You must be satisfied with such admiration as I can honestly give. I call it a very fine country—the hills are steep, the woods seem full of fine timber, and the valley looks comfortable and snug—with rich meadows and several neat farm houses scattered here and there. It exactly answers my idea of a fine country because it unites beauty with utility—and I dare say it is a picturesque one too, because you admire it; I can easily believe it to be full of rocks and promontories, grey moss and brush wood, but these are all lost on me. I know nothing of the picturesque."

"I am afraid it is but too true," said Marianne; "but why should you boast of it?"

"I suspect," said Elinor, "that to avoid one kind of affectation, Edward here falls into another. Because he believes many people pretend to more admiration of the beauties of nature than they really feel, and is disgusted with such pretensions, he affects greater indifference and less discrimination in viewing them himself than he possesses. He is fastidious and will have an affectation of his own."

"It is very true," said Marianne, "that admiration of landscape scenery is become a mere jargon. Every body pretends to feel and tries to describe with the taste and elegance of him who first defined what picturesque beauty was.[1] I detest jargon of every kind, and sometimes I have kept my feelings to myself, because I could find no language to describe them in but what was worn and hackneyed out of all sense and meaning."

[1] *him . . . what picturesque beauty was*: She probably refers to the writer William Gilpin (1724–1804) and his landmark works on the picturesque, including *Observations, Relative Chiefly to Picturesque Beauty* (published in the 1780s and 1790s), *Remarks on Forest Scenery* (1791), and *Three Essays: On Picturesque Beauty* (1792). Austen was also well-acquainted with other influential thinkers and architects of the time who, to a certain degree, also embraced notions of the picturesque, including Uvedale Price (1747–1829), William Payne Knight (1750–1824), and Humphrey Repton (1752–1818).

"I am convinced," said Edward, "that you really feel all the delight in a fine prospect which you profess to feel. But, in return, your sister must allow me to feel no more than I profess. I like a fine prospect, but not on picturesque principles. I do not like crooked, twisted, blasted trees. I admire them much more if they are tall, straight and flourishing. I do not like ruined, tattered cottages. I am not fond of nettles, or thistles, or heath blossoms. I have more pleasure in a snug farm-house than a watch-tower—and a troop of tidy, happy villagers please me better than the finest banditti in the world."

Marianne looked with amazement at Edward, with compassion at her sister. Elinor only laughed.

The subject was continued no farther; and Marianne remained thoughtfully silent, till a new object suddenly engaged her attention. She was sitting by Edward, and in taking his tea from Mrs. Dashwood, his hand passed so directly before her, as to make a ring, with a plait of hair in the centre,[2] very conspicuous on one of his fingers.

"I never saw you wear a ring before, Edward," she cried. "Is that Fanny's hair? I remember her promising to give you some. But I should have thought her hair had been darker."

Marianne spoke inconsiderately what she really felt—but when she saw how much she had pained Edward, her own vexation at her want of thought could not be surpassed by his. He coloured very deeply, and giving a momentary glance at Elinor, replied, "Yes; it is my sister's hair. The setting always casts a different shade on it you know."

Elinor had met his eye, and looked conscious likewise. That the hair was her own, she instantaneously felt as well satisfied as Marianne; the only difference in their conclusions was, that what Marianne considered as a free gift from her sister, Elinor was conscious must have been procured by some theft or contrivance unknown to herself. She was not in a humour,

[2] *ring . . . hair in the centre*: It was not uncommon for locks of hair to be encased in jewelry, especially by lovers or in the case of a beloved relative who had died (i.e., mourning rings).

however, to regard it as an affront, and affecting to take no notice of what passed, by instantly talking of something else, she internally resolved henceforward to catch every opportunity of eyeing the hair and of satisfying herself, beyond all doubt, that it was exactly the shade of her own.

Edward's embarrassment lasted some time, and it ended in an absence of mind still more settled. He was particularly grave the whole morning. Marianne severely censured herself for what she had said; but her own forgiveness might have been more speedy, had she known how little offence it had given her sister.

Before the middle of the day, they were visited by Sir John and Mrs. Jennings, who, having heard of the arrival of a gentleman at the cottage, came to take a survey of the guest. With the assistance of his mother-in-law, Sir John was not long in discovering that the name of Ferrars began with an F and this prepared a future mine of raillery against the devoted Elinor, which nothing but the newness of their acquaintance with Edward could have prevented from being immediately sprung. But, as it was, she only learned from some very significant looks, how far their penetration, founded on Margaret's instructions, extended.

Sir John never came to the Dashwoods without either inviting them to dine at the park the next day, or to drink tea with them that evening. On the present occasion, for the better entertainment of their visitor, towards whose amusement he felt himself bound to contribute, he wished to engage them for both.

"You *must* drink tea with us to night," said he, "for we shall be quite alone—and to-morrow you must absolutely dine with us, for we shall be a large party."

Mrs. Jennings enforced the necessity. "And who knows but you may raise a dance," said she. "And that will tempt *you*, Miss Marianne."

"A dance!" cried Marianne. "Impossible! Who is to dance?"

"Who! why yourselves, and the Careys, and Whitakers to be sure.—What! you thought nobody could dance because a certain person that shall be nameless is gone!"

"I wish with all my soul," cried Sir John, "that Willoughby were among us again."

This, and Marianne's blushing, gave new suspicions to Edward. "And who is Willoughby?" said he, in a low voice, to Miss Dashwood, by whom he was sitting.

She gave him a brief reply. Marianne's countenance was more communicative. Edward saw enough to comprehend, not only the meaning of others, but such of Marianne's expressions as had puzzled him before; and when their visitors left them, he went immediately round to her and said, in a whisper, "I have been guessing. Shall I tell you my guess?"

"What do you mean?"

"Shall I tell you?"

"Certainly."

"Well then; I guess that Mr. Willoughby hunts."

Marianne was surprised and confused, yet she could not help smiling at the quiet archness of his manner, and, after a moment's silence, said,

"Oh! Edward! How can you—But the time will come I hope.... I am sure you will like him."

"I do not doubt it," replied he, rather astonished at her earnestness and warmth; for had he not imagined it to be a joke for the good of her acquaintance in general, founded only on a something or a nothing between Mr. Willoughby and herself, he would not have ventured to mention it.

Chapter XIX

Edward remained a week at the cottage; he was earnestly pressed by Mrs. Dashwood to stay longer; but as if he were bent only on self-mortification, he seemed resolved to be gone when his enjoyment among his friends was at the height. His spirits, during the last two or three days, though still very unequal, were greatly improved—he grew more and more partial to the house and environs—never spoke of going away without a sigh—declared his time to be wholly disengaged—even doubted to what place he should go when he left them—but still, go he must. Never had any week passed so quickly—he could hardly believe it to be gone. He said so repeatedly; other things he said too, which marked the turn of his feelings and gave the lie to his actions. He had no pleasure at Norland; he detested being in town; but either to Norland or London, he must go. He valued their kindness beyond any thing, and his greatest happiness was in being with them. Yet he must leave them at the end of a week, in spite of their wishes and his own, and without any restraint on his time.

Elinor placed[1] all that was astonishing in this way of acting to his mother's account; and it was happy for her that he had a mother whose character was so imperfectly known to her, as to be the general excuse for every thing strange on the part of her son. Disappointed, however, and vexed as she was, and sometimes displeased with his uncertain behaviour to herself, she was very well disposed on the whole to regard his actions with all the candid allowances and generous qualifications, which had been rather more painfully extorted from her, for Willoughby's service, by her mother. His want of spirits, of openness, and of consistency, were most usually attributed to

---

[1] placed: attributed (as in a budget, where she is setting it all in Mrs. Ferrars's column).

his want of independence, and his better knowledge of Mrs. Ferrars's disposition and designs. The shortness of his visit, the steadiness of his purpose in leaving them, originated in the same fettered inclination, the same inevitable necessity of temporising with his mother. The old, well established grievance of duty against will, parent against child, was the cause of all. She would have been glad to know when these difficulties were to cease, this opposition was to yield,—when Mrs. Ferrars would be reformed, and her son be at liberty to be happy. But from such vain wishes, she was forced to turn for comfort to the renewal of her confidence in Edward's affection, to the remembrance of every mark of regard in look or word which fell from him while at Barton, and above all to that flattering proof of it which he constantly wore round his finger.

"I think, Edward," said Mrs. Dashwood, as they were at breakfast the last morning, "you would be a happier man if you had any profession to engage your time and give an interest to your plans and actions. Some inconvenience to your friends, indeed, might result from it—you would not be able to give them so much of your time. But (with a smile) you would be materially benefited in one particular at least—you would know where to go when you left them."

"I do assure you," he replied, "that I have long thought on this point, as you think now. It has been, and is, and probably will always be a heavy misfortune to me, that I have had no necessary business to engage me, no profession to give me employment, or afford me any thing like independence. But unfortunately my own nicety,[2] and the nicety of my friends, have made me what I am, an idle, helpless being. We never could agree in our choice of a profession. I always preferred the church, as I still do. But that was not smart enough for my family. They recommended the army. That was a great deal too smart for me. The law was allowed to be genteel enough; many young men, who had chambers in the Temple,[3] made a very

---

[2] *nicety*: delicacy of breeding and particularity in maintaining a certain status.

[3] *Temple*: i.e., Middle Temple or Inner Temple, one of the Inns of Court (a superior place of lodging).

good appearance in the first circles,[4] and drove about town in very knowing gigs.[5] But I had no inclination for the law, even in this less abstruse study of it, which my family approved. As for the navy, it had fashion on its side, but I was too old[6] when the subject was first started to enter it—and, at length, as there was no necessity for my having any profession at all, as I might be as dashing and expensive without a red coat[7] on my back as with one, idleness was pronounced on the whole to be the most advantageous and honourable, and a young man of eighteen is not in general so earnestly bent on being busy as to resist the solicitations of his friends to do nothing. I was therefore entered at Oxford[8] and have been properly idle ever since."

"The consequence of which, I suppose, will be," said Mrs. Dashwood, "since leisure has not promoted your own happiness, that your sons will be brought up to as many pursuits, employments, professions, and trades as Columella's."[9]

"They will be brought up," said he, in a serious accent,[10] "to be as unlike myself as is possible. In feeling, in action, in condition, in every thing."

"Come, come; this is all an effusion of immediate want of spirits, Edward. You are in a melancholy humour, and fancy that any one unlike yourself must be happy. But remember that the pain of parting from friends will be felt by every body at times, whatever be their education or state. Know your own

[4] *first circles*: most fashionable social circles.

[5] *very knowing gigs*: Here, "very knowing" means smart, chic; a gig is a light, two-wheeled carriage pulled by one horse.

[6] *too old*: training for a naval career began at around the age of eleven or twelve.

[7] *red coat*: Red coats were a recognizable feature of British military uniforms from 1645 through the mid-nineteenth century.

[8] *Oxford*: University of Oxford.

[9] *Columella's*: Chapman identifies Columella (via Mr. A. L. Humphreys in his 1914 *Notes and Queries*) as *Columella; or, The Distressed Anchoret* (1779) by minister and novelist Richard Graves (1715–1804). The novel presents a father who comically sends his sons into varied occupations: "And by these several occupations Columella flattered himself that his sons would be secured from that tedium and disgust of life which *he* experienced, and which he had brought upon himself by a life of indolence and inactivity" (vol. 2, chap. 28).

[10] *accent*: tone.

happiness. You want nothing but patience—or give it a more fascinating name, call it hope. Your mother will secure to you, in time, that independence you are so anxious for; it is her duty, and it will, it must ere long become her happiness to prevent your whole youth from being wasted in discontent. How much may not a few months do?"

"I think," replied Edward, "that I may defy many months to produce any good to me."

This desponding turn of mind, though it could not be communicated to Mrs. Dashwood, gave additional pain to them all in the parting, which shortly took place, and left an uncomfortable impression on Elinor's feelings especially, which required some trouble and time to subdue. But as it was her determination to subdue it, and to prevent herself from appearing to suffer more than what all her family suffered on his going away, she did not adopt the method so judiciously employed by Marianne, on a similar occasion, to augment and fix her sorrow, by seeking silence, solitude, and idleness. Their means were as different as their objects, and equally suited to the advancement of each.

Elinor sat down to her drawing-table as soon as he was out of the house, busily employed herself the whole day, neither sought nor avoided the mention of his name, appeared to interest herself almost as much as ever in the general concerns of the family, and if, by this conduct, she did not lessen her own grief, it was at least prevented from unnecessary increase, and her mother and sisters were spared much solicitude on her account.

Such behaviour as this, so exactly the reverse of her own, appeared no more meritorious to Marianne, than her own had seemed faulty to her. The business of self-command she settled very easily;—with strong affections it was impossible, with calm ones it could have no merit. That her sister's affections *were* calm, she dared not deny, though she blushed to acknowledge it; and of the strength of her own, she gave a very striking proof, by still loving and respecting that sister, in spite of this mortifying conviction.

Without shutting herself up from her family, or leaving the house in determined solitude to avoid them, or lying awake the whole night to indulge meditation, Elinor found every day afforded her leisure enough to think of Edward, and of Edward's behaviour, in every possible variety which the different state of her spirits at different times could produce;—with tenderness, pity, approbation, censure, and doubt. There were moments in abundance, when, if not by the absence of her mother and sisters, at least by the nature of their employments, conversation was forbidden among them, and every effect of solitude was produced. Her mind was inevitably at liberty; her thoughts could not be chained elsewhere; and the past and the future, on a subject so interesting, must be before her, must force her attention, and engross her memory, her reflection, and her fancy.

From a reverie of this kind, as she sat at her drawing-table, she was roused one morning, soon after Edward's leaving them, by the arrival of company. She happened to be quite alone. The closing of the little gate, at the entrance of the green court in front of the house, drew her eyes to the window, and she saw a large party walking up to the door. Amongst them were Sir John and Lady Middleton and Mrs. Jennings, but there were two others, a gentleman and lady, who were quite unknown to her. She was sitting near the window, and as soon as Sir John perceived her, he left the rest of the party to the ceremony of knocking at the door, and stepping across the turf, obliged her to open the casement to speak to him, though the space was so short between the door and the window, as to make it hardly possible to speak at one without being heard at the other.

"Well," said he, "we have brought you some strangers. How do you like them?"

"Hush! they will hear you."

"Never mind if they do. It is only the Palmers. Charlotte is very pretty, I can tell you. You may see her if you look this way."

As Elinor was certain of seeing her in a couple of minutes, without taking that liberty, she begged to be excused.

"Where is Marianne? Has she run away because we are come? I see her instrument is open."

"She is walking, I believe."

They were now joined by Mrs. Jennings, who had not patience enough to wait till the door was opened before she told *her* story. She came hallooing to the window, "How do you do, my dear? How does Mrs. Dashwood do?[11] And where are your sisters? What! all alone! you will be glad of a little company to sit with you. I have brought my other son and daughter to see you. Only think of their coming so suddenly! I thought I heard a carriage last night, while we were drinking our tea, but it never entered my head that it could be them. I thought of nothing but whether it might not be Colonel Brandon come back again; so I said to Sir John, I do think I hear a carriage; perhaps it is Colonel Brandon come back again"—

Elinor was obliged to turn from her, in the middle of her story, to receive the rest of the party; Lady Middleton introduced the two strangers; Mrs. Dashwood and Margaret came down stairs at the same time, and they all sat down to look at one another, while Mrs. Jennings continued her story as she walked through the passage into the parlour, attended by Sir John.

Mrs. Palmer was several years younger than Lady Middleton, and totally unlike her in every respect. She was short and plump, had a very pretty face, and the finest expression of good humour in it that could possibly be. Her manners were by no means so elegant as her sister's, but they were much more prepossessing. She came in with a smile, smiled all the time of her visit, except when she laughed, and smiled when she went away. Her husband was a grave looking young man of five or six and twenty, with an air of more fashion and sense than his wife, but of less willingness to please or be pleased. He entered the room with a look of self-consequence, slightly bowed to the ladies, without speaking a word, and, after briefly surveying

[11] *How do you do ... Mrs. Dashwood do?*: In modern terms, she means, "How are you?" and "How is Mrs. Dashwood?"

them and their apartments, took up a newspaper from the table and continued to read it as long as he staid.

Mrs. Palmer, on the contrary, who was strongly endowed by nature with a turn for being uniformly civil and happy, was hardly seated before her admiration of the parlour and every thing in it burst forth.

"Well! what a delightful room this is! I never saw anything so charming! Only think, mama, how it is improved since I was here last! I always thought it such a sweet place, ma'am! (turning to Mrs. Dashwood,) but you have made it so charming! Only look, sister, how delightful every thing is! How I should like such a house for myself! Should not you, Mr. Palmer?"

Mr. Palmer made her no answer, and did not even raise his eyes from the newspaper.

"Mr. Palmer does not hear me," said she, laughing, "he never does sometimes. It is so ridiculous!"

This was quite a new idea to Mrs. Dashwood, she had never been used to find wit in the inattention of any one, and could not help looking with surprise at them both.

Mrs. Jennings, in the mean time, talked on as loud as she could, and continued her account of their surprise, the evening before, on seeing their friends, without ceasing till every thing was told. Mrs. Palmer laughed heartily at the recollection of their astonishment, and every body agreed, two or three times over, that it had been quite an agreeable surprise.

"You may believe how glad we all were to see them," added Mrs. Jennings, leaning forwards towards Elinor, and speaking in a low voice as if she meant to be heard by no one else, though they were seated on different sides of the room; "but, however, I can't help wishing they had not travelled quite so fast, nor made such a long journey of it, for they came all round by London upon account of some business, for you know (nodding significantly and pointing to her daughter) it was wrong in her situation. I wanted her to stay at home and rest this morning, but she would come with us; she longed so much to see you all!"

Mrs. Palmer laughed, and said it would not do her any harm.

"She expects to be confined[12] in February," continued Mrs. Jennings.

Lady Middleton could no longer endure such a conversation, and therefore exerted herself to ask Mr. Palmer if there was any news in the paper.

"No, none at all," he replied, and read on.

"Here comes Marianne," cried Sir John. "Now, Palmer, you shall see a monstrous pretty girl."

He immediately went into the passage, opened the front door, and ushered her in himself. Mrs. Jennings asked her, as soon as she appeared, if she had not been to Allenham; and Mrs. Palmer laughed so heartily at the question, as to shew she understood it. Mr. Palmer looked up on her entering the room, stared at her some minutes, and then returned to his newspaper. Mrs. Palmer's eye was now caught by the drawings which hung round the room. She got up to examine them.

"Oh! dear, how beautiful these are! Well! how delightful! Do but look, mama, how sweet! I declare they are quite charming; I could look at them for ever." And then sitting down again, she very soon forgot that there were any such things in the room.

When Lady Middleton rose to go away, Mr. Palmer rose also, laid down the newspaper, stretched himself, and looked at them all round.

"My love, have you been asleep?" said his wife, laughing.

He made her no answer; and only observed, after again examining the room, that it was very low pitched, and that the ceiling was crooked. He then made his bow and departed with the rest.

Sir John had been very urgent with them all to spend the next day at the park. Mrs. Dashwood, who did not chuse to dine with them oftener than they dined at the cottage, absolutely refused on her own account; her daughters might do as they pleased. But they had no curiosity to see how Mr. and Mrs. Palmer ate their dinner, and no expectation of pleasure from

[12] *confined*: i.e., to a childbed (to give birth).

them in any other way. They attempted, therefore, likewise to excuse themselves; the weather was uncertain and not likely to be good. But Sir John would not be satisfied—the carriage should be sent for them and they must come. Lady Middleton too, though she did not press their mother, pressed them. Mrs. Jennings and Mrs. Palmer joined their entreaties, all seemed equally anxious to avoid a family party; and the young ladies were obliged to yield.

"Why should they ask us?" said Marianne, as soon as they were gone. "The rent of this cottage is said to be low; but we have it on very hard terms, if we are to dine at the park whenever any one is staying either with them, or with us."

"They mean no less to be civil and kind to us now," said Elinor, "by these frequent invitations than by those which we received from them a few weeks ago. The alteration is not in them, if their parties are grown tedious and dull. We must look for the change elsewhere."

Chapter XX

As the Miss Dashwoods entered the drawing-room of the park the next day, at one door, Mrs. Palmer came running in at the other, looking as good humoured and merry as before. She took them all most affectionately by the hand, and expressed great delight in seeing them again.

"I am so glad to see you!" said she, seating herself between Elinor and Marianne, "for it is so bad a day I was afraid you might not come, which would be a shocking thing, as we go away again tomorrow. We must go, for the Westons come to us next week you know. It was quite a sudden thing our coming at all, and I knew nothing of it till the carriage was coming to the door, and then Mr. Palmer asked me if I would go with him to Barton. He is so droll! He never tells me any thing! I am so sorry we cannot stay longer; however we shall meet again in town very soon, I hope."

They were obliged to put an end to such an expectation.

"Not go to town!" cried Mrs. Palmer, with a laugh, "I shall be quite disappointed if you do not. I could get the nicest house in the world for you, next door to our's, in Hanover-square.[1] You must come, indeed. I am sure I shall be very happy to chaperon you at any time till I am confined, if Mrs. Dashwood should not like to go into public."

They thanked her; but were obliged to resist all her entreaties.

"Oh! my love," cried Mrs. Palmer to her husband, who just then entered the room—"You must help me to persuade the Miss Dashwoods to go to town this winter."

Her love made no answer; and after slightly bowing to the ladies, began complaining of the weather.

"How horrid all this is!" said he. "Such weather makes every thing and every body disgusting. Dulness is as much produced

[1] *Hanover-square*: fashionable residential spot in London.

within doors as without, by rain. It makes one detest all one's acquaintance. What the devil does Sir John mean by not having a billiard room in his house? How few people know what comfort is! Sir John is as stupid as the weather."

The rest of the company soon dropt in.

"I am afraid, Miss Marianne," said Sir John, "you have not been able to take your usual walk to Allenham today."

Marianne looked very grave and said nothing.

"Oh! don't be so sly before us," said Mrs. Palmer; "for we know all about it, I assure you; and I admire your taste very much, for I think he is extremely handsome. We do not live a great way from him in the country, you know. Not above ten miles, I dare say."

"Much nearer thirty," said her husband.

"Ah! well! there is not much difference. I never was at his house; but they say it is a sweet pretty place."

"As vile a spot as I ever saw in my life," said Mr. Palmer.

Marianne remained perfectly silent, though her countenance betrayed her interest in what was said.

"Is it very ugly?" continued Mrs. Palmer—"then it must be some other place that is so pretty I suppose."

When they were seated in the dining room, Sir John observed with regret that they were only eight altogether.

"My dear," said he to his lady, "it is very provoking that we should be so few. Why did not you ask the Gilberts to come to us to-day?"

"Did not I tell you, Sir John, when you spoke to me about it before, that it could not be done? They dined with us last."

"You and I, Sir John," said Mrs. Jennings, "should not stand upon such ceremony."

"Then you would be very ill-bred," cried Mr. Palmer.

"My love, you contradict every body,"—said his wife with her usual laugh. "Do you know that you are quite rude?"

"I did not know I contradicted any body in calling your mother ill-bred."

"Aye, you may abuse me as you please," said the good-natured old lady, "you have taken Charlotte off my hands, and cannot give her back again. So there I have the whip hand[2] of you."

Charlotte laughed heartily to think that her husband could not get rid of her; and exultingly said, she did not care how cross he was to her, as they must live together. It was impossible for any one to be more thoroughly good-natured, or more determined to be happy than Mrs. Palmer. The studied indifference, insolence, and discontent of her husband gave her no pain: and when he scolded or abused her, she was highly diverted.

"Mr. Palmer is so droll!" said she, in a whisper, to Elinor. "He is always out of humour."

Elinor was not inclined, after a little observation, to give him credit for being so genuinely and unaffectedly ill-natured or ill-bred as he wished to appear. His temper might perhaps be a little soured by finding, like many others of his sex, that through some unaccountable bias in favour of beauty, he was the husband of a very silly woman,—but she knew that this kind of blunder was too common for any sensible man to be lastingly hurt by it.—It was rather a wish of distinction she believed, which produced his contemptuous treatment of every body, and his general abuse of every thing before him. It was the desire of appearing superior to other people. The motive was too common to be wondered at; but the means, however they might succeed by establishing his superiority in ill-breeding, were not likely to attach any one to him except his wife.

"Oh! my dear Miss Dashwood," said Mrs. Palmer soon afterwards, "I have got such a favour to ask of you and your sister. Will you come and spend some time at Cleveland this Christmas? Now, pray do,—and come while the Westons are with us. You cannot think how happy I shall be! It will be quite delightful!—My love," applying to her husband, "don't you long to have the Miss Dashwoods come to Cleveland?"

---

[2] *whip hand*: upper hand, advantage (i.e., the hand in which a driver holds a whip).

"Certainly,"—he replied with a sneer—"I came into Devonshire with no other view."

"There now"—said his lady, "you see Mr. Palmer expects you; so you cannot refuse to come."

They both eagerly and resolutely declined her invitation.

"But indeed you must and shall come. I am sure you will like it of all things. The Westons will be with us, and it will be quite delightful. You cannot think what a sweet place Cleveland is; and we are so gay now, for Mr. Palmer is always going about the country canvassing against[3] the election; and so many people come to dine with us that I never saw before, it is quite charming! But, poor fellow! it is very fatiguing to him! for he is forced to make every body like him."

Elinor could hardly keep her countenance as she assented to the hardship of such an obligation.

"How charming it will be," said Charlotte, "when he is in Parliament!—won't it? How I shall laugh! It will be so ridiculous to see all his letters directed to him with an M. P.[4]—But do you know, he says, he will never frank[5] for me? He declares he won't. Don't you, Mr. Palmer?"

Mr. Palmer took no notice of her.

"He cannot bear writing, you know," she continued—"he says it is quite shocking."

"No;" said he, "I never said any thing so irrational. Don't palm all your abuses of language upon me."

"There now; you see how droll he is. This is always the way with him! Sometimes he won't speak to me for half a day together, and then he comes out with something so droll—all about any thing in the world."

She surprised Elinor very much as they returned into the drawing-room by asking her whether she did not like Mr. Palmer excessively.

[3] *canvassing against*: campaigning in.
[4] M.P.: Member of Parliament.
[5] *frank*: Up until 1840, a Member of Parliament could post mail free of charge simply by affixing his signature to the envelope. Normally, postage was calculated according to its weight and the distance it was to travel.

"Certainly;" said Elinor, "he seems very agreeable."

"Well—I am so glad you do. I thought you would, he is so pleasant; and Mr. Palmer is excessively pleased with you and your sisters I can tell you, and you can't think how disappointed he will be if you don't come to Cleveland.—I can't imagine why you should object to it."

Elinor was again obliged to decline her invitation; and by changing the subject, put a stop to her entreaties. She thought it probable that as they lived in the same county, Mrs. Palmer might be able to give some more particular account of Willoughby's general character, than could be gathered from the Middletons' partial acquaintance with him; and she was eager to gain from any one, such a confirmation of his merits as might remove the possibility of fear for Marianne. She began by inquiring if they saw much of Mr. Willoughby at Cleveland, and whether they were intimately acquainted with him.

"Oh! dear, yes; I know him extremely well," replied Mrs. Palmer—"Not that I ever spoke to him indeed; but I have seen him for ever in town. Somehow or other I never happened to be staying at Barton while he was at Allenham. Mama saw him here once before;—but I was with my uncle at Weymouth. However, I dare say we should have seen a great deal of him in Somersetshire, if it had not happened very unluckily that we should never have been in the country together. He is very little at Combe, I believe; but if he were ever so much there, I do not think Mr. Palmer would visit him, for he is in the opposition[6] you know, and besides it is such a way off. I know why you inquire about him, very well; your sister is to marry him. I am monstrous glad of it, for then I shall have her for a neighbour you know."

"Upon my word," replied Elinor, "you know much more of the matter than I do, if you have any reason to expect such a match."

"Don't pretend to deny it, because you know it is what every body talks of. I assure you I heard of it in my way through town."

[6] *opposition*: the political party not in power.

"My dear Mrs. Palmer!"

"Upon my honour I did.—I met Colonel Brandon Monday morning in Bond-street,[7] just before we left town, and he told me of it directly."

"You surprise me very much. Colonel Brandon tell you of it! Surely you must be mistaken. To give such intelligence to a person who could not be interested in it, even if it were true, is not what I should expect Colonel Brandon to do."

"But I do assure you it was so, for all that, and I will tell you how it happened. When we met him, he turned back and walked with us; and so we began talking of my brother and sister, and one thing and another, and I said to him, 'So, Colonel, there is a new family come to Barton cottage, I hear, and mama sends me word they are very pretty, and that one of them is going to be married to Mr. Willoughby of Combe Magna. Is it true, pray? for of course you must know, as you have been in Devonshire so lately.'"

"And what did the Colonel say?"

"Oh!—he did not say much; but he looked as if he knew it to be true, so from that moment I set it down as certain. It will be quite delightful, I declare! When is it to take place?"

"Mr. Brandon was very well I hope."

"Oh! yes, quite well; and so full of your praises, he did nothing but say fine things of you."

"I am flattered by his commendation. He seems an excellent man; and I think him uncommonly pleasing."

"So do I.—He is such a charming man, that it is quite a pity he should be so grave and so dull. Mama says *he* was in love with your sister too.—I assure you it was a great compliment if he was, for he hardly ever falls in love with any body."

"Is Mr. Willoughby much known in your part of Somersetshire?" said Elinor.

"Oh! yes, extremely well; that is, I do not believe many people are acquainted with him, because Combe Magna is so far off; but they all think him extremely agreeable I assure you.

---

[7] *Bond-street*: fashionable London shopping street.

Nobody is more liked than Mr. Willoughby wherever he goes, and so you may tell your sister. She is a monstrous lucky girl to get him, upon my honour; not but that he is much more lucky in getting her, because she is so very handsome and agreeable, that nothing can be good enough for her. However I don't think her hardly at all handsomer than you, I assure you; for I think you both excessively pretty, and so does Mr. Palmer too I am sure, though we could not get him to own it last night."

Mrs. Palmer's information respecting Willoughby was not very material; but any testimony in his favour, however small, was pleasing to her.

"I am so glad we are got acquainted at last," continued Charlotte.—"And now I hope we shall always be great friends. You can't think how much I longed to see you! It is so delightful that you should live at the cottage! Nothing can be like it to be sure! And I am so glad your sister is going to be well married! I hope you will be a great deal at Combe Magna. It is a sweet place by all accounts."

"You have been long acquainted with Colonel Brandon, have not you?"

"Yes, a great while; ever since my sister married.—He was a particular friend of Sir John's. I believe," she added in a low voice, "he would have been very glad to have had me, if he could. Sir John and Lady Middleton wished it very much. But mama did not think the match good enough for me, otherwise Sir John would have mentioned it to the Colonel, and we should have been married immediately."

"Did not Colonel Brandon know of Sir John's proposal to your mother before it was made? Had he never owned his affection to yourself?"

"Oh! no; but if mama had not objected to it, I dare say he would have liked it of all things. He had not seen me then above twice, for it was before I left school. However I am much happier as I am. Mr. Palmer is just the kind of man I like."

Chapter XXI

The Palmers returned to Cleveland the next day, and the two families at Barton were again left to entertain each other. But this did not last long; Elinor had hardly got their last visitors out of her head, had hardly done wondering at Charlotte's being so happy without a cause, at Mr. Palmer's acting so simply, with good abilities, and at the strange unsuitableness which often existed between husband and wife, before Sir John's and Mrs. Jennings's active zeal in the cause of society, procured her some other new acquaintance to see and observe.

In a morning's excursion to Exeter, they had met with two young ladies, whom Mrs. Jennings had the satisfaction of discovering to be her relations, and this was enough for Sir John to invite them directly to the park, as soon as their present engagements at Exeter were over. Their engagements at Exeter instantly gave way before such an invitation, and Lady Middleton was thrown into no little alarm on the return of Sir John, by hearing that she was very soon to receive a visit from two girls whom she had never seen in her life, and of whose elegance,—whose tolerable gentility even, she could have no proof; for the assurances of her husband and mother on that subject went for nothing at all. Their being her relations too made it so much the worse; and Mrs. Jennings's attempts at consolation were therefore unfortunately founded, when she advised her daughter not to care about their being so fashionable; because they were all cousins and must put up with one another. As it was impossible however now to prevent their coming, Lady Middleton resigned herself to the idea of it, with all the philosophy of a well bred woman, contenting herself with merely giving her husband a gentle reprimand on the subject five or six times every day.

The young ladies arrived, their appearance was by no means ungenteel or unfashionable. Their dress was very smart, their

115

manners very civil, they were delighted with the house, and in raptures with the furniture, and they happened to be so doatingly fond of children that Lady Middleton's good opinion was engaged in their favour before they had been an hour at the Park. She declared them to be very agreeable girls indeed, which for her ladyship was enthusiastic admiration. Sir John's confidence in his own judgment rose with this animated praise, and he set off directly for the cottage to tell the Miss Dashwoods of the Miss Steeles' arrival, and to assure them of their being the sweetest girls in the world. From such commendation as this, however, there was not much to be learned; Elinor well knew that the sweetest girls in the world were to be met with in every part of England, under every possible variation of form, face, temper, and understanding. Sir John wanted the whole family to walk to the Park directly and look at his guests. Benevolent, philanthropic man! It was painful to him even to keep a third cousin to himself.

"Do come now," said he—"pray come—you must come—I declare you shall come.—You can't think how you will like them. Lucy is monstrous pretty, and so good humoured and agreeable! The children are all hanging about her already, as if she was an old acquaintance. And they both long to see you of all things, for they have heard at Exeter that you are the most beautiful creatures in the world; and I have told them it is all very true, and a great deal more. You will be delighted with them I am sure. They have brought the whole coach full of playthings for the children. How can you be so cross as not to come? Why they are your cousins, you know, after a fashion. *You* are my cousins, and they are my wife's, so you must be related."

But Sir John could not prevail. He could only obtain a promise of their calling at the Park within a day or two, and then left them in amazement at their indifference, to walk home and boast anew of their attractions to the Miss Steeles, as he had been already boasting of the Miss Steeles to them.

When their promised visit to the Park and consequent introduction to these young ladies took place, they found in the appearance of the eldest, who was nearly thirty, with a very plain and not a sensible face, nothing to admire; but in the other, who was not more than two or three and twenty, they acknowledged considerable beauty; her features were pretty, and she had a sharp quick eye, and a smartness of air, which though it did not give actual elegance or grace, gave distinction to her person.—Their manners were particularly civil, and Elinor soon allowed them credit for some kind of sense, when she saw with what constant and judicious attentions they were making themselves agreeable to Lady Middleton. With her children they were in continual raptures, extolling their beauty, courting their notice, and humouring all their whims; and such of their time as could be spared from the importunate demands which this politeness made on it, was spent in admiration of whatever her ladyship was doing, if she happened to be doing any thing, or in taking patterns of some elegant new dress, in which her appearance the day before had thrown them into unceasing delight. Fortunately for those who pay their court through such foibles, a fond mother, though, in pursuit of praise for her children, the most rapacious of human beings, is likewise the most credulous; her demands are exorbitant; but she will swallow any thing; and the excessive affection and endurance of the Miss Steeles towards her offspring, were viewed therefore by Lady Middleton without the smallest surprise or distrust. She saw with maternal complacency all the impertitinent incroachments and mischievous tricks to which her cousins submitted. She saw their sashes untied, their hair pulled about their ears, their work-bags[1] searched, and their knives and scissars stolen away, and felt no doubt of its being a reciprocal enjoyment. It suggested no other surprise than that Elinor and Marianne should sit so composedly by, without claiming a share in what was passing.

"John is in such spirits to-day!" said she, on his taking Miss Steele's pocket handkerchief, and throwing it out of window—"He is full of monkey tricks."

---

[1] *work-bags*: i.e., bags for needlework.

And soon afterwards, on the second boy's violently pinching one of the same lady's fingers, she fondly observed, "How playful William is!"

"And here is my sweet little Annamaria," she added, tenderly caressing a little girl of three years old, who had not made a noise for the last two minutes; "And she is always so gentle and quiet—Never was there such a quiet little thing!"

But unfortunately in bestowing these embraces, a pin in her ladyship's head dress slightly scratching the child's neck, produced from this pattern of gentleness, such violent screams, as could hardly be outdone by any creature professedly noisy. The mother's consternation was excessive; but it could not surpass the alarm of the Miss Steeles, and every thing was done by all three, in so critical an emergency, which affection could suggest as likely to assuage the agonies of the little sufferer. She was seated in her mother's lap, covered with kisses, her wound bathed with lavender-water,[2] by one of the Miss Steeles, who was on her knees to attend her, and her mouth stuffed with sugar plums by the other. With such a reward for her tears, the child was too wise to cease crying. She still screamed and sobbed lustily, kicked her two brothers for offering to touch her, and all their united soothings were ineffectual till Lady Middleton luckily remembering that in a scene of similar distress last week, some apricot marmalade had been successfully applied for a bruised temple, the same remedy was eagerly proposed for this unfortunate scratch, and a slight intermission of screams in the young lady on hearing it, gave them reason to hope that it would not be rejected.—She was carried out of the room therefore in her mother's arms, in quest of this medicine, and as the two boys chose to follow, though earnestly entreated by their mother to stay behind, the four young ladies were left in a quietness which the room had not known for many hours.

"Poor little creature!" said Miss Steele, as soon as they were gone. "It might have been a very sad accident."

---

[2] *lavender-water*: scented water or perfume; lavender has been used for relaxation and credited with other medicinal properties since antiquity.

"Yet I hardly know how," cried Marianne, "unless it had been under totally different circumstances. But this is the usual way of heightening alarm, where there is nothing to be alarmed at in reality."

"What a sweet woman Lady Middleton is!" said Lucy Steele.

Marianne was silent; it was impossible for her to say what she did not feel, however trivial the occasion; and upon Elinor therefore the whole task of telling lies when politeness required it, always fell. She did her best when thus called on, by speaking of Lady Middleton with more warmth than she felt, though with far less than Miss Lucy.

"And Sir John too," cried the elder sister, "what a charming man he is!"

Here too, Miss Dashwood's commendation, being only simple and just, came in without any éclat.[3] She merely observed that he was perfectly good humoured and friendly.

"And what a charming little family they have! I never saw such fine children in my life.—I declare I quite doat upon them already, and indeed I am always distractedly fond of children."

"I should guess so," said Elinor with a smile, "from what I have witnessed this morning."

"I have a notion," said Lucy, "you think the little Middletons rather too much indulged; perhaps they may be the outside of enough; but it is so natural in Lady Middleton; and for my part, I love to see children full of life and spirits; I cannot bear them if they are tame and quiet."

"I confess," replied Elinor, "that while I am at Barton Park, I never think of tame and quiet children with any abhorrence."

A short pause succeeded this speech, which was first broken by Miss Steele, who seemed very much disposed for conversation, and who now said rather abruptly, "And how do you like Devonshire, Miss Dashwood? I suppose you were very sorry to leave Sussex."

In some surprise at the familiarity of this question, or at least of the manner in which it was spoken, Elinor replied that she was.

---

[3] *éclat*: ostentation or display.

"Norland is a prodigious beautiful place, is not it?" added Miss Steele.

"We have heard Sir John admire it excessively,"[4] said Lucy, who seemed to think some apology necessary for the freedom of her sister.

"I think every one *must* admire it," replied Elinor, "who ever saw the place; though it is not to be supposed that any one can estimate its beauties as we do."

"And had you a great many smart beaux there? I suppose you have not so many in this part of the world; for my part, I think they are a vast addition always."

"But why should you think," said Lucy, looking ashamed of her sister, "that there are not as many genteel young men in Devonshire as Sussex?"

"Nay, my dear, I'm sure I don't pretend to say that there an't. I'm sure there's a vast many smart beaux in Exeter; but you know, how could I tell what smart beaux there might be about Norland; and I was only afraid the Miss Dashwoods might find it dull at Barton, if they had not so many as they used to have. But perhaps you young ladies may not care about the beaux, and had as lief be without them as with them. For my part, I think they are vastly agreeable, provided they dress smart and behave civil. But I can't bear to see them dirty and nasty. Now there's Mr. Rose at Exeter, a prodigious smart young man, quite a beau, clerk to Mr. Simpson you know, and yet if you do but meet him of a morning, he is not fit to be seen.—I suppose your brother was quite a beau, Miss Dashwood, before he married, as he was so rich?"

"Upon my word," replied Elinor, "I cannot tell you, for I do not perfectly comprehend the meaning of the word. But this I can say, that if he ever was a beau before he married, he is one still, for there is not the smallest alteration in him."

"Oh! dear! one never thinks of married men's being beaux— they have something else to do."

[4] *Norland ... excessively*: As Chapman appropriately notes, the mention of Norland *is* overly free and presumptuous, but Lucy's explanation of it is unpersuasive, since Sir John has never seen Norland (cf. p. 23).

"Lord! Anne," cried her sister, "you can talk of nothing but beaux;—you will make Miss Dashwood believe you think of nothing else." And then to turn the discourse, she began admiring the house and the furniture.

This specimen of the Miss Steeles was enough. The vulgar freedom and folly of the eldest left her no recommendation, and as Elinor was not blinded by the beauty, or the shrewd look of the youngest, to her want of real elegance and artlessness, she left the house without any wish of knowing them better.

Not so, the Miss Steeles.—They came from Exeter, well provided with admiration for the use of Sir John Middleton, his family, and all his relations, and no niggardly[5] proportion was now dealt out to his fair cousins, whom they declared to be the most beautiful, elegant, accomplished and agreeable girls they had ever beheld, and with whom they were particularly anxious to be better acquainted.—And to be better acquainted therefore, Elinor soon found was their inevitable lot, for as Sir John was entirely on the side of the Miss Steeles, their party would be too strong for opposition, and that kind of intimacy must be submitted to, which consists of sitting an hour or two together in the same room almost every day. Sir John could do no more; but he did not know that any more was required; to be together was, in his opinion, to be intimate, and while his continual schemes for their meeting were effectual, he had not a doubt of their being established friends.

To do him justice, he did every thing in his power to promote their unreserve, by making the Miss Steeles acquainted with whatever he knew or supposed of his cousins' situations in the most delicate particulars,—and Elinor had not seen them more than twice, before the eldest of them wished her joy on her sister's having been so lucky as to make a conquest of a very smart beau since she came to Barton.

"'Twill be a fine thing to have her married so young to be sure," said she, "and I hear he is quite a beau, and prodigious handsome. And I hope you may have as good luck yourself

---

[5] *niggardly:* stingy or meager.

soon,—but perhaps you may have a friend in the corner already."

Elinor could not suppose that Sir John would be more nice in proclaiming his suspicions of her regard for Edward, than he had been with respect to Marianne; indeed it was rather his favourite joke of the two, as being somewhat newer and more conjectural; and since Edward's visit, they had never dined together, without his drinking to her best affections with so much significancy and so many nods and winks, as to excite general attention. The letter F—had been likewise invariably brought forward, and found productive of such countless jokes, that its character as the wittiest letter in the alphabet had been long established with Elinor.

The Miss Steeles, as she expected, had now all the benefit of these jokes, and in the eldest of them they raised a curiosity to know the name of the gentleman alluded to, which, though often impertinently expressed, was perfectly of a piece with her general inquisitiveness into the concerns of their family. But Sir John did not sport long with the curiosity which he delighted to raise, for he had at least as much pleasure in telling the name, as Miss Steele had in hearing it.

"His name is Ferrars," said he, in a very audible whisper; "but pray do not tell it, for it's a great secret."

"Ferrars!" repeated Miss Steele; "Mr. Ferrars is the happy man, is he? What! your sister-in-law's brother, Miss Dashwood? a very agreeable young man to be sure; I know him very well."

"How can you say so, Anne?" cried Lucy, who generally made an amendment to all her sister's assertions. "Though we have seen him once or twice at my uncle's, it is rather too much to pretend to know him very well."

Elinor heard all this with attention and surprise. "And who was this uncle? Where did he live? How came they acquainted?" She wished very much to have the subject continued, though she did not chuse to join in it herself; but nothing more of it was said, and for the first time in her life, she thought Mrs. Jennings deficient either in curiosity after petty information, or in a disposition to communicate it. The manner in which Miss Steele had spoken of Edward, increased her curiosity; for it struck her as being rather ill-natured, and suggested the suspicion of that lady's knowing, or fancying herself to know something to his disadvantage.—But her curiosity was unavailing, for no farther notice was taken of Mr. Ferrars's name by Miss Steele when alluded to, or even openly mentioned by Sir John.

Chapter XXII

Marianne, who had never much toleration for any thing like impertinence, vulgarity, inferiority of parts,[1] or even difference of taste from herself, was at this time particularly ill-disposed, from the state of her spirits, to be pleased with the Miss Steeles, or to encourage their advances; and to the invariable coldness of her behaviour towards them, which checked every endeavour at intimacy on their side, Elinor principally attributed that preference of herself which soon became evident in the manners of both, but especially of Lucy, who missed no opportunity of engaging her in conversation, or of striving to improve their acquaintance by an easy and frank communication of her sentiments.

Lucy was naturally clever; her remarks were often just and amusing; and as a companion for half an hour Elinor frequently found her agreeable; but her powers had received no aid from education, she was ignorant and illiterate, and her deficiency of all mental improvement,[2] her want of information in the most common particulars, could not be concealed from Miss Dashwood, in spite of her constant endeavour to appear to advantage. Elinor saw, and pitied her for, the neglect of abilities which education might have rendered so respectable; but she saw, with less tenderness of feeling, the thorough want of delicacy, of rectitude, and integrity of mind, which her attentions, her assiduities,[3] her flatteries at the Park betrayed; and she could have no lasting satisfaction in the company of a person who joined insincerity with ignorance; whose want of instruction prevented their meeting in conversation on terms

[1] *parts*: abilities, talents.
[2] *improvement*: cultivation.
[3] *assiduities*: constant attentions (to Elinor).

of equality, and whose conduct towards others, made every shew of attention and deference towards herself perfectly valueless.

"You will think my question an odd one, I dare say," said Lucy to her one day as they were walking together from the park to the cottage—"but, pray, are you personally acquainted with your sister-in-law's mother, Mrs. Ferrars?"

Elinor *did* think the question a very odd one, and her countenance expressed it, as she answered that she had never seen Mrs. Ferrars.

"Indeed!" replied Lucy; "I wonder at that, for I thought you must have seen her at Norland sometimes. Then perhaps you cannot tell me what sort of a woman she is?"

"No;" returned Elinor, cautious of giving her real opinion of Edward's mother, and not very desirous of satisfying, what seemed impertinent curiosity—"I know nothing of her."

"I am sure you think me very strange, for inquiring about her in such a way;" said Lucy, eyeing Elinor attentively as she spoke; "but perhaps there may be reasons—I wish I might venture; but however I hope you will do me the justice of believing that I do not mean to be impertinent."

Elinor made her a civil reply, and they walked on for a few minutes in silence. It was broken by Lucy, who renewed the subject again by saying with some hesitation,

"I cannot bear to have you think me impertinently curious. I am sure I would rather do any thing in the world than be thought so by a person whose good opinion is so well worth having as yours. And I am sure I should not have the smallest fear of trusting *you*; indeed I should be very glad of your advice how to manage in such an uncomfortable situation as I am; but however there is no occasion to trouble *you*. I am sorry you do not happen to know Mrs. Ferrars."

"I am sorry I do *not*," said Elinor, in great astonishment, "if it could be of any use to *you* to know my opinion of her. But really, I never understood that you were at all connected with that family, and therefore I am a little surprised, I confess, at so serious an inquiry into her character."

"I dare say you are, and I am sure I do not at all wonder at it. But if I dared tell you all, you would not be so much surprised. Mrs. Ferrars is certainly nothing to me at present,—but the time *may* come—how soon it will come must depend upon herself—when we may be very intimately connected."

She looked down as she said this, amiably bashful, with only one side glance at her companion to observe its effect on her.

"Good heavens!" cried Elinor, "what do you mean? Are you acquainted with Mr. Robert Ferrars? Can you be—?"[4] And she did not feel much delighted with the idea of such a sister-in-law.

"No;" replied Lucy, "not to Mr. *Robert* Ferrars—I never saw him in my life; but," fixing her eyes upon Elinor, "to his elder brother."

What felt Elinor at that moment? Astonishment, that would have been as painful as it was strong, had not an immediate disbelief of the assertion attended it. She turned towards Lucy in silent amazement, unable to divine the reason or object of such a declaration, and though her complexion varied, she stood firm in incredulity and felt in no danger of an hysterical fit, or a swoon.

"You may well be surprised," continued Lucy; "for to be sure you could have had no idea of it before; for I dare say he never dropped the smallest hint of it to you or any of your family; because it was always meant to be a great secret, and I am sure has been faithfully kept so by me to this hour. Not a soul of all my relations know of it but Anne, and I never should have mentioned it to you, if I had not felt the greatest dependance in the world upon your secrecy; and I really thought my behaviour in asking so many questions about Mrs. Ferrars, must seem so odd, that it ought to be explained. And I do not think Mr. Ferrars can be displeased, when he knows I have trusted you, because I know he has the highest opinion in the world of all your family, and looks upon yourself and the other Miss Dashwoods, quite as his own sisters."—She paused.

[4]*Can you be*—?: This is a conflation of both editions; Lucy's response seems to indicate that the "space" should be filled with "engaged" instead of merely "acquainted".

Elinor for a few moments remained silent. Her astonishment at what she heard was at first too great for words; but at length forcing herself to speak, and to speak cautiously, she said with a calmness of manner, which tolerably well concealed her surprise and solicitude—"May I ask if your engagement is of long standing?"

"We have been engaged these four years."

"Four years!"

"Yes."

Elinor, though greatly shocked, still felt unable to believe it.

"I did not know," said she, "that you were even acquainted till the other day."

"Our acquaintance, however, is of many years date. He was under my uncle's care, you know, a considerable while."

"Your uncle!"

"Yes; Mr. Pratt. Did you never hear him talk of Mr. Pratt?"

"I think I have," replied Elinor, with an exertion of spirits, which increased with her increase of emotion.

"He was four years with my uncle, who lives at Longstaple, near Plymouth. It was there our acquaintance begun, for my sister and me was often staying with my uncle, and it was there our engagement was formed, though not till a year after he had quitted as a pupil; but he was almost always with us afterwards. I was very unwilling to enter into it, as you may imagine, without the knowledge and approbation of his mother; but I was too young and loved him too well to be so prudent as I ought to have been.—Though you do not know him so well as me, Miss Dashwood, you must have seen enough of him to be sensible he is very capable of making a woman sincerely attached to him."

"Certainly," answered Elinor, without knowing what she said; but after a moment's reflection, she added with revived security of Edward's honour and love, and her companion's falsehood—"Engaged to Mr. Edward Ferrars!—I confess myself so totally surprised at what you tell me, that really—I beg your pardon; but surely there must be some mistake of person or name. We cannot mean the same Mr. Ferrars."

"We can mean no other," cried Lucy smiling. "Mr. Edward Ferrars, the eldest son of Mrs. Ferrars of Park-street, and brother of your sister-in-law, Mrs. John Dashwood, is the person I mean; you must allow that *I* am not likely to be deceived, as to the name of the man on who all my happiness depends."

"It is strange," replied Elinor in a most painful perplexity, "that I should never have heard him even mention your name."

"No; considering our situation, it was not strange. Our first care has been to keep the matter secret.—You knew nothing of me, or my family, and therefore there could be no *occasion* for ever mentioning my name to you, and as he was always particularly afraid of his sister's suspecting any thing, *that* was reason enough for his not mentioning it."

She was silent.—Elinor's security sunk; but her self-command did not sink with it.

"Four years you have been engaged," said she with a firm voice.

"Yes; and heaven knows how much longer we may have to wait. Poor Edward! It puts him quite out of heart." Then taking a small miniature from her pocket, she added, "To prevent the possibility of mistake, be so good as to look at this face. It does not do him justice to be sure, but yet I think you cannot be deceived as to the person it was drew for.—I have had it above these three years."

She put it into her hands as she spoke, and when Elinor saw the painting, whatever other doubts her fear of a too hasty decision, or her wish of detecting falsehood might suffer to linger in her mind, she could have none of its being Edward's face. She returned it almost instantly, acknowledging the likeness.

"I have never been able," continued Lucy, "to give him my picture in return, which I am very much vexed at, for he has been always so anxious to get it! But I am determined to set for it the very first opportunity."

"You are quite in the right;" replied Elinor calmly. They then proceeded a few paces in silence. Lucy spoke first.

"I am sure," said she, "I have no doubt in the world of your faithfully keeping this secret, because you must know of what importance it is to us, not to have it reach his mother; for she would never approve of it, I dare say. I shall have no fortune, and I fancy she is an exceeding proud woman."

"I certainly did not seek your confidence," said Elinor; "but you do me no more than justice in imagining that I may be depended on. Your secret is safe with me; but pardon me if I express some surprise at so unnecessary a communication. You must at least have felt that my being acquainted with it could not add to its safety."

As she said this, she looked earnestly at Lucy, hoping to discover something in her countenance; perhaps the falsehood of the greatest part of what she had been saying; but Lucy's countenance suffered no change.

"I was afraid you would think I was taking a great liberty with you," said she, "in telling you all this. I have not known you long to be sure, personally at least, but I have known you and all your family by description a great while; and as soon as I saw you, I felt almost as if you was an old acquaintance. Besides in the present case, I really thought some explanation was due to you after my making such particular inquiries about Edward's mother; and I am so unfortunate, that I have not a creature whose advice I can ask. Anne is the only person that knows of it, and she has no judgment at all; indeed she does me a great deal more harm than good, for I am in constant fear of her betraying me. She does not know how to hold her tongue, as you must perceive, and I am sure I was in the greatest fright in the world t'other day, when Edward's name was mentioned by Sir John, lest she should out with it all. You can't think how much I go through in my mind from it altogether. I only wonder that I am alive after what I have suffered for Edward's sake these last four years. Every thing in such suspense and uncertainty; and seeing him so seldom—we can hardly meet above twice a-year. I am sure I wonder my heart is not quite broke."

Here she took out her handkerchief; but Elinor did not feel very compassionate.

"Sometimes," continued Lucy, after wiping her eyes, "I think whether it would not be better for us both, to break off the matter entirely." As she said this, she looked directly at her companion. "But then at other times I have not resolution enough for it.—I cannot bear the thoughts of making him so miserable, as I know the very mention of such a thing would do. And on my own account too—so dear as he is to me—I don't think I could be equal to it. What would you advise me to do in such a case, Miss Dashwood? What would you do yourself?"

"Pardon me," replied Elinor, startled by the question; "but I can give you no advice under such circumstances. Your own judgment must direct you."

"To be sure," continued Lucy, after a few minutes silence on both sides, "his mother must provide for him sometime or other; but poor Edward is so cast down about it! Did not you think him dreadful low-spirited when he was at Barton? He was so miserable when he left us at Longstaple, to go to you, that I was afraid you would think him quite ill."

"Did he come from your uncle's then, when he visited us?"

"Oh! yes; he had been staying a fortnight with us. Did you think he came directly from town?"

"No," replied Elinor, most feelingly sensible of every fresh circumstance in favour of Lucy's veracity; "I remember he told us, that he had been staying a fortnight with some friends near Plymouth." She remembered too, her own surprise at the time, at his mentioning nothing farther of those friends, at his total silence with respect even to their names.

"Did not you think him sadly out of spirits?" repeated Lucy.

"We did indeed, particularly so when he first arrived."

"I begged him to exert himself for fear you should suspect what was the matter; but it made him so melancholy, not being able to stay more than a fortnight with us, and seeing me so much affected.—Poor fellow!—I am afraid it is just the same with him now; for he writes in wretched spirits. I heard from him just before I left Exeter;" taking a letter from her pocket and carelessly shewing the direction to Elinor. "You know his hand,[5] I dare say, a charming one it is; but that is not written

[5] *his hand*: Cf. footnote 4, p. 80; correspondence here is a proof of the engagement.

so well as usual.—He was tired, I dare say, for he had just filled the sheet to me as full as possible."

Elinor saw that it *was* his hand, and she could doubt no longer. The picture, she had allowed herself to believe, might have been accidentally obtained; it might not have been Edward's gift; but a correspondence between them by letter, could subsist only under a positive engagement, could be authorized by nothing else; for a few moments, she was almost overcome—her heart sunk within her, and she could hardly stand; but exertion was indispensably necessary, and she struggled so resolutely against the oppression of her feelings, that her success was speedy, and for the time complete.

"Writing to each other," said Lucy, returning the letter into her pocket, "is the only comfort we have in such long separations. Yes, *I* have one other comfort in his picture; but poor Edward has not even *that*. If he had but my picture, he says he should be easy. I gave him a lock of my hair set in a ring when he was at Longstaple last, and that was some comfort to him, he said, but not equal to a picture. Perhaps you might notice[6] the ring when you saw him?"

"I did;" said Elinor, with a composure of voice, under which was concealed an emotion and distress beyond any thing she had ever felt before. She was mortified, shocked, confounded.

Fortunately for her, they had now reached the cottage, and the conversation could be continued no farther. After sitting with them a few minutes, the Miss Steeles returned to the Park, and Elinor was then at liberty to think and be wretched.

[6] *might notice*: might have noticed.

VOLUME II

Chapter I

However small Elinor's general dependance on Lucy's veracity might be, it was impossible for her on serious reflection to suspect it in the present case, where no temptation could be answerable to the folly of inventing a falsehood of such a description. What Lucy had asserted to be true, therefore, Elinor could not, dared not longer doubt; supported as it was too on every side by such probabilities and proofs, and contradicted by nothing but her own wishes. Their opportunity of acquaintance in the house of Mr. Pratt was a foundation for the rest, at once indisputable and alarming; and Edward's visit near Plymouth, his melancholy state of mind, his dissatisfaction at his own prospects, his uncertain behaviour towards herself, the intimate knowledge of the Miss Steeles as to Norland and their family connections, which had often surprised her, the picture, the letter, the ring, formed altogether such a body of evidence, as overcame every fear of condemning him unfairly, and established as a fact, which no partiality could set aside, his ill-treatment of herself.—Her resentment of such behaviour, her indignation at having been its dupe, for a short time made her feel only for herself; but other ideas, other considerations soon arose. Had Edward been intentionally deceiving her? Had he feigned a regard for her which he did not feel? Was his engagement to Lucy, an engagement of the heart? No; whatever it might once have been, she could not believe it such at present. His affection was all her own. She could not be deceived in that. Her mother, sisters, Fanny, all had been conscious of his regard for her at Norland; it was not an illusion of her own vanity. He certainly loved her. What a softener of the heart was this persuasion! How much could it not tempt her to forgive! He had been blameable, highly blameable, in remaining at Norland after he first felt her influence over him to be more

than it ought to be. In that, he could not be defended; but if
he had injured her, how much more had he injured himself;
if her case were pitiable, his was hopeless. His imprudence had
made her miserable for a while; but it seemed to have deprived
himself of all chance of ever being otherwise. She might in
time regain tranquility; but *he*, what had he to look forward
to? Could he ever be tolerably happy with Lucy Steele; could
he, were his affection for herself out of the question, with his
integrity, his delicacy, and well-informed mind, be satisfied
with a wife like her—illiterate, artful, and selfish?

The youthful infatuation of nineteen would naturally blind
him to every thing but her beauty and good nature; but the
four succeeding years—years, which if rationally spent, give
such improvement to the understanding, must have opened his
eyes to her defects of education, while the same period of time,
spent on her side in inferior society and more frivolous pursuits, had perhaps robbed her of that simplicity, which might
once have given an interesting character to her beauty.

If in the supposition of his seeking to marry herself, his difficulties from his mother had seemed great, how much greater
were they now likely to be, when the object of his engagement
was undoubtedly inferior in connections, and probably inferior
in fortune to herself. These difficulties, indeed, with an heart
so alienated from Lucy, might not press very hard upon his
patience; but melancholy was the state of the person, by whom
the expectation of family opposition and unkindness, could be
felt as a relief!

As these considerations occurred to her in painful succession,
she wept for him, more than for herself. Supported by the conviction of having done nothing to merit her present unhappiness, and consoled by the belief that Edward had done nothing
to forfeit her esteem, she thought she could even now, under
the first smart of the heavy blow, command herself enough to
guard every suspicion of the truth from her mother and sisters.
And so well was she able to answer her own expectations, that
when she joined them at dinner only two hours after she had
first suffered the extinction of all her dearest hopes, no one

would have supposed from the appearance of the sisters, that Elinor was mourning in secret over obstacles which must divide her for ever from the object of her love, and that Marianne was internally dwelling on the perfections of a man, of whose whole heart she felt thoroughly possessed, and whom she expected to see in every carriage which drove near their house.

The necessity of concealing from her mother and Marianne, what had been entrusted in confidence to herself, though it obliged her to unceasing exertion, was no aggravation of Elinor's distress. On the contrary it was a relief to her, to be spared the communication of what would give such affliction to them, and to be saved likewise from hearing that condemnation of Edward, which would probably flow from the excess of their partial affection for herself, and which was more than she felt equal to support.

From their counsel, or their conversation she knew she could receive no assistance, their tenderness and sorrow must add to her distress, while her self-command would neither receive encouragement from their example nor from their praise. She was stronger alone, and her own good sense so well supported her, that her firmness was as unshaken, her appearance of cheerfulness as invariable, as with regrets so poignant and so fresh, it was possible for them to be.

Much as she had suffered from her first conversation with Lucy on the subject, she soon felt an earnest wish of renewing it; and this for more reasons than one. She wanted to hear many particulars of their engagement repeated again, she wanted more clearly to understand what Lucy really felt for Edward, whether there were any sincerity in her declaration of tender regard for him, and she particularly wanted to convince Lucy, by her readiness to enter on the matter again, and her calmness in conversing on it, that she was no otherwise interested in it than as a friend, which she very much feared her involuntary agitation, in their morning discourse, must have left at least doubtful. That Lucy was disposed to be jealous of her, appeared very probable; it was plain that Edward had always spoken highly in her praise, not merely from Lucy's assertion, but from her venturing to trust her on so short a personal acquaintance, with a secret, so confessedly and evidently important. And even Sir John's joking intelligence must have had some weight. But indeed, while Elinor remained so well assured within herself of being really beloved by Edward, it required no other consideration of probabilities to make it natural that Lucy should be jealous; and that she was so, her very confidence was a proof. What other reason for the disclosure of the affair could there be, but that Elinor might be informed by it of Lucy's superior claims on Edward, and be taught to avoid him in future? She had little difficulty in understanding thus much of her rival's intentions, and while she was firmly resolved to act by her as every principle of honour and honesty directed, to combat her own affection for Edward and to see him as little as possible; she could not deny herself the comfort of endeavouring to convince Lucy that her heart was unwounded. And as she could now have nothing more painful to hear on the subject than had already been told, she did not mistrust her own ability of going through a repetition of particulars with composure.

But it was not immediately that an opportunity of doing so could be commanded, though Lucy was as well disposed as herself to take advantage of any that occurred; for the weather was not often fine enough to allow of their joining in a walk, where they might most easily separate themselves from the others; and though they met at least every other evening either at the park or cottage, and chiefly at the former, they could not be supposed to meet for the sake of conversation. Such a thought would never enter either Sir John or Lady Middleton's head, and therefore very little leisure was ever given for general chat, and none at all for particular discourse. They met for the sake of eating, drinking, and laughing together, playing at cards, or consequences,[1] or any other game that was sufficiently noisy.

---

[1] *consequences*: inventive round game where players construct the "consequences" of the meeting between a lady and a gentleman (though supplying their contributions without knowing what the other players have concocted).

One or two meetings of this kind had taken place, without affording Elinor any chance of engaging Lucy in private, when Sir John called at the cottage one morning, to beg in the name of charity, that they would all dine with Lady Middleton that day, as he was obliged to attend the club at Exeter, and she would otherwise be quite alone, except her mother and the two Miss Steeles. Elinor, who foresaw a fairer opening for the point she had in view, in such a party as this was likely to be, more at liberty among themselves under the tranquil and well-bred direction of Lady Middleton than when her husband united them together in one noisy purpose, immediately accepted the invitation; Margaret, with her mother's permission, was equally compliant, and Marianne, though always unwilling to join any of their parties, was persuaded by her mother, who could not bear to have her seclude herself from any chance of amusement, to go likewise.

The young ladies went, and Lady Middleton was happily preserved from the frightful solitude which had threatened her. The insipidity of the meeting was exactly such as Elinor had expected; it produced not one novelty of thought or expression, and nothing could be less interesting than the whole of their discourse both in the dining parlour and drawing room: to the latter, the children accompanied them, and while they remained there, she was too well convinced of the impossibility of engaging Lucy's attention to attempt it. They quitted it only with the removal of the tea-things. The card-table was then placed, and Elinor began to wonder at herself for having ever entertained a hope of finding time for conversation at the park. They all rose up in preparation for a round game.[2]

"I am glad," said Lady Middleton to Lucy, "you are not going to finish poor little Annamaria's basket this evening; for I am sure it must hurt your eyes to work fillagree[3] by candlelight. And we will make the dear little love some amends for her disappointment tomorrow, and then I hope she will not much mind it."

This hint was enough, Lucy recollected herself instantly and replied, "Indeed you are very much mistaken, Lady Middleton; I am only waiting to know whether you can make your party without me, or I should have been at my fillagree already. I would not disappoint the little angel for all the world, and if you want me at the card-table now, I am resolved to finish the basket after supper."

"You are very good, I hope it won't hurt your eyes—will you ring the bell[4] for some working candles?[5] My poor little girl would be sadly disappointed, I know, if the basket was not finished to-morrow, for though I told her it certainly would not, I am sure she depends upon having it done."

Lucy directly drew her work table near her and reseated herself with an alacrity and cheerfulness which seemed to infer[6] that she could taste no greater delight than in making a fillagree basket for a spoilt child.

Lady Middleton proposed a rubber of Casino[7] to the others. No one made any objection but Marianne, who, with her usual inattention to the forms of general civility, exclaimed, "Your ladyship will have the goodness to excuse *me*—you know I detest cards. I shall go to the pianoforté; I have not touched it since it was tuned." And without farther ceremony, she turned away and walked to the instrument.

Lady Middleton looked as if she thanked heaven that *she* had never made so rude a speech.

"Marianne can never keep long from that instrument you know, ma'am," said Elinor, endeavouring to smooth away the offence; "and I do not much wonder at it; for it is the very best toned pianoforté I ever heard."

The remaining five were now to draw their cards.

[4] *ring the bell*: i.e., summon a servant.
[5] *working candles*: candles used for working feminine pursuits by.
[6] *infer*: imply.
[7] *rubber of Casino*: Italian fishing card game; a rubber is a series of three or five games between two teams.

"Perhaps," continued Elinor, "if I should happen to cut out, I may be of some use to Miss Lucy Steele, in rolling her papers for her; and there is so much still to be done to the basket, that it must be impossible I think for her labour singly, to finish it this evening. I should like the work exceedingly, if she would allow me a share in it."

"Indeed I shall be very much obliged to you for your help," cried Lucy, "for I find there is more to be done to it than I thought there was; and it would be a shocking thing to disappoint dear Annamaria after all."

"Oh! that would be terrible indeed," said Miss Steele—"Dear little soul, how I do love her!"

"You are very kind," said Lady Middleton to Elinor: "and as you really like the work, perhaps you will be as well pleased not to cut in till another rubber, or will you take your chance now?"

Elinor joyfully profited by the first of these proposals, and thus by a little of that address, which Marianne could never condescend to practise, gained her own end, and pleased Lady Middleton at the same time. Lucy made room for her with ready attention, and the two fair rivals were thus seated side by side at the same table, and with the utmost harmony engaged in forwarding the same work. The piano-forté, at which Marianne, wrapt up in her own music and her own thoughts, had by this time forgotten that any body was in the room besides herself, was luckily so near them that Miss Dashwood now judged, she might safely, under the shelter of its noise, introduce the interesting subject, without any risk of being heard at the card-table.

Chapter II

In a firm, though cautious tone, Elinor thus began.

"I should be undeserving of the confidence you have honoured me with, if I felt no desire for its continuance, or no farther curiosity on its subject. I will not apologize therefore for bringing it forward again."

"Thank you," cried Lucy warmly, "for breaking the ice; you have set my heart at ease by it; for I was somehow or other afraid I had offended you by what I told you that Monday."

"Offended me! How could you suppose so? Believe me," and Elinor spoke it with the truest sincerity, "nothing could be farther from my intention, than to give you such an idea. Could you have a motive for the trust, that was not honourable and flattering to me?"

"And yet I do assure you," replied Lucy, her little sharp eyes full of meaning, "there seemed to me to be a coldness and displeasure in your manner, that made me quite uncomfortable. I felt sure that you was angry with me; and have been quarrelling with myself ever since, for having took such a liberty as to trouble you with my affairs. But I am very glad to find it was only my own fancy, and that you do not really blame me. If you knew what a consolation it was to me to relieve my heart by speaking to you of what I am always thinking of every moment of my life, your compassion would make you overlook every thing else I am sure."

"Indeed I can easily believe that it was a very great relief to you, to acknowledge your situation to me, and be assured that you shall never have reason to repent it. Your case is a very unfortunate one; you seem to me to be surrounded with difficulties, and you will have need of all your mutual affection to support you under them. Mr. Ferrars, I believe, is entirely dependent on his mother."

"He has only two thousand pounds of his own; it would be madness to marry upon that, though for my own part, I could give up every prospect of more without a sigh. I have been always used to a very small income, and could struggle with any poverty for him; but I love him too well to be the selfish means of robbing him, perhaps, of all that his mother might give him if he married to please her. We must wait, it may be for many years. With almost every other man in the world, it would be an alarming prospect; but Edward's affection and constancy nothing can deprive me of I know."

"That conviction must be every thing to you; and he is undoubtedly supported by the same trust in your's. If the strength of your reciprocal attachment had failed, as between many people and under many circumstances it naturally would during a four years' engagement, your situation would have been pitiable indeed."

Lucy here looked up; but Elinor was careful in guarding her countenance from every expression that could give her words a suspicious tendency.

"Edward's love for me," said Lucy, "has been pretty well put to the test, by our long, very long absence since we were first engaged, and it has stood the trial so well, that I should be unpardonable to doubt it now. I can safely say that he has never gave me one moment's alarm on that account from the first."

Elinor hardly knew whether to smile or sigh at this assertion.

Lucy went on. "I am rather of a jealous temper too by nature, and from our different situations in life, from his being so much more in the world than me, and our continual separation, I was enough inclined for suspicion, to have found out the truth in an instant, if there had been the slightest alteration in his behaviour to me when we met, or any lowness of spirits that I could not account for, or if he had talked more of one lady than another, or seemed in any respect less happy at Longstaple than he used to be. I do not mean to say that I am particularly observant or quick-sighted in general, but in such a case I am sure I could not be deceived."

"All this," thought Elinor, "is very pretty; but it can impose upon neither of us."

"But what," said she after a short silence, "are your views? or have you none but that of waiting for Mrs. Ferrars's death, which is a melancholy and shocking extremity?—Is her son determined to submit to this, and to all the tediousness of the many years of suspense in which it may involve you, rather than run the risk of her displeasure for a while by owning the truth?"

"If we could be certain that it would be only for a while! But Mrs. Ferrars is a very headstrong proud woman, and in her first fit of anger upon hearing it, would very likely secure every thing to Robert, and the idea of that, for Edward's sake, frightens away all my inclination for hasty measures."

"And for your own sake too, or you are carrying your disinterestedness beyond reason."

Lucy looked at Elinor again, and was silent.

"Do you know Mr. Robert Ferrars?" asked Elinor.

"Not at all—I never saw him; but I fancy he is very unlike his brother—silly and a great coxcomb."[1]

"A great coxcomb!" repeated Miss Steele, whose ear had caught those words by a sudden pause in Marianne's music.— "Oh! they are talking of their favourite beaux, I dare say."

"No, sister," cried Lucy, "you are mistaken there, our favourite beaux are *not* great coxcombs."

"I can answer for it that Miss Dashwood's is not," said Mrs. Jennings, laughing heartily; "for he is one of the modestest, prettiest behaved young men I ever saw; but as for Lucy, she is such a sly little creature, there is no finding out who *she* likes."

"Oh!" cried Miss Steele, looking significantly round at them, "I dare say Lucy's beau is quite as modest and pretty behaved as Miss Dashwood's."

Elinor blushed in spite of herself. Lucy bit her lip, and looked angrily at her sister. A mutual silence took place for some time. Lucy first put an end to it by saying in a lower tone, though

---

[1] *coxcomb*: vain, conceited man.

Marianne was then giving them the powerful protection of a very magnificent concerto—

"I will honestly tell you of one scheme which has lately come into my head, for bringing matters to bear; indeed I am bound to let you into the secret, for you are a party concerned. I dare say you have seen enough of Edward to know that he would prefer the church to every other profession; now my plan is that he should take orders as soon as he can, and then through your interest, which I am sure you would be kind enough to use out of friendship for him, and I hope out of some regard to me, your brother might be persuaded to give him Norland living;[2] which I understand is a very good one, and the present incumbent not likely to live a great while. That would be enough for us to marry upon, and we might trust to time and chance for the rest."

"I should be always happy," replied Elinor, "to shew any mark of my esteem and friendship for Mr. Ferrars; but do not you perceive that my interest on such an occasion would be perfectly unnecessary? He is brother to Mrs. John Dashwood—*that* must be recommendation enough to her husband."

"But Mrs. John Dashwood would not much approve of Edward's going into orders."

"Then I rather suspect that my interest would do very little."

They were again silent for many minutes. At length Lucy exclaimed with a deep sigh,

"I believe it would be the wisest way to put an end to the business at once by dissolving the engagement. We seem so beset with difficulties on every side, that though it would make us miserable for a time, we should be happier perhaps in the end. But you will not give me your advice, Miss Dashwood?"

"No;" answered Elinor, with a smile, which concealed very agitated feelings, "on such a subject I certainly will not. You know very well that my opinion would have no weight with you, unless it were on the side of your wishes."

---

[2] *Norland living*: position, income, and property for a clergyman, falling under the purview of the local landed gentry.

"Indeed you wrong me," replied Lucy with great solemnity; "I know nobody of whose judgment I think so highly as I do of yours; and I do really believe, that if you was to say to me, 'I advise you by all means to put an end to your engagement with Edward Ferrars, it will be more for the happiness of both of you,' I should resolve upon doing it immediately."

Elinor blushed for the insincerity of Edward's future wife, and replied, "this compliment would effectually frighten me from giving any opinion on the subject had I formed one. It raises my influence much too high; the power of dividing two people so tenderly attached is too much for an indifferent person."

"'Tis because you are an indifferent person," said Lucy, with some pique, and laying a particular stress on those words, "that your judgment might justly have such weight with me. If you could be supposed to be biassed in any respect by your own feelings, your opinion would not be worth having."

Elinor thought it wisest to make no answer to this, lest they might provoke each other to an unsuitable increase of ease and unreserve; and was even partly determined never to mention the subject again. Another pause therefore of many minutes' duration, succeeded this speech, and Lucy was still the first to end it.

"Shall you be in town this winter, Miss Dashwood?" said she with all her accustomary complacency.

"Certainly not."

"I am sorry for that," returned the other, while her eyes brightened at the information, "it would have gave me such pleasure to meet you there! But I dare say you will go for all that. To be sure, your brother and sister will ask you to come to them."

"It will not be in my power to accept their invitation if they do."

"How unlucky that is! I had quite depended upon meeting you there. Anne and me are to go the latter end of January to some relations who have been wanting us to visit them these several years! But I only go for the sake of seeing Edward. He will be there in February, otherwise London would have no charms for me; I have not spirits for it."

Elinor was soon called to the card-table by the conclusion of the first rubber,[3] and the confidential discourse of the two ladies was therefore at an end, to which both of them submitted without any reluctance, for nothing had been said on either side, to make them dislike each other less than they had done before; and Elinor sat down to the card table with the melancholy persuasion that Edward was not only without affection for the person who was to be his wife; but that he had not even the chance of being tolerably happy in marriage, which sincere affection on *her* side would have given, for self-interest alone could induce a woman to keep a man to an engagement, of which she seemed so thoroughly aware that he was weary.

From this time the subject was never revived by Elinor, and when entered on by Lucy, who seldom missed an opportunity of introducing it, and was particularly careful to inform her confidante, of her happiness whenever she received a letter from Edward, it was treated by the former with calmness and caution, and dismissed as soon as civility would allow; for she felt such conversations to be an indulgence which Lucy did not deserve, and which were dangerous to herself.

The visit of the Miss Steeles at Barton Park was lengthened far beyond what the first invitation implied. Their favour increased, they could not be spared; Sir John would not hear of their going; and in spite of their numerous and long arranged engagements in Exeter, in spite of the absolute necessity of their returning to fulfil them immediately, which was in full force at the end of every week, they were prevailed on to stay nearly two months at the park, and to assist in the due celebration of that festival which requires a more than ordinary share of private balls and large dinners to proclaim its importance.

[3] *first rubber*: In the first rubber, Elinor was "dummy" (her partner played both of their hands, so Elinor could leave the table).

Chapter III

Though Mrs. Jennings was in the habit of spending a large portion of the year at the houses of her children and friends, she was not without a settled habitation of her own. Since the death of her husband, who had traded with success in a less elegant part of the town, she had resided every winter in a house in one of the streets near Portman-square. Towards this home, she began on the approach of January to turn her thoughts, and thither she one day abruptly, and very unexpectedly by them, asked the elder Miss Dashwoods to accompany her. Elinor, without observing the varying complexion of her sister, and the animated look which spoke no indifference to the plan, immediately gave a grateful but absolute denial for both, in which she believed herself to be speaking their united inclinations. The reason alledged was their determined resolution of not leaving their mother at that time of the year. Mrs. Jennings received the refusal with some surprize, and repeated her invitation immediately.

"Oh! Lord, I am sure your mother can spare you very well, and I *do* beg you will favour me with your company, for I've quite set my heart upon it. Don't fancy that you will be any inconvenience to me, for I shan't put myself at all out of my way for you. It will only be sending Betty by the coach,[1] and I hope I can afford *that*. We three shall be able to go very well in my chaise;[2] and when we are in town, if you do not like to go wherever I do, well and good, you may always go with one of my daughters. I am sure your mother will not object to it; for I have had such good luck in getting my own children off my hands, that she will think me a very fit person to have

[1] *coach*: public stagecoach.
[2] *chaise*: light, horse-drawn, open carriage (employing one or two horses) for up to two people.

the charge of you; and if I don't get one of you at least well married before I have done with you, it shall not be my fault. I shall speak a good word for you to all the young men, you may depend upon it."

"I have a notion," said Sir John, "that Miss Marianne would not object to such a scheme, if her elder sister would come into it. It is very hard indeed that she should not have a little pleasure, because Miss Dashwood does not wish it. So I would advise you two, to set off for town, when you are tired of Barton, without saying a word to Miss Dashwood about it."

"Nay," cried Mrs. Jennings, "I am sure I shall be monstrous glad of Miss Marianne's company, whether Miss Dashwood will go or not, only the more the merrier say I, and I thought it would be more comfortable for them to be together; because if they got tired of me, they might talk to one another, and laugh at my odd ways behind my back. But one or the other, if not both of them, I must have. Lord bless me! how do you think I can live poking by myself, I who have been always used till this winter to have Charlotte with me. Come, Miss Marianne, let us strike[3] hands upon the bargain, and if Miss Dashwood will change her mind by and bye, why so much the better."

"I thank you, ma'am, sincerely thank you," said Marianne, with warmth; "your invitation has insured my gratitude for ever, and it would give me such happiness, yes almost the greatest happiness I am capable of, to be able to accept it. But my mother, my dearest, kindest mother,—I feel the justice of what Elinor has urged, and if she were to be made less happy, less comfortable by our absence—Oh! no, nothing should tempt me to leave her. It should not, must not be a struggle."

Mrs. Jennings repeated her assurance that Mrs. Dashwood could spare them perfectly well; and Elinor, who now understood her sister, and saw to what indifference to almost every thing else, she was carried by her eagerness to be with Willoughby again, made no farther direct opposition to the plan, and merely referred it to her mother's decision, from

[3] *strike*: shake.

whom however she scarcely expected to receive any support in her endeavour to prevent a visit, which she could not approve of for Marianne, and which on her own account she had particular reasons to avoid. Whatever Marianne was desirous of, her mother would be eager to promote—she could not expect to influence the latter to cautiousness of conduct in an affair, respecting which she had never been able to inspire her with distrust; and she dared not explain the motive of her own disinclination for going to London. That Marianne, fastidious as she was, thoroughly acquainted with Mrs. Jennings's manners, and invariably disgusted by them, should overlook every inconvenience of that kind, should disregard whatever must be most wounding to her irritable feelings, in her pursuit of one object, was such a proof, so strong, so full of the importance of that object to her, as Elinor, in spite of all that had passed, was not prepared to witness.

On being informed of the invitation, Mrs. Dashwood, persuaded that such an excursion would be productive of much amusement to both her daughters, and perceiving through all her affectionate attention to herself, how much the heart of Marianne was in it, would not hear of their declining the offer upon *her* account; insisted on their both accepting it directly, and then began to foresee with her usual cheerfulness, a variety of advantages that would accrue to them all, from this separation.

"I am delighted with the plan," she cried, "it is exactly what I could wish. Margaret and I shall be as much benefited by it as yourselves. When you and the Middletons are gone, we shall go on so quietly and happily together with our books and our music! You will find Margaret so improved when you come back again! And I have a little plan of alteration for your bedrooms too, which may now be performed without inconvenience to any one. It is very right that you *should* go to town; I would have every young woman of your condition in life, acquainted with the manners and amusements of London. You will be under the care of a motherly good sort of woman, of whose kindness to you I can have no doubt. And in all probability you will see your brother, and whatever may be his faults, or the faults of his wife, when I consider whose son he is, I cannot bear to have you so wholly estranged from each other."

"Though with your usual anxiety for our happiness," said Elinor, "you have been obviating every impediment to the present scheme which occurred to you, there is still one objection which, in my opinion, cannot be so easily removed."

Marianne's countenance sunk.

"And what," said Mrs. Dashwood, "is my dear prudent Elinor going to suggest? What formidable obstacle is she now to bring forward? Do not let me hear a word about the expense of it."

"My objection is this; though I think very well of Mrs. Jennings's heart, she is not a woman whose society can afford us pleasure, or whose protection will give us consequence."

"That is very true," replied her mother; "but of her society, separately from that of other people, you will scarcely have any thing at all, and you will almost always appear in public with Lady Middleton."

"If Elinor is frightened away by her dislike of Mrs. Jennings," said Marianne, "at least it need not prevent *my* accepting her invitation. I have no such scruples, and I am sure, I could put up with every unpleasantness of that kind with very little effort."

Elinor could not help smiling at this display of indifference towards the manners of a person, to whom she had often had difficulty in persuading Marianne to behave with tolerable politeness: and resolved within herself, that if her sister persisted in going, she would go likewise, as she did not think it proper that Marianne should be left to the sole guidance of her own judgment, or that Mrs. Jennings should be abandoned to the mercy of Marianne for all the comfort of her domestic hours. To this determination she was the more easily reconciled, by recollecting, that Edward Ferrars, by Lucy's account, was not to be in town before February; and that their visit, without any unreasonable abridgment, might be previously finished.

"I will have you *both* go," said Mrs. Dashwood; "these objections are nonsensical. You will have much pleasure in being in

London, and especially in being together; and if Elinor would ever condescend to anticipate enjoyment, she would foresee it there from a variety of sources; she would perhaps expect some from improving her acquaintance with her sister-in-law's family."

Elinor had often wished for an opportunity of attempting to weaken her mother's dependence on the attachment of Edward and herself, that the shock might be the less when the whole truth were revealed, and now on this attack, though almost hopeless of success, she forced herself to begin her design by saying, as calmly as she could, "I like Edward Ferrars very much, and shall always be glad to see him; but as to the rest of the family, it is a matter of perfect indifference to me, whether I am ever known to them or not."

Mrs. Dashwood smiled and said nothing. Marianne lifted up her eyes in astonishment, and Elinor conjectured that she might as well have held her tongue.

After very little farther discourse, it was finally settled that the invitation should be fully accepted. Mrs. Jennings received the information with a great deal of joy, and many assurances of kindness and care; nor was it a matter of pleasure merely to her. Sir John was delighted; for to a man, whose prevailing anxiety was the dread of being alone, the acquisition of two, to the number of inhabitants in London, was something. Even Lady Middleton took the trouble of being delighted, which was putting herself rather out of her way; and as for the Miss Steeles, especially Lucy, they had never been so happy in their lives as this intelligence made them.

Elinor submitted to the arrangement which counteracted her wishes, with less reluctance than she had expected to feel. With regard to herself, it was now a matter of unconcern whether she went to town or not, and when she saw her mother so thoroughly pleased with the plan, and her sister exhilarated by it in look, voice, and manner, restored to all her usual animation, and elevated to more than her usual gaiety, she could not be dissatisfied with the cause, and would hardly allow herself to distrust the consequence.

Marianne's joy was almost a degree beyond happiness, so great was the perturbation of her spirits and her impatience to be gone. Her unwillingness to quit her mother was her only restorative to calmness; and at the moment of parting, her grief on that score was excessive. Her mother's affliction was hardly less, and Elinor was the only one of the three, who seemed to consider the separation as any thing short of eternal.

Their departure took place in the first week in January. The Middletons were to follow in about a week. The Miss Steeles kept their station at the park, and were to quit it only with the rest of the family.

Chapter IV

Elinor could not find herself in the carriage with Mrs. Jennings, and beginning a journey to London under her protection, and as her guest, without wondering at her own situation, so short had their acquaintance with that lady been, so wholly unsuited were they in age and disposition, and so many had been her objections against such a measure only a few days before! But these objections had all, with that happy ardour of youth which Marianne and her mother equally shared, been overcome or overlooked; and Elinor, in spite of every occasional doubt of Willoughby's constancy, could not witness the rapture of delightful expectation which filled the whole soul and beamed in the eyes of Marianne, without feeling how blank was her own prospect, how cheerless her own state of mind in the comparison, and how gladly she would engage in the solicitude of Marianne's situation to have the same animating object in view, the same possibility of hope. A short, a very short time however must now decide what Willoughby's intentions were; in all probability he was already in town. Marianne's eagerness to be gone declared her dependance on finding him there; and Elinor was resolved not only upon gaining every new light as to his character which her own observation or the intelligence of others could give her, but likewise upon watching his behaviour to her sister with such zealous attention, as to ascertain what he was and what he meant, before many meetings had taken place. Should the result of her observations be unfavourable, she was determined at all events to open the eyes of her sister; should it be otherwise, her exertions would be of a different nature—she must then learn to avoid every selfish comparison, and banish every regret which might lessen her satisfaction in the happiness of Marianne.

They were three days on their journey, and Marianne's behaviour as they travelled was a happy specimen of what her future complaisance and companionableness to Mrs. Jennings might be expected to be. She sat in silence almost all the way, wrapt in her own meditations, and scarcely ever voluntarily speaking, except when any object of picturesque beauty within their view drew from her an exclamation of delight exclusively addressed to her sister. To atone for this conduct therefore, Elinor took immediate possession of the post of civility which she had assigned herself, behaved with the greatest attention to Mrs. Jennings, talked with her, laughed with her, and listened to her whenever she could; and Mrs. Jennings on her side treated them both with all possible kindness, was solicitous on every occasion for their ease and enjoyment, and only disturbed that she could not make them choose their own dinners at the inn, nor extort a confession of their preferring salmon to cod, or boiled fowls to veal cutlets. They reached town by three o'clock the third day, glad to be released, after such a journey, from the confinement of a carriage, and ready to enjoy all the luxury of a good fire.

The house was handsome and handsomely fitted up, and the young ladies were immediately put in possession of a very comfortable apartment. It had formerly been Charlotte's, and over the mantlepiece still hung a landscape in coloured silks of her performance, in proof of her having spent seven years at a great school in town to some effect.

As dinner was not to be ready in less than two hours from their arrival, Elinor determined to employ the interval in writing to her mother, and sat down for that purpose. In a few moments Marianne did the same. "I am writing home, Marianne," said Elinor; "had not you better defer your letter for a day or two?"

"I am *not* going to write to my mother," replied Marianne hastily, and as if wishing to avoid any farther inquiry. Elinor said no more; it immediately struck her that she must then be writing to Willoughby, and the conclusion which as instantly followed was, that however mysteriously they might wish to conduct the affair, they must be engaged. This conviction, though not entirely satisfactory, gave her pleasure, and she continued her letter with greater alacrity. Marianne's was finished in a very few minutes; in length it could be no more than a note: it was then folded up, sealed and directed with eager rapidity. Elinor thought she could distinguish a large W. in the direction, and no sooner was it complete than Marianne, ringing the bell, requested the footman who answered it, to get that letter conveyed for her to the two-penny post.[1] This decided the matter at once.

Her spirits still continued very high, but there was a flutter in them which prevented their giving much pleasure to her sister, and this agitation increased as the evening drew on. She could scarcely eat any dinner, and when they afterwards returned to the drawing room, seemed anxiously listening to the sound of every carriage.

It was a great satisfaction to Elinor that Mrs. Jennings, by being much engaged in her own room, could see little of what was passing. The tea things were brought in, and already had Marianne been disappointed more than once by a rap at a neighbouring door, when a loud one was suddenly heard which could not be mistaken for one at any other house. Elinor felt secure of its announcing Willoughby's approach, and Marianne starting up moved towards the door. Every thing was silent; this could not be borne many seconds, she opened the door, advanced a few steps towards the stairs, and after listening half a minute, returned into the room in all the agitation which a conviction of having heard him would naturally produce; in the extasy of her feelings at that instant she could not help exclaiming, "Oh! Elinor, it is Willoughby, indeed it is!" and seemed almost ready to throw herself into his arms, when Colonel Brandon appeared.

It was too great a shock to be borne with calmness, and she immediately left the room. Elinor was disappointed too; but

---

[1] *two-penny post*: London post was delivered four to eight times daily; the postage price increased from one to two cents in 1801.

at the same time her regard for Colonel Brandon ensured his welcome with her, and she felt particularly hurt that a man so partial to her sister should perceive that she experienced nothing but grief and disappointment in seeing him. She instantly saw that it was not unnoticed by him, that he even observed Marianne as she quitted the room, with such astonishment and concern, as hardly left him the recollection of what civility demanded towards herself.

"Is your sister ill?" said he.

Elinor answered in some distress that she was, and then talked of head-aches, low spirits, and over fatigues; and of every thing to which she could decently attribute her sister's behaviour.

He heard her with the most earnest attention, but seeming to recollect himself, said no more on the subject, and began directly to speak of his pleasure at seeing them in London, making the usual inquiries about their journey and the friends they had left behind.

In this calm kind of way, with very little interest on either side, they continued to talk, both of them out of spirits, and the thoughts of both engaged elsewhere. Elinor wished very much to ask whether Willoughby were then in town, but she was afraid of giving him pain by any inquiry after his rival; and at length by way of saying something, she asked if he had been in London ever since she had seen him last. "Yes," he replied, with some embarrassment, "almost ever since; I have been once or twice at Delaford for a few days, but it has never been in my power to return to Barton."

This, and the manner in which it was said, immediately brought back to her remembrance, all the circumstances of his quitting that place, with the uneasiness and suspicions they had caused to Mrs. Jennings, and she was fearful that her question had implied much more curiosity on the subject than she had ever felt.

Mrs. Jennings soon came in. "Oh! Colonel," said she, with her usual noisy cheerfulness, "I am monstrous glad to see you— sorry I could not come before—beg your pardon, but I have been forced to look about me a little, and settle my matters;[2] for it is a long while since I have been at home, and you know one has always a world of little odd things to do after one has been away for any time; and then I have had Cartwright to set-tle with—Lord, I have been as busy as a bee ever since dinner! But pray, Colonel, how came you to conjure out that I should be in town to-day?"

"I had the pleasure of hearing it at Mr. Palmer's, where I have been dining."

"Oh! you did; well, and how do they all do at their house? How does Charlotte do? I warrant you she is a fine size by this time."

"Mrs. Palmer appeared quite well, and I am commissioned to tell you, that you will certainly see her tomorrow."

"Aye, to be sure, I thought as much. Well, Colonel, I have brought two young ladies with me, you see—that is, you see but one of them now, but there is another somewhere. Your friend Miss Marianne, too—which you will not be sorry to hear. I do not know what you and Mr. Willoughby will do between you about her. Aye, it is a fine thing to be young and handsome. Well! I was young once, but I never was very handsome—worse luck for me. However I got a very good husband, and I don't know what the greatest beauty can do more. Ah! poor man! he has been dead these eight years and better. But Colonel, where have you been to since we parted? And how does your business go on? Come, come, let's have no secrets among friends."

He replied with his accustomary mildness to all her inqui-ries, but without satisfying her in any. Elinor now began to make the tea, and Marianne was obliged to appear again.

After her entrance, Colonel Brandon became more thought-ful and silent than he had been before, and Mrs. Jennings could not prevail on him to stay long. No other visitor appeared that evening, and the ladies were unanimous in agreeing to go early to bed.

[2] *matters:* affairs.

Marianne rose the next morning with recovered spirits and happy looks. The disappointment of the evening before seemed forgotten in the expectation of what was to happen that day. They had not long finished their breakfast before Mrs. Palmer's barouche stopt at the door, and in a few minutes she came laughing into the room; so delighted to see them all, that it was hard to say whether she received most pleasure from meeting her mother or the Miss Dashwoods again. So surprised at their coming to town, though it was what she had rather expected all along; so angry at their accepting her mother's invitation after having declined her own, though at the same time she would never have forgiven them if they had not come!

"Mr. Palmer will be so happy to see you," said she; "what do you think he said when he heard of your coming with mama? I forget what it was now, but it was something so droll!"

After an hour or two spent in what her mother called comfortable chat, or in other words, in every variety of inquiry concerning all their acquaintance on Mrs. Jennings's side, and in laughter without cause on Mrs. Palmer's, it was proposed by the latter that they should all accompany her to some shops where she had business that morning, to which Mrs. Jennings and Elinor readily consented, as having likewise some purchases to make themselves; and Marianne, though declining it at first, was induced to go likewise.

Wherever they went, she was evidently always on the watch. In Bond-street especially, where much of their business lay, her eyes were in constant inquiry; and in whatever shop the party were engaged, her mind was equally abstracted from every thing actually before them, from all that interested and occupied the others. Restless and dissatisfied every where, her sister could never obtain her opinion of any article of purchase, however it might equally concern them both; she received no pleasure from any thing; was only impatient to be at home again, and could with difficulty govern her vexation at the tediousness of Mrs. Palmer, whose eye was caught by every thing pretty, expensive, or new; who was wild to buy all, could determine on none, and dawdled away her time in rapture and indecision.

It was late in the morning before they returned home; and no sooner had they entered the house than Marianne flew eagerly up stairs, and when Elinor followed, she found her turning from the table with a sorrowful countenance, which declared that no Willoughby had been there.

"Has no letter been left here for me since we went out?" said she to the footman who then entered with the parcels. She was answered in the negative. "Are you quite sure of it?" she replied. "Are you certain that no servant, no porter has left any letter or note?"

The man replied that none had.

"How very odd!" said she in a low and disappointed voice, as she turned away to the window.

"How odd indeed!" repeated Elinor within herself, regarding her sister with uneasiness. "If she had not known him to be in town she would not have written to him, as she did; she would have written to Combe Magna; and if he is in town, how odd that he should neither come nor write! Oh! my dear mother, you must be wrong in permitting an engagement between a daughter so young, a man so little known, to be carried on in so doubtful, so mysterious a manner! *I* long to inquire; but how will *my* interference be borne!"

She determined after some consideration, that if appearances continued many days longer, as unpleasant as they now were, she would represent in the strongest manner to her mother the necessity of some serious inquiry into the affair.

Mrs. Palmer and two elderly ladies of Mrs. Jennings's intimate acquaintance, whom she had met and invited in the morning, dined with them. The former left them soon after tea to fulfil her evening engagements; and Elinor was obliged to assist in making a whist-table[3] for the others. Marianne was of no use on these occasions, as she would never learn the game, but though her time was therefore at her own disposal, the evening was by no means more productive of pleasure to her than

---

[3] *whist-table*: A whist is a card game, usually for two pairs of players, where points are scored according to the number of tricks won.

to Elinor, for it was spent in all the anxiety of expectation and the pain of disappointment. She sometimes endeavoured for a few minutes to read; but the book was soon thrown aside, and she returned to the more interesting employment of walking backwards and forwards across the room, pausing for a moment whenever she came to the window, in hopes of distinguishing the long-expected rap.

Chapter V

"If this open[1] weather holds much longer," said Mrs. Jennings, when they met at breakfast the following morning, "Sir John will not like leaving Barton next week; 'tis a sad thing for sportsmen to lose a day's pleasure. Poor souls! I always pity them when they do; they seem to take it so much to heart."

"That is true," cried Marianne in a cheerful voice, and walking to the window as she spoke, to examine the day. "I had not thought of *that*. This weather will keep many sportsmen in the country."

It was a lucky recollection, all her good spirits were restored by it. "It is charming weather for *them* indeed," she continued, as she sat down to the breakfast table with a happy countenance. "How much they must enjoy it! But" (with a little return of anxiety) "it cannot be expected to last long. At this time of year, and after such a series of rain, we shall certainly have very little more of it. Frosts will soon set in, and in all probability with severity. In another day or two perhaps; this extreme mildness can hardly last longer—nay, perhaps it may freeze to-night!"

"At any rate," said Elinor, wishing to prevent Mrs. Jennings from seeing her sister's thoughts as clearly as she did, "I dare say we shall have Sir John and Lady Middleton in town by the end of next week."

"Aye, my dear, I'll warrant you we do. Mary always has her own way."

"And now," silently conjectured Elinor, "she will write to Combe by this day's post."

But if she *did*, the letter was written and sent away with a privacy which eluded all her watchfulness to ascertain the fact. Whatever the truth of it might be, and far as Elinor was

[1] *open*: fair, free from frost (friendly to hunters).

162

from feeling thorough contentment about it, yet while she saw
Marianne in spirits, she could not be very uncomfortable herself. And Marianne was in spirits; happy in the mildness of the
weather, and still happier in her expectation of a frost.

The morning was chiefly spent in leaving cards at the houses
of Mrs. Jennings's acquaintance to inform them of her being
in town; and Marianne was all the time busy in observing the
direction of the wind, watching the variations of the sky and
imagining an alteration in the air.

"Don't you find it colder than it was in the morning, Elinor?
There seems to me a very decided difference. I can hardly keep
my hands warm even in my muff. It was not so yesterday, I
think. The clouds seem parting too, the sun will be out in a
moment; and we shall have a clear afternoon."

Elinor was alternately diverted and pained; but Marianne
persevered, and saw every night in the brightness of the fire,
and every morning in the appearance of the atmosphere, the
certain symptoms of approaching frost.

The Miss Dashwoods had no greater reason to be dissatisfied
with Mrs. Jennings's style of living, and set of acquaintance,
than with her behaviour to themselves, which was invariably kind. Every thing in her household arrangements was
conducted on the most liberal plan, and excepting a few old
city[2] friends, whom, to Lady Middleton's regret, she had never
dropped, she visited no one, to whom an introduction could at
all discompose the feelings of her young companions. Pleased
to find herself more comfortably situated in that particular
than she had expected, Elinor was very willing to compound
for the want of much real enjoyment from any of their evening
parties, which, whether at home or abroad, formed only for
cards, could have little to amuse her.

Colonel Brandon, who had a general invitation to the house,
was with them almost every day; he came to look at Marianne
and talk to Elinor, who often derived more satisfaction from
conversing with him than from any other daily occurrence, but

[2] *old city*: less fashionable side of London, the commercial district.

who saw at the same time with much concern his continued regard for her sister. She feared it was a strengthening regard. It grieved her to see the earnestness with which he often watched Marianne, and his spirits were certainly worse than when at Barton.

About a week after their arrival it became certain that Willoughby was also arrived. His card was on the table, when they came in from the morning's drive.

"Good God!" cried Marianne, "he has been here while we were out." Elinor, rejoiced to be assured of his being in London, now ventured to say, "depend upon it he will call again to-morrow." But Marianne seemed hardly to hear her, and on Mrs. Jennings's entrance, escaped with the precious card.

This event, while it raised the spirits of Elinor, restored to those of her sister, all, and more than all, their former agitation. From this moment her mind was never quiet; the expectation of seeing him every hour of the day, made her unfit for anything. She insisted on being left behind, the next morning, when the others went out.

Elinor's thoughts were full of what might be passing in Berkeley-street during their absence; but a moment's glance at her sister when they returned was enough to inform her, that Willoughby had paid no second visit there. A note was just then brought in, and laid on the table.

"For me!" cried Marianne, stepping hastily forward.

"No, ma'am, for my mistress."

But Marianne, not convinced, took it instantly up.

"It is indeed for Mrs. Jennings; how provoking!"

"You are expecting a letter then?" said Elinor, unable to be longer silent.

"Yes, a little—not much."

After a short pause, "you have no confidence in me, Marianne."

"Nay, Elinor, this reproach from *you*—you who have confidence in no one!"

"Me!" returned Elinor in some confusion; "indeed, Marianne, I have nothing to tell."

"Nor I," answered Marianne with energy, "our situations then are alike. We have neither of us any thing to tell; you, because you communicate, and I, because I conceal nothing."

Elinor, distressed by this charge of reserve in herself, which she was not at liberty to do away, knew not how, under such circumstances, to press for greater openness in Marianne.

Mrs. Jennings soon appeared, and the note being given her, she read it aloud. It was from Lady Middleton, announcing their arrival in Conduit-street the night before, and requesting the company of her mother and cousins the following evening. Business on Sir John's part, and a violent cold on her own, prevented their calling in Berkeley-street. The invitation was accepted: but when the hour of appointment drew near, necessary as it was in common civility to Mrs. Jennings, that they should both attend her on such a visit, Elinor had some difficulty in persuading her sister to go, for still she had seen nothing of Willoughby; and therefore was not more indisposed for amusement abroad, than unwilling to run the risk of his calling again in her absence.

Elinor found, when the evening was over, that disposition is not materially altered by a change of abode, for although scarcely settled in town, Sir John had contrived to collect around him, nearly twenty young people, and to amuse them with a ball. This was an affair, however, of which Lady Middleton did not approve. In the country, an unpremeditated dance was very allowable; but in London, where the reputation of elegance was more important and less easily obtained, it was risking too much for the gratification of a few girls, to have it known that Lady Middleton had given a small dance of eight or nine couple, with two violins, and a mere sideboard collation.[3]

Mr. and Mrs. Palmer were of the party; from the former, whom they had not seen before since their arrival in town, as he was careful to avoid the appearance of any attention to his mother-in-law, and therefore never came near her, they

[3] *collation*: light, informal meal.

received no mark of recognition on their entrance. He looked at them slightly, without seeming to know who they were, and merely nodded to Mrs. Jennings from the other side of the room. Marianne gave one glance round the apartment as she entered; it was enough, *he* was not there—and she sat down, equally ill-disposed to receive or communicate pleasure. After they had been assembled about an hour, Mr. Palmer sauntered towards the Miss Dashwoods to express his surprise on seeing them in town, though Colonel Brandon had been first informed of their arrival at his house, and he had himself said something very droll on hearing that they were to come.

"I thought you were both in Devonshire," said he.

"Did you?" replied Elinor.

"When do you go back again?"

"I do not know." And thus ended their discourse.

Never had Marianne been so unwilling to dance in her life, as she was that evening, and never so much fatigued by the exercise. She complained of it as they returned to Berkeley-street.

"Aye, aye," said Mrs. Jennings, "we know the reason of all that very well; if a certain person who shall be nameless, had been there, you would not have been a bit tired: and to say the truth it was not very pretty of him not to give you the meeting[4] when he was invited."

"Invited!" cried Marianne.

"So my daughter Middleton told me, for it seems Sir John met him somewhere in the street this morning." Marianne said no more, but looked exceedingly hurt. Impatient in this situation to be doing something that might lead to her sister's relief, Elinor resolved to write the next morning to her mother, and hoped by awakening her fears for the health of Marianne, to procure those inquiries which had been so long delayed; and she was still more eagerly bent on this measure by perceiving after breakfast on the morrow, that Marianne was again writing to Willoughby, for she could not suppose it to be to any other person.

---

[4] *give you the meeting*: idiomatic expression.

About the middle of the day, Mrs. Jennings went out by herself on business, and Elinor began her letter directly, while Marianne, too restless for employment, too anxious for conversation, walked from one window to the other, or sat down by the fire in melancholy meditation. Elinor was very earnest in her application to her mother, relating all that had passed, her suspicions of Willoughby's inconstancy, urging her by every plea of duty and affection to demand from Marianne, an account of her real situation with respect to him.

Her letter was scarcely finished, when a rap foretold a visitor, and Colonel Brandon was announced. Marianne, who had seen him from the window, and who hated company of any kind, left the room before he entered it. He looked more than usually grave, and though expressing satisfaction at finding Miss Dashwood alone, as if he had somewhat in particular to tell her, sat for some time without saying a word. Elinor, persuaded that he had some communication to make in which her sister was concerned, impatiently expected its opening. It was not the first time of her feeling the same kind of conviction; for more than once before, beginning with the observation of "your sister looks unwell to-day," or "your sister seems out of spirits," he had appeared on the point, either of disclosing, or of inquiring, something particular about her. After a pause of several minutes, their silence was broken, by his asking her in a voice of some agitation, when he was to congratulate her on the acquisition of a brother? Elinor was not prepared for such a question, and having no answer ready, was obliged to adopt the simple and common expedient, of asking what he meant? He tried to smile as he replied, "your sister's engagement to Mr. Willoughby is very generally known."

"It cannot be generally known," returned Elinor, "for her own family do not know it."

He looked surprised and said, "I beg your pardon, I am afraid my inquiry has been impertinent; but I had not supposed any secrecy intended, as they openly correspond, and their marriage is universally talked of."

"How can that be? By whom can you have heard it mentioned?"

"By many—by some of whom you know nothing, by others with whom you are most intimate, Mrs. Jennings, Mrs. Palmer, and the Middletons. But still I might not have believed it, for where the mind is perhaps rather unwilling to be convinced, it will always find something to support its doubts, if I had not, when the servant let me in to-day, accidentally seen a letter in his hand, directed to Mr. Willoughby in your sister's writing. I came to inquire, but I was convinced before I could ask the question. Is every thing finally settled? Is it impossible to—? But I have no right, and I could have no chance of succeeding. Excuse me, Miss Dashwood. I believe I have been wrong in saying so much, but I hardly know what to do, and on your prudence I have the strongest dependence. Tell me that it is all absolutely resolved on, that any attempt, that in short conceal-ment, if concealment be possible, is all that remains."

These words, which conveyed to Elinor a direct avowal of his love for her sister, affected her very much. She was not immediately able to say anything, and even when her spirits were recovered, she debated for a short time, on the answer it would be most proper to give. The real state of things between Willoughby and her sister was so little known to herself, that in endeavouring to explain it, she might be as liable to say too much as too little. Yet as she was convinced that Marianne's affection for Willoughby, could leave no hope of Colonel Brandon's success, whatever the event of that affection might be, and at the same time wished to shield her conduct from censure, she thought it most prudent and kind, after some consideration, to say more than she really knew or believed. She acknowledged, therefore, that though she had never been informed by themselves of the terms on which they stood with each other, of their mutual affection she had no doubt, and of their correspondence she was not astonished to hear.

He listened to her with silent attention, and on her ceasing to speak, rose directly from his seat, and after saying in a voice of emotion, "to your sister I wish all imaginable happiness; to

Willoughby that he may endeavour to deserve her,"—took leave, and went away.

Elinor derived no comfortable feelings from this conversation, to lessen the uneasiness of her mind on other points; she was left, on the contrary, with a melancholy impression of Colonel Brandon's unhappiness, and was prevented even from wishing it removed, by her anxiety for the very event that must confirm it.

Chapter VI

Nothing occurred during the next three or four days, to make Elinor regret what she had done, in applying to her mother; for Willoughby neither came nor wrote. They were engaged about the end of that time to attend Lady Middleton to a party, from which Mrs. Jennings was kept away by the indisposition of her youngest daughter; and for this party, Marianne, wholly dispirited, careless of her appearance, and seeming equally indifferent whether she went or staid, prepared, without one look of hope, or one expression of pleasure. She sat by the drawing room fire after tea, till the moment of Lady Middleton's arrival, without once stirring from her seat, or altering her attitude, lost in her own thoughts and insensible of her sister's presence; and when at last they were told that Lady Middleton waited for them at the door, she started as if she had forgotten that any one was expected.

They arrived in due time at the place of destination, and as soon as the string of carriages before them would allow, alighted, ascended the stairs, heard their names announced from one landing-place[1] to another in an audible voice, and entered a room splendidly lit up, quite full of company, and insufferably hot. When they had paid their tribute of politeness by curtseying to the lady of the house, they were permitted to mingle in the croud,[2] and take their share of the heat and inconvenience, to which their arrival must necessarily add. After some time spent in saying little and doing less, Lady Middleton sat down to Casino, and as Marianne was not in spirits for moving about, she and Elinor luckily succeeding to[3] chairs, placed themselves at no great distance from the table.

[1] *landing-place*: landing (on a staircase).
[2] *croud*: crowd.
[3] *succeeding to*: "inheriting" or obtaining (chairs) when someone else has quit them.

They had not remained in this manner long, before Elinor perceived Willoughby, standing within a few yards of them, in earnest conversation with a very fashionable looking young woman. She soon caught his eye, and he immediately bowed, but without attempting to speak to her, or to approach Marianne, though he could not but see her; and then continued his discourse with the same lady. Elinor turned involuntarily to Marianne, to see whether it could be unobserved by her. At that moment she first perceived him, and her whole countenance glowing with sudden delight, she would have moved towards him instantly, had not her sister caught hold of her.

"Good heavens!" she exclaimed, "he is there—he is there—Oh! why does he not look at me? why cannot I speak to him?"

"Pray, pray be composed," cried Elinor, "and do not betray what you feel to every body present. Perhaps he has not observed you yet."

This however was more than she could believe herself; and to be composed at such a moment was not only beyond the reach of Marianne, it was beyond her wish. She sat in an agony of impatience, which affected every feature.

At last he turned round again, and regarded them both; she started up, and pronouncing his name in a tone of affection, held out her hand to him. He approached, and addressing himself rather to Elinor than Marianne, as if wishing to avoid her eye, and determined not to observe her attitude, inquired in a hurried manner after Mrs. Dashwood, and asked how long they had been in town. Elinor was robbed of all presence of mind by such an address, and was unable to say a word. But the feelings of her sister were instantly expressed. Her face was crimsoned over, and she exclaimed in a voice of the greatest emotion, "Good God! Willoughby, what is the meaning of this? Have you not received my letters? Will you not shake hands with me?"

He could not then avoid it, but her touch seemed painful to him, and he held her hand only for a moment. During all this time he was evidently struggling for composure. Elinor watched his countenance and saw its expression becoming more tranquil. After a moment's pause, he spoke with calmness.

"I did myself the honour of calling in Berkeley-street last Tuesday, and very much regretted that I was not fortunate enough to find yourselves and Mrs. Jennings at home. My card was not lost, I hope."

"But have you not received my notes?" cried Marianne in the wildest anxiety. "Here is some mistake I am sure—some dreadful mistake. What can be the meaning of it? Tell me, Willoughby; for heaven's sake tell me, what is the matter?"

He made no reply; his complexion changed and all his embarrassment returned; but as if, on catching the eye of the young lady with whom he had been previously talking, he felt the necessity of instant exertion, he recovered himself again, and after saying, "Yes, I had the pleasure of receiving the information of your arrival in town, which you were so good as to send me," turned hastily away with a slight bow and joined his friend.

Marianne, now looking dreadfully white, and unable to stand, sunk into her chair, and Elinor, expecting every moment to see her faint, tried to screen her from the observation of others, while reviving her with lavender water.

"Go to him, Elinor," she cried, as soon as she could speak, "and force him to come to me. Tell him I must see him again— must speak to him instantly.—I cannot rest—I shall not have a moment's peace till this is explained—some dreadful misapprehension or other.—Oh go to him this moment."

"How can that be done? No, my dearest Marianne, you must wait. This is not a place for explanations. Wait only till to-morrow."

With difficulty however could she prevent her from following him herself; and to persuade her to check her agitation, to wait, at least, with the appearance of composure, till she might speak to him with more privacy and more effect, was impossible; for Marianne continued incessantly to give way in a low voice to the misery of her feelings, by exclamations of wretchedness. In a short time Elinor saw Willoughby quit the room by the door towards the staircase, and telling Marianne that he was gone, urged the impossibility of speaking to him again that evening, as a fresh argument for her to be calm. She instantly begged her sister would entreat Lady Middleton to take them home, as she was too miserable to stay a minute longer.

Lady Middleton, though in the middle of a rubber, on being informed that Marianne was unwell, was too polite to object for a moment to her wish of going away, and making over her cards to a friend, they departed as soon as the carriage could be found. Scarcely a word was spoken during their return to Berkeley-street. Marianne was in a silent agony, too much oppressed even for tears; but as Mrs. Jennings was luckily not come home, they could go directly to their own room, where hartshorn[4] restored her a little to herself. She was soon undressed and in bed, and as she seemed desirous of being alone, her sister then left her, and while she waited the return of Mrs. Jennings, had leisure enough for thinking over the past.

That some kind of engagement had subsisted between Willoughby and Marianne she could not doubt; and that Willoughby was weary of it, seemed equally clear; for however Marianne might still feed her own wishes, *she* could not attribute such behaviour to mistake or misapprehension of any kind. Nothing but a thorough change of sentiment could account for it. Her indignation would have been still stronger than it was, had she not witnessed that embarrassment which seemed to speak a consciousness of his own misconduct, and prevented her from believing him so unprincipled as to have been sporting with the affections of her sister from the first, without any design that would bear investigation. Absence might have weakened his regard, and convenience might have determined him to overcome it, but that such a regard had formerly existed she could not bring herself to doubt.

[4] *hartshorn*: preparation of ammonia used as smelling salts (a hart's horns were at one time the primary source of ammonia).

As for Marianne, on the pangs which so unhappy a meeting must already have given her, and on those still more severe which might await her in its probable consequence, she could not reflect without the deepest concern. Her own situation gained in the comparison; for while she could *esteem* Edward as much as ever, however they might be divided in future, her mind might be always supported. But every circumstance that could embitter such an evil seemed uniting to heighten the misery of Marianne in a final separation from Willoughby—in an immediate and irreconcileable rupture with him.

Chapter VII

Before the house-maid had lit their fire, the next day, or the sun gained any power over a cold, gloomy, morning in January, Marianne, only half dressed, was kneeling against one of the window-seats for the sake of all the little light she could command from it, and writing as fast as a continual flow of tears would permit her. In this situation, Elinor, roused from sleep by her agitation and sobs, first perceived her; and after observing her for a few moments with silent anxiety, said, in a tone of the most considerate gentleness,

"Marianne, may I ask?"—

"No, Elinor," she replied, "ask nothing; you will soon know all."

The sort of desperate calmness with which this was said, lasted no longer than while she spoke, and was immediately followed by a return of the same excessive affliction. It was some minutes before she could go on with her letter, and the frequent bursts of grief which still obliged her, at intervals, to withhold her pen, were proofs enough of her feeling how more than probable it was that she was writing for the last time to Willoughby.

Elinor paid her every quiet and unobtrusive attention in her power; and she would have tried to soothe and tranquillize her still more, had not Marianne entreated her, with all the eagerness of the most nervous irritability, not to speak to her for the world. In such circumstances, it was better for both that they should not be long together; and the restless state of Marianne's mind not only prevented her from remaining in the room a moment after she was dressed, but requiring at once solitude and continual change of place, made her wander about the house till breakfast time, avoiding the sight of every body.

At breakfast she neither ate, nor attempted to eat any thing; and Elinor's attention was then all employed, not in urging her, not in pitying her, nor in appearing to regard her, but in endeavouring to engage Mrs. Jennings's notice entirely to herself.

As this was a favourite meal with Mrs. Jennings, it lasted a considerable time, and they were just setting themselves, after it, round the common working table, when a letter was delivered to Marianne, which she eagerly caught from the servant, and, turning of a death-like paleness, instantly ran out of the room. Elinor, who saw as plainly by this, as if she had seen the direction, that it must come from Willoughby, felt immediately such a sickness at heart as made her hardly able to hold up her head, and sat in such a general tremour as made her fear it impossible to escape Mrs. Jennings's notice. That good lady, however, saw only that Marianne had received a letter from Willoughby, which appeared to her a very good joke, and which she treated accordingly, by hoping, with a laugh, that she would find it to her liking. Of Elinor's distress, she was too busily employed in measuring lengths of worsted for her rug, to see any thing at all; and calmly continuing her talk, as soon as Marianne disappeared, she said,

"Upon my word I never saw a young woman so desperately in love in my life! My girls were nothing to her, and yet they used to be foolish enough; but as for Miss Marianne, she is quite an altered creature. I hope, from the bottom of my heart, he won't keep her waiting much longer, for it is quite grievous to see her look so ill and forlorn. Pray, when are they to be married?"

Elinor, though never less disposed to speak than at that moment, obliged herself to answer such an attack as this, and, therefore, trying to smile, replied, "And have you really, Ma'am, talked yourself into a persuasion of my sister's being engaged to Mr. Willoughby? I thought it had been only a joke, but so serious a question seems to imply more; and I must beg, therefore, that you will not deceive yourself any longer. I do assure you that nothing would surprise me more than to hear of their being going to be married."

"For shame, for shame, Miss Dashwood! how can you talk so! Don't we all know that it must be a match, that they were over head and ears in love with each other from the first moment they met? Did not I see them together in Devonshire every day, and all day long; and did not I know that your sister came to town with me on purpose to buy wedding clothes? Come, come, this won't do. Because you are so sly about it yourself, you think nobody else has any senses; but it is no such thing, I can tell you, for it has been known all over town this ever so long. I tell every body of it and so does Charlotte."

"Indeed, Ma'am," said Elinor very seriously, "you are mistaken. Indeed, you are doing a very unkind thing in spreading the report, and you will find that you have, though you will not believe me now."

Mrs. Jennings laughed again, but Elinor had not spirits to say more, and eager at all events to know what Willoughby had written, hurried away to their room, where, on opening the door, she saw Marianne stretched on the bed, almost choked by grief, one letter in her hand, and two or three others lying by her. Elinor drew near, but without saying a word; and seating herself on the bed, took her hand, kissed her affectionately several times, and then gave way to a burst of tears, which at first was scarcely less violent than Marianne's. The latter, though unable to speak, seemed to feel all the tenderness of this behaviour, and after some time thus spent in joint affliction, she put all the letters into Elinor's hands; and then covering her face with her handkerchief, almost screamed with agony. Elinor, who knew that such grief, shocking as it was to witness it, must have its course, watched by her till this excess of suffering had somewhat spent itself, and then turning eagerly to Willoughby's letter, read as follows:

Bond Street, January.

My Dear Madam,

I have just had the honour of receiving your letter, for which I beg to return my sincere acknowledgements. I am much concerned to find there was any thing in my behaviour last night that did not meet your approbation; and though I am quite at a loss to discover in what point I could be so unfortunate as to offend you, I entreat your forgiveness of what I can assure you to have been perfectly unintentional. I shall never reflect on my former acquaintance with your family in Devonshire without the most grateful pleasure, and flatter myself it will not be broken by any mistake or misapprehension of my actions. My esteem for your whole family is very sincere; but if I have been so unfortunate as to give rise to a belief of more than I felt, or meant to express, I shall reproach myself for not having been more guarded in my professions of that esteem. That I should ever have meant more you will allow to be impossible, when you understand that my affections have been long engaged elsewhere, and it will not be many weeks, I believe, before this engagement is fulfilled. It is with great regret that I obey your commands of returning the letters, with which I have been honoured from you, and the lock of hair, which you so obligingly bestowed on me.

> I am, dear Madam,
> Your most obedient
> humble Servant,
> JOHN WILLOUGHBY.

With what indignation such a letter as this must be read by Miss Dashwood, may be imagined. Though aware, before she began it, that it must bring a confession of his inconstancy, and confirm their separation for ever, she was not aware that such language could be suffered to announce it! nor could she have supposed Willoughby capable of departing so far from the appearance of every honourable and delicate feeling—so far from the common decorum of a gentleman, as to send a letter so impudently cruel: a letter which, instead of bringing with his desire of a release any professions of regret, acknowledged no breach of faith, denied all peculiar affection whatever—a letter of which every line was an insult, and which proclaimed its writer to be deep in hardened villainy.

She paused over it for some time with indignant astonishment; then read it again and again; but every perusal only served to increase her abhorrence of the man, and so bitter were her feelings against him, that she dared not trust herself to speak, lest she might wound Marianne still deeper by treating their disengagement,[1] not as a loss to her of any possible good but as an escape from the worst and most irremediable of all evils, a connection, for life, with an unprincipled man, as a deliverance the most real, a blessing the most important.

In her earnest meditations on the contents of the letter, on the depravity of that mind which could dictate it, and, probably, on the very different mind of a very different person, who had no other connection whatever with the affair than what her heart gave him with every thing that passed, Elinor forgot the immediate distress of her sister, forgot that she had three letters on her lap yet unread, and so entirely forgot how long she had been in the room, that when on hearing a carriage drive up to the door, she went to the window to see who could be coming so unreasonably early, she was all astonishment to perceive Mrs. Jennings's chariot,[2] which she knew had not been ordered till one. Determined not to quit Marianne, though hopeless of contributing, at present, to her ease, she hurried away to excuse herself from attending Mrs. Jennings, on account of her sister being indisposed. Mrs. Jennings, with a thoroughly good-humoured concern for its cause, admitted the excuse most readily, and Elinor, after seeing her safe off, returned to Marianne, whom she found attempting to rise from the bed, and whom she reached just in time to prevent her from falling on the floor, faint and giddy from a long want of proper rest and food; for it was many days since she had any appetite, and many nights since she had really slept; and now, when her mind was no longer supported by the fever of suspense, the consequence of all this was felt in an aching head, a weakened stomach, and a general nervous faintness. A glass of wine, which Elinor procured for her directly, made her more comfortable, and she was at last able to express some sense of her kindness, by saying,

[1] *disengagement*: broken engagement.
[2] *chariot*: fancy carriage.

"Poor Elinor! how unhappy I make you!"

"I only wish," replied her sister, "there were any thing I *could* do, which might be of comfort to you."

This, as every thing else would have been, was too much for Marianne, who could only exclaim, in the anguish of her heart, "Oh! Elinor, I am miserable indeed," before her voice was entirely lost in sobs.

Elinor could no longer witness this torrent of unresisted grief in silence.

"Exert yourself, dear Marianne," she cried, "if you would not kill yourself and all who love you. Think of your mother; think of her misery while *you* suffer; for her sake you must exert yourself."

"I cannot, I cannot," cried Marianne; "leave me, leave me, if I distress you; leave me, hate me, forget me! but do not torture me so. Oh! how easy for those who have no sorrow of their own to talk of exertion! Happy, happy Elinor, *you* cannot have an idea of what I suffer."

"Do you call *me* happy, Marianne? Ah! if you knew!—And can you believe me to be so, while I see you so wretched!"

"Forgive me, forgive me," throwing her arms round her sister's neck; "I know you feel for me; I know what a heart you have; but yet you are—you must be happy; Edward loves you—what, oh! what can do away such happiness as that?"

"Many, many circumstances," said Elinor, solemnly.

"No, no, no," cried Marianne wildly, "he loves you, and only you. You *can* have no grief."

"I can have no pleasure while I see you in this state."

"And you will never see me otherwise. Mine is a misery which nothing can do away."

"You must not talk so, Marianne. Have you no comforts? no friends? Is your loss such as leaves no opening for consolation? Much as you suffer now, think of what you would have suffered if the discovery of his character had been delayed to a later period—if your engagement had been carried on for months and months, as it might have been, before he chose to put an end to it. Every additional day of unhappy confidence, on your side, would have made the blow more dreadful."

"Engagement!" cried Marianne, "there has been no engagement."

"No engagement!"

"No, he is not so unworthy as you believe him. He has broken no faith with me."

"But he told you that he loved you?"—

"Yes—no—never absolutely. It was every day implied, but never professedly declared. Sometimes I thought it had been—but it never was."

"Yet you wrote to him?"—

"Yes—could that be wrong after all that had passed?—But I cannot talk."

Elinor said no more, and turning again to the three letters which now raised a much stronger curiosity than before, directly ran over the contents of all. The first, which was what her sister had sent him on their arrival in town, was to this effect.

Berkeley Street, January.

How surprised you will be, Willoughby, on receiving this; and I think you will feel something more than surprise, when you know that I am in town. An opportunity of coming hither, though with Mrs. Jennings, was a temptation we could not resist. I wish you may[3] receive this in time to come here to-night, but I will not depend on it. At any rate I shall expect you to-morrow. For the present, adieu.

M. D.

Her second note, which had been written on the morning after the dance at the Middletons', was in these words:—

"I cannot express my disappointment in having missed you the day before yesterday, nor my astonishment at not having received any answer to a note which I sent you above a week ago. I have been expecting to hear from you, and still more to see you, every hour of the day. Pray call again as soon as possible, and explain the reason of my having expected this in

[3] *wish you may:* hope you will.

vain. You had better come earlier another time, because we are generally out by one. We were last night at Lady Middleton's, where there was a dance. I have been told that you were asked to be of the party. But could it be so? You must be very much altered indeed since we parted, if that could be the case, and you not there. But I will not suppose this possible, and I hope very soon to receive your personal assurance of its being otherwise."

M. D.

The contents of her last note to him were these:—

"What am I to imagine, Willoughby, by your behaviour last night? Again I demand an explanation of it. I was prepared to meet you with the pleasure which our separation naturally produced, with the familiarity which our intimacy at Barton appeared to me to justify. I was repulsed indeed! I have passed a wretched night in endeavouring to excuse a conduct which can scarcely be called less than insulting; but though I have not yet been able to form any reasonable apology for your behaviour, I am perfectly ready to hear your justification of it. You have perhaps been misinformed, or purposely deceived, in something concerning me, which may have lowered me in your opinion. Tell me what it is, explain the grounds on which you acted, and I shall be satisfied, in being able to satisfy you. It would grieve me indeed to be obliged to think ill of you; but if I am to do it, if I am to learn that you are not what we have hitherto believed you, that your regard for us all was insincere, that your behaviour to me was intended only to deceive, let it be told as soon as possible. My feelings are at present in a state of dreadful indecision; I wish to acquit you, but certainty on either side will be ease to what I now suffer. If your sentiments are no longer what they were, you will return my notes, and the lock of my hair which is in your possession."

M. D.

That such letters, so full of affection and confidence, could have been so answered, Elinor, for Willoughby's sake, would have been unwilling to believe. But her condemnation of him did not blind her to the impropriety of their having been written at all; and she was silently grieving over the imprudence which had hazarded such unsolicited proofs of tenderness, not warranted by anything preceding, and most severely condemned by the event, when Marianne, perceiving that she had finished the letters, observed to her that they contained nothing but what any one would have written in the same situation.

"I felt myself," she added, "to be as solemnly engaged to him, as if the strictest legal covenant had bound us to each other."

"I can believe it," said Elinor; "but unfortunately he did not feel the same."

"He *did* feel the same, Elinor—for weeks and weeks he felt it. I know he did. Whatever may have changed him now, (and nothing but the blackest art employed against me can have done it,) I was once as dear to him as my own soul could wish. This lock of hair, which now he can so readily give up, was begged of me with the most earnest supplication. Had you seen his look, his manner, had you heard his voice at that moment! Have you forgot the last evening of our being together at Barton? The morning that we parted too! When he told me that it might be many weeks before we meet again—his distress—can I ever forget his distress!"

For a moment or two she could say no more; but when this emotion had passed away, she added, in a firmer tone,

"Elinor, I have been cruelly used; but not by Willoughby."

"Dearest Marianne, who but himself? By whom can he have been instigated?"

"By all the world, rather than by his own heart. I could rather believe every creature of my acquaintance leagued together to ruin me in his opinion, than believe his nature capable of such cruelty. This woman of whom he writes—whoever she be—or any one, in short, but your own dear self, mama, and Edward, may have been so barbarous to bely me. Beyond you three, is there a creature in the world whom I would not rather suspect of evil than Willoughby, whose heart I know so well?"

Elinor would not contend, and only replied, "Whoever may have been so detestably your enemy, let them be cheated of their malignant triumph, my dear sister, by seeing how nobly the consciousness of your own innocence and good intentions supports your spirits. It is a reasonable and laudable pride which resists such malevolence."

"No, no," cried Marianne, "misery such as mine has no pride. I care not who knows that I am wretched. The triumph of seeing me so may be open to all the world. Elinor, Elinor, they who suffer little may be proud and independent as they like—may resist insult, or return mortification—but I cannot. I must feel—I must be wretched—and they are welcome to enjoy the consciousness of it that can."

"But for my mother's sake and mine"—

"I would do more than for my own. But to appear happy when I am so miserable—Oh! who can require it?"

Again they were both silent. Elinor was employed in walking thoughtfully from the fire to the window, from the window to the fire, without knowing that she received warmth from one, or discerning objects through the other; and Marianne, seated at the foot of the bed, with her head leaning against one of its posts, again took up Willoughby's letter, and after shuddering over every sentence, exclaimed—

"It is too much! Oh! Willoughby, Willoughby, could this be yours! Cruel, cruel—nothing can acquit you. Elinor, nothing can. Whatever he might have heard against me—ought he not to have suspended his belief? ought he not to have told me of it, to have given me the power of clearing myself? 'The lock of hair, (repeating it from the letter,) which you so obligingly bestowed on me'—That is unpardonable. Willoughby, where was your heart, when you wrote those words? Oh! barbarously insolent!—Elinor, can he be justified?"

"No, Marianne, in no possible way."

"And yet this woman—who knows what her art may have been—how long it may have been premeditated, and how deeply contrived by her!—Who is she?—Who can she be?— Whom did I ever hear him talk of as young and attractive among his female acquaintance?—Oh! no one, no one—he talked to me only of myself."

Another pause ensued; Marianne was greatly agitated, and it ended thus.

"Elinor, I must go home. I must go and comfort mama. Cannot we be gone to-morrow?"

"To-morrow, Marianne!"

"Yes; why should I stay here? I came only for Willoughby's sake—and now who cares for me? Who regards me?"

"It would be impossible to go to-morrow. We owe Mrs. Jennings much more than civility; and civility of the commonest kind must prevent such a hasty removal as that."

"Well then, another day or two perhaps; but I cannot stay here long, I cannot stay to endure the questions and remarks of all these people. The Middletons and Palmers—how am I to bear their pity? The pity of such a woman as Lady Middleton! Oh! what would *he* say to that!"

Elinor advised her to lie down again, and for a moment she did so; but no attitude could give her ease; and in restless pain of mind and body she moved from one posture to another, till growing more and more hysterical, her sister could with difficulty keep her on the bed at all, and for some time was fearful of being constrained to call for assistance. Some lavender drops, however, which she was at length persuaded to take, were of use; and from that time till Mrs. Jennings returned, she continued on the bed quiet and motionless.

Chapter VIII

Mrs. Jennings came immediately to their room on her return, and without waiting to have her request of admittance answered, opened the door and walked in with a look of real concern.

"How do you do my dear?"—said she in a voice of great compassion to Marianne, who turned away her face without attempting to answer.

"How is she, Miss Dashwood?—Poor thing! she looks very bad.—No wonder. Aye, it is but too true. He is to be married very soon—a good-for-nothing fellow! I have no patience with him. Mrs. Taylor told me of it half an hour ago, and she was told it by a particular friend of Miss Grey herself, else I am sure I should not have believed it; and I was almost ready to sink as it was. Well, said I, all I can say is, that if it is true, he has used a young lady of my acquaintance abominably ill, and I wish with all my soul his wife may plague his heart out. And so I shall always say, my dear, you may depend on it. I have no notion of men's going on in this way: and if ever I meet him again, I will give him such a dressing[1] as he has not had this many a day. But there is one comfort, my dear Miss Marianne; he is not the only young man in the world worth having; and with your pretty face you will never want admirers. Well, poor thing! I won't disturb her any longer, for she had better have her cry out at once and have done with it. The Parrys and Sandersons luckily are coming to-night you know, and that will amuse her."

She then went away, walking on tiptoe out of the room, as if she supposed her young friend's affliction could be increased by noise.

[1] *dressing*: dressing down, scolding.

Marianne, to the surprise of her sister, determined on dining with them. Elinor even advised her against it. But "no, she would go down; she could bear it very well, and the bustle about her would be less." Elinor, pleased to have her governed for a moment by such a motive, though believing it hardly possible that she could sit out the dinner, said no more; and adjusting her dress for her as well as she could, while Marianne still remained on the bed, was ready to assist her into the dining room as soon as they were summoned to it.

When there, though looking most wretchedly, she ate more and was calmer than her sister had expected. Had she tried to speak, or had she been conscious of half Mrs. Jennings's well-meant but ill-judged attentions to her, this calmness could not have been maintained; but not a syllable escaped her lips, and the abstraction of her thoughts preserved her in ignorance of every thing that was passing before her.

Elinor, who did justice to Mrs. Jennings's kindness, though its effusions were often distressing, and sometimes almost ridiculous, made her those acknowledgements, and returned her those civilities, which her sister could not make or return for herself. Their good friend saw that Marianne was unhappy, and felt that every thing was due to her which might make her at all less so. She treated her therefore, with all the indulgent fondness of a parent towards a favourite child on the last day of its holidays. Marianne was to have the best place by the fire, was to be tempted to eat by every delicacy in the house, and to be amused by the relation of all the news of the day. Had not Elinor, in the sad countenance of her sister, seen a check to all mirth, she could have been entertained by Mrs. Jennings's endeavours to cure a disappointment in love, by a variety of sweetmeats and olives, and a good fire. As soon, however, as the consciousness of all this was forced by continual repetition on Marianne, she could stay no longer. With an hasty exclamation of Misery, and a sign to her sister not to follow her, she directly got up and hurried out of the room.

"Poor soul!" cried Mrs. Jennings, as soon as she was gone, "how it grieves me to see her! And I declare if she is not gone away without finishing her wine! And the dried cherries too! Lord! nothing seems to do her any good. I am sure if I knew of any thing she would like, I would send all over the town for it. Well, it is the oddest thing to me, that a man should use such a pretty girl so ill! But when there is plenty of money on one side, and next to none on the other, Lord bless you! they care no more about such things!—"

"The lady then—Miss Grey I think you called her—is very rich?"

"Fifty thousand pounds, my dear. Did you ever see her? a smart, stilish girl they say, but not handsome. I remember her aunt very well, Biddy Henshawe; she married a very wealthy man. But the family are all rich together. Fifty thousand pounds! and by all accounts it won't come before it's wanted; for they say he is all to pieces. No wonder! dashing about with his curricle and hunters! Well, it don't signify talking, but when a young man, be he who he will, comes and makes love to a pretty girl, and promises marriage, he has no business to fly off from his word only because he grows poor, and a richer girl is ready to have him. Why don't he, in such a case, sell his horses, let his house, turn off his servants, and make a thorough reform at once? I warrant you, Miss Marianne would have been ready to wait till matters came round. But that won't do, now-a-days; nothing in the way of pleasure can ever be given up by the young men of this age."

"Do you know what kind of a girl Miss Grey is? Is she said to be amiable?"

"I never heard any harm of her; indeed I hardly ever heard her mentioned; except that Mrs. Taylor did say this morning, that one day Miss Walker hinted to her, that she believed Mr. and Mrs. Ellison would not be sorry to have Miss Grey married, for she and Mrs. Ellison could never agree."—

"And who are the Ellisons?"

"Her guardians, my dear. But now she is of age and may choose for herself; and a pretty choice she has made!—What now," after pausing a moment—"your poor sister is gone to her own room I suppose to moan by herself. Is there nothing one can get to comfort her? Poor dear, it seems quite cruel to let her be alone. Well, by-and-by we shall have a few friends, and that will amuse her a little. What shall we play at? She hates whist I know; but is there no round game she cares for?"

"Dear Ma'am, this kindness is quite unnecessary. Marianne I dare say will not leave her room again this evening. I shall persuade her if I can to go early to bed, for I am sure she wants rest."

"Aye, I believe that will be best for her. Let her name her own supper, and go to bed. Lord! no wonder she has been looking so bad and so cast down this last week or two, for this matter I suppose has been hanging over her head as long as that. And so the letter that came to-day finished it! Poor soul! I am sure if I had had a notion of it, I would not have joked her about it for all my money. But then you know, how should I guess such a thing? I made sure of its being nothing but a common love letter, and you know young people like to be laughed at about them. Lord! how concerned Sir John and my daughters will be when they hear it! If I had had my senses about me I might have called in Conduit-street in my way home, and told them of it. But I shall see them tomorrow."

"It would be unnecessary I am sure, for you to caution Mrs. Palmer and Sir John against ever naming Mr. Willoughby, or making the slightest allusion to what has passed, before my sister. Their own good-nature must point out to them the real cruelty of appearing to know any thing about it when she is present; and the less that may ever be said to myself on the subject, the more my feelings will be spared, as you my dear madam will easily believe."

"Oh! Lord! yes, that I do indeed. It must be terrible for you to hear it talked of; and as for your sister, I am sure I would not mention a word about it to her for the world. You saw I did not all dinner time. No more would Sir John nor my daughters, for they are all very thoughtful and considerate; especially if I give them a hint, as I certainly will. For my part, I think the less that is said about such things, the better, the sooner 'tis blown over and forgot. And what good does talking ever do you know?"

"In this affair it can only do harm; more so perhaps than in many cases of a similar kind, for it has been attended by circumstances which, for the sake of every one concerned in it, make it unfit to become the public conversation.[2] I must do *this* justice to Mr. Willoughby—he has broken no positive engagement with my sister."

"Law, my dear! Don't pretend to defend him. No positive engagement indeed! after taking her all over Allenham House, and fixing on the very rooms they were to live in hereafter!"

Elinor, for her sister's sake, could not press the subject farther, and she hoped it was not required of her for Willoughby's; since, though Marianne might lose much, he could gain very little by the inforcement of the real truth. After a short silence on both sides, Mrs. Jennings, with all her natural hilarity, burst forth again.

"Well, my dear, 'tis a true saying about an ill wind, for it will be all the better for Colonel Brandon. He will have her at last; aye, that he will. Mind me, now, if they an't married by Midsummer.[3] Lord! how he'll chuckle over this news! I hope he will come tonight. It will be all to one a better match for your sister. Two thousand a year without debt or drawback— except the little love-child,[4] indeed; aye, I had forgot her; but she may be 'prenticed[5] out at small cost, and then what does it signify? Delaford is a nice place, I can tell you; exactly what I call a nice old fashioned place, full of comforts and conveniences; quite shut in with great garden walls that are covered with the best fruit-trees in the country: and such a mulberry tree in one corner! Lord! how Charlotte and I did stuff the only time we were there! Then, there is a dove-cote,[6] some

---

[2] *public conversation*: i.e., subject of public conversation.

[3] *Midsummer*: June 24, "St. John's Day" (the feast of St. John the Baptist), and the period surrounding (associated with the summer solstice and actually counted as the first day of summer, and not technically its midpoint).

[4] *love-child*: illegitimate child; cf. p. 66.

[5] *'prenticed*: apprenticed; sent to learn a trade. (Mrs. Jennings assumes the illegitimate child will be raised to be of the servant class.)

[6] *dove-cote*: shelter with nest holes for domesticated pigeons.

delightful stewponds,[7] and a very pretty canal; and every thing, in short, that one could wish for: and, moreover, it is close to the church, and only a quarter of a mile from the turnpike-road, so 'tis never dull, for if you only go and sit up in an old yew arbour behind the house, you may see all the carriages that pass along. Oh! 'tis a nice place! A butcher hard by in the village, and the parsonage-house within a stone's throw. To my fancy, a thousand times prettier than Barton Park, where they are forced to send three miles for their meat, and have not a neighbour nearer than your mother. Well, I shall spirit up the Colonel as soon as I can. One shoulder of mutton, you know, drives another down.[8] If we *can* but put Willoughby out of her head!"

"Aye, if we can but do *that*, Ma'am," said Elinor, "we shall do very well with or without Colonel Brandon." And then rising, she went away to join Marianne, whom she found, as she expected, in her own room, leaning, in silent misery, over the small remains of a fire, which, till Elinor's entrance, had been her only light.

"You had better leave me," was all the notice that her sister received from her.

"I will leave you," said Elinor, "if you will go to bed." But this, from the momentary perverseness of impatient suffering, she at first refused to do. Her sister's earnest, though gentle persuasion, however, soon softened her to compliance, and Elinor saw her lay her aching head on the pillow, and saw her, as she hoped, in a way to get some quiet rest before she left her.

In the drawing-room, whither she then repaired, she was soon joined by Mrs. Jennings, with a wine-glass, full of something, in her hand.

"My dear," said she, entering, "I have just recollected that I have some of the finest old Constantia wine[9] in the house, that

---

[7] *stewponds*: fishponds.

[8] *One ... down*: Per Chapman, this is a proverbial expression similar to the French: *En mangeant l'appetit vient*.

[9] *Constantia wine*: sweet wine from a farm near Cape Town, South Africa.

ever was tasted, so I have brought a glass of it for your sister. My poor husband! how fond he was of it! Whenever he had a touch of his old cholicky gout, he said it did him more good than any thing else in the world. Do take it to your sister."

"Dear Ma'am," replied Elinor, smiling at the difference of the complaints for which it was recommended, "how good you are! But I have just left Marianne in bed, and, I hope, almost asleep; and as I think nothing will be of so much service to her as rest, if you will give me leave, I will drink the wine myself."

Mrs. Jennings, though regretting that she had not been five minutes earlier, was satisfied with the compromise; and Elinor, as she swallowed the chief of it, reflected that, though its good effects on a cholicky gout were, at present, of little importance to her, its healing powers on a disappointed heart might be as reasonably tried on herself as on her sister.

Colonel Brandon came in while the party were at tea, and by his manner of looking round the room for Marianne, Elinor immediately fancied that he neither expected, nor wished to see her there, and, in short, that he was already aware of what occasioned her absence. Mrs. Jennings was not struck by the same thought; for, soon after his entrance, she walked across the room to the tea-table where Elinor presided, and whispered—"The Colonel looks as grave as ever you see. He knows nothing of it; do tell him, my dear."

He shortly afterwards drew a chair close to her's, and, with a look which perfectly assured her of his good information, inquired after her sister.

"Marianne is not well," said she. "She has been indisposed all day, and we have persuaded her to go to bed."

"Perhaps, then," he hesitatingly replied, "what I heard this morning may be—there may be more truth in it than I could believe possible at first."

"What did you hear?"

"That a gentleman, whom I had reason to think—in short, that a man, whom I *knew* to be engaged—but how shall I tell you? If you know it already, as surely you must, I may be spared."

"You mean," answered Elinor, with forced calmness, "Mr. Willoughby's marriage with Miss Grey. Yes, we *do* know it all. This seems to have been a day of general elucidation, for this very morning first unfolded it to us. Mr. Willoughby is unfathomable! Where did you hear it?"

"In a stationer's shop in Pall Mall,[10] where I had business. Two ladies were waiting for their carriage, and one of them was giving the other an account of the intended match, in a voice so little attempting concealment, that it was impossible for me not to hear all. The name of Willoughby, John Willoughby, frequently repeated, first caught my attention, and what followed was a positive assertion that every thing was now finally settled respecting his marriage with Miss Grey—it was no longer to be a secret—it would take place even within a few weeks, with many particulars of preparations and other matters. One thing, especially, I remember, because it served to identify the man still more:—as soon as the ceremony was over, they were to go to Combe Magna, his seat in Somersetshire. My astonishment!—but it would be impossible to describe what I felt. The communicative lady I learnt, on inquiry, for I staid in the shop till they were gone, was a Mrs. Ellison, and that, as I have been since informed, is the name of Miss Grey's guardian."

"It is. But have you likewise heard that Miss Grey has fifty thousand pounds? In that, if in any thing, we may find an explanation."

"It may be so; but Willoughby is capable—at least I think"—he stopped a moment; then added in a voice which seemed to distrust itself, "And your sister—how did she—"

"Her sufferings have been very severe. I have only to hope that they may be proportionably short. It has been, it is a most cruel affliction. Till yesterday, I believe, she never doubted his regard; and even now, perhaps—but I am almost convinced that he never was really attached to her. He has been very deceitful! and, in some points, there seems a hardness of heart about him."

[10] *Pall Mall*: fashionable street in London's West End.

"Ah!" said Colonel Brandon, "there is, indeed! But your sister does not—I think you said so—she does not consider it quite as you do?"

"You know her disposition, and may believe how eagerly she would still justify him if she could."

He made no answer; and soon afterwards, by the removal of the tea-things, and the arrangement of the card parties, the subject was necessarily dropped. Mrs. Jennings, who had watched them with pleasure while they were talking, and who expected to see the effect of Miss Dashwood's communication, in such an instantaneous gaiety on Colonel Brandon's side, as might have become a man in the bloom of youth, of hope and happiness, saw him, with amazement, remain the whole evening more serious and thoughtful than usual.

Chapter IX

From a night of more sleep than she had expected, Marianne awoke the next morning to the same consciousness of misery in which she had closed her eyes.

Elinor encouraged her as much as possible to talk of what she felt; and before breakfast was ready, they had gone through the subject again and again; with the same steady conviction and affectionate counsel on Elinor's side, the same impetuous feelings and varying opinions on Marianne's, as before. Sometimes she could believe Willoughby to be as unfortunate and as innocent as herself, and at others, lost every consolation in the impossibility of acquitting him. At one moment she was absolutely indifferent to the observation of all the world, at another she would seclude herself from it for ever, and at a third could resist it with energy. In one thing, however, she was uniform, when it came to the point, in avoiding, where it was possible, the presence of Mrs. Jennings, and in a determined silence when obliged to endure it. Her heart was hardened against the belief of Mrs. Jennings's entering into her sorrows with any compassion.

"No, no, no, it cannot be," she cried; "she cannot feel. Her kindness is not sympathy; her good nature is not tenderness. All that she wants is gossip, and she only likes me now because I supply it."

Elinor had not needed this to be assured of the injustice to which her sister was often led in her opinion of others, by the irritable refinement of her own mind, and the too great importance placed by her on the delicacies of a strong sensibility, and the graces of a polished manner. Like half the rest of the world, if more than half there be that are clever and good, Marianne, with excellent abilities and an excellent disposition, was neither reasonable nor candid. She expected from other people the same opinions and feelings as her own, and she judged of their motives by the immediate effect of their actions on herself. Thus a circumstance occurred, while the sisters were together in their own room after breakfast, which sunk the heart of Mrs. Jennings still lower in her estimation; because, through her own weakness, it chanced to prove a source of fresh pain to herself, though Mrs. Jennings was governed in it by an impulse of the utmost good-will.

With a letter in her out-stretched hand, and countenance gaily smiling, from the persuasion of bringing comfort, she entered their room, saying,

"Now, my dear, I bring you something that I am sure will do you good."

Marianne heard enough. In one moment her imagination placed before her a letter from Willoughby, full of tenderness and contrition, explanatory of all that had passed, satisfactory, convincing; and instantly followed by Willoughby himself, rushing eagerly into the room to inforce, at her feet, by the eloquence of his eyes, the assurances of his letter. The work of one moment was destroyed by the next. The hand writing of her mother, never till then unwelcome, was before her; and, in the acuteness of the disappointment which followed such an extasy of more than hope, she felt as if, till that instant, she had never suffered.

The cruelty of Mrs. Jennings no language, within her reach in her moments of happiest eloquence, could have expressed; and now she could reproach her only by the tears which streamed from her eyes with passionate violence—a reproach, however, so entirely lost on its object, that after many expressions of pity, she withdrew, still referring her to the letter for comfort. But the letter, when she was calm enough to read it, brought little comfort. Willoughby filled every page. Her mother, still confident of their engagement, and relying as warmly as ever on his constancy, had only been roused by Elinor's application, to intreat from Marianne greater openness towards them both; and this, with such tenderness towards her, such affection for Willoughby, and such a conviction of their future happiness in each other, that she wept with agony through the whole of it.

All her impatience to be at home again now returned; her mother was dearer to her than ever; dearer through the very excess of her mistaken confidence in Willoughby, and she was wildly urgent to be gone. Elinor, unable herself to determine whether it were better for Marianne to be in London or at Barton, offered no counsel of her own except of patience till their mother's wishes could be known; and at length she obtained her sister's consent to wait for that knowledge.

Mrs. Jennings left them earlier than usual; for she could not be easy till the Middletons and Palmers were able to grieve as much as herself; and positively refusing Elinor's offered attendance, went out alone for the rest of the morning. Elinor, with a very heavy heart, aware of the pain she was going to communicate, and perceiving by Marianne's letter how ill she had succeeded in laying any foundation for it, then sat down to write her mother an account of what had passed, and intreat her directions for the future; while Marianne, who came into the drawing-room on Mrs. Jennings's going away, remained fixed at the table where Elinor wrote, watching the advancement of her pen, grieving over her for the hardship of such a task, and grieving still more fondly over its effect on her mother.

In this manner they had continued about a quarter of an hour, when Marianne, whose nerves could not then bear any sudden noise, was startled by a rap at the door.

"Who can this be?" cried Elinor. "So early too! I thought we *had* been safe."

Marianne moved to the window—

"It is Colonel Brandon!" said she, with vexation. "We are never safe from *him*."

"He will not come in, as Mrs. Jennings is from home."

"I will not trust to *that*," retreating to her own room. "A man who has nothing to do with his own time has no conscience in his intrusion on that of others."

The event proved her conjecture right, though it was founded on injustice and error; for Colonel Brandon *did* come in; and Elinor, who was convinced that solicitude for Marianne brought him thither, and who saw *that* solicitude in his disturbed and melancholy look, and in his anxious though brief inquiry after her, could not forgive her sister for esteeming him so lightly.

"I met Mrs. Jennings in Bond-street," said he, after the first salutation, "and she encouraged me to come on; and I was the more easily encouraged, because I thought it probable that I might find you alone, which I was very desirous of doing. My object—my wish—my sole wish in desiring it—I hope, I believe it is—is to be a means of giving comfort;—no, I must not say comfort—not present comfort—but conviction, lasting conviction to your sister's mind. My regard for her, for yourself, for your mother—will you allow me to prove it, by relating some circumstances, which nothing but a *very* sincere regard—nothing but an earnest desire of being useful——I think I am justified—though where so many hours have been spent in convincing myself that I am right, is there not some reason to fear I may be wrong?'" He stopped.

"I understand you," said Elinor. "You have something to tell me of Mr. Willoughby, that will open his character farther. Your telling it will be the greatest act of friendship that can be shewn Marianne. My gratitude will be insured immediately by any information tending to that end, and *her's* must be gained by it in time. Pray, pray let me hear it."

"You shall; and, to be brief, when I quitted Barton last October—but this will give you no idea—I must go farther back. You will find me a very awkward narrator, Miss Dashwood; I hardly know where to begin. A short account of myself, I believe, will be necessary, and it *shall* be a short one. On such a subject," sighing heavily, "I can have little temptation to be diffuse."

He stopt a moment for recollection, and then, with another sigh, went on.

"You have probably entirely forgotten a conversation—(it is not to be supposed that it could make any impression on you)—a conversation between us one evening at Barton

Park—it was the evening of a dance—in which I alluded to a lady I had once known, as resembling, in some measure, your sister Marianne."

"Indeed," answered Elinor, "I have *not* forgotten it." He looked pleased by this remembrance, and added;

"If I am not deceived by the uncertainty, the partiality of tender recollection, there is a very strong resemblance between them, as well in mind as person. The same warmth of heart, the same eagerness of fancy and spirits. This lady was one of my nearest relations, an orphan from her infancy, and under the guardianship of my father. Our ages were nearly the same, and from our earliest years we were playfellows and friends. I cannot remember the time when I did not love Eliza; and my affection for her, as we grew up, was such, as perhaps, judging from my present forlorn and cheerless gravity, you might think me incapable of having ever felt. Her's, for me, was, I believe, fervent as the attachment of your sister to Mr. Willoughby, and it was, though from a different cause, no less unfortunate. At seventeen, she was lost to me for ever. She was married—married against her inclination to my brother. Her fortune was large, and our family estate much encumbered. And this, I fear, is all that can be said for the conduct of one, who was at once her uncle and guardian. My brother did not deserve her; he did not even love her. I had hoped that her regard for me would support her under any difficulty, and for some time it did; but at last the misery of her situation, for she experienced great unkindness, overcame all her resolution, and though she had promised me that nothing—but how blindly I relate! I have never told you how this was brought on. We were within a few hours of eloping together for Scotland.[1] The treachery, or the folly, of my cousin's maid betrayed us. I was banished to the house of a relation far distant, and she was allowed no liberty, no society, no

[1] *eloping ... Scotland:* There were significantly fewer restrictions for marriage under Scottish law; eloping couples could be married immediately and without parental consent.

amusement, till my father's point was gained. I had depended on her fortitude too far, and the blow was a severe one—but had her marriage been happy, so young as I then was, a few months must have reconciled me to it, or at least I should not have now to lament it. This however was not the case. My brother had no regard for her; his pleasures were not what they ought to have been, and from the first he treated her unkindly. The consequence of this, upon a mind so young, so lively, so inexperienced as Mrs. Brandon's, was but too natural. She resigned herself at first to all the misery of her situation; and happy had it been if she had not lived to overcome those regrets which the remembrance of me occasioned. But can we wonder that with such a husband to provoke inconstancy, and without a friend to advise or restrain her, (for my father lived only a few months after their marriage, and I was with my regiment in the East Indies) she should fall? Had I remained in England, perhaps—but I meant to promote the happiness of both by removing from her for years, and for that purpose had procured my exchange.[2] The shock which her marriage had given me," he continued, in a voice of great agitation, "was of trifling weight—was nothing—to what I felt when I heard, about two years afterwards, of her divorce.[3] It was *that* which threw this gloom,—even now the recollection of what I suffered—"

He could say no more, and rising hastily walked for a few minutes about the room. Elinor, affected by his relation,[4] and still more by his distress, could not speak. He saw her concern, and coming to her, took her hand, pressed it, and kissed it with grateful respect. A few minutes more of silent exertion enabled him to proceed with composure.

---

[2] *exchange*: transfer to another regiment.

[3] *divorce*: more likely a judicial separation in the Ecclesiastical Court. Until the Matrimonial Causes Act of 1857, divorce fell under the jurisdiction of the Ecclesiastical Court rather than the civil. Legal divorce was uncommon, expensive, and very publicly conducted, since a legal divorce essentially required a private Act of Parliament. Adultery was the only acceptable ground for divorce.

[4] *relation*: narrative.

"It was nearly three years after this unhappy period before I returned to England. My first care, when I *did* arrive, was of course to seek for her; but the search was as fruitless as it was melancholy. I could not trace her beyond her first seducer, and there was every reason to fear that she had removed from him only to sink deeper in a life of sin. Her legal allowance[5] was not adequate to her fortune, nor sufficient for her comfortable maintenance, and I learnt from my brother, that the power of receiving it had been made over some months before to another person. He imagined, and calmly could he imagine it, that her extravagance and consequent distress had obliged her to dispose of it for some immediate relief. At last, however, and after I had been six months in England, I *did* find her. Regard for a former servant of my own, who had since fallen into misfortune, carried me to visit him in a spunging-house,[6] where he was confined for debt; and there, in the same house, under a similar confinement, was my unfortunate sister. So altered—so faded—worn down by acute suffering of every kind! hardly could I believe the melancholy and sickly figure before me, to be the remains of the lovely, blooming, healthful girl, on whom I had once doated. What I endured in so beholding her—but I have no right to wound your feelings by attempting to describe it—I have pained you too much already. That she was, to all appearance, in the last stage of a consumption,[7] was—yes, in such a situation it was my greatest comfort. Life could do nothing for her, beyond giving time for a better preparation for death; and that was given. I saw her placed in comfortable lodgings, and under proper attendants; I visited her every day during the rest of her short life; I was with her in her last moments."

[5] *legal allowance*: A House of Commons official (the "Lady's Friend") was tasked with ensuring that a divorced woman received suitable but moderate provision from her husband.

[6] *spunging-house*: house for debtors, like a small debtor's prison, with a sheriff or bailiff presiding over it.

[7] *consumption*: wasting disease, often tuberculosis; an established literary means for carrying off fallen women.

Again he stopped to recover himself; and Elinor spoke her feelings in an exclamation of tender concern, at the fate of his unfortunate friend.

"Your sister, I hope, cannot be offended," said he, "by the resemblance I have fancied between her and my poor disgraced relation. Their fates, their fortunes cannot be the same; and had the natural sweet disposition of the one been guarded by a firmer mind, or an happier marriage, she might have been all that you will live to see the other be. But to what does all this lead? I seem to have been distressing you for nothing. Ah! Miss Dashwood—a subject such as this—untouched for four-teen years—it is dangerous to handle it at all! I *will* be more collected—more concise. She left to my care her only child, a little girl, the offspring of her first guilty connection, who was then about three years old. She loved the child, and had always kept it with her. It was a valued, a precious trust to me; and gladly would I have discharged it in the strictest sense, by watching over her education myself, had the nature of our sit-uations allowed it; but I had no family, no home; and my little Eliza was therefore placed at school. I saw her there whenever I could, and after the death of my brother, (which happened about five years ago, and which left to me the possession of the family property,) she frequently visited me at Delaford. I called her a distant relation; but I am well aware that I have in general been suspected of a much nearer connection with her. It is now three years ago, (she had just reached her fourteenth year,) that I removed her from school, to place her under the care of a very respectable woman, residing in Dorsetshire, who had the charge of four or five other girls of about the same time of life; and for two years I had every reason to be pleased with her situation. But last February, almost a twelvemonth back, she suddenly disappeared. I had allowed her, (imprudently, as it has since turned out,) at her earnest desire, to go to Bath with one of her young friends, who was attending her father there for his health. I knew him to be a very good sort of man, and I thought well of his daughter—better than she deserved, for, with a most obstinate and ill-judged secrecy, she would tell nothing, would give no clue, though she certainly knew all. He, her father, a well-meaning, but not a quick-sighted man, could really, I believe, give no information; for he had been generally confined to the house, while the girls were ranging over the town and making what acquaintance they chose; and he tried to convince me, as thoroughly as he was convinced himself, of his daughter's being entirely unconcerned in the business. In short, I could learn nothing but that she was gone; all the rest, for eight long months, was left to conjecture. What I thought, what I feared, may be imagined; and what I suffered too."

"Good heavens!" cried Elinor, "could it be—could Willoughby!—"

"The first news that reached me of her," he continued, "came in a letter from herself, last October. It was forwarded to me from Delaford, and I received it on the very morning of our intended party to Whitwell; and this was the reason of my leaving Barton so suddenly, which I am sure must at the time have appeared strange to every body, and which I believe gave offence to some. Little did Mr. Willoughby imagine, I suppose, when his looks censured me for incivility in breaking up the party, that I was called away to the relief of one, whom he had made poor and miserable; but *had* he known it, what would it have availed? Would he have been less gay or less happy in the smiles of your sister? No, he had already done that, which no man who *can* feel for another, would do. He had left the girl whose youth and innocence he had seduced, in a situation of the utmost distress, with no creditable home, no help, no friends, ignorant of his address! He had left her promising to return; he neither returned, nor wrote, nor relieved her."

"This is beyond every thing!" exclaimed Elinor.

"His character is now before you; expensive,[8] dissipated, and worse than both. Knowing all this, as I have now known it many weeks, guess what I must have felt on seeing your sister as fond of him as ever, and on being assured that she was to

[8] *expensive*: extravagant.

marry him; guess what I must have felt for all your sakes. When I came to you last week and found you alone, I came determined to know the truth; though irresolute what to do when it *was* known. My behaviour must have seemed strange to you then; but now you will comprehend it. To suffer you all to be so deceived; to see your sister—but what could I do? I had no hope of interfering with success; and sometimes I thought your sister's influence might yet reclaim him. But now, after such dishonourable usage, who can tell what were his designs on her? Whatever they may have been, however, she may now, and hereafter doubtless *will*, turn with gratitude towards her own condition, when she compares it with that of my poor Eliza, when she considers the wretched and hopeless situation of this poor girl, and pictures her to herself, with an affection for him as strong, still as strong as her own, and with a mind tormented by self-reproach, which must attend her through life. Surely this comparison must have its use with her. She will feel her own sufferings to be nothing. They proceed from no misconduct, and can bring no disgrace. On the contrary, every friend must be made still more her friend by them. Concern for her unhappiness, and respect for her fortitude under it, must strengthen every attachment. Use your own discretion, however, in communicating to her what I have told you. You must know best what will be its effect; but had I not seriously, and from my heart believed it might be of service, might lessen her regrets, I would not have suffered myself to trouble you with this account of my family afflictions, with a recital which may seem to have been intended to raise myself at the expense of others."

Elinor's thanks followed this speech with grateful earnestness; attended too with the assurance of her expecting material advantage to Marianne from the communication of what had passed.

"I have been more pained," said she, "by her endeavours to acquit him than by all the rest; for it irritates her mind more than the most perfect conviction of his unworthiness can do. Now, though at first she will suffer much, I am sure she will soon become easier. Have you," she continued, after a short silence, "ever seen Mr. Willoughby since you left him at Barton?"

"Yes," he replied gravely, "once I have. One meeting was unavoidable."

Elinor, startled by his manner, looked at him anxiously, saying,

"What? have you met him to—"

"I could meet him in no other way. Eliza had confessed to me, though most reluctantly, the name of her lover; and when he returned to town, which was within a fortnight after myself, we met by appointment, he to defend, I to punish his conduct.[9] We returned unwounded, and the meeting, therefore, never got abroad."

Elinor sighed over the fancied necessity of this; but to a man and a soldier, she presumed not to censure it.

"Such," said Colonel Brandon, after a pause, "has been the unhappy resemblance between the fate of mother and daughter! and so imperfectly have I discharged my trust!"

"Is she still in town?"

"No; as soon as she recovered from her lying-in, for I found her near her delivery, I removed her and her child into the country, and there she remains."

Recollecting, soon afterwards, that he was probably dividing Elinor from her sister, he put an end to his visit, receiving from her again the same grateful acknowledgements, and leaving her full of compassion and esteem for him.

[9] *we met . . . conduct:* i.e., in a duel; dueling, though illegal, was the established means of settling questions of honor (and a highly Romantic proceeding to boot).

Chapter X

When the particulars of this conversation were repeated by Miss Dashwood to her sister, as they very soon were, the effect on her was not entirely such as the former had hoped to see. Not that Marianne appeared to distrust the truth of any part of it, for she listened to it all with the most steady and submissive attention, made neither objection nor remark, attempted no vindication of Willoughby, and seemed to shew by her tears that she felt it to be impossible. But though this behaviour assured Elinor that the conviction of his guilt *was* carried home to her mind, though she saw with satisfaction the effect of it, in her no longer avoiding Colonel Brandon when he called, in her speaking to him, even voluntarily speaking, with a kind of compassionate respect, and though she saw her spirits less violently irritated than before, she did not see her less wretched. Her mind did become settled, but it was settled in a gloomy dejection. She felt the loss of Willoughby's character yet more heavily than she had felt the loss of his heart; his seduction and desertion of Miss Williams, the misery of that poor girl, and the doubt of what his designs might *once* have been on herself, preyed altogether so much on her spirits, that she could not bring herself to speak of what she felt even to Elinor; and brooding over her sorrows in silence, gave more pain to her sister than could have been communicated by the most open and most frequent confession of them.

To give the feelings or the language of Mrs. Dashwood on receiving and answering Elinor's letter, would be only to give a repetition of what her daughters had already felt and said; of a disappointment hardly less painful than Marianne's, and an indignation even greater than Elinor's. Long letters from her, quickly succeeding each other, arrived to tell all that she suffered and thought; to express her anxious solicitude for

Marianne, and entreat she would bear up with fortitude under this misfortune. Bad indeed must the nature of Marianne's affliction be, when her mother could talk of fortitude! mortifying and humiliating must be the origin of those regrets, which *she* could wish her not to indulge!

Against the interest of her own individual comfort, Mrs. Dashwood had determined that it would be better for Marianne to be anywhere, at that time, than at Barton, where every thing within her view would be bringing back the past in the strongest and most afflicting manner, by constantly placing Willoughby before her, such as she had always seen him there. She recommended it to her daughters, therefore, by all means not to shorten their visit to Mrs. Jennings; the length of which, though never exactly fixed, had been expected by all to comprise at least five or six weeks. A variety of occupations, of objects, and of company, which could not be procured at Barton, would be inevitable there, and might yet, she hoped, cheat Marianne, at times, into some interest beyond herself, and even into some amusement, much as the idea of both might now be spurned by her.

From all danger of seeing Willoughby again, her mother considered her to be at least equally safe in town as in the country, since his acquaintance must now be dropped by all who called themselves her friends. Design could never bring them in each other's way: negligence could never leave them exposed to a surprise; and chance had less in its favour in the croud of London than even in the retirement of Barton, where it might force him before her while paying that visit at Allenham on his marriage, which Mrs. Dashwood, from foreseeing at first as a probable event, had brought herself to expect as a certain one.

She had yet another reason for wishing her children to remain where they were; a letter from her son-in-law had told her that he and his wife were to be in town before the middle of February, and she judged it right that they should sometimes see their brother.

Marianne had promised to be guided by her mother's opinion, and she submitted to it therefore without opposition, though it proved perfectly different from what she wished and expected, though she felt it to be entirely wrong, formed on mistaken grounds, and that by requiring her longer continuance in London it deprived her of the only possible alleviation of her wretchedness, the personal sympathy of her mother, and doomed her to such society and such scenes as must prevent her ever knowing a moment's rest.

But it was a matter of great consolation to her, that what brought evil to herself would bring good to her sister; and Elinor, on the other hand, suspecting that it would not be in her power to avoid Edward entirely, comforted herself by thinking, that though their longer stay would therefore militate against her own happiness, it would be better for Marianne than an immediate return into Devonshire.

Her carefulness in guarding her sister from ever hearing Willoughby's name mentioned, was not thrown away. Marianne, though without knowing it herself, reaped all its advantage; for neither Mrs. Jennings, nor Sir John, nor even Mrs. Palmer herself, ever spoke of him before her. Elinor wished that the same forbearance could have extended towards herself, but that was impossible, and she was obliged to listen day after day to the indignation of them all.

Sir John could not have thought it possible. "A man of whom he had always had such reason to think well! Such a good-natured fellow! He did not believe there was a bolder rider in England! It was an unaccountable business. He wished him at the devil with all his heart. He would not speak another word to him, meet him where he might, for all the world! No, not if it were to be by the side of Barton covert, and they were kept waiting for two hours together. Such a scoundrel of a fellow! such a deceitful dog! It was only the last time they met that he had offered him one of Folly's puppies! and this was the end of it!"

Mrs. Palmer, in her way, was equally angry. "She was determined to drop his acquaintance immediately, and she was very thankful that she had never been acquainted with him at all. She wished with all her heart Combe Magna was not so near Cleveland; but it did not signify, for it was a great deal too far off to visit; she hated him so much that she was resolved never to mention his name again, and she should tell everybody she saw, how good-for-nothing he was."

The rest of Mrs. Palmer's sympathy was shewn in procuring all the particulars in her power of the approaching marriage, and communicating them to Elinor. She could soon tell at what coach-maker's the new carriage was building, by what painter Mr. Willoughby's portrait was drawn, and at what warehouse[1] Miss Grey's clothes might be seen.

The calm and polite unconcern of Lady Middleton on the occasion was an happy relief to Elinor's spirits, oppressed as they often were by the clamorous kindness of the others. It was a great comfort to her, to be sure of exciting no interest in *one* person at least among their circle of friends; a great comfort to know that there was *one* who would meet her without feeling any curiosity after particulars, or any anxiety for her sister's health.

Every qualification[2] is raised at times, by the circumstances of the moment, to more than its real value; and she was sometimes worried down by officious condolence to rate good-breeding as more indispensable to comfort than good-nature.

Lady Middleton expressed her sense of the affair about once every day, or twice, if the subject occured very often, by saying, "It is very shocking indeed!" and by the means of this continual though gentle vent, was able not only to see the Miss Dashwoods from the first without the smallest emotion, but very soon to see them without recollecting a word of the matter; and having thus supported the dignity of her own sex, and spoken her decided censure of what was wrong in the other, she thought herself at liberty to attend to the interest of her own assemblies, and therefore determined (though rather against the opinion of Sir John) that as Mrs. Willoughby would at once be a woman of elegance and fortune, to leave her card with her as soon as she married.

---

[1] *warehouse*: shop (a fashionable term).
[2] *qualification*: quality.

Colonel Brandon's delicate unobtrusive inquiries were never unwelcome to Miss Dashwood. He had abundantly earned the privilege of intimate discussion of her sister's disappointment, by the friendly zeal with which he had endeavoured to soften it, and they always conversed with confidence. His chief reward for the painful exertion of disclosing past sorrows and present humiliations, was given in the pitying eye with which Marianne sometimes observed him, and the gentleness of her voice whenever (though it did not often happen) she was obliged, or could oblige herself to speak to him. *These* assured him that his exertion had produced an increase of good-will towards himself, and *these* gave Elinor hopes of its being farther augmented hereafter; but Mrs. Jennings, who knew nothing of all this, who knew only that the Colonel continued as grave as ever, and that she could neither prevail on him to make the offer himself, nor commission her to make it for him, began, at the end of two days, to think that, instead of Midsummer, they would not be married till Michaelmas,[3] and by the end of a week that it would not be a match at all. The good understanding between the Colonel and Miss Dashwood seemed rather to declare that the honours of the mulberry-tree, the canal, and the yew arbour, would all be made over to *her*; and Mrs. Jennings had for some time ceased to think at all of Mr. Ferrars.

Early in February, within a fortnight from the receipt of Willoughby's letter, Elinor had the painful office of informing her sister that he was married. She had taken care to have the intelligence conveyed to herself, as soon as it was known that the ceremony was over, as she was desirous that Marianne should not receive the first notice of it from the public papers, which she saw her eagerly examining every morning.

She received the news with resolute composure; made no observation on it, and at first shed no tears; but after a short time they would burst out, and for the rest of the day, she was in a state hardly less pitiable than when she first learnt to expect the event.

[3] *Michaelmas*: September 29, the feast of St. Michael the Archangel.

The Willoughbys left town as soon as they were married; and Elinor now hoped, as there could be no danger of her seeing either of them, to prevail on her sister, who had never yet left the house since the blow first fell, to go out again by degrees as she had done before.

About this time, the two Miss Steeles, lately arrived at their cousin's house in Bartlett's Buildings, Holborn,[4] presented themselves again before their more grand relations in Conduit and Berkeley-street;[5] and were welcomed by them all with great cordiality.

Elinor only was sorry to see them. Their presence always gave her pain, and she hardly knew how to make a very gracious return to the overpowering delight of Lucy in finding her *still* in town.

"I should have been quite disappointed if I had not found you here *still*," said she repeatedly, with a strong emphasis on the word. "But I always thought I *should*. I was almost sure you would not leave London yet awhile; though you *told* me, you know, at Barton, that you should not stay above a *month*. But I thought, at the time, that you would most likely change your mind when it came to the point. It would have been such a great pity to have went away before your brother and sister came. And now to be sure you will be in no *hurry* to be gone. I am amazingly glad you did not keep to *your word*."

Elinor perfectly understood her, and was forced to use all her self-command to make it appear that she did *not*.

"Well, my dear," said Mrs. Jennings, "and how did you travel?"

"Not in the stage, I assure you," replied Miss Steele, with quick exultation; "we came post all the way, and had a very smart beau to attend us. Dr. Davies was coming to town, and so we thought we'd join him in a post-chaise; and he behaved very genteelly, and paid ten or twelve shillings more than we did."

[4] *Bartlett's Buildings, Holborn*: actual residential buildings in an area of central London.
[5] *Conduit and Berkeley-street*: an area and residential block in central London, respectively.

"Oh, oh!" cried Mrs. Jennings; "very pretty, indeed! and the Doctor is a single man, I warrant you."

"There now," said Miss Steele, affectedly simpering, "everybody laughs at me so about the Doctor, and I cannot think why. My cousins say they are sure I have made a conquest; but for my part I declare I never think about him from one hour's end to another. 'Lord! here comes your beau, Nancy,' my cousin said t'other day, when she saw him crossing the street to the house. My beau, indeed! said I—I cannot think who you mean. The Doctor is no beau of mine."

"Aye, aye, that is very pretty talking—but it won't do—the Doctor is the man, I see."

"No, indeed!" replied her cousin, with affected earnestness, "and I beg you will contradict it, if you ever hear it talked of."

Mrs. Jennings directly gave her the gratifying assurance that she certainly would *not*, and Miss Steele was made completely happy.

"I suppose you will go and stay with your brother and sister, Miss Dashwood, when they come to town," said Lucy, returning, after a cessation of hostile hints, to the charge.

"No, I do not think we shall."

"Oh, yes, I dare say you will."

Elinor would not humour her by farther opposition.

"What a charming thing it is that Mrs. Dashwood can spare you both for so long a time together!"

"Long a time, indeed!" interposed Mrs. Jennings. "Why, their visit is but just begun!"

Lucy was silenced.

"I am sorry we cannot see your sister, Miss Dashwood," said Miss Steele. "I am sorry she is not well;" for Marianne had left the room on their arrival.

"You are very good. My sister, will be equally sorry to miss the pleasure of seeing you; but she has been very much plagued lately with nervous head-aches, which make her unfit for company or conversation."

"Oh, dear, that is a great pity! but such old friends as Lucy and me!—I think she might see *us*; and I am sure we would not speak a word."

Elinor, with great civility, declined the proposal. Her sister was perhaps laid down upon the bed, or in her dressing gown, and therefore not able to come to them.

"Oh, if that's all," cried Miss Steele, "we can just as well go and see *her*."

Elinor began to find this impertinence too much for her temper; but she was saved the trouble of checking it, by Lucy's sharp reprimand, which now, as on many occasions, though it did not give much sweetness to the manners of one sister, was of advantage in governing those of the other.

Chapter XI

After some opposition, Marianne yielded to her sister's entreaties, and consented to go out with her and Mrs. Jennings one morning for half an hour. She expressly conditioned, however, for paying no visits, and would do no more than accompany them to Gray's in Sackville-street,[1] where Elinor was carrying on a negociation for the exchange of a few old-fashioned jewels of her mother.

When they stopped at the door, Mrs. Jennings recollected that there was a lady at the other end of the street, on whom she ought to call; and as she had no business at Gray's, it was resolved, that while her young friends transacted their's, she should pay her visit and return for them.

On ascending the stairs, the Miss Dashwoods found so many people before them in the room, that there was not a person at liberty to attend to their orders; and they were obliged to wait. All that could be done was, to sit down at that end of the counter which seemed to promise the quickest succession; one gentleman only was standing there, and it is probable that Elinor was not without hope of exciting his politeness to a quicker dispatch. But the correctness of his eye, and the delicacy of his taste, proved to be beyond his politeness. He was giving orders for a toothpick-case for himself, and till its size, shape, and ornaments were determined, all of which, after examining and debating for a quarter of an hour over every toothpick-case in the shop, were finally arranged by his own inventive fancy, he had no leisure to bestow any other attention on the two ladies, than what was comprised in three or four very broad stares; a kind of notice which served to imprint on Elinor the remembrance of a person and face, of strong,

[1] *Gray's in Sackville-street*: actual jeweler in Piccadilly (fashionable West End London) (per Chapman).

natural, sterling insignificance, though adorned in the first style of fashion.

Marianne was spared from the troublesome feelings of contempt and resentment, on this impertinent examination of their features, and on the puppyism[2] of his manner in deciding on all the different horrors of the different toothpick-cases presented to his inspection, by remaining unconscious of it all; for she was as well able to collect her thoughts within herself, and be as ignorant of what was passing around her, in Mr. Gray's shop, as in her own bed-room.

At last the affair was decided. The ivory, the gold, and the pearls, all received their appointment, and the gentleman having named the last day on which his existence could be continued without the possession of the toothpick-case, drew on his gloves with leisurely care, and bestowing another glance on the Miss Dashwoods, but such a one as seemed rather to demand than express admiration, walked off with an happy air of real conceit and affected indifference.

Elinor lost no time in bringing her business forward, and was on the point of concluding it, when another gentleman presented himself at her side. She turned her eyes towards his face, and found him with some surprise to be her brother.

Their affection and pleasure in meeting, was just enough to make a very creditable appearance in Mr. Gray's shop. John Dashwood was really far from being sorry to see his sisters again; it rather gave them satisfaction; and his inquiries after their mother were respectful and attentive.

Elinor found that he and Fanny had been in town two days.

"I wished very much to call upon you yesterday," said he, "but it was impossible, for we were obliged to take Harry to see the wild beasts at Exeter Exchange:[3] and we spent the rest of the day with Mrs. Ferrars. Harry was vastly pleased. *This* morning I had fully intended to call on you, if I could possibly find a spare half hour, but one has always so much to do on first coming to

---

[2] *puppyism*: affectation, conceit.
[3] *Exeter Exchange*: popular menagerie (early zoo).

town. I am come here to bespeak[4] Fanny a seal. But to-morrow I think I shall certainly be able to call in Berkeley-street, and be introduced to your friend Mrs. Jennings. I understand she is a woman of very good fortune. And the Middletons too, you must introduce me to *them*. As my mother-in-law's relations, I shall be happy to shew them every respect. They are excellent neighbours to you in the country, I understand."

"Excellent indeed. Their attention to our comfort, their friendliness in every particular, is more than I can express."

"I am extremely glad to hear it, upon my word; extremely glad indeed. But so it ought to be; they are people of large fortune, they are related to you, and every civility and accommodation that can serve to make your situation pleasant, might be reasonably expected. And so you are most comfortably settled in your little cottage and want for nothing! Edward brought us a most charming account of the place; the most complete thing of its kind, he said, that ever was, and you all seemed to enjoy it beyond any thing. It was a great satisfaction to us to hear it, I assure you."

Elinor did feel a little ashamed of her brother; and was not sorry to be spared the necessity of answering him, by the arrival of Mrs. Jennings's servant, who came to tell her that his mistress waited for them at the door.

Mr. Dashwood attended them down stairs, was introduced to Mrs. Jennings at the door of her carriage, and repeating his hope of being able to call on them the next day, took leave.

His visit was duly paid. He came with a pretence at an apology from their sister-in-law, for not coming too; "but she was so much engaged with her mother, that really she had no leisure for going any where." Mrs. Jennings, however, assured him directly, that she should not stand upon ceremony, for they were all cousins, or something like it, and she should certainly wait on Mrs. John Dashwood very soon, and bring her sisters to see her. His manners to *them*, though calm, were perfectly kind; to Mrs. Jennings most attentively civil; and on Colonel

---

[4] *bespeak*: order.

Brandon's coming in soon after himself, he eyed him with a curiosity which seemed to say, that he only wanted to know him to be rich, to be equally civil to *him*.

After staying with them half an hour, he asked Elinor to walk with him to Conduit-street, and introduce him to Sir John and Lady Middleton. The weather was remarkably fine, and she readily consented. As soon as they were out of the house, his enquiries began.

"Who is Colonel Brandon? Is he a man of fortune?"

"Yes; he has very good property in Dorsetshire."

"I am glad of it. He seems a most gentlemanlike man; and I think, Elinor, I may congratulate you on the prospect of a very respectable establishment in life."

"Me, brother! what do you mean?"

"He likes you. I observed him narrowly, and am convinced of it. What is the amount of his fortune?"

"I believe about two thousand a-year."

"Two thousand a-year;" and then working himself up to a pitch of enthusiastic generosity, he added, "Elinor, I wish, with all my heart, it were *twice* as much, for your sake."

"Indeed I believe you," replied Elinor; "but I am very sure that Colonel Brandon has not the smallest wish of marrying *me*."

"You are mistaken, Elinor; you are very much mistaken. A very little trouble on your side secures him. Perhaps just at present he may be undecided; the smallness of your fortune may make him hang back; his friends may all advise him against it. But some of those little attentions and encouragements which ladies can so easily give, will fix him, in spite of himself. And there can be no reason why you should not try for him. It is not to be supposed that any prior attachment on your side—in short, you know as to an attachment of that kind, it is quite out of the question, the objections are insurmountable—you have too much sense not to see all that. Colonel Brandon must be the man; and no civility shall be wanting on my part, to make him pleased with you and your family. It is a match that must give universal satisfaction. In short, it is a kind of thing that"—lowering his voice to an important whisper—"will be exceedingly welcome to *all parties*." Recollecting himself, however, he added, "That is, I mean to say—your friends are all truly anxious to see you well settled; Fanny particularly, for she has your interest very much at heart, I assure you. And her mother too, Mrs. Ferrars, a very good-natured woman, I am sure it would give her great pleasure; she said as much the other day."

Elinor would not vouchsafe any answer.

"It would be something remarkable now," he continued, "something droll, if Fanny should have a brother and I a sister settling at the same time. And yet it is not very unlikely."

"Is Mr. Edward Ferrars," said Elinor, with resolution, "going to be married?"

"It is not actually settled, but there is such a thing in agitation. He has a most excellent mother. Mrs. Ferrars, with the utmost liberality, will come forward, and settle on him a thousand a-year, if the match takes place. The lady is the Hon. Miss Morton, only daughter of the late Lord Morton, with thirty thousand pounds. A very desirable connection on both sides, and I have not a doubt of its taking place in time. A thousand a-year is a great deal for a mother to give away, to make over for ever; but Mrs. Ferrars has a noble spirit. To give you another instance of her liberality:—The other day, as soon as we came to town, aware that money could not be very plenty with us just now, she put bank-notes into Fanny's hands to the amount of two hundred pounds. And extremely acceptable it is, for we must live at a great expense while we are here."

He paused for her assent and compassion; and she forced herself to say,

"Your expenses both in town and country must certainly be considerable, but your income is a large one."

"Not so large, I dare say, as many people suppose. I do not mean to complain, however; it is undoubtedly a comfortable one, and I hope will in time be better. The inclosure[5] of

---

[5] *inclosure*: The Inclosure Act of 1773 and subsequent Acts of Parliament enabled landowners to enclose lands that were previously open to public use.

Norland Common, now carrying on, is a most serious drain. And then I have made a little purchase within this half year; East Kingham Farm, you must remember the place, where old Gibson used to live. The land was so very desirable for me in every respect, so immediately adjoining my own property, that I felt it my duty to buy it. I could not have answered it to my conscience to let it fall into any other hands. A man must pay for his convenience; and it *has* cost me a vast deal of money."

"More than you think it really and intrinsically worth."

"Why, I hope not that. I might have sold it again the next day, for more than I gave: but with regard to the purchase-money, I might have been very unfortunate indeed; for the stocks were at that time so low, that if I had not happened to have the necessary sum in my banker's hands, I must have sold out to very great loss."

Elinor could only smile.

"Other great and inevitable expenses too we have had on first coming to Norland. Our respected father, as you well know, bequeathed all the Stanhill effects that remained at Norland (and very valuable they were), to your mother. Far be it from me to repine at his doing so; he had an undoubted right to dispose of his own property as he chose. But, in consequence of it, we have been obliged to make large purchases of linen, china, &c. to supply the place of what was taken away. You may guess, after all these expenses, how very far we must be from being rich, and how acceptable Mrs. Ferrars's kindness is."

"Certainly," said Elinor; "and assisted by her liberality, I hope you may yet live to be in easy circumstances."

"Another year or two may do much towards it," he gravely replied; "but however there is still a great deal to be done. There is not a stone laid of Fanny's greenhouse, and nothing but the plan of the flower-garden marked out."

"Where is the green-house to be?"

"Upon the knoll behind the house. The old walnut trees are all come down to make room for it. It will be a very fine object from many parts of the park, and the flower-garden will slope down just before it, and be exceedingly pretty. We have cleared away all the old thorns that grew in patches over the brow."

Elinor kept her concern and her censure to herself; and was very thankful that Marianne was not present, to share the provocation.

Having now said enough to make his poverty clear, and to do away the necessity of buying a pair of ear-rings for each of his sisters, in his next visit at Gray's, his thoughts took a cheerfuller turn, and he began to congratulate Elinor on having such a friend as Mrs. Jennings.

"She seems a most valuable woman indeed.—Her house, her style of living, all bespeak an exceeding good income; and it is an acquaintance that has not only been of great use to you hitherto, but in the end may prove materially advantageous.— Her inviting you to town is certainly a vast thing in your favour; and indeed, it speaks altogether so great a regard for you, that in all probability when she dies you will not be forgotten.— She must have a great deal to leave."

"Nothing at all, I should rather suppose; for she has only her jointure, which will descend to her children."

"But it is not to be imagined that she lives up to her income. Few people of common prudence will do *that*; and whatever she saves, she will be able to dispose of."

"And do you not think it more likely that she should leave it to her daughters, than to us?"

"Her daughters are both exceedingly well married, and therefore I cannot perceive the necessity of her remembering them farther. Whereas, in my opinion, by her taking so much notice of you, and treating you in this kind of way, she has given you a sort of claim on her future consideration, which a conscientious woman would not disregard. Nothing can be kinder than her behaviour; and she can hardly do all this, without being aware of the expectation she raises."

"But she raises none in those most concerned. Indeed, brother, your anxiety for our welfare and prosperity carries you too far."

"Why to be sure," said he, seeming to recollect himself, "people have little, have very little in their power. But, my dear Elinor, what is the matter with Marianne?—she looks very unwell, has lost her colour, and is grown quite thin. Is she ill?"

"She is not well, she has had a nervous complaint on her for several weeks."

"I am sorry for that. At her time of life, any thing of an illness destroys the bloom for ever! Her's has been a very short one! She was as handsome a girl last September, as any I ever saw; and as likely to attract the men. There was something in her style of beauty, to please them particularly. I remember Fanny used to say that she would marry sooner and better than you did; not but what she is exceedingly fond of *you*, but so it happened to strike her. She will be mistaken, however. I question whether Marianne *now*, will marry a man worth more than five or six hundred a-year, at the utmost, and I am very much deceived if *you* do not do better. Dorsetshire! I know very little of Dorsetshire; but, my dear Elinor, I shall be exceedingly glad to know more of it; and I think I can answer for your having Fanny and myself among the earliest and best pleased of your visitors."

Elinor tried very seriously to convince him that there was no likelihood of her marrying Colonel Brandon; but it was an expectation of too much pleasure to himself to be relinquished, and he was really resolved on seeking an intimacy with that gentleman, and promoting the marriage by every possible attention. He had just compunction enough for having done nothing for his sisters himself, to be exceedingly anxious that everybody else should do a great deal; and an offer from Colonel Brandon, or a legacy from Mrs. Jennings, was the easiest means of atoning for his own neglect.

They were lucky enough to find Lady Middleton at home, and Sir John came in before their visit ended. Abundance of civilities passed on all sides. Sir John was ready to like anybody, and though Mr. Dashwood did not seem to know much about horses, he soon set him down as a very good-natured fellow: while Lady Middleton saw enough of fashion in his appearance, to think his acquaintance worth having; and Mr. Dashwood went away delighted with both.

"I shall have a charming account to carry to Fanny," said he, as he walked back with his sister. "Lady Middleton is really a most elegant woman! Such a woman as I am sure Fanny will be glad to know. And Mrs. Jennings too, an exceeding well-behaved woman, though not so elegant as her daughter. Your sister need not have any scruple even of visiting *her*, which, to say the truth, has been a little the case, and very naturally; for we only knew that Mrs. Jennings was the widow of a man who had got all his money in a low way; and Fanny and Mrs. Ferrars were both strongly prepossessed that neither she nor her daughters were such kind of women as Fanny would like to associate with. But now I can carry her a most satisfactory account of both."

Chapter XII

Mrs. John Dashwood had so much confidence in her husband's judgment that she waited the very next day both on Mrs. Jennings and her daughter; and her confidence was rewarded by finding even the former, even the woman with whom her sisters were staying, by no means unworthy her notice; and as for Lady Middleton, she found her one of the most charming women in the world!

Lady Middleton was equally pleased with Mrs. Dashwood. There was a kind of cold hearted selfishness on both sides, which mutually attracted them; and they sympathised with each other in an insipid propriety of demeanour, and a general want of understanding.

The same manners however, which recommended Mrs. John Dashwood to the good opinion of Lady Middleton, did not suit the fancy of Mrs. Jennings, and to *her* she appeared nothing more than a little proud-looking woman of uncordial address, who met her husband's sisters without any affection, and almost without having any thing to say to them; for of the quarter of an hour bestowed on Berkeley-street, she sat at least seven minutes and a half in silence.

Elinor wanted very much to know, though she did not chuse to ask, whether Edward was then in town; but nothing would have induced Fanny voluntarily to mention his name before her, till able to tell her that his marriage with Miss Morton was resolved on, or till her husband's expectations on Colonel Brandon were answered; because she believed them still so very much attached to each other, that they could not be too sedulously[1] divided in word and deed on every occasion. The intelligence however, which *she* would not give, soon flowed from another quarter. Lucy came very shortly to claim Elinor's

---

[1] *sedulously*: with careful perseverance.

compassion on being unable to see Edward, though he had arrived in town with Mr. and Mrs. Dashwood. He dared not come to Bartlett's Buildings for fear of detection, and though their mutual impatience to meet, was not to be told, they could do nothing at present but write.

Edward assured them himself of his being in town, within a very short time, by twice calling in Berkeley-street. Twice was his card found on the table, when they returned from their morning's engagements. Elinor was pleased that he had called; and still more pleased that she had missed him.

The Dashwoods were so prodigiously delighted with the Middletons, that though not much in the habit of giving any thing, they determined to give them—a dinner; and soon after their acquaintance began, invited them to dine in Harley-street,[2] where they had taken a very good house for three months. Their sisters and Mrs. Jennings were invited likewise, and John Dashwood was careful to secure Colonel Brandon, who, always glad to be where the Miss Dashwoods were, received his eager civilities with some surprise, but much more pleasure. They were to meet Mrs. Ferrars; but Elinor could not learn whether her sons were to be of the party. The expectation of seeing *her*, however, was enough to make her interested in the engagement; for though she could now meet Edward's mother without that strong anxiety which had once promised to attend such an introduction, though she could now see her with perfect indifference as to her opinion of herself, her desire of being in company with Mrs. Ferrars, her curiosity to know what she was like, was as lively as ever.

The interest with which she thus anticipated the party, was soon afterwards increased, more powerfully than pleasantly, by her hearing that the Miss Steeles were also to be at it.

So well had they recommended themselves to Lady Middleton, so agreeable had their assiduities made them to her, that

[2] *Harley-street*: This prestigious London street has long been known as home to many medical specialists, but in this case it refers merely to the location of the Dashwood's London house.

though Lucy was certainly not elegant, and her sister not even genteel, she was as ready as Sir John to ask them to spend a week or two in Conduit-street: and it happened to be particularly convenient to the Miss Steeles, as soon as the Dashwoods' invitation was known, that their visit should begin a few days before the party took place.

Their claims to the notice of Mrs. John Dashwood, as the nieces of the gentleman who for many years had had the care of her brother, might not have done much, however, towards procuring them seats at her table; but as Lady Middleton's guests they must be welcome; and Lucy, who had long wanted to be personally known to the family, to have a nearer view of their characters and her own difficulties, and to have an opportunity of endeavouring to please them, had seldom been happier in her life than she was on receiving Mrs. John Dashwood's card.

On Elinor its effect was very different. She began immediately to determine that Edward who lived with his mother, must be asked as his mother was, to a party given by his sister; and to see him for the first time after all that passed, in the company of Lucy!—she hardly knew how she could bear it!

These apprehensions perhaps were not founded entirely on reason, and certainly not at all on truth. They were relieved however, not by her own recollection but by the good will of Lucy, who believed herself to be inflicting a severe disappointment when she told her that Edward certainly would not be in Harley-street on Tuesday, and even hoped to be carrying the pain still farther by persuading her, that he was kept away by that extreme affection for herself, which he could not conceal when they were together.

The important Tuesday came that was to introduce the two young ladies to this formidable mother-in-law.

"Pity me, dear Miss Dashwood!" said Lucy, as they walked up the stairs together—for the Middletons arrived so directly after Mrs. Jennings, that they all followed the servant at the same time—"There is nobody here but you, that can feel for me.—I declare I can hardly stand. Good gracious!—In a moment I shall see the person that all my happiness depends on—that is to be my mother!"—

Elinor could have given her immediate relief by suggesting the possibility of its being Miss Morton's mother, rather than her own, whom they were about to behold; but instead of doing that, she assured her, and with great sincerity, that she did pity her,—to the utter amazement of Lucy, who, though really uncomfortable herself, hoped at least to be an object of irrepressible envy to Elinor.

Mrs. Ferrars was a little, thin woman, upright, even to formality, in her figure, and serious, even to sourness, in her aspect. Her complexion was sallow; and her features small, without beauty, and naturally without expression; but a lucky contraction of the brow had rescued her countenance from the disgrace of insipidity, by giving it the strong characters of pride and ill nature. She was not a woman of many words: for, unlike people in general, she proportioned them to the number of her ideas; and of the few syllables that did escape her, not one fell to the share of Miss Dashwood, whom she eyed with the spirited determination of disliking her at all events.

Elinor could not *now* be made unhappy by this behaviour.—A few months ago it would have hurt her exceedingly; but it was not in Mrs. Ferrars's power to distress her by it now;—and the difference of her manners to the Miss Steeles, a difference which seemed purposely made to humble her more, only amused her. She could not but smile to see the graciousness of both mother and daughter towards the very person—for Lucy was particularly distinguished—whom of all others, had they known as much as she did, they would have been most anxious to mortify; while she herself, who had comparatively no power to wound them, sat pointedly slighted by both. But while she smiled at a graciousness so misapplied, she could not reflect on the mean-spirited folly from which it sprung, nor observe the studied attentions with which the Miss Steeles courted its continuance, without thoroughly despising them all four.

Lucy was all exultation on being so honourably distinguished; and Miss Steele wanted only to be teazed about Dr. Davies to be perfectly happy.

The dinner was a grand one, the servants were numerous, and every thing bespoke the Mistress's inclination for shew, and the Master's ability to support it. In spite of the improvements and additions which were making to the Norland estate, and in spite of its owner having once been within some thousand pounds of being obliged to sell out at a loss, nothing gave any symptom of that indigence which he had tried to infer from it;—no poverty of any kind, except of conversation, appeared—but there, the deficiency was considerable. John Dashwood had not much to say for himself that was worth hearing, and his wife had still less. But there was no peculiar disgrace in this, for it was very much the case with the chief of their visitors, who almost all laboured under one or other of these disqualifications for being agreeable—Want of sense, either natural or improved—want of elegance—want of spirits—or want of temper.

When the ladies withdrew to the drawing-room after dinner, this poverty was particularly evident, for the gentlemen *had* supplied the discourse with some variety—the variety of politics, inclosing land, and breaking horses—but then it was all over; and one subject only engaged the ladies till coffee came in, which was the comparative heights of Harry Dashwood, and Lady Middleton's second son William, who were nearly of the same age.

Had both the children been there, the affair might have been determined too easily by measuring them at once; but as Harry only was present, it was all conjectural assertion on both sides, and everybody had a right to be equally positive in their opinion, and to repeat it over and over again as often as they liked.

The parties stood thus:

The two mothers, though each really convinced that her own son was the tallest, politely decided in favour of the other.

The two grandmothers, with not less partiality, but more sincerity, were equally earnest in support of their own descendant.

Lucy, who was hardly less anxious to please one parent than the other, thought the boys were both remarkably tall for their age, and could not conceive that there could be the smallest difference in the world between them; and Miss Steele, with yet greater address gave it, as fast as she could, in favour of each.

Elinor, having once delivered her opinion on William's side, by which she offended Mrs. Ferrars and Fanny still more, did not see the necessity of enforcing it by any farther assertion; and Marianne, when called on for her's, offended them all, by declaring that she had no opinion to give, as she had never thought about it.

Before her removing from Norland, Elinor had painted a very pretty pair of screens[3] for her sister-in-law, which being now just mounted and brought home, ornamented her present drawing room; and these screens, catching the eye of John Dashwood on his following the other gentlemen into the room, were officiously handed by him to Colonel Brandon for his admiration.

"These are done by my eldest sister," said he; "and you, as a man of taste, will, I dare say, be pleased with them. I do not know whether you ever happened to see any of her performances before, but she is in general reckoned to draw extremely well."

The Colonel, though disclaiming all pretensions to connoisseur-ship, warmly admired the screens, as he would have done any thing painted by Miss Dashwood; and the curiosity of the others being of course excited, they were handed round for general inspection. Mrs. Ferrars, not aware of their being Elinor's work, particularly requested to look at them; and after they had received the gratifying testimony of Lady Middleton's approbation, Fanny presented them to her mother, considerately informing her at the same time, that they were done by Miss Dashwood.

[3] *screens*: i.e., fire screens.

"Hum"—said Mrs. Ferrars—"very pretty,"—and without regarding[4] them at all, returned them to her daughter.

Perhaps Fanny thought for a moment that her mother had been quite rude enough,—for, colouring a little, she immediately said,

"They are very pretty, ma'am—an't they?" But then again, the dread of having been too civil, too encouraging herself, probably came over her, for she presently added,

"Do you not think they are something in Miss Morton's style of painting, ma'am?—*She does* paint most delightfully!—How beautifully her last landscape is done!"

"Beautifully indeed! But *she* does every thing well."

Marianne could not bear this.—She was already greatly displeased with Mrs. Ferrars; and such ill-timed praise of another, at Elinor's expense, though she had not any notion of what was principally meant by it, provoked her immediately to say with warmth,

"This is admiration of a very particular kind!—what is Miss Morton to us?—who knows, or who cares, for her?—it is Elinor of whom *we* think and speak."

And so saying, she took the screens out of her sister-in-law's hands, to admire them herself as they ought to be admired.

Mrs. Ferrars looked exceedingly angry, and drawing herself up more stiffly than ever, pronounced in retort this bitter phillippic;[5] "Miss Morton is Lord Morton's daughter."

Fanny looked very angry too, and her husband was all in a fright at his sister's audacity. Elinor was much more hurt by Marianne's warmth, than she had been by what produced it; but Colonel Brandon's eyes, as they were fixed on Marianne, declared that he noticed only what was amiable in it, the affectionate heart which could not bear to see a sister slighted in the smallest point.

Marianne's feelings did not stop here. The cold insolence of Mrs. Ferrars's general behaviour to her sister, seemed, to her,

[4] *regarding*: looking at.
[5] *phillippic*: tirade, discourse of bitter condemnation.

to foretel such difficulties and distresses to Elinor, as her own wounded heart taught her to think of with horror; and urged by a strong impulse of affectionate sensibility, she moved, after a moment, to her sister's chair, and putting one arm round her neck, and one cheek close to her's, said in a low, but eager, voice.

"Dear, dear Elinor, don't mind them. Don't let them make *you* unhappy."

She could say no more; her spirits were quite overcome, and hiding her face on Elinor's shoulder, she burst into tears.— Every body's attention was called, and almost every body was concerned.—Colonel Brandon rose up and went to them without knowing what he did.—Mrs. Jennings, with a very intelligent "Ah! poor dear," immediately gave her, her salts;[6] and Sir John felt so desperately enraged against the author of this nervous distress, that he instantly changed his seat to one close by Lucy Steele, and gave her, in a whisper, a brief account of the whole shocking affair.

In a few minutes, however, Marianne was recovered enough to put an end to the bustle, and sit down among the rest; though her spirits retained the impression of what had passed, the whole evening.

"Poor Marianne!" said her brother to Colonel Brandon in a low voice, as soon as he could secure his attention,—"She has not such good health as her sister,—she is very nervous,—she has not Elinor's constitution;—and one must allow that there is something very trying to a young woman who *has been* a beauty, in the loss of her personal attractions. You would not think it perhaps, but Marianne *was* remarkably handsome a few months ago; quite as handsome as Elinor.—Now you see it is all gone."

[6] *salts*: i.e., smelling salts.

Chapter XIII

Elinor's curiosity to see Mrs. Ferrars was satisfied.—She had found in her every thing that could tend to make a farther connection between the families, undesirable.—She had seen enough of her pride, her meanness, and her determined prejudice against herself, to comprehend all the difficulties that must have perplexed the engagement, and retarded the marriage, of Edward and herself, had he been otherwise free;—and she had seen almost enough to be thankful for her *own* sake, that one greater obstacle preserved her from suffering under any other of Mrs. Ferrars's creation, preserved her from all dependence upon her caprice, or any solicitude for her good opinion. Or at least, if she did not bring herself quite to rejoice in Edward's being fettered to Lucy, she determined, that had Lucy been more amiable, she *ought* to have rejoiced.

She wondered that Lucy's spirits could be so very much elevated by the civility of Mrs. Ferrars;—that her interest and her vanity should so very much blind her, as to make the attention which seemed only paid her because she was *not Elinor*, appear a compliment to herself—or to allow her to derive encouragement from a preference only given her, because her real situation was unknown. But that it was so, had not only been declared by Lucy's eyes at the time, but was declared over again the next morning more openly, for at her particular desire, Lady Middleton set her down in Berkeley-street on the chance of seeing Elinor alone, to tell her how happy she was.

The chance proved a lucky one, for a message from Mrs. Palmer soon after she arrived, carried Mrs. Jennings away.

"My dear friend," cried Lucy as soon as they were by themselves, "I come to talk to you of my happiness. Could any thing be so flattering as Mrs. Ferrars's way of treating me yesterday? So exceeding affable as she was!—You know how I dreaded

the thoughts of seeing her;—but the very moment I was introduced, there was such an affability in her behaviour as really
should seem to say, she had quite took a fancy to me. Now was
not it so?—You saw it all; and was not you quite struck with
it?"

"She was certainly very civil to you."

"Civil!—Did you see nothing but only civility?—I saw a vast
deal more. Such kindness as fell to the share of nobody but
me!—No pride, no hauteur, and your sister just the same—all
sweetness and affability!"

Elinor wished to talk of something else, but Lucy still pressed
her to own that she had reason for her happiness; and Elinor
was obliged to go on.—

"Undoubtedly, if they had known your engagement," said
she, "nothing could be more flattering than their treatment of
you;—but as that was not the case"—

"I guessed you would say so"—replied Lucy quickly—"but
there was no reason in the world why Mrs. Ferrars should seem
to like me, if she did not, and her liking me is every thing. You
shan't talk me out of my satisfaction. I am sure it will all end
well, and there will be no difficulties at all, to what I used to
think. Mrs. Ferrars is a charming woman, and so is your sister.
They are both delightful women indeed!—I wonder I should
never hear you say how agreeable Mrs. Dashwood was!"

To this, Elinor had no answer to make, and did not attempt
any.

"Are you ill, Miss Dashwood?—you seem low—you don't
speak;—sure you an't well."

"I never was in better health."

"I am glad of it with all my heart, but really you did not look
it. I should be so sorry to have *you* ill; you, that have been the
greatest comfort to me in the world!—Heaven knows what I
should have done without your friendship."—

Elinor tried to make a civil answer, though doubting her own
success. But it seemed to satisfy Lucy, for she directly replied,

"Indeed I am perfectly convinced of your regard for me, and
next to Edward's love, it is the greatest comfort I have.—Poor

Edward!—But now, there is one good thing, we shall be able to meet, and meet pretty often, for Lady Middleton's delighted with Mrs. Dashwood, so we shall be a good deal in Harley-street, I dare say, and Edward spends half his time with his sister—besides, Lady Middleton and Mrs. Ferrars will visit now;—and Mrs. Ferrars and your sister were both so good to say more than once, they should always be glad to see me.—They are such charming women!—I am sure if ever you tell your sister what I think of her, you cannot speak too high."

But Elinor would not give her any encouragement to hope that she *should* tell her sister. Lucy continued.

"I am sure I should have seen it in a moment, if Mrs. Ferrars had took a dislike to me. If she had only made me a formal curtsey, for instance, without saying a word, and never after had took any notice of me, and never looked at me in a pleasant way—you know what I mean,—if I had been treated in that forbidding sort of way, I should have gave it all up in despair. I could not have stood it. For where she *does* dislike, I know it is most violent."

Elinor was prevented from making any reply to this civil triumph, by the door's being thrown open, the servant's announcing Mr. Ferrars, and Edward's immediately walking in.

It was a very awkward moment; and the countenance of each shewed that it was so. They all looked exceedingly foolish; and Edward seemed to have as great an inclination to walk out of the room again, as to advance farther into it. The very circumstance, in its unpleasantest form, which they would each have been most anxious to avoid, had fallen on them—They were not only all three together, but were together without the relief of any other person. The ladies recovered themselves first. It was not Lucy's business to put herself forward, and the appearance of secrecy must still be kept up. She could therefore only *look* her tenderness, and after slightly addressing him, said no more.

But Elinor had more to do; and so anxious was she, for his sake and her own, to do it well, that she forced herself, after a moment's recollection, to welcome him, with a look and manner that were almost easy, and almost open; and another struggle, another effort still improved them. She would not allow the presence of Lucy, nor the consciousness of some injustice towards herself, to deter her from saying that she was happy to see him, and that she had very much regretted being from home, when he called before in Berkeley-street. She would not be frightened from paying him those attentions which, as a friend and almost a relation, were his due, by the observant eyes of Lucy, though she soon perceived them to be narrowly watching her.

Her manners gave some re-assurance to Edward, and he had courage enough to sit down; but his embarrassment still exceeded that of the ladies in a proportion, which the case rendered reasonable, though his sex might make it rare; for his heart had not the indifference of Lucy's, nor could his conscience have quite the ease of Elinor's.

Lucy, with a demure and settled air, seemed determined to make no contribution to the comfort of the others, and would not say a word; and almost every thing that *was* said, proceeded from Elinor, who was obliged to volunteer all the information about her mother's health, their coming to town, &c. which Edward ought to have inquired about, but never did.

Her exertions did not stop here; for she soon afterwards felt herself so heroically disposed as to determine, under pretence of fetching Marianne, to leave the others by themselves: and she really did it, and *that* in the handsomest manner, for she loitered away several minutes on the landing-place, with the most high-minded fortitude, before she went to her sister. When that was once done, however, it was time for the raptures of Edward to cease; for Marianne's joy hurried her into the drawing-room immediately. Her pleasure in seeing him was like every other of her feelings, strong in itself, and strongly spoken. She met him with a hand that would be taken, and a voice that expressed the affection of a sister.

"Dear Edward!" she cried, "this is a moment of great happiness!—This would almost make amends for every thing!"

Edward tried to return her kindness as it deserved, but before such witnesses he dared not say half what he really felt. Again they all sat down, and for a moment or two all were silent; while Marianne was looking with the most speaking tenderness, sometimes at Edward and sometimes at Elinor, regretting only that their delight in each other should be checked by Lucy's unwelcome presence. Edward was the first to speak, and it was to notice Marianne's altered looks, and express his fear of her not finding London agree with her.

"Oh! don't think of me!" she replied, with spirited earnestness, though her eyes were filled with tears as she spoke, "don't think of *my* health. Elinor is well, you see. That must be enough for us both."

This remark was not calculated to make Edward or Elinor more easy, nor to conciliate the good will of Lucy, who looked up at Marianne with no very benignant expression.

"Do you like London?" said Edward, willing to say any thing that might introduce another subject.

"Not at all. I expected much pleasure in it, but I have found none. The sight of you, Edward, is the only comfort it has afforded; and thank Heaven! you are what you always were!"

She paused—no one spoke.

"I think, Elinor," she presently added, "we must employ Edward to take care of us in our return to Barton. In a week or two, I suppose, we shall be going; and, I trust, Edward will not be very unwilling to accept the charge."

Poor Edward muttered something, but what it was, nobody knew, not even himself. But Marianne, who saw his agitation, and could easily trace it to whatever cause best pleased herself, was perfectly satisfied, and soon talked of something else.

"We spent such a day, Edward, in Harley-street yesterday! So dull, so wretchedly dull!—But I have much to say to you on that head, which cannot be said now."

And with this admirable discretion did she defer the assurance of her finding their mutual relatives more disagreeable than ever, and of her being particularly disgusted with his mother, till they were more in private.

"But why were you not there, Edward?—Why did you not come?"

"I was engaged elsewhere."

"Engaged! But what was that, when such friends were to be met?"

"Perhaps, Miss Marianne," cried Lucy, eager to take some revenge on her, "you think young men never stand upon engagements, if they have no mind to keep them, little as well as great."

Elinor was very angry, but Marianne seemed entirely insensible of the sting; for she calmly replied,

"Not so, indeed; for, seriously speaking, I am very sure that conscience only kept Edward from Harley-street. And I really believe he *has* the most delicate conscience in the world; the most scrupulous in performing every engagement however minute, and however it may make against his interest or pleasure. He is the most fearful of giving pain, of wounding expectation, and the most incapable of being selfish, of any body I ever saw. Edward, it is so and I will say it. What! are you never to hear yourself praised!—Then, you must be no friend of mine; for those who will accept of my love and esteem, must submit to my open commendation."

The nature of her commendation, in the present case, however, happened to be particularly ill-suited to the feelings of two thirds of her auditors, and was so very unexhilarating to Edward, that he very soon got up to go away.

"Going so soon!" said Marianne; "my dear Edward this must not be."

And drawing him a little aside, she whispered her persuasion that Lucy could not stay much longer. But even this encouragement failed, for he would go; and Lucy, who would have outstaid him had his visit lasted two hours, soon afterwards went away.

"What can bring her here so often!" said Marianne, on her leaving them. "Could she not see that we wanted her gone!—how teazing to Edward!"

"Why so?—we were all his friends, and Lucy has been the longest known to him of any. It is but natural that he should like to see her as well as ourselves."

Marianne looked at her steadily, and said, "You know, Elinor, that this is a kind of talking which I cannot bear. If you only hope to have your assertion contradicted, as I must suppose to be the case, you ought to recollect that I am the last person in the world to do it. I cannot descend to be tricked out of assurances, that are not really wanted."

She then left the room; and Elinor dared not follow her to say more, for bound as she was by her promise of secrecy to Lucy, she could give no information that would convince Marianne; and painful as the consequences of her still continuing in an error might be, she was obliged to submit to it. All that she could hope, was that Edward would not often expose her or himself to the distress of hearing Marianne's mistaken warmth, nor to the repetition of any other part of the pain that had attended their recent meeting—and this she had every reason to expect.

Chapter XIV

Within a few days after this meeting, the newspapers announced to the world, that the Lady[1] of Thomas Palmer, Esq. was safely delivered of a son and heir; a very interesting and satisfactory paragraph, at least to all those intimate connections who knew it before.

This event, highly important to Mrs. Jennings's happiness, produced a temporary alteration in the disposal of her time, and influenced, in a like degree, the engagements of her young friends; for as she wished to be as much as possible with Charlotte, she went thither every morning as soon as she was dressed and did not return till late in the evening; and the Miss Dashwoods, at the particular request of the Middletons, spent the whole of every day in Conduit-street. For their own comfort, they would much rather have remained, at least all the morning, in Mrs. Jennings's house; but it was not a thing to be urged against the wishes of everybody. Their hours were therefore made over to Lady Middleton and the two Miss Steeles, by whom their company was in fact as little valued, as it was professedly sought.

They had too much sense to be desirable companions to the former; and by the latter they were considered with a jealous eye, as intruding on *their* ground, and sharing the kindness which they wanted to monopolize. Though nothing could be more polite than Lady Middleton's behaviour to Elinor and Marianne, she did not really like them at all. Because they neither flattered herself nor her children, she could not believe them good-natured; and because they were fond of reading, she fancied them satirical: perhaps without exactly knowing what it was to be satirical; but *that* did not signify. It was censure in common use, and easily given.

[1] *Lady*: i.e., wife.

Their presence was a restraint both on her and on Lucy. It checked the idleness of one, and the business of the other. Lady Middleton was ashamed of doing nothing before them, and the flattery which Lucy was proud to think of and administer at other times, she feared they would despise her for offering. Miss Steele was the least discomposed of the three, by their presence; and it was in their power to reconcile her to it entirely. Would either of them, only have given her a full and minute account of the whole affair between Marianne and Mr. Willoughby, she would have thought herself amply rewarded for the sacrifice of the best place by the fire after dinner, which their arrival occasioned. But this conciliation was not granted; for though she often threw out expressions of pity for her sister to Elinor, and more than once dropt a reflection on the inconstancy of beaux before Marianne, no effect was produced, but a look of indifference from the former, or of disgust in the latter. An effort even yet lighter might have made her their friend. Would they only have laughed at her about the Doctor! But so little were they, any more than the others, inclined to oblige her, that if Sir John dined from home, she might spend a whole day without hearing any other raillery on the subject, than what she was kind enough to bestow on herself.

All these jealousies and discontents, however, were so totally unsuspected by Mrs. Jennings, that she thought it a delightful thing for the girls to be together; and generally congratulated her young friends every night, on having escaped the company of a stupid old woman so long. She joined them sometimes at Sir John's, and sometimes at her own house; but wherever it was, she always came in excellent spirits, full of delight and importance, attributing Charlotte's well doing to her own care, and ready to give so exact, so minute a detail of her situation, as only Miss Steele had curiosity enough to desire. One thing *did* disturb her; and of that she made her daily complaint. Mr. Palmer maintained the common, but unfatherly opinion among his sex, of all infants being alike; and though she could plainly perceive at different times, the most striking resemblance between this baby and every one of his relations on both sides, there was no convincing his father of it; no persuading him to believe that it was not exactly like every other baby of the same age; nor could he even be brought to acknowledge the simple proposition of its being the finest child in the world.

I come now to the relation of a misfortune, which about this time befell Mrs. John Dashwood. It so happened that while her two sisters with Mrs. Jennings were first calling on her in Harley-street, another of her acquaintance had dropt in—a circumstance in itself not apparently likely to produce evil to her. But while the imaginations of other people will carry them away to form wrong judgments of our conduct, and to decide on it by slight appearances, one's happiness must in some measure be always at the mercy of chance. In the present instance, this last-arrived lady allowed her fancy so far to outrun truth and probability, that on merely hearing the name of the Miss Dashwoods, and understanding them to be Mr. Dashwood's sisters, she immediately concluded them to be staying in Harley-street; and this misconstruction produced within a day or two afterwards, cards of invitation for them as well as for their brother and sister, to a small musical party at her house. The consequence of which was, that Mrs. John Dashwood was obliged to submit not only to the exceedingly great inconvenience of sending her carriage for the Miss Dashwoods; but, what was still worse, must be subject to all the unpleasantness of appearing to treat them with attention: and who could tell that they might not expect to go out with her a second time? The power of disappointing them, it was true, must always be her's. But that was not enough; for when people are determined on a mode of conduct which they know to be wrong, they feel injured by the expectation of any thing better from them.

Marianne had now been brought by degrees, so much into the habit of going out every day, that it was become a matter of indifference to her, whether she went or not: and she prepared quietly and mechanically for every evening's engagement, though without expecting the smallest amusement from any, and very often without knowing till the last moment, where it was to take her.

To her dress and appearance she was grown so perfectly indifferent, as not to bestow half the consideration on it, during the whole of her toilette,[2] which it received from Miss Steele in the first five minutes of their being together, when it was finished. Nothing escaped *her* minute observation and general curiosity; she saw every thing, and asked every thing; was never easy till she knew the price of every part of Marianne's dress; could have guessed the number of her gowns altogether with better judgment than Marianne herself, and was not without hopes of finding out before they parted, how much her washing cost per week, and how much she had every year to spend upon herself. The impertinence of these kind of scrutinies, moreover, was generally concluded with a compliment, which though meant as its douceur,[3] was considered by Marianne as the greatest impertinence of all; for after undergoing an examination into the value and make of her gown, the colour of her shoes, and the arrangement of her hair, she was almost sure of being told that upon "her word she looked vastly smart, and she dared to say would make a great many conquests."

With such encouragement as this, was she dismissed on the present occasion to her brother's carriage; which they were ready to enter five minutes after it stopped at the door, a punctuality not very agreeable to their sister-in-law, who had preceded them to the house of her acquaintance, and was there hoping for some delay on their part that might inconvenience either herself or her coachman.

The events of the evening were not very remarkable. The party, like other musical parties, comprehended a great many people who had real taste for the performance, and a great many more who had none at all; and the performers themselves were, as usual, in their own estimation, and that of their immediate friends, the first[4] private performers in England.

[2] *toilette*: process of dressing and grooming.
[3] *douceur*: financial inducement or bribe (here, a conciliatory gesture).
[4] *first*: primary, most talented, finest.

As Elinor was neither musical, nor affecting to be so, she made no scruple of turning away her eyes from the grand pianoforté, whenever it suited her, and unrestrained even by the presence of a harp, and a violon-cello, would fix them at pleasure on any other object in the room. In one of these excursive glances she perceived among a group of young men, the very he, who had given them a lecture on toothpick-cases at Gray's. She perceived him soon afterwards looking at herself, and speaking familiarly to her brother; and had just determined to find out his name from the latter, when they both came towards her, and Mr. Dashwood introduced him to her as Mr. Robert Ferrars.

He addressed her with easy civility, and twisted his head into a bow which assured her as plainly as words could have done, that he was exactly the coxcomb she had heard him described to be by Lucy. Happy had it been for her, if her regard for Edward had depended less on his own merit, than on the merit of his nearest relations! For then his brother's bow must have given the finishing stroke to what the ill-humour of his mother and sister would have begun. But while she wondered at the difference of the two young men, she did not find that the emptiness and conceit of the one, put her at all out of charity with the modesty and worth of the other. Why they *were* different, Robert explained to her himself in the course of a quarter of an hour's conversation; for, talking of his brother, and lamenting the extreme *gaucherie*[5] which he really believed kept him from mixing in proper society, he candidly and generously attributed it much less to any natural deficiency, than to the misfortune of a private education; while he himself, though probably without any particular, any material superiority by nature, merely from the advantage of a public school, was as well fitted to mix in the world as any other man.

"Upon my soul," he added, "I believe it is nothing more; and so I often tell my mother, when she is grieving about it. 'My dear Madam,' I always say to her, 'you must make yourself easy.

---

[5] *gaucherie*: French for awkward, embarrassing, or unsophisticated ways.

The evil is now irremediable, and it has been entirely your own doing. Why would you be persuaded by my uncle, Sir Robert, against your own judgment, to place Edward under private tuition,[6] at the most critical time of his life? If you had only sent him to Westminster[7] as well as myself, instead of sending him to Mr. Pratt's, all this would have been prevented.' This is the way in which I always consider the matter, and my mother is perfectly convinced of her error."

Elinor would not oppose his opinion, because, whatever might be her general estimation of the advantage of a public school, she could not think of Edward's abode in Mr. Pratt's family, with any satisfaction.

"You reside in Devonshire, I think"—was his next observation, "in a cottage near Dawlish."[8]

Elinor set him right as to its situation, and it seemed rather surprising to him that anybody could live in Devonshire, without living near Dawlish. He bestowed his hearty approbation however on their species of house.

"For my own part," said he, "I am excessively fond of a cottage;[9] there is always so much comfort, so much elegance about them. And I protest, if I had any money to spare, I should buy a little land and build one myself, within a short distance of London, where I might drive myself down at any time, and collect a few friends about me, and be happy. I advise every body who is going to build, to build a cottage. My friend Lord Courtland came to me the other day on purpose to ask my advice, and laid before me three different plans of Bonomi's.[10] I was to decide on the best of them. 'My dear Courtland,' said I, immediately throwing them all into the fire, 'do not adopt

---

[6] *under private tuition*: Robert puts forward what was a widespread debate over private education (with a tutor at home) or public education.

[7] *Westminster*: prestigious public boarding school (established in 1560 by Queen Elizabeth).

[8] *Dawlish*: coastal town and seaside resort in Devon.

[9] *cottage*: in this case, a *cottage ornés* ("decorated cottage"), a highly stylized construction illustrative of romantic notions of rusticity.

[10] *Bonomi's*: Joseph Bonomi (1739–1808), a fashionable architect.

either of them, but by all means build a cottage.' And that, I fancy, will be the end of it.

"Some people imagine that there can be no accommodations, no space in a cottage; but this is all a mistake. I was last month at my friend Elliott's near Dartford. Lady Elliott wished to give a dance. 'But how can it be done?' said she; 'my dear Ferrars, do tell me how it is to be managed. There is not a room in this cottage that will hold ten couple, and where can the supper be?' I immediately saw that there could be no difficulty in it, so I said, 'My dear Lady Elliott, do not be uneasy. The dining parlour will admit eighteen couple with ease; card-tables may be placed in the drawing-room; the library may be open for tea and other refreshments; and let the supper be set out in the saloon.' Lady Elliott was delighted with the thought. We measured the dining-room, and found it would hold exactly eighteen couple, and the affair was arranged precisely after my plan. So that, in fact, you see, if people do but know how to set about it, every comfort may be as well enjoyed in a cottage as in the most spacious dwelling."

Elinor agreed to it all, for she did not think he deserved the compliment of rational opposition.

As John Dashwood had no more pleasure in music than his eldest sister, his mind was equally at liberty to fix on any thing else; and a thought struck him during the evening, which he communicated to his wife, for her approbation, when they got home. The consideration of Mrs. Dennison's mistake, in supposing his sisters their guests, had suggested the propriety of their being really invited to become such, while Mrs. Jennings's engagements kept her from home. The expense would be nothing, the inconvenience not more; and it was altogether an attention, which the delicacy of his conscience pointed out to be requisite to its complete enfranchisement from his promise to his father. Fanny was startled at the proposal.

"I do not see how it can be done," said she, "without affronting Lady Middleton, for they spend every day with her; otherwise I should be exceedingly glad to do it. You know I am always ready to pay them any attention in my power, as my taking them out this evening shews. But they are Lady Middleton's visitors. How can I ask them away from her?"

Her husband, but with great humility, did not see the force of her objection. "They had already spent a week in this manner in Conduit-street, and Lady Middleton could not be displeased at their giving the same number of days to such near relations."

Fanny paused a moment, and then, with fresh vigour, said,

"My love, I would ask them with all my heart, if it was in my power. But I had just settled within myself to ask the Miss Steeles to spend a few days with us. They are very well behaved, good kind of girls; and I think the attention is due to them, as their uncle did so very well by Edward. We can ask your sisters some other year, you know; but the Miss Steeles may not be in town any more. I am sure you will like them; indeed, you *do* like them, you know, very much already, and so does my mother; and they are such favourites with Harry!"

Mr. Dashwood was convinced. He saw the necessity of inviting the Miss Steeles immediately, and his conscience was pacified by the resolution of inviting his sisters another year; at the same time, however, slyly suspecting that another year would make the invitation needless, by bringing Elinor to town as Colonel Brandon's wife, and Marianne as *their* visitor.

Fanny, rejoicing in her escape, and proud of the ready wit that had procured it, wrote the next morning to Lucy, to request her company and her sister's, for some days, in Harley-street, as soon as Lady Middleton could spare them. This was enough to make Lucy really and reasonably happy. Mrs. Dashwood seemed actually working for her, herself; cherishing all her hopes, and promoting all her views! Such an opportunity of being with Edward and his family was, above all things, the most material to her interest, and such an invitation the most gratifying to her feelings! It was an advantage that could not be too gratefully acknowledged, nor too speedily made use of; and the visit to Lady Middleton, which had not before had any precise limits, was instantly discovered to have been always meant to end in two days time.

When the note was shewn to Elinor, as it was within ten minutes after its arrival, it gave her, for the first time, some share in the expectations of Lucy; for such a mark of uncommon kindness, vouchsafed on so short an acquaintance, seemed to declare that the good will towards her arose from something more than merely malice against herself; and might be brought, by time and address, to do every thing that Lucy wished. Her flattery had already subdued the pride of Lady Middleton, and made an entry into the close heart of Mrs. John Dashwood; and these were effects that laid open the probability of greater.

The Miss Steeles removed to Harley-street, and all that reached Elinor of their influence there, strengthened her expectation of the event.[11] Sir John, who called on them more than once, brought home such accounts of the favour they were in, as must be universally striking. Mrs. Dashwood had never been so much pleased with any young women in her life, as she was with them; had given each of them a needle book,[12] made by some emigrant; called Lucy by her christian name; and did not know whether she should ever be able to part with them.

[11] *event*: outcome.
[12] *needle book*: needle case (shaped like a booklet); made by a French emigrant and purchased as a form of charity.

VOLUME III

VOLUME III

Chapter I

Mrs. Palmer was so well at the end of a fortnight, that her mother felt it no longer necessary to give up the whole of her time to her; and contenting herself with visiting her once or twice a day, returned from that period to her own home, and her own habits, in which she found the Miss Dashwoods very ready to reassume their former share.

About the third or fourth morning after their being thus re-settled in Berkeley-street, Mrs. Jennings, on returning from her ordinary visit to Mrs. Palmer, entered the drawing-room, where Elinor was sitting by herself, with an air of such hurrying importance as prepared her to hear something wonderful; and giving her time only to form that idea, began directly to justify it by saying,

"Lord! my dear Miss Dashwood! have you heard the news!"

"No, ma'am. What is it?"

"Something so strange! But you shall hear it all.—When I got to Mr. Palmer's, I found Charlotte quite in a fuss about the child. She was sure it was very ill—it cried, and fretted, and was all over pimples. So I looked at it directly, and, 'Lord! my dear,' says I, 'it is nothing in the world but the red-gum;'[1] and nurse said just the same. But Charlotte, she would not be satisfied, so Mr. Donavan was sent for; and luckily he happened to be just come in from Harley-street, so he stepped over directly, and as soon as ever he saw the child, he said just as we did, that it was nothing in the world but the red-gum, and then Charlotte was easy. And so, just as he was going away again, it came into my head, I am sure I do not know how I happened to think of it, but it came into my head to ask him if there was any news. So upon that, he smirked, and simpered, and looked

---

[1] *red-gum*: form of teething rash (per Chapman).

grave, and seemed to know something or other, and at last he
said in a whisper, 'For fear any unpleasant report should reach
the young ladies under your care as to their sister's indisposition, I think it advisable to say, that I believe there is no great
reason for alarm; I hope Mrs. Dashwood will do very well.'"

"What! is Fanny ill?"

"That is exactly what I said, my dear. 'Lord!' says I, 'is Mrs.
Dashwood ill?' So then it all came out; and the long and the
short of the matter, by all I can learn, seems to be this. Mr.
Edward Ferrars, the very young man I used to joke with you
about (but however, as it turns out, I am monstrous glad there
never was any thing in it), Mr. Edward Ferrars, it seems, has
been engaged above this twelvemonth to my cousin Lucy!—
There's for you, my dear!—And not a creature knowing a syllable of the matter except Nancy!—Could you have believed
such a thing possible?—There is no great wonder in their liking one another; but that matters should be brought so forward between them, and nobody suspect it! *That* is strange!—I
never happened to see them together, or I am sure I should
have found it out directly. Well, and so this was kept a great
secret, for fear of Mrs. Ferrars, and neither she nor your brother
or sister suspected a word of the matter;—till this very morning, poor Nancy, who, you know, is a well-meaning creature,
but no conjurer,[2] popt it all out. 'Lord!' thinks she to herself,
'they are all so fond of Lucy, to be sure they will make no difficulty about it;' and so, away she went to your sister, who was
sitting all alone at her carpet-work, little suspecting what was
to come—for she had just been saying to your brother, only
five minutes before, that she thought to make a match between
Edward and some Lord's daughter or other, I forget who. So
you may think what a blow it was to all her vanity and pride.
She fell into violent hysterics immediately, with such screams
as reached your brother's ears, as he was sitting in his own
dressing-room down stairs, thinking about writing a letter to
his steward in the country. So up he flew directly, and a terrible

[2] *conjurer*: i.e., one with powers of conjecture or understanding.

scene took place, for Lucy was come to them by that time, little
dreaming what was going on. Poor soul! I pity *her*. And I must
say, I think she was used very hardly; for your sister scolded
like any fury, and soon drove her into a fainting fit. Nancy, she
fell upon her knees, and cried bitterly; and your brother, he
walked about the room, and said he did not know what to do.
Mrs. Dashwood declared they should not stay a minute longer
in the house, and your brother was forced to go down upon *his*
knees too, to persuade her to let them stay till they had packed
up their clothes. *Then* she fell into hysterics again, and he was
so frightened that he would send for Mr. Donavan, and Mr.
Donavan found the house in all this uproar. The carriage was
at the door ready to take my poor cousins away, and they were
just stepping in as he came off; poor Lucy in such a condition,
he says, she could hardly walk; and Nancy, she was almost as
bad. I declare, I have no patience with your sister; and I hope,
with all my heart, it will be a match in spite of her. Lord! what
a taking poor Mr. Edward will be in when he hears of it! To
have his love used so scornfully! for they say he is monstrous
fond of her, as well he may. I should not wonder, if he was to
be in the greatest of a passion!—and Mr. Donavan thinks just
the same. He and I had a great deal of talk about it; and the
best of all is, that he is gone back again to Harley-street, that
he may be within call when Mrs. Ferrars is told of it, for she
was sent for as soon as ever my cousins left the house, for your
sister was sure *she* would be in hysterics too; and so she may, for
what I care. I have no pity for either of them. I have no notion
of people's making such a to-do about money and greatness.
There is no reason on earth why Mr. Edward and Lucy should
not marry; for I am sure Mrs. Ferrars may afford to do very well
by her son, and though Lucy has next to nothing herself, she
knows better than any body how to make the most of every
thing; and I dare say, if Mrs. Ferrars would only allow him five
hundred a-year, she would make as good an appearance with it
as any body else would with eight. Lord! how snug they might
live in such another cottage as yours—or a little bigger—with
two maids and two men; and I believe I could help them to a

housemaid, for my Betty has a sister out of place,[3] that would fit them exactly."

Here Mrs. Jennings ceased, and as Elinor had had time enough to collect her thoughts, she was able to give such an answer, and make such observations, as the subject might naturally be supposed to produce. Happy to find that she was not suspected of any extraordinary interest in it; that Mrs. Jennings (as she had of late often hoped might be the case) had ceased to imagine her at all attached to Edward; and happy above all the rest, in the absence of Marianne, she felt very well able to speak of the affair without embarrassment, and to give her judgment, as she believed, with impartiality on the conduct of every one concerned in it.

She could hardly determine what her own expectation of its event really was; though she earnestly tried to drive away the notion of its being possible to end otherwise at last, than in the marriage of Edward and Lucy. What Mrs. Ferrars would say and do, though there could not be a doubt of its nature, she was anxious to hear; and still more anxious to know how Edward would conduct himself. For *him* she felt much compassion;— for Lucy very little—and it cost her some pains to procure that little;—for the rest of the party none at all.

As Mrs. Jennings could talk on no other subject, Elinor soon saw the necessity of preparing Marianne for its discussion. No time was to be lost in undeceiving her, in making her acquainted with the real truth, and in endeavouring to bring her to hear it talked of by others, without betraying that she felt any uneasiness for her sister, or any resentment against Edward.

Elinor's office was a painful one.—She was going to remove what she really believed to be her sister's chief consolation,—to give such particulars of Edward, as she feared would ruin him for ever in her good opinion,—and to make Marianne, by a resemblance in their situations, which to *her* fancy would seem strong, feel all her own disappointment over again. But

[3] *out of place*: lacking a "situation" or job.

unwelcome as such a task must be, it was necessary to be done, and Elinor therefore hastened to perform it.

She was very far from wishing to dwell on her own feelings, or to represent herself as suffering much, any otherwise than as the self-command she had practised since her first knowledge of Edward's engagement, might suggest a hint of what was practicable to Marianne. Her narration was clear and simple; and though it could not be given without emotion, it was not accompanied by violent agitation, nor impetuous grief.—*That* belonged rather to the hearer, for Marianne listened with horror, and cried excessively. Elinor was to be the comforter of others in her own distresses, no less than in theirs; and all the comfort that could be given by assurances of her own composure of mind, and a very earnest vindication of Edward from every charge but of imprudence, was readily offered.

But Marianne for some time would give credit to neither. Edward seemed a second Willoughby; and acknowledging as Elinor did, that she *had* loved him most sincerely, could she feel less than herself! As for Lucy Steele, she considered her so totally unamiable, so absolutely incapable of attaching a sensible man, that she could not be persuaded at first to believe, and afterwards to pardon, any former affection of Edward for her. She would not even admit it to have been natural; and Elinor left her to be convinced that it was so, by that which only could convince her, a better knowledge of mankind.

Her first communication had reached no farther than to state the fact of the engagement, and the length of time it had existed.—Marianne's feelings had then broken in, and put an end to all regularity of detail; and for some time all that could be done was to soothe her distress, lessen her alarms, and combat her resentment. The first question on her side, which led to farther particulars, was,

"How long has this been known to you, Elinor? has he written to you?"

"I have known it these four months. When Lucy first came to Barton-park last November, she told me in confidence of her engagement."

At these words, Marianne's eyes expressed the astonish-ment, which her lips could not utter. After a pause of wonder, she exclaimed,

"Four months!—Have you known of this four months?"—

Elinor confirmed it.

"What!—while attending me in all my misery, has this been on your heart?—and I have reproached you for being happy!"—

"It was not fit that you should then know how much I was the reverse."—

"Four months!"—cried Marianne again.—"So calm!—so cheerful!—how have you been supported?"—

"By feeling that I was doing my duty.—My promise to Lucy, obliged me to be secret. I owed it to her, therefore, to avoid giving any hint of the truth; and I owed it to my family and friends, not to create in them a solicitude about me, which it could not be in my power to satisfy."

Marianne seemed much struck.—

"I have very often wished to undeceive yourself and my mother," added Elinor; "and once or twice I have attempted it;—but without betraying my trust, I never could have con-vinced you."

"Four months!—and yet you loved him!"—

"Yes. But I did not love only him;—and while the comfort of others was dear to me, I was glad to spare them from knowing how much I felt. Now, I can think and speak of it with little emotion. I would not have you suffer on my account; for I assure you I no longer suffer materially myself. I have many things to support me. I am not conscious of having provoked the disap-pointment by any imprudence of my own, and I have borne it as much as possible without spreading it farther. I acquit Edward of all essential misconduct. I wish him very happy; and I am so sure of his always doing his duty, that though now he may har-bour some regret, in the end he must become so. Lucy does not want sense, and that is the foundation on which every thing good may be built.—And after all, Marianne, after all that is bewitching in the idea of a single and constant attachment, and all that can be said of one's happiness depending entirely on any particular person, it is not meant—it is not fit—it is not possible that it should be so.—Edward will marry Lucy; he will marry a woman superior in person and understanding to half her sex; and time and habit will teach him to forget that he ever thought another superior to *her*."—

"If such is your way of thinking," said Marianne, "if the loss of what is most valued is so easily to be made up by something else, your resolution, your self-command, are, perhaps, a little less to be wondered at.—They are brought more within my comprehension."

"I understand you.—You do not suppose that I have ever felt much.—For four months, Marianne, I have had all this hanging on my mind, without being at liberty to speak of it to a single creature; knowing that it would make you and my mother most unhappy whenever it were explained to you, yet unable to prepare you for it in the least.—It was told me,—it was in a manner forced on me by the very person herself, whose prior engagement ruined all my prospects; and told me, as I thought, with triumph.—This person's suspicions, therefore, I have had to oppose, by endeavouring to appear indifferent where I have been most deeply interested;—and it has not been only once;—I have had her hopes and exultation to listen to again and again.—I have known myself to be divided from Edward for ever, without hearing one circumstance that could make me less desire the connection.—Nothing has proved him unworthy; nor has any thing declared him indifferent to me.—I have had to contend against the unkindness of his sister, and the insolence of his mother; and have suffered the punishment of an attachment, without enjoying its advantages.—And all this has been going on at a time, when, as you too well know, it has not been my only unhappiness.—If you can think me capable of ever feeling—surely you may suppose that I have suffered *now*. The composure of mind with which I have brought myself at present to consider the matter, the consolation that I have been willing to admit, have been the effect of constant and painful exertion;—they did not spring up of themselves;—they did not occur to relieve my spirits at first—No, Marianne.—*Then*, if I had not been bound to silence, perhaps nothing could have kept me entirely—not even what I owed to my dearest friends—from openly shewing that I was *very* unhappy."—

Marianne was quite subdued.—

"Oh! Elinor," she cried, "you have made me hate myself for ever.—How barbarous have I been to you!—you, who have been my only comfort, who have borne with me in all my misery, who have seemed to be only suffering for me!—Is this my gratitude!—Is this the only return I can make you?—Because your merit cries out upon myself, I have been trying to do it away."

The tenderest caresses followed this confession. In such a frame of mind as she was now in, Elinor had no difficulty in obtaining from her whatever promise she required; and at her request, Marianne engaged never to speak of the affair to any one with the least appearance of bitterness;—to meet Lucy without betraying the smallest increase of dislike to her;—and even to see Edward himself, if chance should bring them together, without any diminution of her usual cordiality.—These were great concessions;—but where Marianne felt that she had injured, no reparation could be too much for her to make.

She performed her promise of being discreet, to admiration.— She attended to all that Mrs. Jennings had to say upon the subject, with an unchanging complexion, dissented from her in nothing, and was heard three times to say, "Yes, ma'am."—She listened to her praise of Lucy with only moving from one chair to another, and when Mrs. Jennings talked of Edward's affection, it cost her only a spasm in her throat.—Such advances towards heroism in her sister, made Elinor feel equal to any thing herself.

The next morning brought a farther trial of it, in a visit from their brother, who came with a most serious aspect to talk over the dreadful affair, and bring them news of his wife.

"You have heard, I suppose," said he with great solemnity, as soon as he was seated, "of the very shocking discovery that took place under our roof yesterday."

They all looked their assent; it seemed too awful a moment for speech.

"Your sister," he continued, "has suffered dreadfully. Mrs. Ferrars too—in short it has been a scene of such complicated distress—but I will hope that the storm may be weathered without our being any of us quite overcome. Poor Fanny! she was in hysterics all yesterday. But I would not alarm you too much. Donavan says there is nothing materially to be apprehended; her constitution is a good one, and her resolution equal to any thing. She has borne it all, with the fortitude of an angel! She says she never shall think well of anybody again; and one cannot wonder at it, after being so deceived!—meeting with such ingratitude, where so much kindness had been shewn, so much confidence had been placed! It was quite out of the benevolence of her heart, that she had asked these young women to her house; merely because she thought they deserved some attention, were harmless, well-behaved girls, and would be pleasant companions; for otherwise we both wished very much to have invited you and Marianne to be with us, while your kind friend there, was attending her daughter. And now to be so rewarded! 'I wish with all my heart,' says poor Fanny in her affectionate way, 'that we had asked your sisters instead of them.'"

Here he stopped to be thanked; which being done, he went on.

"What poor Mrs. Ferrars suffered, when first Fanny broke it to her, is not to be described. While she with the truest affection had been planning a most eligible connection for him, was it to be supposed that he could be all the time secretly engaged to another person!—such a suspicion could never have entered her head! If she suspected *any* prepossession elsewhere, it could not be in *that* quarter. '*There*, to be sure,' said she, 'I might have thought myself safe.' She was quite in an agony. We consulted together, however, as to what should be done, and at last she determined to send for Edward. He came. But I am sorry to relate what ensued. All that Mrs. Ferrars could say to make him put an end to the engagement, assisted too as you may well suppose by my arguments, and Fanny's entreaties, was of no avail. Duty, affection, every thing was disregarded. I never thought Edward so stubborn, so unfeeling before. His mother explained to him her liberal designs, in case of his marrying Miss Morton; told him she would settle on him the Norfolk estate, which, clear of land-tax, brings in a good thousand a-year; offered even, when matters grew desperate, to make it twelve hundred; and in opposition to this, if he still persisted in this low connection, represented to him the certain penury that must attend the match. His own two thousand pounds she protested should be his all; she would never see him again; and so far would she be from affording him the smallest assistance, that if he were to enter into any profession with a view of better support, she would do all in her power to prevent his advancing in it."

Here Marianne, in an ecstacy of indignation, clapped her hands together, and cried, "Gracious God! can this be possible!"

"Well may you wonder, Marianne," replied her brother, "at the obstinacy which could resist such arguments as these. Your exclamation is very natural."

Marianne was going to retort, but she remembered her promises, and forbore.

"All this, however," he continued, "was urged in vain. Edward said very little; but what he did say, was in the most determined manner. Nothing should prevail on him to give up his engagement. He would stand to it, cost him what it might."

"Then," cried Mrs. Jennings with blunt sincerity, no longer able to be silent, "he has acted like an honest man! I beg your pardon, Mr. Dashwood, but if he had done otherwise, I should have thought him a rascal. I have some little concern in the business, as well as yourself, for Lucy Steele is my cousin, and I believe there is not a better kind of girl in the world, nor one who more deserves a good husband."

John Dashwood was greatly astonished; but his nature was calm, not open to provocation, and he never wished to offend anybody, especially anybody of good fortune. He therefore replied without any resentment.

"I would by no means speak disrespectfully of any relation of your's, madam. Miss Lucy Steele is, I dare say, a very deserving young woman, but in the present case you know, the connection must be impossible. And to have entered into a secret engagement with a young man under her uncle's care, the son of a woman especially of such very large fortune as Mrs. Ferrars, is perhaps altogether a little extraordinary. In short, I do not mean to reflect upon the behaviour of any person whom you have a regard for, Mrs. Jennings. We all wish her extremely happy, and Mrs. Ferrars's conduct throughout the whole, has been such as every conscientious, good mother, in like circumstances, would adopt. It has been dignified and liberal. Edward has drawn his own lot, and I fear it will be a bad one."

Marianne sighed out her similar apprehension; and Elinor's heart wrung for the feelings of Edward, while braving his mother's threats, for a woman who could not reward him.

"Well, sir," said Mrs. Jennings, "and how did it end?"

"I am sorry to say, ma'am, in a most unhappy rupture:— Edward is dismissed for ever from his mother's notice. He left her house yesterday, but where he is gone or whether he is still in town, I do not know; for *we* of course can make no inquiry."

"Poor young man!—and what is to become of him?"

"What, indeed, ma'am! It is a melancholy consideration. Born to the prospect of such affluence! I cannot conceive a situation more deplorable. The interest of two thousand pounds— how can a man live on it!—and when to that is added the recollection, that he might, but for his own folly, within three months have been in the receipt of two thousand, five hundred a-year, (for Miss Morton has thirty thousand pounds,) I cannot picture to myself a more wretched condition. We must all feel for him; and the more so, because it is totally out of our power to assist him."

"Poor young man!" cried Mrs. Jennings, "I am sure he should be very welcome to bed and board at my house; and so I would tell him if I could see him. It is not fit that he should be living about at his own charge now, at lodgings and taverns."

Elinor's heart thanked her for such kindness towards Edward, though she could not forbear smiling at the form of it.

"If he would only have done as well by himself," said John Dashwood, "as all his friends were disposed to do by him, he might now have been in his proper situation, and would have wanted for nothing. But as it is, it must be out of anybody's power to assist him. And there is one thing more preparing against him, which must be worse than all—his mother has determined, with a very natural kind of spirit, to settle *that* estate upon Robert immediately, which might have been Edward's, on proper conditions. I left her this morning with her lawyer, talking over the business."

"Well!" said Mrs. Jennings, "that is *her* revenge. Everybody has a way of their own. But I don't think mine would be, to make one son independent, because another had plagued me."

Marianne got up, and walked about the room.

"Can any thing be more galling to the spirit of a man," continued John, "than to see his younger brother in possession of an estate which might have been his own? Poor Edward! I feel for him sincerely."

A few minutes more spent in the same kind of effusion, concluded his visit; and with repeated assurances to his sisters that he really believed there was no material danger in Fanny's indisposition, and that they need not therefore be very uneasy about it, he went away; leaving the three ladies unanimous in their sentiments on the present occasion, as far at least as it regarded Mrs. Ferrars's conduct, the Dashwoods' and Edward's.

Marianne's indignation burst forth as soon as he quitted the room; and as her vehemence made reserve impossible in Elinor, and unnecessary in Mrs. Jennings, they all joined in a very spirited critique upon the party.

Chapter II

Mrs. Jennings was very warm in her praise of Edward's conduct, but only Elinor and Marianne understood its true merit. *They* only knew how little he had had to tempt him to be disobedient, and how small was the consolation, beyond the consciousness of doing right, that could remain to him in the loss of friends and fortune. Elinor gloried in his integrity; and Marianne forgave all his offences in compassion for his punishment. But though confidence between them was, by this public discovery, restored to its proper state, it was not a subject on which either of them were fond of dwelling when alone. Elinor avoided it upon principle, as tending to fix still more upon her thoughts, by the too warm, too positive assurances of Marianne, that belief of Edward's continued affection for herself which she rather wished to do away; and Marianne's courage soon failed her, in trying to converse upon a topic which always left her more dissatisfied with herself than ever, by the comparison it necessarily produced between Elinor's conduct and her own.

She felt all the force of that comparison; but not as her sister had hoped, to urge her to exertion now; she felt it with all the pain of continual self-reproach, regretted most bitterly that she had never exerted herself before; but it brought only the torture of penitence, without the hope of amendment. Her mind was so much weakened that she still fancied present exertion impossible, and therefore it only dispirited her more.

Nothing new was heard by them, for a day or two afterwards, of affairs in Harley-street, or Bartlett's Buildings. But though so much of the matter was known to them already, that Mrs. Jennings might have had enough to do in spreading that knowledge farther, without seeking after more, she had resolved from the first to pay a visit of comfort and inquiry to her cousins as soon as she could; and nothing but the hindrance of more visitors than usual, had prevented her going to them within that time.

The third day succeeding their knowledge of the particulars, was so fine, so beautiful a Sunday as to draw many to Kensington Gardens,[1] though it was only the second week in March. Mrs. Jennings and Elinor were of the number; but Marianne, who knew that the Willoughbys were again in town, and had a constant dread of meeting them, chose rather to stay at home, than venture into so public a place.

An intimate acquaintance of Mrs. Jennings joined them soon after they entered the Gardens, and Elinor was not sorry that by her continuing with them, and engaging all Mrs. Jennings's conversation, she was herself left to quiet reflection. She saw nothing of the Willoughbys, nothing of Edward, and for some time nothing of anybody who could by any chance whether grave or gay, be interesting to her. But at last she found herself with some surprise, accosted by Miss Steele, who, though looking rather shy, expressed great satisfaction in meeting them, and on receiving encouragement from the particular kindness of Mrs. Jennings, left her own party for a short time, to join their's. Mrs. Jennings immediately whispered to Elinor,

"Get it all out of her, my dear. She will tell you any thing if you ask. You see I cannot leave Mrs. Clarke."

It was lucky, however, for Mrs. Jennings's curiosity and Elinor's too, that she would tell any thing *without* being asked, for nothing would otherwise have been learnt.

"I am so glad to meet you;" said Miss Steele, taking her familiarly by the arm—"for I wanted to see you of all things in the world." And then lowering her voice, "I suppose Mrs. Jennings has heard all about it. Is she angry?"

"Not at all, I believe, with you."

"That is a good thing. And Lady Middleton, is *she* angry?"

"I cannot suppose it possible that she should."

---

[1] *Kensington Gardens*: The gardens of London's Kensington Palace were, from the eighteenth century, open to the public and highly popular.

"I am monstrous glad of it. Good gracious! I have had such a time of it! I never saw Lucy in such a rage in my life. She vowed at first she would never trim me up a new bonnet, nor do any thing else for me again, so long as she lived; but now she is quite come to,[2] and we are as good friends as ever. Look, she made me this bow to my hat, and put in the feather last night. There now, *you* are going to laugh at me too. But why should not I wear pink ribbons? I do not care if it *is* the Doctor's favourite colour. I am sure, for my part, I should never have known he *did* like it better than any other colour, if he had not happened to say so. My cousins have been so plaguing me!—I declare sometimes I do not know which way to look before them."

She had wandered away to a subject on which Elinor had nothing to say, and therefore soon judged it expedient to find her way back again to the first.

"Well, but Miss Dashwood," speaking triumphantly, "people may say what they chuse about Mr. Ferrars's declaring he would not have Lucy, for it's no such a thing I can tell you; and it's quite a shame for such ill-natured reports to be spread abroad. Whatever Lucy might think about it herself, you know, it was no business of other people to set it down for certain."

"I never heard anything of the kind hinted at before, I assure you," said Elinor.

"Oh! did not you? But it *was* said, I know, very well, and by more than one; for Miss Godby told Miss Sparks, that nobody in their senses could expect Mr. Ferrars to give up a woman like Miss Morton, with thirty thousand pounds to her fortune, for Lucy Steele that had nothing at all; and I had it from Miss Sparks myself. And besides that, my cousin Richard said himself, that when it came to the point, he was afraid Mr. Ferrars would be off; and when Edward did not come near us for three days, I could not tell what to think myself; and I believe in my heart Lucy gave it all up for lost; for we came away from your brother's Wednesday, and we saw nothing of him not all Thursday, Friday, and Saturday, and did not know what was

---

[2] *is quite come to*: has relented, has "come around".

become with him. Once Lucy thought to write to him, but
then her spirit rose against that. However this morning he
came just as we came home from church; and then it all came
out, how he had been sent for Wednesday to Harley-street,
and been talked to by his mother and all of them, and how he
had declared before them all that he loved nobody but Lucy,
and nobody but Lucy would he have. And how he had been so
worried by what passed, that as soon as he had went away from
his mother's house, he had got upon his horse, and rid into the
country some where or other; and how he had staid about at
an inn all Thursday and Friday, on purpose to get the better
of it. And after thinking it all over and over again, he said, it
seemed to him as if, now he had no fortune, and no nothing at
all, it would be quite unkind to keep her on to the engagement,
because it must be for her loss, for he had nothing but two thousand pounds, and no hope of any thing else; and if he was to
go into orders,[3] as he had some thoughts, he could get nothing
but a curacy,[4] and how was they to live upon that?—He could
not bear to think of her doing no better, and so he begged,
if she had the least mind for it, to put an end to the matter
directly, and leave him to shift for himself. I heard him say all
this as plain as could possibly be. And it was entirely for *her*
sake, and upon *her* account, that he said a word about being
off, and not upon his own. I will take my oath he never dropt
a syllable of being tired of her, or of wishing to marry Miss
Morton, or anything like it. But, to be sure, Lucy would not
give ear to such kind of talking; so she told him directly (with
a great deal about sweet and love, you know, and all that—Oh,
la! one can't repeat such kind of things you know)—she told
him directly, she had not the least mind in the world to be
off, for she could live with him upon a trifle, and how little so
ever he might have, she should be very glad to have it all, you
know, or something of the kind. So then he was monstrous

[3] *to go . . . orders*: i.e., to be ordained to the Anglican priesthood.
[4] *curacy*: Curates, assistant clergymen without benefices, frequently served for
absentee incumbents.

happy, and talked on some time about what they should do, and they agreed he should take orders directly, and they must wait to be married till he got a living. And just then I could not hear any more, for my cousin called from below to tell me Mrs. Richardson was come in her coach, and would take one of us to Kensington Gardens; so I was forced to go into the room and interrupt them, to ask Lucy if she would like to go, but she did not care to leave Edward; so I just run up stairs and put on a pair of silk stockings, and came off with the Richardsons."

"I do not understand what you mean by interrupting them," said Elinor; "you were all in the same room together, were not you?"

"No, indeed, not us. La! Miss Dashwood, do you think people make love when any body else is by? Oh for shame!—To be sure you must know better than that. (Laughing affectedly.)—No, no; they were shut up in the drawing-room together, and all I heard was only by listening at the door."

"How!" cried Elinor; "have you been repeating to me what you only learnt yourself by listening at the door? I am sorry I did not know it before; for I certainly would not have suffered you to give me particulars of a conversation which you ought not to have known yourself. How could you behave so unfairly by your sister?"

"Oh, la! there is nothing in *that*. I only stood at the door, and heard what I could. And I am sure Lucy would have done just the same by me; for a year or two back, when Martha Sharpe and I had so many secrets together, she never made any bones of hiding in a closet, or behind a chimney-board,[5] on purpose to hear what we said."

Elinor tried to talk of something else; but Miss Steele could not be kept beyond a couple of minutes, from what was uppermost in her mind.

"Edward talks of going to Oxford soon," said she, "but now he is lodging at No.—, Pall Mall. What an ill-natured woman his mother is, an't she? And your brother and sister were not

[5] *chimney-board*: board used to close up a chimney.

very kind! However, I shan't say anything against them to *you*; and to be sure they did send us home in their own chariot, which was more than I looked for. And for my part, I was all in a fright for fear your sister should ask us for the huswifes[6] she had gave us a day or two before; but however, nothing was said about them, and I took care to keep mine out of sight. Edward have got some business at Oxford, he says; so he must go there for a time; and after *that*, as soon as he can light upon a Bishop, he will be ordained. I wonder what curacy he will get!—Good gracious! (gigling as she spoke) I'd lay my life I know what my cousins will say, when they hear of it. They will tell me I should write to the Doctor, to get Edward the curacy of his new living. I know they will; but I am sure I would not do such a thing for all the world.—'La!' I shall say directly, 'I wonder how you could think of such a thing. *I* write to the Doctor, indeed!'"

"Well," said Elinor, "it is a comfort to be prepared against the worst. You have got your answer ready."

Miss Steele was going to reply on the same subject, but the approach of her own party made another more necessary.

"Oh, la! here come the Richardsons. I had a vast deal more to say to you, but I must not stay away from them not any longer. I assure you they are very genteel people. He makes a monstrous deal of money, and they keep their own coach. I have not time to speak to Mrs. Jennings about it myself, but pray tell her I am quite happy to hear she is not in anger against us, and Lady Middleton the same; and if any thing should happen to take you and your sister away, and Mrs. Jennings should want company, I am sure we should be very glad to come and stay with her for as long a time as she likes. I suppose Lady Middleton won't ask us any more this bout. Good bye; I am sorry Miss Marianne was not here. Remember me kindly to her. La! if you have not got your best spotted muslin on!—I wonder you was not afraid of its being torn."

Such was her parting concern; for after this, she had time only to pay her farewell compliments to Mrs. Jennings before

---

[6] *huswifes*: sewing cases.

her company was claimed by Mrs. Richardson; and Elinor was left in possession of knowledge which might feed her powers of reflection some time, though she had learnt very little more than what had been already foreseen and foreplanned in her own mind. Edward's marriage with Lucy was as firmly determined on, and the time of its taking place remained as absolutely uncertain, as she had concluded it would be;—every thing depended, exactly after her expectation, on his getting that preferment,[7] of which, at present, there seemed not the smallest chance.

As soon as they returned to the carriage, Mrs. Jennings was eager for information; but as Elinor wished to spread as little as possible intelligence that had in the first place been so unfairly obtained, she confined herself to the brief repetition of such simple particulars, as she felt assured that Lucy, for the sake of her own consequence, would chuse to have known. The continuance of their engagement, and the means that were to be taken for promoting its end, was all her communication; and this produced from Mrs. Jennings the following natural remark.

"Wait for his having a living!—aye, we all know how *that* will end;—they will wait a twelvemonth, and finding no good comes of it, will set down upon a curacy of fifty pounds a-year, with the interest of his two thousand pounds, and what little matter Mr. Steele and Mr. Pratt can give her.—Then they will have a child every year! and Lord help 'em! how poor they will be!—I must see what I can give them towards furnishing their house. Two maids and two men indeed!—as I talked of t'other day.—No, no, they must get a stout girl of all works.—Betty's sister would never do for them *now*."

The next morning brought Elinor a letter by the two-penny post from Lucy herself. It was as follows:

Bartlett's Buildings, March.
I hope my dear Miss Dashwood will excuse the liberty I take of writing to her; but I know your friendship for me

[7]*preferment*: appointment to a living.

will make you pleased to hear such a good account of myself
and my dear Edward, after all the troubles we have went
through lately, therefore will make no more apologies, but
proceed to say that, thank God! though we have suffered
dreadfully, we are both quite well now, and as happy as we
must always be in one another's love. We have had great trials, and great persecutions, but however, at the same time,
gratefully acknowledge many friends, yourself not the least
among them, whose great kindness I shall always thankfully
remember, as will Edward too, who I have told of it. I am
sure you will be glad to hear, as likewise dear Mrs. Jennings,
I spent two happy hours with him yesterday afternoon, he would
not hear of our parting, though earnestly did I, as I thought my
duty required, urge him to it for prudence sake, and would have
parted for ever on the spot, would he consent to it; but he said
it should never be, he did not regard his mother's anger, while
he could have my affections; our prospects are not very bright,
to be sure, but we must wait, and hope for the best; he will be
ordained shortly, and should it ever be in your power to recommend him to any body that has a living to bestow, am very
sure you will not forget us, and dear Mrs. Jennings too, trust
she will speak a good word for us to Sir John, or Mr. Palmer,
or any friend that may be able to assist us.—Poor Anne was
much to blame for what she did, but she did it for the best, so I
say nothing; hope Mrs. Jennings won't think it too much trouble to give us a call, should she come this way any morning,
'twould be a great kindness, and my cousins would be proud to
know her.—My paper reminds me to conclude,[8] and begging
to be most gratefully and respectfully remembered to her, and
to Sir John, and Lady Middleton, and the dear children, when
you chance to see them, and love to Miss Marianne,

I am, &c. &c.

As soon as Elinor had finished it, she performed what she
concluded to be its writer's real design, by placing it in the

---

[8] *My paper . . . conclude*: The paper would be folded to serve as its own envelope, so she has run out of writable space.

hands of Mrs. Jennings, who read it aloud with many comments of satisfaction and praise.

"Very well indeed!—how prettily she writes!—aye, that was quite proper to let him be off if he would. That was just like Lucy.—Poor soul! I wish I *could* get him a living with all my heart.—She calls me dear Mrs. Jennings, you see. She is a good-hearted girl as ever lived.—Very well upon my word. That sentence is very prettily turned. Yes, yes, I will go and see her, sure enough. How attentive she is, to think of every body!—Thank you, my dear, for shewing it me. It is as pretty a letter as ever I saw, and does Lucy's head and heart great credit."

Chapter III

The Miss Dashwoods had now been rather more than two months in town, and Marianne's impatience to be gone increased every day. She sighed for the air, the liberty, the quiet of the country; and fancied that if any place could give her ease, Barton must do it. Elinor was hardly less anxious than herself for their removal, and only so much less bent on its being effected immediately, as that she was conscious of the difficulties of so long a journey, which Marianne could not be brought to acknowledge. She began, however, seriously to turn her thoughts towards its accomplishment, and had already mentioned their wishes to their kind hostess, who resisted them with all the eloquence of her good-will, when a plan was suggested, which, though detaining them from home yet a few weeks longer, appeared to Elinor altogether much more eligible than any other. The Palmers were to remove to Cleveland about the end of March, for the Easter holidays; and Mrs. Jennings, with both her friends, received a very warm invitation from Charlotte to go with them. This would not, in itself, have been sufficient for the delicacy of Miss Dashwood;—but it was inforced with so much real politeness by Mr. Palmer himself, as, joined to the very great amendment of his manners towards them since her sister had been known to be unhappy, induced her to accept it with pleasure.

When she told Marianne what she had done, however, her first reply was not very auspicious.

"Cleveland!"—she cried, with great agitation. "No, I cannot go to Cleveland."—

"You forget," said Elinor, gently, "that its situation is not ... that it is not in the neighbourhood of...."

"But it is in Somersetshire.—I cannot go into Somersetshire.—There, where I looked forward to going ... No, Elinor, you cannot expect me to go there."

Elinor would not argue upon the propriety of overcoming such feelings;—she only endeavoured to counteract them by working on others;—and represented it, therefore, as a measure which would fix the time of her returning to that dear mother, whom she so much wished to see, in a more eligible, more comfortable manner, than any other plan could do, and perhaps without any greater delay. From Cleveland, which was within a few miles of Bristol, the distance to Barton was not beyond one day, though a long day's journey; and their mother's servant might easily come there to attend them down; and as there could be no occasion for their staying above a week at Cleveland, they might now be at home in little more than three weeks' time. As Marianne's affection for her mother was sincere, it must triumph, with little difficulty, over the imaginary evils she had started.

Mrs. Jennings was so far from being weary of her guests, that she pressed them very earnestly to return with her again from Cleveland. Elinor was grateful for the attention, but it could not alter their design; and their mother's concurrence being readily gained, every thing relative to their return was arranged as far as it could be;—and Marianne found some relief in drawing up a statement of the hours, that were yet to divide her from Barton.

"Ah! Colonel, I do not know what you and I shall do without the Miss Dashwoods;"—was Mrs. Jennings's address to him when he first called on her, after their leaving her was settled—"for they are quite resolved upon going home from the Palmers;—and how forlorn we shall be, when I come back!—Lord! we shall sit and gape at one another as dull as two cats."

Perhaps Mrs. Jennings was in hopes, by this vigorous sketch of their future ennui, to provoke him to make that offer, which might give himself an escape from it;—and if so, she had soon afterwards good reason to think her object gained; for, on Elinor's moving to the window to take more expeditiously the dimensions of a print, which she was going to copy for her friend, he followed her to it with a look of particular meaning, and conversed with her there for several minutes. The effect of his discourse on the lady too, could not escape her observation, for though she was too honourable to listen, and had even changed her seat, on purpose that she might *not* hear, to one close by the piano forté on which Marianne was playing, she could not keep herself from seeing that Elinor changed colour, attended with agitation, and was too intent on what he said, to pursue her employment.—Still farther in confirmation of her hopes, in the interval of Marianne's turning from one lesson to another, some words of the Colonel's inevitably reached her ear, in which he seemed to be apologizing for the badness of his house. This set the matter beyond a doubt. She wondered indeed at his thinking it necessary to do so;—but supposed it to be the proper etiquette. What Elinor said in reply she could not distinguish, but judged from the motion of her lips that she did not think *that* any material objection;—and Mrs. Jennings commended her in her heart for being so honest. They then talked on for a few minutes longer without her catching a syllable, when another lucky stop in Marianne's performance brought her these words in the Colonel's calm voice,

"I am afraid it cannot take place very soon."

Astonished and shocked at so unlover-like a speech, she was almost ready to cry out, "Lord! what should hinder it?"—but checking her desire, confined herself to this silent ejaculation.

"This is very strange!—sure he need not wait to be older."—

This delay on the Colonel's side, however, did not seem to offend or mortify his fair companion in the least, for on their breaking up the conference soon afterwards, and moving different ways, Mrs. Jennings very plainly heard Elinor say, and with a voice which shewed her to feel what she said,

"I shall always think myself very much obliged to you."

Mrs. Jennings was delighted with her gratitude, and only wondered, that after hearing such a sentence, the Colonel should be able to take leave of them, as he immediately did, with the utmost sang-froid,[1] and go away without making her

---

[1] *sang-froid*: self-possession, even under strain.

any reply!—She had not thought her old friend could have made so indifferent a suitor.

What had really passed between them was to this effect.

"I have heard," said he, with great compassion, "of the injustice your friend Mr. Ferrars has suffered from his family; for if I understand the matter right, he has been entirely cast off by them for persevering in his engagement with a very deserving young woman—Have I been rightly informed?—Is it so?"— Elinor told him that it was.

"The cruelty, the impolitic cruelty,"—he replied, with great feeling—"of dividing, or attempting to divide, two young people long attached to each other, is terrible—Mrs. Ferrars does not know what she may be doing—what she may drive her son to. I have seen Mr. Ferrars two or three times in Harley-street, and am much pleased with him. He is not a young man with whom one can be intimately acquainted in a short time, but I have seen enough of him to wish him well for his own sake, and as a friend of yours, I wish it still more. I understand that he intends to take orders. Will you be so good as to tell him that the living of Delaford, now just vacant, as I am informed by this day's post, is his, if he think it worth his acceptance— but *that*, perhaps, so unfortunately circumstanced as he is now, it may be nonsense to appear to doubt, I only wish it were more valuable.—It is a rectory, but a small one; the late incumbent, I believe, did not make more than 200 *l*.[2] per annum, and though it is certainly capable of improvement, I fear, not to such an amount as to afford him a very comfortable income. Such as it is, however, my pleasure in presenting him to it, will be very great. Pray assure him of it."

Elinor's astonishment at this commission could hardly have been greater, had the Colonel been really making her an offer of his hand. The preferment, which only two days before she had considered as hopeless for Edward, was already provided to enable him to marry;—and *she*, of all people in the world, was

---

[2] *200 l.*: two hundred pounds (equivalent, according to Copeland's estimates, to $16,000).

fixed on to bestow it!—Her emotion was such as Mrs. Jennings had attributed to a very different cause;—but whatever minor feelings less pure, less pleasing, might have a share in that emotion, her esteem for the general benevolence, and her gratitude for the particular friendship, which together prompted Colonel Brandon to this act, were strongly felt, and warmly expressed. She thanked him for it with all her heart, spoke of Edward's principles and disposition with that praise which she knew them to deserve; and promised to undertake the commission with pleasure, if it were really his wish to put off so agreeable an office to another. But at the same time, she could not help thinking that no one could so well perform it as himself. It was an office in short, from which, unwilling to give Edward the pain of receiving an obligation from *her*, she would have been very glad to be spared herself;—but Colonel Brandon, on motives of equal delicacy, declining it likewise, still seemed so desirous of its being given through her means, that she would not on any account make farther opposition. Edward, she believed, was still in town, and fortunately she had heard his address from Miss Steele. She could undertake therefore to inform him of it, in the course of the day. After this had been settled, Colonel Brandon began to talk of his own advantage in securing so respectable and agreeable a neighbour, and *then* it was that he mentioned with regret, that the house was small and indifferent;—an evil which Elinor, as Mrs. Jennings had supposed her to do, made very light of, at least as far as regarded its size.

"The smallness of the house," said she, "I cannot imagine any inconvenience to them, for it will be in proportion to their family and income."

By which the Colonel was surprised to find that *she* was considering Mr. Ferrars's marriage as the certain consequence of the presentation; for he did not suppose it possible that Delaford living could supply such an income, as any body in his style of life would venture to settle on—and he said so.

"This little rectory *can* do no more than make Mr. Ferrars comfortable as a bachelor; it cannot enable him to marry. I am sorry to say that my patronage ends with this; and my interest[3] is hardly more extensive. If, however, by any unforeseen chance it should be in my power to serve him farther, I must think very differently of him from what I now do, if I am not as ready to be useful to him then, as I sincerely wish I could be at present. What I am now doing indeed, seems nothing at all, since it can advance him so little towards what must be his principal, his only object of happiness. His marriage must still be a distant good;—at least, I am afraid it cannot take place very soon.—"

Such was the sentence which, when misunderstood, so justly offended the delicate feelings of Mrs. Jennings; but after this narration of what really passed between Colonel Brandon and Elinor, while they stood at the window, the gratitude expressed by the latter on their parting, may perhaps appear in general, not less reasonably excited, nor less properly worded than if it had arisen from an offer of marriage.

[3] *interest*: influence.

Chapter IV

"Well, Miss Dashwood," said Mrs. Jennings, sagaciously smiling, as soon as the gentleman had withdrawn, "I do not ask you what the Colonel has been saying to you; for though, upon my honour, I *tried* to keep out of hearing, I could not help catching enough to understand his business. And I assure you I never was better pleased in my life, and I wish you joy of it with all my heart."

"Thank you, ma'am," said Elinor. "It *is* a matter of great joy to me; and I feel the goodness of Colonel Brandon most sensibly. There are not many men who would act as he has done. Few people who have so compassionate an heart! I never was more astonished in my life."

"Lord! my dear, you are very modest! I an't the least astonished at it in the world, for I have often thought of late, there was nothing more likely to happen."

"You judged from your knowledge of the Colonel's general benevolence; but at least you could not foresee that the opportunity would so very soon occur."

"Opportunity!" repeated Mrs. Jennings—"Oh! as to that, when a man has once made up his mind to such a thing, somehow or other he will soon find an opportunity. Well, my dear, I wish you joy of it again and again; and if ever there was a happy couple in the world, I think I shall soon know where to look for them."

"You mean to go to Delaford after them I suppose," said Elinor, with a faint smile.

"Aye, my dear, that I do, indeed. And as to the house being a bad one, I do not know what the Colonel would be at, for it is as good a one as ever I saw."

"He spoke of its being out of repair."

"Well, and whose fault is that? why don't he repair it?—who should do it but himself?"

They were interrupted by the servant's coming in, to announce the carriage being at the door; and Mrs. Jennings immediately preparing to go, said—

"Well, my dear, I must be gone before I have had half my talk out. But, however, we may have it all over in the evening, for we shall be quite alone. I do not ask you to go with me, for I dare say your mind is too full of the matter to care for company; and besides, you must long to tell your sister all about it."

Marianne had left the room before the conversation began.

"Certainly, ma'am, I shall tell Marianne of it; but I shall not mention it at present to any body else."

"Oh! very well," said Mrs. Jennings rather disappointed. "Then you would not have me tell it Lucy, for I think of going as far as Holborn to-day."

"No, ma'am, not even Lucy if you please. One day's delay will not be very material; and till I have written to Mr. Ferrars, I think it ought not to be mentioned to any body else. I shall do *that* directly. It is of importance that no time should be lost with him, for he will of course have much to do relative to his ordination."

This speech at first puzzled Mrs. Jennings exceedingly. Why Mr. Ferrars was to be written to about it in such a hurry, she could not immediately comprehend. A few moments' reflection, however, produced a very happy idea, and she exclaimed;—

"Oh ho!—I understand you. Mr. Ferrars is to be the man. Well, so much the better for him. Aye, to be sure, he must be ordained in readiness; and I am very glad to find things are so forward between you. But, my dear, is not this rather out of character? Should not the Colonel write himself?—sure, he is the proper person."

Elinor did not quite understand the beginning of Mrs. Jennings's speech; neither did she think it worth inquiring into; and therefore only replied to its conclusion.

"Colonel Brandon is so delicate a man, that he rather wished any one to announce his intentions to Mr. Ferrars than himself."

"And so *you* are forced to do it. Well, *that* is an odd kind of delicacy! However, I will not disturb you (seeing her preparing to write.) You know your own concerns best. So good bye, my dear. I have not heard of any thing to please me so well since Charlotte was brought to bed."

And away she went; but returning again in a moment,

"I have just been thinking of Betty's sister, my dear. I should be very glad to get her so good a mistress. But whether she would do for a lady's maid, I am sure I can't tell. She is an excellent housemaid, and works very well at her needle. However, you will think of all that at your leisure."

"Certainly, ma'am," replied Elinor, not hearing much of what she said, and more anxious to be alone, than to be mistress of the subject.

How she should begin—how she should express herself in her note to Edward, was now all her concern. The particular circumstances between them made a difficulty of that which to any other person would have been the easiest thing in the world; but she equally feared to say too much or too little, and sat deliberating over her paper, with the pen in her hand, till broken in on by the entrance of Edward himself.

He had met Mrs. Jennings at the door in her way to the carriage, as he came to leave his farewell card; and she, after apologising for not returning herself, had obliged him to enter, by saying that Miss Dashwood was above, and wanted to speak with him on very particular business.

Elinor had just been congratulating herself, in the midst of her perplexity, that however difficult it might be to express herself properly by letter, it was at least preferable to giving the information by word of mouth, when her visitor entered, to force her upon this greatest exertion of all. Her astonishment and confusion were very great on his so sudden appearance. She had not seen him before since his engagement became public, and therefore not since his knowing her to be acquainted with it; which, with the consciousness of what she had been thinking of, and what she had to tell him, made her feel particularly uncomfortable for some minutes. He too was much distressed, and they sat down together in a most promising state of embarrassment.—Whether he had asked her pardon for his intrusion on first coming into the room, he could not recollect; but determining to be on the safe side, he made his apology in form as soon as he could say any thing, after taking a chair.

"Mrs. Jennings told me," said he, "that you wished to speak with me, at least I understood her so—or I certainly should not have intruded on you in such a manner; though at the same time, I should have been extremely sorry to leave London without seeing you and your sister; especially as it will most likely be some time—it is not probable that I should soon have the pleasure of meeting you again. I go to Oxford to-morrow."

"You would not have gone, however," said Elinor recovering herself, and determined to get over what she so much dreaded as soon as possible, "without receiving our good wishes, even if we had not been able to give them in person. Mrs. Jennings was quite right in what she said. I have something of consequence to inform you of, which I was on the point of communicating by paper. I am charged with a most agreeable office, (breathing rather faster than usual as she spoke.) Colonel Brandon, who was here only ten minutes ago, has desired me to say that, understanding you mean to take orders, he has great pleasure in offering you the living of Delaford, now just vacant, and only wishes it were more valuable. Allow me to congratulate you on having so respectable and well-judging a friend, and to join in his wish that the living—it is about two hundred a-year—were much more considerable, and such as might better enable you to—as might be more than a temporary accommodation to yourself—such in short, as might establish all your views of happiness."

What Edward felt, as he could not say it himself, it cannot be expected that any one else should say for him. He *looked* all the astonishment which such unexpected, such unthought-of information could not fail of exciting; but he said only these two words,

"Colonel Brandon!"

"Yes," continued Elinor, gathering more resolution, as some of the worst was over; "Colonel Brandon means it as a testimony of his concern for what has lately passed—for the cruel situation in which the unjustifiable conduct of your family has placed you—a concern which I am sure Marianne, myself, and all your friends must share; and likewise as a proof of his high esteem for your general character, and his particular approbation of your behaviour on the present occasion."

"Colonel Brandon give *me* a living!—Can it be possible?"

"The unkindness of your own relations has made you astonished to find friendship any where."

"No," replied he, with sudden consciousness, "not to find it in you; for I cannot be ignorant that to you, to your goodness I owe it all.—I feel it—I would express it if I could—but, as you well know, I am no orator."

"You are very much mistaken. I do assure you that you owe it entirely, at least almost entirely, to your own merit, and Colonel Brandon's discernment of it. I have had no hand in it. I did not even know, till I understood his design, that the living was vacant; nor had it ever occurred to me that he might have had such a living in his gift. As a friend of mine, of my family, he may perhaps—indeed I know he *has*, still greater pleasure in bestowing it; but, upon my word, you owe nothing to my solicitation."

Truth obliged her to acknowledge some small share in the action, but she was at the same time so unwilling to appear as the benefactress of Edward, that she acknowledged it with hesitation; which probably contributed to fix that suspicion in his mind which had recently entered it. For a short time he sat deep in thought, after Elinor had ceased to speak;—at last, and as if it were rather an effort, he said,

"Colonel Brandon seems a man of great worth and respectability. I have always heard him spoken of as such, and your brother I know esteems him highly. He is undoubtedly a sensible man, and in his manners perfectly the gentleman."

"Indeed," replied Elinor, "I believe that you will find him, on farther acquaintance, all that you have heard him to be; and as you will be such very near neighbours, (for I understand the parsonage is almost close to the mansion-house,) it is particularly important that he *should* be all this."

Edward made no answer; but when she had turned away her head, gave her a look so serious, so earnest, so uncheerful, as seemed to say, that he might hereafter wish the distance between the parsonage and the mansion-house much greater.

"Colonel Brandon, I think, lodges in St. James's-street," said he, soon afterwards, rising from his chair.

Elinor told him the number of the house.

"I must hurry away then, to give him those thanks which you will not allow me to give *you*; to assure him that he has made me a very—an exceedingly happy man."

Elinor did not offer to detain him; and they parted, with a very earnest assurance on *her* side of her unceasing good wishes for his happiness in every change of situation that might befal him; on *his*, with rather an attempt to return the same good will, than the power of expressing it.

"When I see him again," said Elinor to herself, as the door shut him out, "I shall see him the husband of Lucy."

And with this pleasing anticipation, she sat down to reconsider the past, recal the words and endeavour to comprehend all the feelings of Edward; and, of course, to reflect on her own with discontent.[1]

When Mrs. Jennings came home, though she returned from seeing people whom she had never seen before, and of whom therefore she must have a great deal to say, her mind was so much more occupied by the important secret in her possession, than by anything else, that she reverted to it again as soon as Elinor appeared.

"Well, my dear," she cried, "I sent you up the young man. Did not I do right?—And I suppose you had no great difficulty—You did not find him very unwilling to accept your proposal?"

"No, ma'am; *that* was not very likely."

---

[1] *discontent:* discontentment, dissatisfaction.

"Well, and how soon will he be ready?—For it seems all to depend upon that."

"Really," said Elinor, "I know so little of these kind of forms, that I can hardly even conjecture as to the time, or the preparation necessary; but I suppose two or three months will complete his ordination."

"Two or three months!" cried Mrs. Jennings; "Lord! my dear, how calmly you talk of it; and can the Colonel wait two or three months! Lord bless me!—I am sure it would put *me* quite out of patience!—And though one would be very glad to do a kindness by poor Mr. Ferrars, I do think it is not worth while to wait two or three months for him. Sure, somebody else might be found that would do as well; somebody that is in orders already."

"My dear ma'am," said Elinor "what can you be thinking of?—Why, Colonel Brandon's only object is to be of use to Mr. Ferrars."

"Lord bless you, my dear!—Sure you do not mean to persuade me that the Colonel only marries you for the sake of giving ten guineas to Mr. Ferrars!"

The deception could not continue after this; and an explanation immediately took place; by which both gained considerable amusement for the moment, without any material loss of happiness to either, for Mrs. Jennings only exchanged one form of delight for another, and still without forfeiting her expectation of the first.

"Aye, aye, the parsonage is but a small one," said she, after the first ebullition of surprise and satisfaction was over, "and very likely *may* be out of repair; but to hear a man apologising, as I thought, for a house that to my knowledge has five sitting rooms on the ground-floor, and I think the housekeeper told me, could make up fifteen beds!—and to you too, that had been used to live in Barton cottage!—It seemed quite ridiculous. But, my dear, we must touch up[2] the Colonel to do

---

[2] *touch up*: stimulate, inspire (from "touching up" a horse with a whip to inspire the horse to move).

something to the parsonage, and make it comfortable for them, before Lucy goes to it."

"But Colonel Brandon does not seem to have any idea of the living's being enough to allow them to marry."

"The Colonel is a ninny, my dear; because he has two thousand a-year himself, he thinks that nobody else can marry on less. Take my word for it, that, if I am alive, I shall be paying a visit at Delaford Parsonage before Michaelmas; and I am sure I sha'nt go if Lucy an't there."

Elinor was quite of her opinion, as to the probability of their not waiting for any thing more.

Chapter V

Edward, having carried his thanks to Colonel Brandon, proceeded with his happiness to Lucy; and such was the excess of it by the time he reached Bartlett's Buildings, that she was able to assure Mrs. Jennings, who called on her again the next day with her congratulations, that she had never seen him in such spirits before in her life.

Her own happiness, and her own spirits, were at least very certain; and she joined Mrs. Jennings most heartily in her expectation of their being all comfortably together in Delaford Parsonage before Michaelmas. So far was she, at the same time, from any backwardness to give Elinor that credit which Edward *would* give her, that she spoke of her friendship for them both with the most grateful warmth, was ready to own all their obligation to her, and openly declared that no exertion for their good on Miss Dashwood's part, either present or future, would ever surprise her, for she believed her capable of doing anything in the world for those she really valued. As for Colonel Brandon, she was not only ready to worship him as a saint, but was moreover truly anxious that he should be treated as one in all worldly concerns; anxious that his tythes[1] should be raised to the utmost; and secretly resolved to avail herself, at Delaford, as far as she possibly could, of his servants, his carriage, his cows, and his poultry.

It was now above a week since John Dashwood had called in Berkeley-street, and as since that time no notice had been taken by them of his wife's indisposition, beyond one verbal inquiry, Elinor began to feel it necessary to pay her a visit.— This was an obligation, however, which not only opposed

[1] *tythes*: A minister was morally entitled to one-tenth of farmers' produce.

her own inclination, but which had not the assistance of any encouragement from her companions. Marianne, not contented with absolutely refusing to go herself, was very urgent to prevent her sister's going at all; and Mrs. Jennings, though her carriage was always at Elinor's service, so very much disliked Mrs. John Dashwood, that not even her curiosity to see how she looked after the late discovery, nor her strong desire to affront her by taking Edward's part, could overcome her unwillingness to be in her company again. The consequence was, that Elinor set out by herself to pay a visit, for which no one could really have less inclination, and to run the risk of a tête-à-tête[2] with a woman, whom neither of the others had so much reason to dislike.

Mrs. Dashwood was denied;[3] but before the carriage could turn from the house, her husband accidentally came out. He expressed great pleasure in meeting Elinor, told her that he had been just going to call in Berkeley-street, and assuring her that Fanny would be very glad to see her, invited her to come in.

They walked up stairs into the drawing-room.—Nobody was there.

"Fanny is in her own room, I suppose," said he;—"I will go to her presently, for I am sure she will not have the least objection in the world to seeing *you*.—Very far from it indeed. *Now* especially there cannot be—but however, you and Marianne were always great favourites.—Why would not Marianne come?"—

Elinor made what excuse she could for her.

"I am not sorry to see you alone," he replied, "for I have a good deal to say to you. This living of Colonel Brandon's—can it be true?—has he really given it to Edward?—I heard it yesterday by chance, and was coming to you on purpose to inquire farther about it."

"It is perfectly true.—Colonel Brandon has given the living of Delaford to Edward."

---

[2] *tête-à-tête*: private conversation between two people.
[3] *denied*: She has declared herself to be "not at home" (i.e., not open to receiving guests).

"Really!—Well, this is very astonishing!—no relationship! —no connection between them!—and now that livings fetch such a price!⁴—what was the value of this?"

"About two hundred a-year."

"Very well—and for the next presentation to a living of that value—supposing the late incumbent to have been old and sickly, and likely to vacate it soon—he might have got I dare say—fourteen hundred pounds. And how came he not to have settled that matter before this person's death?—*Now* indeed it would be too late to sell it, but a man of Colonel Brandon's sense!—I wonder he should be so improvident in a point of such common, such natural, concern!—Well, I am convinced that there is a vast deal of inconsistency in almost every human char-acter. I suppose, however—on recollection—that the case may probably be *this*. Edward is only to hold the living till the per-son to whom the Colonel has really sold the presentation, is old enough to take it.—Aye, aye, that is the fact, depend upon it."

Elinor contradicted it, however, very positively; and by relating that she had herself been employed in conveying the offer from Colonel Brandon to Edward, and therefore must understand the terms on which it was given, obliged him to submit to her authority.

"It is truly astonishing!"—he cried, after hearing what she said—"what could be the Colonel's motive?"

"A very simple one—to be of use to Mr. Ferrars."

"Well, well; whatever Colonel Brandon may be, Edward is a very lucky man!—You will not mention the matter to Fanny, however, for though I have broke it to her, and she bears it vastly well,—she will not like to hear it much talked of."

Elinor had some difficulty here to refrain from observing, that she thought Fanny might have borne with composure, an acquisition of wealth to her brother, by which neither she nor her child could be possibly impoverished.

"Mrs. Ferrars," added he, lowering his voice to the tone becoming so important a subject, "knows nothing about it at

⁴ *such a price*: When livings did not pass directly to "youngest sons" in a family, they could be sold by the patron.

present, and I believe it will be best to keep it entirely concealed from her as long as may be.—When the marriage takes place, I fear she must hear of it all."

"But why should such precaution be used?—Though it is not to be supposed that Mrs. Ferrars can have the smallest satisfaction in knowing that her son has money enough to live upon,—for *that* must be quite out of the question; yet why, after her late behaviour, is she supposed to feel at all?—she has done with her son, she has cast him off for ever, and has made all those over whom she had any influence, cast him off likewise. Surely, after doing so, she cannot be imagined liable to any impression of sorrow or of joy on his account—she cannot be interested in any thing that befalls him.—She would not be so weak as to throw away the comfort of a child, and yet retain the anxiety of a parent!"

"Ah! Elinor," said John, "your reasoning is very good, but it is founded on ignorance of human nature. When Edward's unhappy match takes place, depend upon it his mother will feel as much as if she had never discarded him; and therefore every circumstance that may accelerate that dreadful event, must be concealed from her as much as possible. Mrs. Ferrars can never forget that Edward is her son."

"You surprise me; I should think it must nearly have escaped her memory by *this* time."

"You wrong her exceedingly. Mrs. Ferrars is one of the most affectionate mothers in the world."

Elinor was silent.

"We think *now*"—said Mr. Dashwood, after a short pause, "of *Robert's* marrying Miss Morton."

Elinor, smiling at the grave and decisive importance of her brother's tone, calmly replied,

"The lady, I suppose, has no choice in the affair."

"Choice!—how do you mean?"—

"I only mean, that I suppose from your manner of speaking, it must be the same to Miss Morton whether she marry Edward or Robert."

"Certainly, there can be no difference; for Robert will now to all intents and purposes be considered as the eldest son;—and as to any thing else, they are both very agreeable young men, I do not know that one is superior to the other."

Elinor said no more, and John was also for a short time silent.—His reflections ended thus.

"Of *one* thing, my dear sister," kindly taking her hand, and speaking in an awful whisper—"I may assure you;—and I *will* do it, because I know it must gratify you. I have good reason to think—indeed I have it from the best authority, or I should not repeat it, for otherwise it would be very wrong to say any thing about it—but I have it from the very best authority— not that I ever precisely heard Mrs. Ferrars say it herself—but her daughter *did*, and I have it from her—That in short, what- ever objections there might be against a certain—a certain connection—you understand me—it would have been far pref- erable to her, it would not have given her half the vexation that *this* does. I was exceedingly pleased to hear that Mrs. Ferrars considered it in that light—a very gratifying circumstance you know to us all. 'It would have been beyond comparison,' she said, 'the least evil of the two, and she would be glad to com- pound *now* for nothing worse.' But however, all that is quite out of the question—not to be thought of or mentioned—as to any attachment you know—it never could be—all that is gone by. But I thought I would just tell you of this, because I knew how much it must please you. Not that you have any rea- son to regret, my dear Elinor. There is no doubt of your doing exceedingly well—quite as well, or better, perhaps, all things considered. Has Colonel Brandon been with you lately?"

Elinor had heard enough, if not to gratify her vanity, and raise her self-importance, to agitate her nerves and fill her mind;— and she was therefore glad to be spared from the necessity of saying much in reply herself, and from the danger of hearing any thing more from her brother, by the entrance of Mr. Robert Ferrars. After a few moments' chat, John Dashwood, recollect- ing that Fanny was yet uninformed of his sister's being there, quitted the room in quest of her; and Elinor was left to improve her acquaintance with Robert, who, by the gay unconcern, the happy self-complacency of his manner while enjoying so unfair a division of his mother's love and liberality, to the prejudice of his banished brother, earned only by his own dissipated course of life, and that brother's integrity, was confirming her most unfavourable opinion of his head and heart.

They had scarcely been two minutes by themselves, before he began to speak of Edward; for he too had heard of the living, and was very inquisitive on the subject. Elinor repeated the particulars of it, as she had given them to John; and their effect on Robert, though very different, was not less striking than it had been on *him*. He laughed most immoderately. The idea of Edward's being a clergyman, and living in a small parsonage-house, diverted him beyond measure;—and when to that was added the fanciful imagery of Edward reading prayers in a white surplice, and publishing the banns of marriage between John Smith and Mary Brown, he could conceive nothing more ridiculous.

Elinor, while she waited in silence, and immovable gravity, the conclusion of such folly, could not restrain her eyes from being fixed on him with a look that spoke all the contempt it excited. It was a look, however, very well bestowed, for it relieved her own feelings, and gave no intelligence to him. He was recalled from wit to wisdom, not by any reproof of her's, but by his own sensibility.

"We may treat it as a joke," said he at last, recovering from the affected laugh which had considerably lengthened out the genuine gaiety of the moment—"but upon my soul, it is a most serious business. Poor Edward! he is ruined for ever. I am extremely sorry for it—for I know him to be a very good-hearted creature; as well-meaning a fellow perhaps, as any in the world. You must not judge of him, Miss Dashwood, from *your* slight acquaintance.—Poor Edward!—His manners are certainly not the happiest in nature.—But we are not all born, you know, with the same powers—the same address.—Poor fellow!—to see him in a circle of strangers!—to be sure it was pitiable enough!—but, upon my soul, I believe he has as good a heart as any in the kingdom; and I declare and protest to you I never was so shocked in my life, as when it all burst forth.

I could not believe it.—My mother was the first person who told me of it, and I, feeling myself called on to act with resolution, immediately said to her, 'My dear madam, I do not know what you may intend to do on the occasion, but as for myself, I must say, that if Edward does marry this young woman, *I* never will see him again.' That was what I said immediately,—I was most uncommonly shocked indeed!—Poor Edward!—he has done for himself completely—shut himself out for ever from all decent society!—but, as I directly said to my mother, I am not in the least surprised at it; from his style of education it was always to be expected. My poor mother was half frantic."

"Have you ever seen the lady?"

"Yes; once, while she was staying in this house, I happened to drop in for ten minutes; and I saw quite enough of her. The merest awkward country girl, without style, or elegance, and almost without beauty—I remember her perfectly. Just the kind of girl I should suppose likely to captivate poor Edward. I offered immediately, as soon as my mother related the affair to me, to talk to him myself, and dissuade him from the match; but it was too late *then*, I found, to do any thing, for unluckily, I was not in the way[5] at first, and knew nothing of it till after the breach had taken place, when it was not for me, you know, to interfere. But had I been informed of it a few hours earlier—I think it is most probable—that something might have been hit on. I certainly should have represented it to Edward in a very strong light. 'My dear fellow,' I should have said, 'consider what you are doing. You are making a most disgraceful connection, and such a one as your family are unanimous in disapproving.' I cannot help thinking, in short, that means might have been found. But now it is all too late. He must be starved, you know;—that is certain; absolutely starved."

He had just settled this point with great composure, when the entrance of Mrs. John Dashwood put an end to the subject. But though *she* never spoke of it out of her own family, Elinor could see its influence on her mind, in the something

---

[5] *in the way*: i.e., in the way of knowing.

like confusion of countenance with which she entered, and an attempt at cordiality in her behaviour to herself. She even proceeded so far as to be concerned to find that Elinor and her sister were so soon to leave town, as she had hoped to see more of them;—an exertion in which her husband, who attended her into the room, and hung enamoured over her accents, seemed to distinguish every thing that was most affectionate and graceful.

Chapter VI

One other short call in Harley-street, in which Elinor received her brother's congratulations on their travelling so far towards Barton without any expense, and on Colonel Brandon's being to follow them to Cleveland in a day or two, completed the intercourse of the brother and sisters in town;—and a faint invitation from Fanny, to come to Norland whenever it should happen to be in their way, which of all things was the most unlikely to occur, with a more warm, though less public, assurance, from John to Elinor, of the promptitude with which he should come to see her at Delaford, was all that foretold any meeting in the country.

It amused her to observe that all her friends seemed determined to send her to Delaford;—a place, in which, of all others, she would now least chuse to visit, or wish to reside; for not only was it considered as her future home by her brother and Mrs. Jennings, but even Lucy, when they parted, gave her a pressing invitation to visit her there.

Very early in April, and tolerably early in the day, the two parties from Hanover-square and Berkeley-street set out from their respective homes, to meet, by appointment, on the road. For the convenience of Charlotte and her child, they were to be more than two days on their journey, and Mr. Palmer, travelling more expeditiously with Colonel Brandon, was to join them at Cleveland soon after their arrival.

Marianne, few as had been her hours of comfort in London, and eager as she had long been to quit it, could not, when it came to the point, bid adieu to the house in which she had for the last time enjoyed those hopes, and that confidence, in Willoughby, which were now extinguished for ever, without great pain. Nor could she leave the place in which Willoughby remained, busy in new engagements, and new schemes, in which *she* could have no share, without shedding many tears.

Elinor's satisfaction at the moment of removal, was more positive. She had no such object for her lingering thoughts to fix on, she left no creature behind, from whom it would give her a moment's regret to be divided for ever, she was pleased to be free herself from the persecution of Lucy's friendship, she was grateful for bringing her sister away unseen by Willoughby since his marriage, and she looked forward with hope to what a few months of tranquility at Barton might do towards restoring Marianne's peace of mind, and confirming her own.

Their journey was safely performed. The second day brought them into the cherished, or the prohibited, county of Somerset, for as such was it dwelt on by turns in Marianne's imagination; and in the forenoon of the third they drove up to Cleveland.

Cleveland was a spacious, modern-built house, situated on a sloping lawn. It had no park,[1] but the pleasure-grounds[2] were tolerably extensive; and like every other place of the same degree of importance, it had its open shrubbery, and closer wood walk, a road of smooth gravel winding round a plantation, led to the front, the lawn was dotted over with timber, the house itself was under the guardianship of the fir, the mountain-ash, and the acacia, and a thick screen of them altogether, interspersed with tall Lombardy poplars, shut out the offices.

Marianne entered the house with an heart swelling with emotion from the consciousness of being only eighty miles from Barton, and not thirty from Combe Magna; and before she had been five minutes within its walls, while the others were busily helping Charlotte shew her child to the housekeeper, she quitted it again, stealing away through the winding shrubberies, now just beginning to be in beauty, to gain a distant eminence; where, from its Grecian temple,[3] her eye, wandering over a wide tract of country to the south-east, could fondly rest on the farthest ridge of hills in the horizon, and fancy that from their summits Combe Magna might be seen.

[1] *park*: land surrounding a country house, with woods, lakes, and pasturage.
[2] *pleasure-grounds*: piece of land adapted for lawn games, etc.
[3] *Grecian temple*: pseudoclassical building, a popular affectation among certain circles.

In such moments of precious, of invaluable misery, she rejoiced in tears of agony to be at Cleveland; and as she returned by a different circuit to the house, feeling all the happy privilege of country liberty, of wandering from place to place in free and luxurious solitude, she resolved to spend almost every hour of every day while she remained with the Palmers, in the indulgence of such solitary rambles.

She returned just in time to join the others as they quitted the house, on an excursion through its more immediate premises; and the rest of the morning was easily whiled away, in lounging round the kitchen garden, examining the bloom upon its walls, and listening to the gardener's lamentations upon blights,—in dawdling through the green-house, where the loss of her favourite plants, unwarily exposed, and nipped by the lingering frost, raised the laughter of Charlotte,—and in visiting her poultry-yard, where, in the disappointed hopes of her dairy-maid, by hens forsaking their nests, or being stolen by a fox, or in the rapid decease of a promising young brood, she found fresh sources of merriment.

The morning was fine and dry, and Marianne, in her plan of employment abroad, had not calculated for any change of weather during their stay at Cleveland. With great surprise therefore, did she find herself prevented by a settled rain from going out again after dinner. She had depended on a twilight walk to the Grecian temple, and perhaps all over the grounds, and an evening merely cold or damp would not have deterred her from it; but an heavy and settled rain even she could not fancy dry or pleasant weather for walking.

Their party was small, and the hours passed quietly away. Mrs. Palmer had her child, and Mrs. Jennings her carpet-work; they talked of the friends they had left behind, arranged Lady Middleton's engagements, and wondered whether Mr. Palmer and Colonel Brandon would get farther than Reading that night. Elinor, however little concerned in it, joined in their discourse, and Marianne, who had the knack of finding her way in every house to the library, however it might be avoided by the family in general, soon procured herself a book.

Nothing was wanting on Mrs. Palmer's side that constant and friendly good-humour could do, to make them feel themselves welcome. The openness and heartiness of her manner, more than atoned for that want of recollection and elegance, which made her often deficient in the forms of politeness; her kindness, recommended by so pretty a face, was engaging; her folly, though evident, was not disgusting, because it was not conceited; and Elinor could have forgiven every thing but her laugh.

The two gentlemen arrived the next day to a very late dinner, affording a pleasant enlargement of the party, and a very welcome variety to their conversation, which a long morning of the same continued rain had reduced very low.

Elinor had seen so little of Mr. Palmer, and in that little had seen so much variety in his address to her sister and herself, that she knew not what to expect to find him in his own family. She found him, however, perfectly the gentleman in his behaviour to all his visitors, and only occasionally rude to his wife and her mother; she found him very capable of being a pleasant companion, and only prevented from being so always, by too great an aptitude to fancy himself as much superior to people in general, as he must feel himself to be to Mrs. Jennings and Charlotte. For the rest of his character and habits, they were marked, as far as Elinor could perceive, with no traits at all unusual in his sex and time of life. He was nice in his eating, uncertain in his hours; fond of his child, though affecting to slight it; and idled away the mornings at billiards, which ought to have been devoted to business. She liked him, however, upon the whole much better than she had expected, and in her heart was not sorry that she could like him no more;— not sorry to be driven by the observation of his Epicurism, his selfishness, and his conceit, to rest with complacency on the remembrance of Edward's generous temper, simple taste, and diffident feelings.

Of Edward, or at least of some of his concerns, she now received intelligence from Colonel Brandon, who had been into Dorsetshire lately; and who, treating her at once as the disinterested friend of Mr. Ferrars, and the kind confidante of himself, talked to her a great deal of the Parsonage at Delaford, described its deficiencies, and told her what he meant to do himself towards removing them.—His behaviour to her in this, as well as in every other particular, his open pleasure in meeting her after an absence of only ten days, his readiness to converse with her, and his deference for her opinion, might very well justify Mrs. Jennings's persuasion of his attachment, and would have been enough, perhaps, had not Elinor still, as from the first, believed Marianne his real favourite, to make her suspect it herself. But as it was, such a notion had scarcely ever entered her head, except by Mrs. Jennings's suggestion; and she could not help believing herself the nicest observer of the two;—she watched his eyes, while Mrs. Jennings thought only of his behaviour;—and while his looks of anxious solicitude on Marianne's feeling, in her head and throat, the beginning of an heavy cold, because unexpressed by words, entirely escaped the latter lady's observation;—*she* could discover in them the quick feelings, and needless alarm of a lover.

Two delightful twilight walks on the third and fourth evenings of her being there, not merely on the dry gravel of the shrubbery, but all over the grounds, and especially in the most distant parts of them, where there was something more of wildness than in the rest, where the trees were the oldest, and the grass was the longest and wettest, had—assisted by the still greater imprudence of sitting in her wet shoes and stockings—given Marianne a cold so violent, as, though for a day or two trifled with or denied, would force itself by increasing ailments, on the concern of every body, and the notice of herself. Prescriptions poured in from all quarters, and as usual, were all declined. Though heavy and feverish, with a pain in her limbs, a cough, and a sore throat, a good night's rest was to cure her entirely; and it was with difficulty that Elinor prevailed on her, when she went to bed, to try one or two of the simplest of the remedies.

Chapter VII

Marianne got up the next morning at her usual time; to every inquiry replied that she was better, and tried to prove herself so, by engaging in her accustomary employments. But a day spent in sitting shivering over the fire with a book in her hand, which she was unable to read, or in lying, weary and languid, on a sofa, did not speak much in favour of her amendment; and when, at last, she went early to bed, more and more indisposed, Colonel Brandon was only astonished at her sister's composure, who, though attending and nursing her the whole day, against Marianne's inclination, and forcing proper medicines on her at night, trusted, like Marianne, to the certainty and efficacy of sleep, and felt no real alarm.

A very restless and feverish night, however, disappointed the expectation of both; and when Marianne, after persisting in rising, confessed herself unable to sit up, and returned voluntarily to her bed, Elinor was very ready to adopt Mrs. Jennings's advice, of sending for the Palmers' apothecary.

He came, examined his patient, and though encouraging Miss Dashwood to expect that a very few days would restore her sister to health, yet, by pronouncing her disorder to have a putrid tendency, and allowing the word "infection" to pass his lips, gave instant alarm to Mrs. Palmer on her baby's account. Mrs. Jennings, who had been inclined from the first to think Marianne's complaint more serious than Elinor, now looked very grave on Mr. Harris's report, and confirming Charlotte's fears and caution, urged the necessity of her immediate removal with her infant; and Mr. Palmer, though treating their apprehensions as idle, found the anxiety and importunity of his wife too great to be withstood. Her departure therefore was fixed on; and, within an hour after Mr. Harris's arrival, she set off, with her little boy and his nurse, for the house of a near relation of

Mr. Palmer's, who lived a few miles on the other side of Bath; whither her husband promised, at her earnest entreaty, to join her in a day or two; and whither she was almost equally urgent with her mother to accompany her. Mrs. Jennings, however, with a kindness of heart which made Elinor really love her, declared her resolution of not stirring from Cleveland as long as Marianne remained ill, and of endeavouring, by her own attentive care, to supply to her the place of the mother she had taken her from; and Elinor found her on every occasion a most willing and active helpmate, desirous to share in all her fatigues, and often by her better experience in nursing, of material use.

Poor Marianne, languid and low from the nature of her malady, and feeling herself universally ill, could no longer hope that tomorrow would find her recovered; and the idea of what to-morrow would have produced, but for this unlucky illness, made every ailment more severe; for on that day they were to have begun their journey home; and, attended the whole way by a servant of Mrs. Jennings, were to have taken their mother by surprise on the following forenoon. The little that she said, was all in lamentation of this inevitable delay; though Elinor tried to raise her spirits, and make her believe, as she *then* really believed herself, that it would be a very short one.

The next day produced little or no alteration in the state of the patient; she certainly was not better, and except that there was no amendment, did not appear worse. Their party was now farther reduced; for Mr. Palmer, though very unwilling to go, as well from real humanity and good-nature, as from a dislike of appearing to be frightened away by his wife, was persuaded at last by Colonel Brandon to perform his promise of following her; and while he was preparing to go, Colonel Brandon himself, with a much greater exertion, began to talk of going likewise.—Here, however, the kindness of Mrs. Jennings interposed most acceptably; for to send the Colonel away while his love was in so much uneasiness on her sister's account, would be to deprive them both, she thought, of every comfort; and therefore telling him at once that his stay at Cleveland was necessary to herself, that she should want him to play at piquet[1] of an evening, while Miss Dashwood was above with her sister, &c. she urged him so strongly to remain, that he, who was gratifying the first wish of his own heart by a compliance, could not long even affect to demur; especially as Mrs. Jennings's entreaty was warmly seconded by Mr. Palmer, who seemed to feel a relief to himself, in leaving behind him a person so well able to assist or advise Miss Dashwood in any emergency.

Marianne was of course kept in ignorance of all these arrangements. She knew not that she had been the means of sending the owners of Cleveland away, in about seven days from the time of their arrival. It gave her no surprise that she saw nothing of Mrs. Palmer; and as it gave her likewise no concern, she never mentioned her name.

Two days passed away from the time of Mr. Palmer's departure, and her situation continued, with little variation, the same. Mr. Harris, who attended her every day, still talked boldly of a speedy recovery, and Miss Dashwood was equally sanguine; but the expectation of the others was by no means so cheerful. Mrs. Jennings had determined very early in the seisure that Marianne would never get over it, and Colonel Brandon, who was chiefly of use in listening to Mrs. Jennings's forebodings, was not in a state of mind to resist their influence. He tried to reason himself out of fears, which the different judgment of the apothecary seemed to render absurd; but the many hours of each day in which he was left entirely alone, were but too favourable for the admission of every melancholy idea, and he could not expel from his mind the persuasion that he should see Marianne no more.

On the morning of the third day however, the gloomy anticipations of both were almost done away; for when Mr. Harris arrived, he declared his patient materially better. Her pulse was much stronger, and every symptom more favourable than on the preceding visit. Elinor, confirmed in every pleasant hope, was all cheerfulness; rejoicing that in her letters to her mother,

---

[1] *piquet*: two-person, trick-taking card game.

she had pursued her own judgment rather than her friend's, in making very light of the indisposition which delayed them at Cleveland; and almost fixing on the time when Marianne would be able to travel.

But the day did not close so auspiciously as it began.— Towards the evening, Marianne became ill again, growing more heavy, restless, and uncomfortable than before. Her sister, however, still sanguine, was willing to attribute the change to nothing more than the fatigue of having set up to have her bed made; and carefully administering the cordials prescribed, saw her with satisfaction sink at last into a slumber, from which she expected the most beneficial effects. Her sleep, though not so quiet as Elinor wished to see it, lasted a considerable time; and anxious to observe the result of it herself, she resolved to sit with her during the whole of it. Mrs. Jennings, knowing nothing of any change in the patient, went unusually early to bed; her maid, who was one of the principal nurses, was recreating[2] herself in the housekeeper's room, and Elinor remained alone with Marianne.

The repose of the latter became more and more disturbed; and her sister, who watched with unremitting attention her continual change of posture, and heard the frequent but inarticulate sounds of complaint which passed her lips, was almost wishing to rouse her from so painful a slumber, when Marianne, suddenly awakened by some accidental noise in the house, started hastily up, and with feverish wildness, cried out—

"Is mama coming?—"

"Not yet," replied the other, concealing her terror, and assisting Marianne to lie down again, "but she will be here, I hope, before it is long. It is a great way, you know, from hence to Barton."

"But she must not go round by London," cried Marianne, in the same hurried manner, "I shall never see her, if she goes by London."

Elinor perceived with alarm that she was not quite herself, and while attempting to soothe her, eagerly felt her pulse. It was

---

[2] *recreating*: resting (taking recreation).

lower and quicker than ever! and Marianne, still talking wildly of mama, her alarm increased so rapidly, as to determine her on sending instantly for Mr. Harris, and dispatching a messenger to Barton for her mother. To consult with Colonel Brandon on the best means of effecting the latter, was a thought which immediately followed the resolution of its performance; and as soon as she had rung up the maid to take her place by her sister, she hastened down to the drawing-room, where she knew he was generally to be found at a much later hour than the present.

It was no time for hesitation. Her fears and her difficulties were immediately before him. Her fears, he had no courage, no confidence to attempt the removal of;—he listened to them in silent despondence;—but her difficulties were instantly obviated, for with a readiness that seemed to speak the occasion, and the service prearranged in his mind, he offered himself as the messenger who should fetch Mrs. Dashwood. Elinor made no resistance that was not easily overcome. She thanked him with brief, though fervent gratitude, and while he went to hurry off his servant with a message to Mr. Harris, and an order for post-horses[3] directly, she wrote a few lines to her mother.

The comfort of such a friend at that moment as Colonel Brandon—of such a companion for her mother,—how gratefully was it felt!—a companion whose judgment would guide, whose attendance must relieve, and whose friendship might soothe her!—as far as the shock of such a summons *could* be lessened to her, his presence, his manners, his assistance, would lessen it.

He, meanwhile, whatever he might feel, acted with all the firmness of a collected mind, made every necessary arrangement with the utmost dispatch, and calculated with exactness the time in which she might look for his return. Not a moment was lost in delay of any kind. The horses arrived even before they were expected, and Colonel Brandon only pressing her hand with a look of solemnity, and a few words spoken too

---

[3] *post-horses:* horses used for a post chaise (cf. footnote 4, p. 65).

low to reach her ear, hurried into the carriage. It was then about twelve o'clock, and she returned to her sister's apartment to wait for the arrival of the apothecary, and to watch by her the rest of the night. It was a night of almost equal suffering to both. Hour after hour passed away in sleepless pain and delirium on Marianne's side, and in the most cruel anxiety on Elinor's, before Mr. Harris appeared. Her apprehensions once raised, paid by their excess for all her former security; and the servant who sat up with her, for she would not allow Mrs. Jennings to be called, only tortured her more, by hints of what her mistress had always thought.

Marianne's ideas were still, at intervals, fixed incoherently on her mother, and whenever she mentioned her name, it gave a pang to the heart of poor Elinor, who, reproaching herself for having trifled with so many days of illness, and wretched for some immediate relief, fancied that all relief might soon be in vain, that every thing had been delayed too long, and pictured to herself her suffering mother arriving too late to see this darling child, or to see her rational.

She was on the point of sending again for Mr. Harris, or if *he* could not come, for some other advice, when the former— but not till after five o'clock—arrived. His opinion, however, made some little amends for his delay, for though acknowledging a very unexpected and unpleasant alteration in his patient, he would not allow the danger to be material, and talked of the relief which a fresh mode of treatment must procure, with a confidence which, in a lesser degree, was communicated to Elinor. He promised to call again in the course of three or four hours, and left both the patient and her anxious attendant more composed than he had found them.

With strong concern, and with many reproaches for not being called to their aid, did Mrs. Jennings hear in the morning of what had passed. Her former apprehensions, now with greater reason restored, left her no doubt of the event; and though trying to speak comfort to Elinor, her conviction of her sister's danger would not allow her to offer the comfort of hope. Her heart was really grieved. The rapid decay, the early death of a girl so young, so lovely as Marianne, must have struck a less interested person with concern. On Mrs. Jennings's compassion she had other claims. She had been for three months her companion, was still under her care, and she was known to have been greatly injured, and long unhappy. The distress of her sister too, particularly a favourite, was before her;—and as for their mother, when Mrs. Jennings considered that Marianne might probably be to *her* what Charlotte was to herself, her sympathy in *her* sufferings was very sincere.

Mr. Harris was punctual in his second visit;—but he came to be disappointed in his hopes of what the last would produce. His medicines had failed;—the fever was unabated; and Marianne only more quiet—not more herself—remained in an heavy stupor. Elinor, catching all, and more than all, his fears in a moment, proposed to call in farther advice. But he judged it unnecessary; he had still something more to try, some fresh application, of whose success he was almost as confident as the last, and his visit concluded with encouraging assurances which reached the ear, but could not enter the heart, of Miss Dashwood. She was calm, except when she thought of her mother, but she was almost hopeless; and in this state she continued till noon, scarcely stirring from her sister's bed, her thoughts wandering from one image of grief, one suffering friend to another, and her spirits oppressed to the utmost by the conversation of Mrs. Jennings, who scrupled not to attribute the severity and danger of this attack, to the many weeks of previous indisposition which Marianne's disappointment had brought on. Elinor felt all the reasonableness of the idea, and it gave fresh misery to her reflections.

About noon, however, she began—but with a caution—a dread of disappointment, which for some time kept her silent, even to her friend—to fancy, to hope she could perceive a slight amendment in her sister's pulse;—she waited, watched, and examined it again and again;—and at last, with an agitation more difficult to bury under exterior calmness, than all her foregoing distress, ventured to communicate her hopes. Mrs. Jennings, though forced, on examination, to acknowledge a temporary revival, tried to keep her young friend from indulging a thought of its continuance;—and Elinor, conning over every injunction of distrust, told herself likewise not to hope. But it was too late. Hope had already entered; and feeling all its anxious flutter, she bent over her sister to watch—she hardly knew for what. Half an hour passed away, and the favourable symptom yet blessed her. Others even arose to confirm it. Her breath, her skin, her lips, all flattered Elinor with signs of amendment, and Marianne fixed her eyes on her with a rational, though languid, gaze. Anxiety and hope now oppressed her in equal degrees, and left her no moment of tranquillity till the arrival of Mr. Harris at four o'clock,—when his assurances, his felicitations on a recovery in her sister even surpassing his expectation, gave her confidence, comfort, and tears of joy.

Marianne was in every respect materially better, and he declared her entirely out of danger. Mrs. Jennings, perhaps satisfied with the partial justification of her forebodings which had been found in their late alarm, allowed herself to trust in his judgment, and admitted with unfeigned joy, and soon with unequivocal cheerfulness, the probability of an entire recovery.

Elinor could not be cheerful. Her joy was of a different kind, and led to anything rather than to gaiety. Marianne restored to life, health, friends, and to her doating mother, was an idea to fill her heart with sensations of exquisite comfort, and expand it in fervent gratitude;—but it led to no outward demonstrations of joy, no words, no smiles. All within Elinor's breast was satisfaction, silent and strong.

She continued by the side of her sister with little intermission the whole afternoon, calming every fear, satisfying every inquiry of her enfeebled spirits, supplying every succour, and watching almost every look and every breath. The possibility of a relapse would of course, in some moments, occur to remind her of what anxiety was—but when she saw, on her frequent and minute examination, that every symptom of recovery continued, and saw Marianne at six o'clock sink into a quiet, steady, and to all appearance comfortable, sleep, she silenced every doubt.

The time was now drawing on, when Colonel Brandon might be expected back. At ten o'clock, she trusted, or at least not much later, her mother would be relieved from the dreadful suspense in which she must now be travelling towards them. The Colonel too!—perhaps scarcely less an object of pity!—Oh!—how slow was the progress of time which yet kept them in ignorance!

At seven o'clock, leaving Marianne still sweetly asleep, she joined Mrs. Jennings in the drawing-room to tea. Of breakfast she had been kept by her fears, and of dinner by their sudden reverse, from eating much;—and the present refreshment, therefore, with such feelings of content as she brought to it, was particularly welcome. Mrs. Jennings would have persuaded her at its conclusion to take some rest before her mother's arrival, and allow *her* to take her place by Marianne; but Elinor had no sense of fatigue, no capability of sleep at that moment about her, and she was not to be kept away from her sister an unnecessary instant. Mrs. Jennings therefore attending her up stairs into the sick chamber, to satisfy herself that all continued right, left her there again to her charge and her thoughts, and retired to her own room to write letters and sleep.

The night was cold and stormy. The wind roared round the house, and the rain beat against the windows; but Elinor, all happiness within, regarded it not. Marianne slept through every blast, and the travellers—they had a rich reward in store, for every present inconvenience.

The clock struck eight. Had it been ten, Elinor would have been convinced that at that moment she heard a carriage driving up to the house; and so strong was the persuasion that she *did*, in spite of the *almost* impossibility of their being already come, that she moved into the adjoining dressing-closet and opened a window-shutter, to be satisfied of the truth. She instantly saw that her ears had not deceived her. The flaring lamps of a carriage were immediately in view. By their uncertain light she thought she could discern it to be drawn by four horses; and this, while it told the excess of her poor mother's alarm, gave some explanation to such unexpected rapidity.

Never in her life had Elinor found it so difficult to be calm, as at that moment. The knowledge of what her mother must be feeling as the carriage stopt at the door,—of her doubt—her dread—perhaps her despair!—and of what *she* had to tell!—with such knowledge it was impossible to be calm. All that remained to be done, was to be speedy; and therefore staying only till she could leave Mrs. Jennings's maid with her sister, she hurried down stairs.

The bustle in the vestibule, as she passed along an inner lobby, assured her that they were already in the house. She rushed forwards towards the drawing-room,—she entered it,—and saw only Willoughby.

Chapter VIII

Elinor, starting back with a look of horror at the sight of him, obeyed the first impulse of her heart in turning instantly to quit the room, and her hand was already on the lock, when its action was suspended by his hastily advancing, and saying, in a voice rather of command than supplication,

"Miss Dashwood, for half an hour—for ten minutes—I entreat you to stay."

"No, sir," she replied with firmness, "I shall *not* stay. Your business cannot be with *me*. The servants, I suppose, forgot to tell you that Mr. Palmer was not in the house."

"Had they told me," he cried with vehemence, "that Mr. Palmer and all his relations were at the devil, it would not have turned me from the door. My business is with you, and only you."

"With me!"—in the utmost amazement—"well, sir—be quick—and if you can—less violent."

"Sit down, and I will be both."

She hesitated; she knew not what to do. The possibility of Colonel Brandon's arriving and finding him there, came across her. But she had promised to hear him, and her curiosity no less than her honour was engaged. After a moment's recollection, therefore, concluding that prudence required dispatch, and that her acquiescence would best promote it, she walked silently towards the table, and sat down. He took the opposite chair, and for half a minute not a word was said by either.

"Pray be quick, sir"—said Elinor impatiently—"I have no time to spare."

He was sitting in an attitude of deep meditation, and seemed not to hear her.

"Your sister," said he, with abruptness, a moment afterwards—"is out of danger. I heard it from the servant. God be praised!—But is it true?—is it really true?"

Elinor would not speak. He repeated the inquiry with yet greater eagerness.

"For God's sake tell me, is she out of danger, or is she not?"

"We hope she is."

He rose up, and walked across the room.

"Had I known as much half an hour ago—But since I *am* here"—speaking with a forced vivacity as he returned to his seat—"what does it signify?—For once, Miss Dashwood—it will be the last time, perhaps—let us be cheerful together.—I am in a fine mood for gaiety.—Tell me honestly"—a deeper glow overspreading his cheeks—"do you think me most a knave or a fool?"

Elinor looked at him with greater astonishment than ever. She began to think that he must be in liquor;—the strangeness of such a visit, and of such manners, seemed no otherwise intelligible; and with this impression she immediately rose, saying,

"Mr. Willoughby, I advise you at present to return to Combe.—I am not at leisure to remain with you longer.—Whatever your business may be with me, it will be better recollected and explained to-morrow."

"I understand you," he replied, with an expressive smile, and a voice perfectly calm, "yes, I am very drunk. A pint of porter[1] with my cold beef at Marlborough was enough to over-set me."

"At Marlborough!"—cried Elinor, more and more at a loss to understand what he would be at.

"Yes—I left London this morning at eight o'clock, and the only ten minutes I have spent out of my chaise since that time, procured me a nuncheon[2] at Marlborough."

The steadiness of his manner, and the intelligence of his eye as he spoke, convincing Elinor, that whatever other unpardonable folly might bring him to Cleveland, he was not brought there by intoxication, she said, after a moment's recollection,

"Mr. Willoughby, you *ought* to feel, and I certainly *do*—that after what has passed—your coming here in this manner,

[1] *porter*: dark beer.
[2] *nuncheon*: inter-meal snack.

and forcing yourself upon my notice, requires a very particular excuse.—What is it, that you mean by it?"—

"I mean"—said he, with serious energy—"if I can, to make you hate me one degree less than you do *now*. I mean to offer some kind of explanation, some kind of apology, for the past; to open my whole heart to you, and by convincing you, that though I have been always a blockhead, I have not been always a rascal, to obtain something like forgiveness from Ma—from your sister."

"Is this the real reason of your coming?"

"Upon my soul it is,"—was his answer, with a warmth which brought all the former Willoughby to her remembrance, and in spite of herself made her think him sincere.

"If that is all, you may be satisfied already,—for Marianne *does*—she has *long* forgiven you."

"Has she!"—he cried, in the same eager tone.—"Then she has forgiven me before she ought to have done it. But she shall forgive me again, and on more reasonable grounds.—*Now* will you listen to me?"

Elinor bowed her assent.

"I do not know," said he, after a pause of expectation on her side, and thoughtfulness on his own,—"how *you* may have accounted for my behaviour to your sister, or what diabolical motive you may have imputed to me.—Perhaps you will hardly think the better of me,—it is worth the trial however, and you shall hear every thing. When I first became intimate in your family, I had no other intention, no other view in the acquaintance than to pass my time pleasantly while I was obliged to remain in Devonshire, more pleasantly than I had ever done before. Your sister's lovely person and interesting manners could not but please me; and her behaviour to me almost from the first, was of a kind—It is astonishing, when I reflect on what it was, and what *she* was, that my heart should have been so insensible!—But at first I must confess, my vanity only was elevated by it. Careless of her happiness, thinking only of my own amusement, giving way to feelings which I had always been too much in the habit of indulging, I endeavoured, by every means in my power, to make myself pleasing to her, without any design of returning her affection."

Miss Dashwood at this point, turning her eyes on him with the most angry contempt, stopped him, by saying,

"It is hardly worth while, Mr. Willoughby, for you to relate, or for me to listen any longer. Such a beginning as this cannot be followed by any thing.—Do not let me be pained by hearing any thing more on the subject."

"I insist on your hearing the whole of it," he replied. "My fortune was never large, and I had always been expensive, always in the habit of associating with people of better income than myself. Every year since my coming of age, or even before, I believe, had added to my debts; and though the death of my old cousin, Mrs. Smith, was to set me free; yet that event being uncertain, and possibly far distant, it had been for some time my intention to re-establish my circumstances by marrying a woman of fortune. To attach myself to your sister, therefore, was not a thing to be thought of;—and with a meanness, selfishness, cruelty—which no indignant, no contemptuous look, even of yours, Miss Dashwood, can ever reprobate too much—I was acting in this manner, trying to engage her regard, without a thought of returning it.—But one thing may be said for me, even in that horrid state of selfish vanity, I did not know the extent of the injury I meditated, because I did not *then* know what it was to love. But have I ever known it?—Well may it be doubted; for, had I really loved, could I have sacrificed my feelings to vanity, to avarice?—or, what is more, could I have sacrificed her's?—But I have done it. To avoid a comparative poverty, which her affection and her society would have deprived of all its horrors, I have, by raising myself to affluence, lost every thing that could make it a blessing."

"You did then," said Elinor, a little softened, "believe yourself at one time attached to her."

"To have resisted such attractions, to have withstood such tenderness!—Is there a man on earth who could have done it!—Yes, I found myself, by insensible degrees, sincerely fond of her; and the happiest hours of my life were what I spent with her when I felt my intentions were strictly honourable, and my feelings blameless. Even *then*, however, when fully determined on paying my addresses to her, I allowed myself most improperly to put off, from day to day, the moment of doing it, from an unwillingness to enter into an engagement while my circumstances were so greatly embarrassed. I will not reason here—nor will I stop for *you* to expatiate[3] on the absurdity, and the worse than absurdity, of scrupling to engage my faith where my honour was already bound. The event has proved, that I was a cunning fool, providing with great circumspection for a possible opportunity of making myself contemptible and wretched for ever. At last, however, my resolution was taken, and I had determined, as soon as I could engage her alone, to justify the attentions I had so invariably paid her, and openly assure her of an affection which I had already taken such pains to display. But in the interim—in the interim of the very few hours that were to pass, before I could have an opportunity of speaking with her in private—a circumstance occurred—an unlucky circumstance, to ruin all my resolution, and with it all my comfort. A discovery took place,"—here he hesitated and looked down.—"Mrs. Smith had somehow or other been informed, I imagine by some distant relation, whose interest it was to deprive me of her favour, of an affair, a connection— but I need not explain myself farther," he added, looking at her with an heightened colour and an inquiring eye,—"your particular intimacy—you have probably heard the whole story long ago."

"I have," returned Elinor, colouring likewise and hardening her heart anew against any compassion for him, "I have heard it all. And how you will explain away any part of your guilt in that dreadful business, I confess is beyond my comprehension."

"Remember," cried Willoughby, "from whom you received the account. Could it be an impartial one? I acknowledge that her situation and her character ought to have been respected by me. I do not mean to justify myself, but at the same time

[3] *expatiate*: enlarge in discourse or writing.

cannot leave you to suppose that I have nothing to urge—that because she was injured she was irreproachable, and because I was a libertine, *she* must be a saint. If the violence of her passions, the weakness of her understanding—I do not mean, however, to defend myself. Her affection for me deserved better treatment, and I often, with great self-reproach, recal the tenderness which, for a very short time, had the power of creating any return. I wish—I heartily wish it had never been. But I have injured more than herself; and I have injured one, whose affection for me—(may I say it?) was scarcely less warm than her's; and whose mind—Oh! how infinitely superior!"—

"Your indifference, however, towards that unfortunate girl—I must say it, unpleasant to me as the discussion of such a subject may well be—your indifference is no apology for your cruel neglect of her. Do not think yourself excused by any weakness, any natural defect of understanding on her side, in the wanton cruelty so evident on yours. You must have known that while you were enjoying yourself in Devonshire, pursuing fresh schemes, always gay, always happy, she was reduced to the extremest indigence."

"But, upon my soul, I did *not* know it," he warmly replied; "I did not recollect that I had omitted to give her my direction; and common sense might have told her how to find it out."

"Well, sir, and what said Mrs. Smith?"

"She taxed me with the offence at once, and my confusion may be guessed. The purity of her life, the formality of her notions, her ignorance of the world—every thing was against me. The matter itself I could not deny, and vain was every endeavour to soften it. She was previously disposed, I believe, to doubt the morality of my conduct in general, and was moreover discontented with the very little attention, the very little portion of my time that I had bestowed on her, in my present visit. In short, it ended in a total breach. By one measure I might have saved myself. In the height of her morality, good woman! she offered to forgive the past, if I would marry Eliza. That could not be—and I was formally dismissed from her favour and her house. The night following this affair—I was to go the next morning—was spent by me in deliberating on what my future conduct should be. The struggle was great—but it ended too soon. My affection for Marianne, my thorough conviction of her attachment to me—it was all insufficient to outweigh that dread of poverty, or get the better of those false ideas of the necessity of riches, which I was naturally inclined to feel, and expensive society had increased. I had reason to believe myself secure of my present wife, if I chose to address her, and I persuaded myself to think that nothing else in common prudence remained for me to do. An heavy scene however awaited me, before I could leave Devonshire;—I was engaged to dine with you on that very day; some apology was therefore necessary for my breaking the engagement. But whether I should write this apology, or deliver it in person, was a point of long debate. To see Marianne, I felt would be dreadful, and I even doubted whether I could see her again and keep to my resolution. In that point, however, I undervalued my own magnanimity, as the event declared; for I went, I saw her, and saw her miserable, and left her miserable—and left her hoping never to see her again."

"Why did you call, Mr. Willoughby?" said Elinor, reproachfully; "a note would have answered every purpose.—Why was it necessary to call?"

"It was necessary to my own pride. I could not bear to leave the country in a manner that might lead you, or the rest of the neighbourhood, to suspect any part of what had really passed between Mrs. Smith and myself—and I resolved therefore on calling at the cottage, in my way to Honiton. The sight of your dear sister, however, was really dreadful; and to heighten the matter, I found her alone. You were all gone I do not know where. I had left her only the evening before, so fully, so firmly resolved within myself on doing right! A few hours were to have engaged her to me for ever; and I remember how happy, how gay were my spirits, as I walked from the cottage to Allenham, satisfied with myself, delighted with every body! But in this, our last interview of friendship, I approached her with a sense of guilt that almost took from me the power of dissembling. Her sorrow, her disappointment, her deep regret, when I told her that I was obliged to leave Devonshire so immediately—I never shall forget it—united too with such reliance, such confidence in me!—Oh, God!—what an hard-hearted rascal I was!"

They were both silent for a few moments. Elinor first spoke.

"Did you tell her that you should soon return?"

"I do not know what I told her," he replied, impatiently; "less than was due to the past, beyond a doubt, and in all likelihood much more than was justified by the future. I cannot think of it.—It won't do.—Then came your dear mother to torture me farther, with all her kindness and confidence. Thank Heaven! it *did* torture me. I was miserable. Miss Dashwood, you cannot have an idea of the comfort it gives me to look back on my own misery. I owe such a grudge to myself for the stupid, rascally folly of my own heart, that all my past sufferings under it are only triumph and exultation to me now. Well, I went, left all that I loved, and went to those to whom, at best, I was only indifferent. My journey to town—travelling with my own horses, and therefore so tediously—no creature to speak to—my own reflections so cheerful—when I looked forward everything so inviting!—when I looked back at Barton, the picture so soothing!—oh! it was a blessed journey!"

He stopt.

"Well, sir," said Elinor, who, though pitying him, grew impatient for his departure, "and this is all?"

"All!—no,—have you forgot what passed in town?—That infamous letter—Did she shew it you?"

"Yes, I saw every note that passed."

"When the first of her's reached me, (as it immediately did, for I was in town the whole time,) what I felt is—in the common phrase, not to be expressed; in a more simple one—perhaps too simple to raise any emotion—my feelings were very, very painful.—Every line, every word was—in the hackneyed metaphor which their dear writer, were she here, would forbid—a dagger to my heart. To know that Marianne was in town was—in the same language—a thunderbolt.—Thunderbolts and daggers!—what a reproof would she have given me!—her taste, her opinions—I believe they are better known to me than my own,—and I am sure they are dearer."

Elinor's heart, which had undergone many changes in the course of this extraordinary conversation, was now softened again;—yet she felt it her duty to check such ideas in her companion as the last.

"This is not right, Mr. Willoughby.—Remember that you are married. Relate only what in your conscience you think necessary for me to hear."

"Marianne's note, by assuring me that I was still as dear to her as in former days, that in spite of the many, many weeks we had been separated, she was as constant in her own feelings, and as full of faith in the constancy of mine as ever, awakened all my remorse. I say awakened, because time and London, business and dissipation, had in some measure quieted it, and I had been growing a fine hardened villain, fancying myself indifferent to her, and chusing to fancy that she too must have become indifferent to me; talking to myself of our past attachment as a mere idle, trifling, business, shrugging up my shoulders in proof of its being so, and silencing every reproach, overcoming every scruple, by secretly saying now and then, 'I shall be heartily glad to hear she is well married.'—But this note made me know myself better. I felt that she was infinitely dearer to me than any other woman in the world, and that I was using her infamously. But everything was then just settled between Miss Grey and me. To retreat was impossible. All that I had to do, was to avoid you both. I sent no answer to Marianne, intending by that means to preserve myself from her farther notice; and for some time I was even determined not to call in Berkeley-street;—but at last, judging it wiser to affect the air of a cool, common acquaintance than anything else, I watched you all safely out of the house one morning, and left my name."

"Watched us out of the house!"

"Even so. You would be surprised to hear how often I watched you, how often I was on the point of falling in with you. I have entered many a shop to avoid your sight, as the carriage drove by. Lodging as I did in Bond-street, there was hardly a day in which I did not catch a glimpse of one or other of you; and nothing but the most constant watchfulness on my side, a most invariably prevailing desire to keep out of your sight, could have separated us so long. I avoided the Middletons as much as possible, as well as everybody else who was likely to prove an acquaintance in common. Not aware of their being in town, however, I blundered on Sir John, I believe, the first day of his coming, and the day after I had called at Mrs. Jennings's. He asked me to a party, a dance at his house in the evening.— Had he *not* told me as an inducement that you and your sister were to be there, I should have felt it too certain a thing, to trust myself near him. The next morning brought another short note from Marianne—still affectionate, open, artless, confiding—everything that could make *my* conduct most hateful. I could not answer it. I tried—but could not frame a sentence. But I thought of her, I believe, every moment of the day. If you *can* pity me, Miss Dashwood, pity my situation as it was *then*. With my head and heart full of your sister, I was forced to play the happy lover to another woman!—Those three or four weeks were worse than all. Well, at last, as I need not tell you, you were forced on me; and what a sweet figure I cut!—what an evening of agony it was!—Marianne, beautiful as an angel on one side, calling me Willoughby in such a tone!—Oh! God!—holding out her hand to me, asking me for an explanation with those bewitching eyes fixed in such speaking solicitude on my face!—and Sophia, jealous as the devil on the other hand, looking all that was—Well, it does not signify; it is over now.—Such an evening!—I ran away from you all as soon as I could; but not before I had seen Marianne's sweet face as white as death.—*That* was the last, last look I ever had of her;—the last manner in which she appeared to me. It was a horrid sight!—Yet when I thought of her to-day as really dying, it was a kind of comfort to me to imagine that I knew exactly how she would appear to those, who saw her last in this world. She was before me, constantly before me, as I travelled, in the same look and hue."

A short pause of mutual thoughtfulness succeeded. Willoughby first rousing himself, broke it thus:

"Well, let me make haste and be gone. Your sister is certainly better, certainly out of danger?"

"We are assured of it."

"Your poor mother too!—doting on Marianne."

"But the letter, Mr. Willoughby, your own letter; have you anything to say about that?"

"Yes, yes, *that* in particular. Your sister wrote to me again, you know, the very next morning. You saw what she said. I was breakfasting at the Ellisons,—and her letter, with some others, was brought to me there from my lodgings. It happened to catch Sophia's eye before it caught mine—and its size, the elegance of the paper, the hand-writing altogether, immediately gave her a suspicion. Some vague report had reached her before of my attachment to some young lady in Devonshire, and what had passed within her observation the preceding evening had marked who the young lady was, and made her more jealous than ever. Affecting that air of playfulness, therefore, which is delightful in a woman one loves, she opened the letter directly, and read its contents. She was well paid for her impudence. She read what made her wretched. Her wretchedness I could have borne, but her passion—her malice—At all events it must be appeased. And in short—what do you think of my wife's style of letter-writing?—delicate—tender—truly feminine—was it not?"

"Your wife!—The letter was in your own hand writing."

"Yes, but I had only the credit of servilely copying such sentences as I was ashamed to put my name to. The original was all her own—her own happy thoughts and gentle diction. But what could I do?—we were engaged, every thing in preparation, the day almost fixed—But I am talking like a fool. Preparation!—day!—In honest words, her money was necessary to me, and in a situation like mine, any thing was to be done to prevent a rupture. And after all, what did it signify to my character in the opinion of Marianne and her friends, in what language my answer was couched?—It must have been only to one end. My business was to declare myself a scoundrel, and whether I did it with a bow or a bluster was of little importance.—'I am ruined for ever in their opinion'—said I to myself—'I am shut out for ever from their society, they already think me an unprincipled fellow, this letter will only make them think me a blackguard one.' Such were my reasonings, as, in a sort of desperate carelessness, I copied my wife's words, and parted with the last relics of Marianne. Her three notes—unluckily they were all in my pocket-book, or I should have denied their existence, and hoarded them for ever—I was forced to put them up,[4] and could not even kiss them. And the lock of hair—that too I had always carried about me in the same pocket-book, which was now searched by Madam with the most ingratiating virulence,—the dear lock—all, every memento was torn from me."

"You are very wrong, Mr. Willoughby, very blameable," said Elinor, while her voice, in spite of herself, betrayed her compassionate emotion; "you ought not to speak in this way, either of Mrs. Willoughby or my sister. You have made your own choice. It was not forced on you. Your wife has a claim to your politeness, to your respect, at least. She must be attached to you, or she would not have married you. To treat her with unkindness, to speak of her slightingly is no atonement to Marianne—nor can I suppose it a relief to your own conscience."

"Do not talk to me of my wife," said he with an heavy sigh.—"She does not deserve your compassion.—She knew I had no regard for her when we married.—Well, married we were, and came down to Combe Magna to be happy, and afterwards returned to town to be gay.—And now do you pity me, Miss Dashwood?—or have I said all this to no purpose?—Am I—be it only one degree—am I less guilty in your opinion than I was before?—My intentions were not always wrong. Have I explained away any part of my guilt?"

"Yes, you have certainly removed something—a little.—You have proved yourself, on the whole, less faulty than I had

[4] *up*: away.

believed you. You have proved your heart less wicked, much less wicked. But I hardly know—the misery that you have inflicted—I hardly know what could have made it worse."

"Will you repeat to your sister when she is recovered, what I have been telling you?—Let me be a little lightened too in her opinion as well as in yours. You tell me that she has forgiven me already. Let me be able to fancy that a better knowledge of my heart, and of my present feelings, will draw from her a more spontaneous, more natural, more gentle, less dignified, forgiveness. Tell her of my misery and my penitence—tell her that my heart was never inconstant to her, and if you will, that at this moment she is dearer to me than ever."

"I will tell her all that is necessary to what may comparatively be called, your justification. But you have not explained to me the particular reason of your coming now, nor how you heard of her illness."

"Last night, in Drury-lane lobby,[5] I ran against Sir John Middleton, and when he saw who I was—for the first time these two months—he spoke to me.—That he had cut me ever since my marriage, I had seen without surprise or resentment. Now, however, his good-natured, honest, stupid soul, full of indignation against me, and concern for your sister, could not resist the temptation of telling me what he knew ought to—though probably he did not think it *would*—vex me horridly.—As bluntly as he could speak it, therefore, he told me that Marianne Dashwood was dying of a putrid fever at Cleveland—a letter that morning received from Mrs. Jennings declared her danger most imminent—the Palmers all gone off in a fright, &c.—I was too much shocked to be able to pass myself off as insensible even to the undiscerning Sir John. His heart was softened in seeing mine suffer; and so much of his ill-will was done away, that when we parted, he almost shook me by the hand while he reminded me of an old promise about a pointer puppy. What I felt on hearing that your sister was dying—and dying too,

[5] *Drury-lane lobby*: Theatre Royal, Drury Lane, was (and is) one of the most famous playhouses in London's fashionable West End.

believing me the greatest villain upon earth, scorning, hating me in her latest moments—for how could I tell what horrid projects might not have been imputed? *One* person I was sure would represent me as capable of anything—What I felt was dreadful!—My resolution was soon made, and at eight o'clock this morning I was in my carriage. Now you know all."

Elinor made no answer. Her thoughts were silently fixed on the irreparable injury which too early an independence and its consequent habits of idleness, dissipation, and luxury, had made in the mind, the character, the happiness, of a man who, to every advantage of person and talents, united a disposition naturally open and honest, and a feeling, affectionate temper. The world had made him extravagant and vain—Extravagance and vanity had made him cold-hearted and selfish. Vanity, while seeking its own guilty triumph at the expense of another, had involved him in a real attachment, which extravagance, or at least its offspring, necessity, had required to be sacrificed. Each faulty propensity in leading him to evil, had led him likewise to punishment. The attachment, from which against honour, against feeling, against every better interest he had outwardly torn himself, now, when no longer allowable, governed every thought; and the connection, for the sake of which he had, with little scruple, left her sister to misery, was likely to prove a source of unhappiness to himself of a far more incurable nature. From a reverie of this kind she was recalled at the end of some minutes by Willoughby, who, rousing himself from a reverie at least equally painful, started up in preparation for going, and said,

"There is no use in staying here; I must be off."

"Are you going back to town?"

"No—to Combe Magna. I have business there; from thence to town in a day or two. Good bye."

He held out his hand. She could not refuse to give him her's;—he pressed it with affection.

"And you *do* think something better of me than you did?"—said he, letting it fall, and leaning against the mantle-piece as if forgetting he was to go.

Elinor assured him that she did;—that she forgave, pitied, wished him well—was even interested in his happiness—and added some gentle counsel as to the behaviour most likely to promote it. His answer was not very encouraging.

"As to that," said he, "I must rub through the world as well as I can. Domestic happiness is out of the question. If, however, I am allowed to think that you and yours feel an interest in my fate and actions, it may be the means—it may put me on my guard—at least, it will be something to live for. Marianne to be sure is lost to me for ever. Were I even by any blessed chance at liberty again"—

Elinor stopped him with a reproof.

"Well"—he replied—"once more good bye. I shall now go away and live in dread of one event."

"What do you mean?"

"Your sister's marriage."

"You are very wrong. She can never be more lost to you than she is now."

"But she will be gained by some one else. And if that some one should be the very he whom, of all others, I could least bear—But I will not stay to rob myself of all your compassionate goodwill, by shewing that where I have most injured I can least forgive. Good bye,—God bless you!"

And with these words, he almost ran out of the room.

Chapter IX

Elinor, for some time after he left her, for some time even after the sound of his carriage had died away, remained too much oppressed by a croud of ideas, widely differing in themselves, but of which sadness was the general result, to think even of her sister.

Willoughby, he, whom only half an hour ago she had abhorred as the most worthless of men, Willoughby, in spite of all his faults, excited a degree of commiseration for the sufferings produced by them, which made her think of him as now separated for ever from her family with a tenderness, a regret, rather in proportion, as she soon acknowledged within herself—to his wishes than to his merits. She felt that his influence over her mind was heightened by circumstances which ought not in reason to have weight; by that person of uncommon attraction, that open, affectionate, and lively manner which it was no merit to possess; and by that still ardent love for Marianne, which it was not even innocent to indulge. But she felt that it was so, long, long before she could feel his influence less.

When at last she returned to the unconscious Marianne, she found her just awaking, refreshed by so long and sweet a sleep to the extent of her hopes. Elinor's heart was full. The past, the present, the future, Willoughby's visit, Marianne's safety, and her mother's expected arrival, threw her altogether into an agitation of spirits which kept off every indication of fatigue, and made her only fearful of betraying herself to her sister. Short was the time, however, in which that fear could affect her, for within half an hour after Willoughby's leaving the house, she was again called down stairs by the sound of another carriage.—Eager to save her mother from every unnecessary moment's horrible suspense, she ran immediately into the hall, and reached the outward door just in time to receive and support her as she entered it.

Mrs. Dashwood, whose terror as they drew near the house had produced almost the conviction of Marianne's being no more, had no voice to inquire after her, no voice even for Elinor; but *she*, waiting neither for salutation nor inquiry, instantly gave the joyful relief;—and her mother, catching it with all her usual warmth, was in a moment as much overcome by her happiness, as she had been before by her fears. She was supported into the drawing-room between her daughter and her friend;—and there, shedding tears of joy, though still unable to speak, embraced Elinor again and again, turning from her at intervals to press Colonel Brandon's hand, with a look which spoke at once her gratitude, and her conviction of his sharing with herself in the bliss of the moment. He shared it, however, in a silence even greater than her own.

As soon as Mrs. Dashwood had recovered herself, to see Marianne was her first desire; and in two minutes she was with her beloved child, rendered dearer to her than ever by absence, unhappiness, and danger. Elinor's delight, as she saw what each felt in the meeting, was only checked by an apprehension of its robbing Marianne of farther sleep;—but Mrs. Dashwood could be calm, could be even prudent, when the life of a child was at stake, and Marianne, satisfied in knowing her mother was near her, and conscious of being too weak for conversation, submitted readily to the silence and quiet prescribed by every nurse around her. Mrs. Dashwood *would* sit up with her all night, and Elinor, in compliance with her mother's entreaty, went to bed. But the rest, which one night entirely sleepless, and many hours of the most wearing anxiety seemed to make requisite, was kept off by irritation of spirits. Willoughby, "poor Willoughby," as she now allowed herself to call him, was constantly in her thoughts; she would not but have heard his vindication for the world, and now blamed, now acquitted herself for having judged him so harshly before. But her promise of relating it to her sister was invariably painful. She dreaded the performance of it, dreaded what its effect on Marianne might be; doubted whether after such an explanation she could ever be happy with another; and for a moment wished Willoughby a widower. Then, remembering Colonel Brandon, reproved herself, felt that to *his* sufferings and *his* constancy far more than to his rival's, the reward of her sister was due, and wished any thing rather than Mrs. Willoughby's death.

The shock of Colonel Brandon's errand at Barton had been much softened to Mrs. Dashwood by her own previous alarm; for so great was her uneasiness about Marianne, that she had already determined to set out for Cleveland on that very day, without waiting for any farther intelligence, and had so far settled her journey before his arrival, that the Careys were then expected every moment to fetch Margaret away, as her mother was unwilling to take her where there might be infection.

Marianne continued to mend every day, and the brilliant cheerfulness of Mrs. Dashwood's looks and spirits proved her to be, as she repeatedly declared herself, one of the happiest women in the world. Elinor could not hear the declaration, nor witness its proofs without sometimes wondering whether her mother ever recollected Edward. But Mrs. Dashwood, trusting to the temperate account of her own disappointment which Elinor had sent her, was led away by the exuberance of her joy to think only of what would increase it. Marianne was restored to her from a danger in which, as she now began to feel, her own mistaken judgment in encouraging the unfortunate attachment to Willoughby, had contributed to place her;—and in her recovery she had yet another source of joy unthought of by Elinor. It was thus imparted to her, as soon as any opportunity of private conference between them occurred.

"At last we are alone. My Elinor, you do not yet know all my happiness. Colonel Brandon loves Marianne. He has told me so himself."

Her daughter, feeling by turns both pleased and pained, surprised and not surprised, was all silent attention.

"You are never like me, dear Elinor, or I should wonder at your composure now. Had I sat down to wish for any possible good to my family, I should have fixed on Colonel Brandon's marrying one of you as the object most desirable. And I believe Marianne will be the most happy with him of the two."

Elinor was half inclined to ask her reason for thinking so, because satisfied that none founded on an impartial consideration of their age, characters, or feelings, could be given;—but her mother must always be carried away by her imagination on any interesting subject, and therefore instead of an inquiry, she passed it off with a smile.

"He opened his whole heart to me yesterday as we travelled. It came out quite unawares, quite undesignedly. I, you may well believe, could talk of nothing but my child;—he could not conceal his distress; I saw that it equalled my own, and he perhaps, thinking that mere friendship, as the world now goes, would not justify so warm a sympathy—or rather not thinking at all, I suppose—giving way to irresistible feelings, made me acquainted with his earnest, tender, constant, affection for Marianne. He has loved her, my Elinor, ever since the first moment of seeing her."

Here, however, Elinor perceived,—not the language, not the professions of Colonel Brandon, but the natural embellishments of her mother's active fancy, which fashioned every thing delightful to her, as it chose.

"His regard for her, infinitely surpassing anything that Willoughby ever felt or feigned, as much more warm, as more sincere or constant—which ever we are to call it—has subsisted through all the knowledge of dear Marianne's unhappy prepossession for that worthless young man!—and without selfishness—without encouraging a hope!—could he have seen her happy with another—Such a noble mind!—such openness, such sincerity!—no one can be deceived in *him*."

"Colonel Brandon's character," said Elinor, "as an excellent man, is well established."

"I know it is"—replied her mother seriously, "or after such a warning, I should be the last to encourage such affection, or even to be pleased by it. But his coming for me as he did, with such active, such ready friendship, is enough to prove him one of the worthiest of men."

"His character, however," answered Elinor, "does not rest on *one* act of kindness, to which his affection for Marianne, were humanity out of the case, would have prompted him. To Mrs. Jennings, to the Middletons, he has been long and intimately known; they equally love and respect him; and even my own knowledge of him, though lately acquired, is very considerable; and so highly do *I* value and esteem him, that if Marianne can be happy with him, I shall be as ready as yourself to think our connection the greatest blessing to us in the world. What answer did you give him?—Did you allow him to hope?"

"Oh! my love, I could not then talk of hope to him or to myself. Marianne might at that moment be dying. But he did not ask for hope or encouragement. His was an involuntary confidence, an irrepressible effusion to a soothing friend—not an application to a parent. Yet after a time I *did* say, for at first I was quite overcome—that if she lived, as I trusted she might, my greatest happiness would lie in promoting their marriage; and since our arrival, since our delightful security I have repeated it to him more fully, have given him every encouragement in my power. Time, a very little time, I tell him, will do everything;—Marianne's heart is not to be wasted for ever on such a man as Willoughby.—His own merits must soon secure it."

"To judge from the Colonel's spirits, however, you have not yet made him equally sanguine."

"No.—He thinks Marianne's affection too deeply rooted for any change in it under a great length of time, and even supposing her heart again free, is too diffident of himself to believe, that with such a difference of age and disposition, he could ever attach her. There, however, he is quite mistaken. His age is only so much beyond her's, as to be an advantage, as to make his character and principles fixed;—and his disposition, I am well convinced, is exactly the very one to make your sister happy. And his person, his manners too, are all in his favour. My partiality does not blind me; he certainly is not so handsome as Willoughby—but at the same time, there is something much more pleasing in his countenance.—There was always a something,—if you remember,—in Willoughby's eyes at times, which I did not like."

Elinor could *not* remember it;—but her mother, without waiting for her assent, continued,

"And his manners, the Colonel's manners are not only more pleasing to me than Willoughby's ever were, but they are of a kind I well know to be more solidly attaching to Marianne. Their gentleness, their genuine attention to other people, and their manly unstudied simplicity is much more accordant with her real disposition, than the liveliness—often artificial, and often ill-timed of the other. I am very sure myself, that had Willoughby turned out as really amiable, as he has proved himself the contrary, Marianne would yet never have been so happy with *him*, as she will be with Colonel Brandon."

She paused.—Her daughter could not quite agree with her, but her dissent was not heard, and therefore gave no offence.

"At Delaford, she will be within an easy distance of me," added Mrs. Dashwood, "even if I remain at Barton; and in all probability,—for I hear it is a large village,—indeed there certainly *must* be some small house or cottage close by, that would suit us quite as well as our present situation."

Poor Elinor!—here was a new scheme for getting her to Delaford!—but her spirit was stubborn.

"His fortune too!—for at my time of life you know, everybody cares about *that*;—and though I neither know, nor desire to know, what it really is, I am sure it must be a good one."

Here they were interrupted by the entrance of a third person, and Elinor withdrew to think it all over in private, to wish success to her friend, and yet in wishing it, to feel a pang for Willoughby.

Chapter X

Marianne's illness, though weakening in its kind, had not been long enough to make her recovery slow; and with youth, natural strength, and her mother's presence in aid, it proceeded so smoothly as to enable her to remove within four days after the arrival of the latter, into Mrs. Palmer's dressing-room. When there, at her own particular request, for she was impatient to pour forth her thanks to him for fetching her mother, Colonel Brandon was invited to visit her.

His emotion in entering the room, in seeing her altered looks, and in receiving the pale hand which she immediately held out to him, was such, as, in Elinor's conjecture, must arise from something more than his affection for Marianne, or the consciousness of its being known to others; and she soon discovered in his melancholy eye and varying complexion as he looked at her sister, the probable recurrence of many past scenes of misery to his mind, brought back by that resemblance between Marianne and Eliza already acknowledged, and now strengthened by the hollow eye, the sickly skin, the posture of reclining weakness, and the warm acknowledgement of peculiar obligation.

Mrs. Dashwood, not less watchful of what passed than her daughter, but with a mind very differently influenced, and therefore watching to very different effect, saw nothing in the Colonel's behaviour but what arose from the most simple and self-evident sensations, while in the actions and words of Marianne she persuaded herself to think that something more than gratitude already dawned.

At the end of another day or two, Marianne growing visibly stronger every twelve hours, Mrs. Dashwood, urged equally by her own and her daughter's wishes, began to talk of removing to Barton. On *her* measures depended those of her two friends; Mrs. Jennings could not quit Cleveland during the Dashwoods' stay, and Colonel Brandon was soon brought, by their united request, to consider his own abode there as equally determinate, if not equally indispensable. At his and Mrs. Jennings's united request in return, Mrs. Dashwood was prevailed on to accept the use of his carriage on her journey back, for the better accommodation of her sick child; and the Colonel, at the joint invitation of Mrs. Dashwood and Mrs. Jennings, whose active good-nature made her friendly and hospitable for other people as well as herself, engaged with pleasure to redeem it by a visit at the cottage, in the course of a few weeks.

The day of separation and departure arrived; and Marianne, after taking so particular and lengthened a leave of Mrs. Jennings, one so earnestly grateful, so full of respect and kind wishes as seemed due to her own heart from a secret acknowledgement of past inattention, and bidding Colonel Brandon farewel with the cordiality of a friend, was carefully assisted by him into the carriage, of which he seemed anxious that she should engross at least half. Mrs. Dashwood and Elinor then followed, and the others were left by themselves, to talk of the travellers, and feel their own dulness, till Mrs. Jennings was summoned to her chaise to take comfort in the gossip of her maid for the loss of her two young companions; and Colonel Brandon immediately afterwards took his solitary way to Delaford.

The Dashwoods were two days on the road, and Marianne bore her journey on both, without essential fatigue. Every thing that the most zealous affection, the most solicitous care could do to render her comfortable, was the office of each watchful companion, and each found their reward in her bodily ease, and her calmness of spirits. To Elinor, the observation of the latter was particularly grateful. She, who had seen her week after week so constantly suffering, oppressed by anguish of heart which she had neither courage to speak of, nor fortitude to conceal, now saw with a joy, which no other could equally share, an apparent composure of mind, which, in being the result as she trusted of serious reflection, must eventually lead her to contentment and cheerfulness.

As they approached Barton indeed, and entered on scenes, of which every field and every tree brought some peculiar, some painful recollection, she grew silent and thoughtful, and turning away her face from their notice, sat earnestly gazing through the window. But here, Elinor could neither wonder nor blame; and when she saw, as she assisted Marianne from the carriage, that she had been crying, she saw only an emotion too natural in itself to raise anything less tender than pity, and in its unobtrusiveness entitled to praise. In the whole of her subsequent manner, she traced the direction of a mind awakened to reasonable exertion; for no sooner had they entered their common sitting-room, than Marianne turned her eyes around it with a look of resolute firmness, as if determined at once to accustom herself to the sight of every object with which the remembrance of Willoughby could be connected.— She said little, but every sentence aimed at cheerfulness, and though a sigh sometimes escaped her, it never passed away without the atonement of a smile. After dinner she would try her pianoforté. She went to it; but the music on which her eye first rested was an opera, procured for her by Willoughby, containing some of their favourite duets, and bearing on its outward leaf her own name in his hand writing.—That would not do.—She shook her head, put the music aside, and after running over the keys for a minute complained of feebleness in her fingers, and closed the instrument again; declaring however with firmness as she did so, that she should in future practise much.

The next morning produced no abatement in these happy symptoms. On the contrary, with a mind and body alike strengthened by rest, she looked and spoke with more genuine spirit, anticipating the pleasure of Margaret's return, and talking of the dear family party which would then be restored, of their mutual pursuits and cheerful society as the only happiness worth a wish.

"When the weather is settled, and I have recovered my strength," said she, "we will take long walks together every day. We will walk to the farm at the edge of the down, and

see how the children go on; we will walk to Sir John's new
plantations at Barton-Cross, and the Abbeyland; and we will
often go to the old ruins of the Priory, and try to trace its foun-
dations as far as we are told they once reached. I know we shall
be happy. I know the summer will pass happily away. I mean
never to be later in rising than six, and from that time till dinner I shall divide every moment between music and reading. I
have formed my plan, and am determined to enter on a course
of serious study. Our own library is too well known to me, to
be resorted to for anything beyond mere amusement. But there
are many works well worth reading, at the Park; and there are
others of more modern production which I know I can borrow
of Colonel Brandon. By reading only six hours a-day, I shall
gain in the course of a twelvemonth a great deal of instruction
which I now feel myself to want."

Elinor honoured her for a plan which originated so nobly
as this; though smiling to see the same eager fancy which had
been leading her to the extreme of languid indolence and selfish repining, now at work in introducing excess into a scheme
of such rational employment and virtuous self-controul. Her
smile however changed to a sigh when she remembered that
her promise to Willoughby was yet unfulfilled, and feared she
had that to communicate which might again unsettle the
mind of Marianne, and ruin at least for a time this fair prospect
of busy tranquility. Willing therefore to delay the evil hour,
she resolved to wait till her sister's health were more secure,
before she appointed it. But the resolution was made only to
be broken.

Marianne had been two or three days at home, before the
weather was fine enough for an invalid like herself to venture
out. But at last a soft, genial morning appeared; such as might
tempt the daughter's wishes and the mother's confidence; and
Marianne, leaning on Elinor's arm, was authorised to walk as
long as she could without fatigue, in the lane before the house.

The sisters set out at a pace, slow as the feebleness of Marianne in an exercise hitherto untried since her illness required;—
and they had advanced only so far beyond the house as to

admit a full view of the hill, the important hill behind, when pausing with her eyes turned towards it, Marianne calmly said,

"There, exactly there"—pointing with one hand, "on that projecting mound,—there I fell; and there I first saw Willoughby."

Her voice sunk with the word, but presently reviving she added,

"I am thankful to find that I can look with so little pain on the spot!—shall we ever talk on that subject, Elinor?"— hesitatingly it was said.—"Or will it be wrong?—I *can* talk of it now, I hope, as I ought to do."—

Elinor tenderly invited her to be open.

"As for regret," said Marianne, "I have done with that, as far as *he* is concerned. I do not mean to talk to you of what my feelings have been for him, but what they are *now*.—At present, if I could be satisfied on one point, if I could be allowed to think that he was not *always* acting a part, not *always* deceiving me;—but above all, if I could be assured that he never was so *very* wicked as my fears have sometimes fancied him, since the story of that unfortunate girl"—

She stopt.—Elinor joyfully treasured her words as she answered,

"If you could be assured of that, you think you should be easy."

"Yes. My peace of mind is doubly involved in it;—for not only is it horrible to suspect a person, who has been what *he* has been to *me*, of such designs,—but what must it make me appear to myself?—What in a situation like mine, but a most shamefully unguarded affection could expose me to"—

"How then," asked her sister, "would you account for his behaviour?"

"I would suppose him,—Oh! how gladly would I suppose him, only fickle, very, very fickle."

Elinor said no more. She was debating within herself on the eligibility of beginning her story directly, or postponing it till Marianne were in stronger health;—and they crept on for a few minutes in silence.

"I am not wishing him too much good," said Marianne at last with a sigh, "when I wish his secret reflections may be no more unpleasant than my own. He will suffer enough in them."

"Do you compare your conduct with his?"

"No. I compare it with what it ought to have been; I compare it with yours."

"Our situations have borne little resemblance."

"They have borne more than our conduct.—Do not, my dearest Elinor, let your kindness defend what I know your judgment must censure. My illness has made me think—It has given me leisure and calmness for serious recollection. Long before I was enough recovered to talk, I was perfectly able to reflect. I considered the past; I saw in my own behaviour since the beginning of our acquaintance with him last autumn, nothing but a series of imprudence towards myself, and want of kindness to others. I saw that my own feelings had prepared my sufferings, and that my want of fortitude under them had almost led me to the grave. My illness, I well knew, had been entirely brought on by myself by such negligence of my own health, as I had felt even at the time to be wrong. Had I died,—it would have been self-destruction.* I did not know my danger till the danger was removed; but with such feelings as these reflections gave me, I wonder at my recovery,—wonder that the very eagerness of my desire to live, to have time for atonement to my God, and to you all, did not kill me at once. Had I died,—in what peculiar misery should I have left you, my nurse, my friend, my sister!—You, who had seen all the fretful selfishness of my latter days; who had known all the murmurings of my heart!—How should I have lived in *your* remembrance!—My mother too! How could you have consoled her!—I cannot express my own abhorrence of myself. Whenever I looked towards the past, I saw some duty neglected, or some failing indulged. Every body seemed injured by me. The kindness, the unceasing kindness

---

Had I died . . . self-destruction: Suicide was condemned by Christianity, but it was (in fiction and in fact) associated with despairing females in unhappy love relationships.

of Mrs. Jennings, I had repaid with ungrateful contempt. To the Middletons, the Palmers, the Steeles, to every common acquaintance even, I had been insolent and unjust; with an heart hardened against their merits, and a temper irritated by their very attention.—To John, to Fanny,—yes, even to them, little as they deserve, I had given less than their due. But you,—you above all, above my mother, had been wronged by me. I, and only I, knew your heart and its sorrows; yet, to what did it influence me?—not to any compassion that could benefit you or myself.—Your example was before me: but to what avail?—Was I more considerate of you and your comfort? Did I imitate your forbearance, or lessen your restraints, by taking any part in those offices of general complaisance or particular gratitude which you had hitherto been left to discharge alone?—No;—not less when I knew you to be unhappy, than when I had believed you at ease, did I turn away from every exertion of duty or friendship; scarcely allowing sorrow to exist but with me, regretting only *that* heart which had deserted and wronged me, and leaving you, for whom I professed an unbounded affection, to be miserable for my sake."

Here ceased the rapid flow of her self-reproving spirit; and Elinor, impatient to soothe, though too honest to flatter, gave her instantly that praise and support which her frankness and her contrition so well deserved. Marianne pressed her hand and replied,

"You are very good.—The future must be my proof. I have laid down my plan, and if I am capable of adhering to it—my feelings shall be governed and my temper improved. They shall no longer worry others, nor torture myself. I shall now live solely for my family. You, my mother, and Margaret, must henceforth be all the world to me; you will share my affections entirely between you. From you, from my home, I shall never again have the smallest incitement to move; and if I do mix in other society it will be only to show that my spirit is humbled, my heart amended, and that I can practise the civilities, the lesser duties of life, with gentleness, and forbearance. As for Willoughby—to say that I shall soon or that I shall ever forget him, would be idle. His remembrance can be overcome by no change of circumstances or opinions. But it shall be regulated, it shall be checked by religion, by reason, by constant employment."

She paused—and added in a lower voice, "If I could but know his heart, everything would become easy."

Elinor, who had now been for some time reflecting on the propriety or impropriety of speedily hazarding her narration, without feeling at all nearer decision than at first, heard this; and perceiving that as reflection did nothing, resolution must do all, soon found herself leading to the fact.

She managed the recital, as she hoped, with address; prepared her anxious listener with caution; related simply and honestly the chief points on which Willoughby grounded his apology; did justice to his repentance, and softened only his protestations of present regard. Marianne said not a word.— She trembled, her eyes were fixed on the ground, and her lips became whiter than even sickness had left them. A thousand inquiries sprung up from her heart, but she dared not urge one. She caught every syllable with panting eagerness; her hand, unknowingly to herself, closely pressed her sister's, and tears covered her cheeks.

Elinor, dreading her being tired, led her towards home; and till they reached the door of the cottage, easily conjecturing what her curiosity must be though no question was suffered to speak it, talked of nothing but Willoughby, and their conversation together; and was carefully minute in every particular of speech and look, where minuteness could be safely indulged. As soon as they entered the house, Marianne with a kiss of gratitude and these two words just articulate through her tears, "Tell mama," withdrew from her sister and walked slowly up stairs. Elinor would not attempt to disturb a solitude so reasonable as what she now sought; and with a mind anxiously pre-arranging its result, and a resolution of reviving the subject again, should Marianne fail to do it, she turned into the parlour to fulfil her parting injunction.

Chapter XI

Mrs. Dashwood did not hear unmoved the vindication of her former favourite. She rejoiced in his being cleared from some part of his imputed guilt;—she was sorry for him;—she wished him happy. But the feelings of the past could not be recalled.— Nothing could restore him with a faith unbroken—a character unblemished, to Marianne. Nothing could do away the knowledge of what the latter had suffered through his means, nor remove the guilt of his conduct towards Eliza. Nothing could replace him, therefore, in her former esteem, nor injure the interests of Colonel Brandon.

Had Mrs. Dashwood, like her daughter, heard Willoughby's story from himself—had she witnessed his distress, and been under the influence of his countenance and his manner, it is probable that her compassion would have been greater. But it was neither in Elinor's power, nor in her wish, to rouse such feelings in another, by her retailed[1] explanation, as had at first been called forth in herself. Reflection had given calmness to her judgment, and sobered her own opinion of Willoughby's deserts;—she wished, therefore, to declare only the simple truth, and lay open such facts as were really due to his character, without any embellishment of tenderness to lead the fancy astray.

In the evening, when they were all three together, Marianne began voluntarily to speak of him again;—but that it was not without an effort, the restless, unquiet thoughtfulness in which she had been for some time previously sitting—her rising colour, as she spoke—and her unsteady voice, plainly shewed.

"I wish to assure you both," said she, "that I see every thing—as you can desire me to do."

[1] *retailed*: recounted, passed along to others.

Mrs. Dashwood would have interrupted her instantly with soothing tenderness, had not Elinor, who really wished to hear her sister's unbiassed opinion, by an eager sign, engaged her silence. Marianne slowly continued—

"It is a great relief to me—what Elinor told me this morning —I have now heard exactly what I wished to hear."—For some moments her voice was lost; but recovering herself, she added, and with greater calmness than before—"I am now perfectly satisfied, I wish for no change. I never could have been happy with him, after knowing, as sooner or later I must have known, all this.—I should have had no confidence, no esteem. Nothing could have done it away to my feelings."

"I know it—I know it," cried her mother. "Happy with a man of libertine practices!—With one who had so injured the peace of the dearest of our friends, and the best of men!— No—my Marianne has not a heart to be made happy with such a man!—Her conscience, her sensitive conscience, would have felt all that the conscience of her husband ought to have felt."

Marianne sighed, and repeated—"I wish for no change."

"You consider the matter," said Elinor, "exactly as a good mind and a sound understanding must consider it; and I dare say, you perceive, as well as myself, not only in this, but in many other circumstances, reason enough to be convinced that your marriage must have involved you in many certain troubles and disappointments, in which you would have been poorly supported by an affection, on his side, much less certain. Had you married, you must have been always poor. His expensiveness is acknowledged even by himself, and his whole conduct declares that self-denial is a word hardly understood by him. His demands and your inexperience together on a small, very small income, must have brought on distresses which would not be the *less* grievous to you, from having been entirely unknown and unthought of before. *Your* sense of honour and honesty would have led you, I know, when aware of your situation, to attempt all the economy that would appear to you possible; and perhaps, as long as your frugality retrenched only on your own comfort, you might have been suffered to practise it, but beyond that—and how little could the utmost of your single management do to stop the ruin which had begun before your marriage?—Beyond *that*, had you endeavoured, however reasonably, to abridge *his* enjoyments, is it not to be feared, that instead of prevailing on feelings so selfish to consent to it, you would have lessened your own influence on his heart, and made him regret the connection which had involved him in such difficulties?"

Marianne's lips quivered, and she repeated the word "Selfish?" in a tone that implied—"do you really think him selfish?"

"The whole of his behaviour," replied Elinor, "from the beginning to the end of the affair, has been grounded on self-ishness. It was selfishness which first made him sport with your affections; which afterwards, when his own were engaged, made him delay the confession of it, and which finally carried him from Barton. His own enjoyment, or his own ease, was, in every particular, his ruling principle."

"It is very true. My happiness never was his object."

"At present," continued Elinor, "he regrets what he has done. And why does he regret it?—Because he finds it has not answered towards himself. It has not made him happy. His circumstances are now unembarrassed—he suffers from no evil of that kind; and he thinks only that he has married a woman of a less amiable temper than yourself. But does it thence follow that had he married you, he would have been happy?—The inconveniencies would have been different. He would then have suffered under the pecuniary distresses which, because they are removed, he now reckons as nothing. He would have had a wife of whose temper he could make no complaint, but he would have been always necessitous—always poor; and probably would soon have learnt to rank the innumerable comforts of a clear estate and good income as of far more importance, even to domestic happiness, than the mere temper of a wife."

"I have not a doubt of it," said Marianne; "and I have nothing to regret—nothing but my own folly."

"Rather say your mother's imprudence, my child," said Mrs. Dashwood; "*she* must be answerable."

Marianne would not let her proceed;—and Elinor, satisfied that each felt their own error, wished to avoid any survey of the past that might weaken her sister's spirits; she therefore, pursuing the first subject, immediately continued,

"*One* observation may, I think, be fairly drawn from the whole of the story—that all Willoughby's difficulties have arisen from the first offence against virtue, in his behaviour to Eliza Williams. That crime has been the origin of every lesser one, and of all his present discontents."

Marianne assented most feelingly to the remark; and her mother was led by it to an enumeration of Colonel Brandon's injuries and merits, warm as friendship and design could unitedly dictate. Her daughter did not look, however, as if much of it were heard by her.

Elinor, according to her expectation, saw on the two or three following days, that Marianne did not continue to gain strength as she had done; but while her resolution was unsubdued, and she still tried to appear cheerful and easy, her sister could safely trust to the effect of time upon her health.

Margaret returned, and the family were again all restored to each other, again quietly settled at the cottage, and if not pursuing their usual studies with quite so much vigour as when they first came to Barton, at least planning a vigorous prosecution of them in future.

Elinor grew impatient for some tidings of Edward. She had heard nothing of him since her leaving London, nothing new of his plans, nothing certain even of his present abode. Some letters had passed between her and her brother, in consequence of Marianne's illness; and in the first of John's, there had been this sentence:—"We know nothing of our unfortunate Edward, and can make no inquiries on so prohibited a subject, but conclude him to be still at Oxford;" which was all the intelligence of Edward afforded her by the correspondence, for his name was not even mentioned in any of the succeeding letters. She was not doomed, however, to be long in ignorance of his measures.[2]

Their man-servant had been sent one morning to Exeter on business; and when, as he waited at table, he had satisfied the inquiries of his mistress as to the event of his errand, this was his voluntary communication—

"I suppose you know, ma'am, that Mr. Ferrars is married."

Marianne gave a violent start, fixed her eyes upon Elinor, saw her turning pale, and fell back in her chair in hysterics. Mrs. Dashwood, whose eyes, as she answered the servants inquiry, had intuitively taken the same direction, was shocked to perceive by Elinor's countenance how much she really suffered, and in a moment afterwards, alike distressed by Marianne's situation, knew not on which child to bestow her principal attention.

The servant, who saw only that Miss Marianne was taken ill, had sense enough to call one of the maids, who, with Mrs. Dashwood's assistance, supported her into the other room. By that time, Marianne was rather better, and her mother leaving her to the care of Margaret and the maid, returned to Elinor, who, though still much disordered, had so far recovered the use of her reason and voice as to be just beginning an inquiry of Thomas, as to the source of his intelligence. Mrs. Dashwood immediately took all that trouble on herself; and Elinor had the benefit of the information without the exertion of seeking it.

"Who told you that Mr. Ferrars was married, Thomas?"

"I see Mr. Ferrars myself, ma'am, this morning in Exeter, and his lady too, Miss Steele as was. They was stopping in a chaise at the door of the New London Inn, as I went there with a message from Sally at the Park to her brother, who is one of the post-boys. I happened to look up as I went by the chaise, and so I see directly it was the youngest Miss Steele; so I took off my hat, and she knew me and called to me, and inquired after you, ma'am, and the young ladies, especially Miss Marianne, and

[2] *measures*: course of action.

bid me I should give her compliments and Mr. Ferrars's, their best compliments and service, and how sorry they was they had not time to come on and see you, but they was in a great hurry to go forwards, for they was going further down for a little while, but howsever, when they come back, they'd make sure to come and see you."

"But did she tell you she was married, Thomas?"

"Yes, ma'am. She smiled, and said how she had changed her name since she was in these parts. She was always a very affable and free-spoken young lady, and very civil behaved. So, I made free to wish her joy."

"Was Mr. Ferrars in the carriage with her?"

"Yes, ma'am, I just see him leaning back in it, but he did not look up;—he never was a gentleman much for talking."

Elinor's heart could easily account for his not putting himself forward; and Mrs. Dashwood probably found the same explanation.

"Was there no one else in the carriage?"

"No, ma'am, only they two."

"Do you know where they came from?"

"They come straight from town, as Miss Lucy—Mrs. Ferrars told me."

"And are going farther westward?"

"Yes, ma'am—but not to bide long. They will soon be back again, and then they'd be sure and call here."

Mrs. Dashwood now looked at her daughter; but Elinor knew better than to expect them. She recognised the whole of Lucy in the message, and was very confident that Edward would never come near them. She observed, in a low voice, to her mother, that they were probably going down to Mr. Pratt's, near Plymouth.

Thomas's intelligence seemed over. Elinor looked as if she wished to hear more.

"Did you see them off, before you came away?"

"No, ma'am—the horses was just coming out, but I could not bide any longer; I was afraid of being late."

"Did Mrs. Ferrars look well?"

"Yes, ma'am, she said how she was very well; and to my mind she was always a very handsome young lady—and she seemed vastly contented."

Mrs. Dashwood could think of no other question, and Thomas and the table-cloth, now alike needless, were soon afterwards dismissed. Marianne had already sent to say that she should eat nothing more. Mrs. Dashwood's and Elinor's appetites were equally lost, and Margaret might think herself very well off, that with so much uneasiness as both her sisters had lately experienced, so much reason as they had often had to be careless of their meals, she had never been obliged to go without her dinner before.

When the dessert and the wine were arranged, and Mrs. Dashwood and Elinor were left by themselves, they remained long together in a similarity of thoughtfulness and silence. Mrs. Dashwood feared to hazard any remark, and ventured not to offer consolation. She now found that she had erred in relying on Elinor's representation of herself; and justly concluded that every thing had been expressly softened at the time, to spare her from an increase of unhappiness, suffering as she then had suffered for Marianne. She found that she had been misled by the careful, the considerate attention of her daughter, to think the attachment, which once she had so well understood, much slighter in reality, than she had been wont to believe, or than it was now proved to be. She feared that under this persuasion she had been unjust, inattentive, nay, almost unkind, to her Elinor;—that Marianne's affliction, because more acknowledged, more immediately before her, had too much engrossed her tenderness, and led her away to forget that in Elinor she might have a daughter suffering almost as much, certainly with less self-provocation, and greater fortitude.

Chapter XII

Elinor now found the difference between the expectation of an unpleasant event, however certain the mind may be told to consider it, and certainty itself. She now found, that in spite of herself, she had always admitted a hope, while Edward remained single, that something would occur to prevent his marrying Lucy; that some resolution of his own, some mediation of friends, or some more eligible opportunity of establishment for the lady, would arise to assist the happiness of all. But he was now married, and she condemned her heart for the lurking flattery, which so much heightened the pain of the intelligence.

That he should be married so soon, before (as she imagined) he could be in orders, and consequently before he could be in possession of the living, surprised her a little at first. But she soon saw how likely it was that Lucy, in her self-provident care, in her haste to secure him, should overlook every thing but the risk of delay. They were married, married in town, and now hastening down to her uncle's. What had Edward felt on being within four miles of Barton, on seeing her mother's servant, on hearing Lucy's message!

They would soon, she supposed, be settled at Delaford.—Delaford,—that place in which so much conspired to give her an interest; which she wished to be acquainted with, and yet desired to avoid. She saw them in an instant in their parsonage-house; saw in Lucy, the active, contriving manager, uniting at once a desire of smart appearance, with the utmost frugality, and ashamed to be suspected of half her economical practices;—pursuing her own interest in every thought, courting the favour of Colonel Brandon, of Mrs. Jennings, and of every wealthy friend. In Edward,—she knew not what she saw, nor what she wished to see;—happy or unhappy,—nothing pleased her; she turned away her head from every sketch of him.

Elinor flattered herself that some one of their connections in London would write to them to announce the event, and give farther particulars,—but day after day passed off, and brought no letter, no tidings. Though uncertain that any one were to blame, she found fault with every absent friend. They were all thoughtless or indolent.

"When do you write to Colonel Brandon, ma'am?" was an inquiry which sprung from the impatience of her mind to have something going on.

"I wrote to him, my love, last week, and rather expect to see, than to hear from him again. I earnestly pressed his coming to us, and should not be surprised to see him walk in to-day or to-morrow, or any day."

This was gaining something, some thing to look forward to. Colonel Brandon *must* have some information to give.

Scarcely had she so determined it, when the figure of a man on horseback drew her eyes to the window. He stopt at their gate. It was a gentleman, it was Colonel Brandon himself. Now she should hear more; and she trembled in expectation of it. But—it was *not* Colonel Brandon—neither his air—nor his height. Were it possible, she should say it must be Edward. She looked again. He had just dismounted;—she could not be mistaken;—it *was* Edward. She moved away and sat down. "He comes from Mr. Pratt's purposely to see us. I *will* be calm; I *will* be mistress of myself."

In a moment she perceived that the others were likewise aware of the mistake. She saw her mother and Marianne change colour; saw them look at herself, and whisper a few sentences to each other. She would have given the world to be able to speak—and to make them understand that she hoped no coolness, no slight, would appear in their behaviour to him;—but she had no utterance, and was obliged to leave all to their own discretion.

Not a syllable passed aloud. They all waited in silence for the appearance of their visitor. His footsteps were heard along the gravel path; in a moment he was in the passage; and in another, he was before them.

His countenance, as he entered the room, was not too happy, even for Elinor. His complexion was white with agitation, and he looked as if fearful of his reception, and conscious that he merited no kind one. Mrs. Dashwood, however, conforming, as she trusted, to the wishes of that daughter, by whom she then meant in the warmth of her heart to be guided in every-thing, met him with a look of forced complacency, gave him her hand, and wished him joy.

He coloured, and stammered out an unintelligible reply. Elinor's lips had moved with her mother's, and when the moment of action was over, she wished that she had shaken hands with him too. But it was then too late, and with a coun-tenance meaning to be open, she sat down again and talked of the weather.

Marianne had retreated as much as possible out of sight, to conceal her distress; and Margaret, understanding some part, but not the whole, of the case, thought it incumbent on her to be dignified, and therefore took a seat as far from him as she could, and maintained a strict silence.

When Elinor had ceased to rejoice in the dryness of the season, a very awful pause took place. It was put an end to by Mrs. Dashwood, who felt obliged to hope that he had left Mrs. Ferrars very well. In an hurried manner, he replied in the affirmative.

Another pause.

Elinor, resolving to exert herself, though fearing the sound of her own voice, now said,

"Is Mrs. Ferrars at Longstaple?"

"At Longstaple!" he replied, with an air of surprise—"No, my mother is in town."

"I meant," said Elinor, taking up some work from the table, "to inquire after Mrs. *Edward* Ferrars."

She dared not look up;—but her mother and Marianne both turned their eyes on him. He coloured, seemed perplexed, looked doubtingly, and after some hesitation, said,

"Perhaps you mean—my brother—you mean Mrs.—Mrs. *Robert* Ferrars."

"Mrs. Robert Ferrars!"—was repeated by Marianne and her mother, in an accent of the utmost amazement;—and though Elinor could not speak, even *her* eyes were fixed on him with the same impatient wonder. He rose from his seat and walked to the window, apparently from not knowing what to do; took up a pair of scissars that lay there, and while spoiling both them and their sheath by cutting the latter to pieces as he spoke, said, in an hurried voice,

"Perhaps you do not know—you may not have heard that my brother is lately married to—to the youngest—to Miss Lucy Steele."

His words were echoed with unspeakable astonishment by all but Elinor, who sat with her head leaning over her work, in a state of such agitation as made her hardly know where she was.

"Yes," said he, "they were married last week, and are now at Dawlish."

Elinor could sit it no longer. She almost ran out of the room, and as soon as the door was closed, burst into tears of joy, which at first she thought would never cease. Edward, who had till then looked any where, rather than at her, saw her hurry away, and perhaps saw—or even heard, her emotion; for immediately afterwards he fell into a reverie, which no remarks, no inquiries, no affectionate address of Mrs. Dashwood could penetrate, and at last, without saying a word, quitted the room, and walked out towards the village—leaving the others in the greatest astonishment and perplexity on a change in his situation, so wonderful and so sudden;—a perplexity which they had no means of lessening but by their own conjectures.

Chapter XIII

Unaccountable, however, as the circumstances of his release might appear to the whole family, it was certain that Edward was free: and to what purpose that freedom would be employed was easily pre-determined by all;—for after experiencing the blessings of *one* imprudent engagement, contracted without his mother's consent, as he had already done for more than four years, nothing less could be expected of him in the failure of *that*, than the immediate contraction of another.

His errand at Barton, in fact, was a simple one. It was only to ask Elinor to marry him;—and considering that he was not altogether inexperienced in such a question, it might be strange that he should feel so uncomfortable in the present case as he really did, so much in need of encouragement and fresh air.

How soon he had walked himself into the proper resolution, however, how soon an opportunity of exercising it occurred, in what manner he expressed himself, and how he was received, need not be particularly told. This only need be said;—that when they all sat down to table at four o'clock, about three hours after his arrival, he had secured his lady, engaged her mother's consent, and was not only in the rapturous profession of the lover, but in the reality of reason and truth, one of the happiest of men. His situation indeed was more than commonly joyful. He had more than the ordinary triumph of accepted love to swell his heart, and raise his spirits. He was released without any reproach to himself, from an entanglement which had long formed his misery, from a woman whom he had long ceased to love;—and elevated at once to that security with another, which he must have thought of almost with despair, as soon as he had learnt to consider it with desire. He was brought, not from doubt or suspense, but from misery to

347

happiness;—and the change was openly spoken in such a gen-uine, flowing, grateful cheerfulness, as his friends had never witnessed in him before.

His heart was now open to Elinor, all its weaknesses, all its errors confessed, and his first boyish attachment to Lucy treated with all the philosophic dignity of twenty-four.

"It was a foolish, idle inclination on my side," said he, "the consequence of ignorance of the world—and want of employment. Had my mother given me some active profession when I was removed at eighteen from the care of Mr. Pratt, I think—nay, I am sure, it would never have happened; for though I left Longstaple with what I thought, at the time, a most unconquerable preference for his niece, yet had I then had any pursuit, any object to engage my time and keep me at a distance from her for a few months, I should very soon have outgrown the fancied attachment, especially by mixing more with the world, as in such a case I must have done. But instead of having anything to do, instead of having any pro-fession chosen for me, or being allowed to chuse any myself, I returned home to be completely idle; and for the first twelve-month afterwards, I had not even the nominal employment, which belonging to the university would have given me, for I was not entered at Oxford till I was nineteen. I had therefore nothing in the world to do, but to fancy myself in love; and as my mother did not make my home in every respect com-fortable, as I had no friend, no companion in my brother, and disliked new acquaintance, it was not unnatural for me to be very often at Longstaple, where I always felt myself at home, and was always sure of a welcome; and accordingly I spent the greatest part of my time there from eighteen to nineteen: Lucy appeared every thing that was amiable and obliging. She was pretty too—at least I thought so *then*, and I had seen so little of other women, that I could make no comparisons, and see no defects. Considering everything, therefore, I hope, foolish as our engagement was, foolish as it has since in every way been proved, it was not at the time an unnatural, or an inexcusable piece of folly."

The change which a few hours had wrought in the minds and the happiness of the Dashwoods, was such—so great—as promised them all, the satisfaction of a sleepless night. Mrs. Dashwood, too happy to be comfortable, knew not how to love Edward, nor praise Elinor enough, how to be enough thankful for his release without wounding his delicacy, nor how at once to give them leisure for unrestrained conversation together, and yet enjoy, as she wished, the sight and society of both.

Marianne could speak *her* happiness only by tears. Comparisons would occur—regrets would arise;—and her joy, though sincere as her love for her sister, was of a kind to give her neither spirits nor language.

But Elinor—How are *her* feelings to be described?—From the moment of learning that Lucy was married to another, that Edward was free, to the moment of his justifying the hopes which had so instantly followed, she was everything by turns but tranquil. But when the second moment had passed, when she found every doubt, every solicitude removed, compared her situation with what so lately it had been,—saw him honourably released from his former engagement, saw him instantly profiting by the release, to address herself and declare an affection as tender, as constant as she had ever supposed it to be,—she was oppressed, she was overcome by her own felicity;—and happily disposed as is the human mind to be easily familiarized with any change for the better, it required several hours to give sedateness to her spirits, or any degree of tranquility to her heart.

Edward was now fixed at the cottage at least for a week;—for whatever other claims might be made on him, it was impossible that less than a week should be given up to the enjoyment of Elinor's company, or suffice to say half that was to be said of the past, the present, and the future;—for though a very few hours spent in the hard labour of incessant talking will dispatch more subjects than can really be in common between any two rational creatures, yet with lovers it is different. Between *them* no subject is finished, no communication is even made, till it has been made at least twenty times over.

Lucy's marriage, the unceasing and reasonable wonder among them all, formed of course one of the earliest discussions of the lovers;—and Elinor's particular knowledge of each party made it appear to her in every view, as one of the most extraordinary and unaccountable circumstances she had ever heard. How they could be thrown together, and by what attraction Robert could be drawn on to marry a girl, of whose beauty she had herself heard him speak without any admiration,—a girl too already engaged to his brother, and on whose account that brother had been thrown off by his family—it was beyond her comprehension to make out. To her own heart it was a delightful affair, to her imagination it was even a ridiculous one, but to her reason, her judgment, it was completely a puzzle.

Edward could only attempt an explanation by supposing, that perhaps at first accidentally meeting, the vanity of the one had been so worked on by the flattery of the other, as to lead by degrees to all the rest. Elinor remembered what Robert had told her in Harley-street, of his opinion of what his own mediation in his brother's affairs might have done, if applied to in time. She repeated it to Edward.

"*That* was exactly like Robert,"—was his immediate observation.—"And *that*," he presently added, "might perhaps be in his head when the acquaintance between them first began. And Lucy perhaps at first might think only of procuring his good offices in my favour. Other designs might afterwards arise."

How long it had been carrying on between them, however, he was equally at a loss with herself to make out; for at Oxford, where he had remained by choice ever since his quitting London, he had had no means of hearing of her but from herself, and her letters to the very last were neither less frequent, nor less affectionate than usual. Not the smallest suspicion, therefore, had ever occurred to prepare him for what followed;—and when at last it burst on him in a letter from Lucy herself, he had been for some time, he believed, half stupified between the wonder, the horror, and the joy of such a deliverance. He put the letter into Elinor's hands.

"DEAR SIR,

BEING very sure I have long lost your affections, I have thought myself at liberty to bestow my own on another, and have no doubt of being as happy with him as I once used to think I might be with you; but I scorn to accept a hand while the heart was another's. Sincerely wish you happy in your choice, and it shall not be my fault if we are not always good friends, as our near relationship now makes proper. I can safely say I owe you no ill-will, and am sure you will be too generous to do us any ill offices. Your brother has gained my affections entirely, and as we could not live without one another, we are just returned from the altar, and are now on our way to Dawlish for a few weeks, which place your dear brother has great curiosity to see, but thought I would first trouble you with these few lines, and shall always remain,

Your sincere well-wisher, friend, and sister,   LUCY FERRARS.

I have burnt all your letters, and will return your picture the first opportunity. Please to destroy my scrawls—but the ring with my hair you are very welcome to keep."

Elinor read and returned it without any comment.

"I will not ask your opinion of it as a composition," said Edward.—"For worlds would not I have had a letter of her's seen by *you* in former days.—In a sister it is bad enough, but in a wife!—how I have blushed over the pages of her writing!—and I believe I may say that since the first half year of our foolish—business—this is the only letter I ever received from her, of which the substance made me any amends for the defect of the style."

"However it may have come about," said Elinor, after a pause—"they are certainly married. And your mother has brought on herself a most appropriate punishment. The independence she settled on Robert, through resentment against you, has put it in his power to make his own choice; and she has actually been bribing one son with a thousand a-year, to do the very deed which she disinherited the other for intending to do. She will hardly be less hurt, I suppose, by Robert's marrying Lucy, than she would have been by your marrying her."

"She will be more hurt by it, for Robert always was her favourite.—She will be more hurt by it, and on the same principle will forgive him much sooner."

In what state the affair stood at present between them, Edward knew not, for no communication with any of his family had yet been attempted by him. He had quitted Oxford within four and twenty hours after Lucy's letter arrived, and with only one object before him, the nearest road to Barton, had had no leisure to form any scheme of conduct, with which that road did not hold the most intimate connection. He could do nothing till he were assured of his fate with Miss Dashwood; and by his rapidity in seeking *that* fate, it is to be supposed, in spite of the jealousy with which he had once thought of Colonel Brandon, in spite of the modesty with which he rated his own deserts, and the politeness with which he talked of his doubts, he did not, upon the whole, expect a very cruel reception. It was his business, however, to say that he *did*, and he said it very prettily. What he might say on the subject a twelvemonth after, must be referred to the imagination of husbands and wives.

That Lucy had certainly meant to deceive, to go off with a flourish of malice against him in her message by Thomas, was perfectly clear to Elinor; and Edward himself, now thoroughly enlightened on her character, had no scruple in believing her capable of the utmost meanness of wanton ill-nature. Though his eyes had been long opened, even before his acquaintance with Elinor began, to her ignorance and a want of liberality in some of her opinions—they had been equally imputed, by him, to her want of education; and till her last letter reached him, he had always believed her to be a well-disposed, good-hearted girl, and thoroughly attached to himself. Nothing but such a persuasion could have prevented his putting an end to an engagement, which, long before the discovery of it laid him open to his mother's anger, had been a continual source of disquiet and regret to him.

"I thought it my duty," said he, "independent of my feelings, to give her the option of continuing the engagement or not, when I was renounced by my mother, and stood to all appearance without a friend in the world to assist me. In such a situation as that, where there seemed nothing to tempt the avarice or the vanity of any living creature, how could I suppose, when she so earnestly, so warmly insisted on sharing my fate, whatever it might be, that any thing but the most disinterested affection was her inducement? And even now, I cannot comprehend on what motive she acted, or what fancied advantage it could be to her, to be fettered to a man for whom she had not the smallest regard, and who had only two thousand pounds in the world. She could not foresee that Colonel Brandon would give me a living."

"No, but she might suppose that something would occur in your favour; that your own family might in time relent. And at any rate, she lost nothing by continuing the engagement, for she has proved that it fettered neither her inclination nor her actions. The connection was certainly a respectable one, and probably gained her consideration among her friends; and, if nothing more advantageous occurred, it would be better for her to marry *you* than be single."

Edward was of course immediately convinced that nothing could have been more natural than Lucy's conduct, nor more self-evident than the motive of it.

Elinor scolded him, harshly as ladies always scold the imprudence which compliments themselves, for having spent so much time with them at Norland, when he must have felt his own inconstancy.

"Your behaviour was certainly very wrong," said she, "because—to say nothing of my own conviction, our relations were all led away by it to fancy and expect *what*, as you were *then* situated, could never be."

He could only plead an ignorance of his own heart, and a mistaken confidence in the force of his engagement.

"I was simple enough to think, that because my *faith* was plighted to another, there could be no danger in my being with you; and that the consciousness of my engagement was to keep my heart as safe and sacred as my honour. I felt that I admired you, but I told myself it was only friendship; and till I began to make comparisons between yourself and Lucy, I did not know how far I was got. After that, I suppose, I *was* wrong in remaining so much in Sussex, and the arguments with which I reconciled myself to the expediency of it, were no better than these:—The danger is my own; I am doing no injury to anybody but myself."

Elinor smiled, and shook her head.

Edward heard with pleasure of Colonel Brandon's being expected at the Cottage, as he really wished not only to be better acquainted with him, but to have an opportunity of convincing him that he no longer resented his giving him the living of Delaford—"Which, at present," said he, "after thanks so ungraciously delivered as mine were on the occasion, he must think I have never forgiven him for offering."

Now he felt astonished himself that he had never yet been to the place. But so little interest had he taken in the matter that he owed all his knowledge of the house, garden, and glebe*, extent of the parish, condition of the land, and rate of the tythes, to Elinor herself, who had heard so much of it from Colonel Brandon, and heard it with so much attention, as to be entirely mistress of the subject.

One question after this only remained undecided between them, one difficulty only was to be overcome. They were brought together by mutual affection, with the warmest approbation of their real friends, their intimate knowledge of each other seemed to make their happiness certain—and they only wanted something to live upon. Edward had two thousand pounds, and Elinor one, which, with Delaford living, was all that they could call their own; for it was impossible that Mrs. Dashwood should advance anything, and they were neither of them quite enough in love to think that three hundred and fifty pounds a-year would supply them with the comforts of life.

* *glebe*: plot of cultivated land.

Edward was not entirely without hopes of some favourable change in his mother towards him; and on *that* he rested for the residue of their income. But Elinor had no such dependance; for since Edward would still be unable to marry Miss Morton, and his chusing herself had been spoken of in Mrs. Ferrars's flattering language as only a lesser evil than his chusing Lucy Steele, she feared that Robert's offence would serve no other purpose than to enrich Fanny.

About four days after Edward's arrival Colonel Brandon appeared, to complete Mrs. Dashwood's satisfaction, and to give her the dignity of having, for the first time since her living at Barton, more company with her than her house would hold. Edward was allowed to retain the privilege of first comer, and Colonel Brandon therefore walked every night to his old quarters at the Park; from whence he usually returned in the morning, early enough to interrupt the lovers' first tête-à-tête before breakfast.

A three weeks' residence at Delaford, where, in his evening hours at least, he had little to do but to calculate the disproportion between thirty-six and seventeen, brought him to Barton in a temper of mind which needed all the improvement in Marianne's looks, all the kindness of her welcome, and all the encouragement of her mother's language, to make it cheerful. Among such friends, however, and such flattery, he did revive. No rumour of Lucy's marriage had yet reached him;—he knew nothing of what had passed; and the first hours of his visit were consequently spent in hearing and in wondering. Every thing was explained to him by Mrs. Dashwood, and he found fresh reason to rejoice in what he had done for Mr. Ferrars, since eventually it promoted the interest of Elinor.

It would be needless to say, that the gentlemen advanced in the good opinion of each other, as they advanced in each other's acquaintance, for it could not be otherwise. Their resemblance in good principles and good sense, in disposition and manner of thinking, would probably have been sufficient to unite them in friendship, without any other attraction; but their being in love with two sisters, and two sisters fond of each other, made that mutual regard inevitable and immediate, which might otherwise have waited the effect of time and judgment.

The letters from town, which a few days before would have made every nerve in Elinor's body thrill with transport, now arrived to be read with less emotion than mirth. Mrs. Jennings wrote to tell the wonderful tale, to vent her honest indignation against the jilting girl, and pour forth her compassion towards poor Mr. Edward, who, she was sure, had quite doted upon the worthless hussey, and was now, by all accounts, almost broken-hearted, at Oxford.—"I do think," she continued, "nothing was ever carried on so sly; for it was but two days before Lucy called and sat a couple of hours with me. Not a soul suspected anything of the matter, not even Nancy, who, poor soul! came crying to me the day after, in a great fright for fear of Mrs. Ferrars, as well as not knowing how to get to Plymouth; for Lucy it seems borrowed all her money before she went off to be married, on purpose we suppose to make a shew with, and poor Nancy had not seven shillings in the world;—so I was very glad to give her five guineas to take her down to Exeter, where she thinks of staying three or four weeks with Mrs. Burgess, in hopes, as I tell her, to fall in with the Doctor again. And I must say that Lucy's crossness not to take her along with them in the chaise is worse than all. Poor Mr. Edward! I cannot get him out of my head, but you must send for him to Barton, and Miss Marianne must try to comfort him."

Mr. Dashwood's strains were more solemn. Mrs. Ferrars was the most unfortunate of women—poor Fanny had suffered agonies of sensibility—and he considered the existence of each, under such a blow, with grateful wonder. Robert's offence was unpardonable, but Lucy's was infinitely worse. Neither of them was ever again to be mentioned to Mrs. Ferrars; and even, if she might hereafter be induced to forgive her son, his wife should never be acknowledged as her daughter, nor be permitted to appear in her presence. The secrecy with which every thing had been carried on between them, was rationally treated as enormously heightening the crime, because, had any suspicion of it occurred to the others, proper measures would have been taken to prevent the marriage; and he called on Elinor to join with him in regretting that Lucy's engagement with Edward had not rather been fulfilled, than that she should thus be the means of spreading misery farther in the family.—He thus continued:

"Mrs. Ferrars has never yet mentioned Edward's name, which does not surprise us; but to our great astonishment, not a line has been received from him on the occasion. Perhaps, however, he is kept silent by his fear of offending, and I shall, therefore, give him a hint, by a line to Oxford, that his sister and I both think a letter of proper submission from him addressed perhaps to Fanny, and by her shewn to her mother, might not be taken amiss; for we all know the tenderness of Mrs. Ferrars's heart, and that she wishes for nothing so much as to be on good terms with her children."

This paragraph was of some importance to the prospects and conduct of Edward. It determined him to attempt a reconciliation, though not exactly in the manner pointed out by their brother and sister.

"A letter of proper submission!" repeated he; "would they have me beg my mother's pardon for Robert's ingratitude to *her*, and breach of honour to *me*?—I can make no submission—I am grown neither humble nor penitent by what has passed.— I am grown very happy, but that would not interest.—I know of no submission that is proper for me to make."

"You may certainly ask to be forgiven," said Elinor, "because you have offended;—and I should think you might *now* venture so far as to profess some concern for having ever formed the engagement which drew on you your mother's anger."

He agreed that he might.

"And when she has forgiven you, perhaps a little humility may be convenient while acknowledging a second engagement, almost as imprudent in *her* eyes, as the first."

He had nothing to urge against it, but still resisted the idea of a letter of proper submission; and therefore, to make it easier to him, as he declared a much greater willingness to make mean concessions by word of mouth than on paper, it was resolved that, instead of writing to Fanny, he should go to London, and personally intreat her good offices in his favour.—"And if they really *do* interest themselves," said Marianne, in her new character of candour, "in bringing about a reconciliation, I shall think that even John and Fanny are not entirely without merit."

After a visit on Colonel Brandon's side of only three or four days, the two gentlemen quitted Barton together.—They were to go immediately to Delaford, that Edward might have some personal knowledge of his future home, and assist his patron and friend in deciding on what improvements were needed to it; and from thence, after staying there a couple of nights, he was to proceed on his journey to town.

Chapter XIV

After a proper resistance on the part of Mrs. Ferrars, just so violent and so steady as to preserve her from that reproach which she always seemed fearful of incurring, the reproach of being too amiable, Edward was admitted to her presence, and pronounced to be again her son.

Her family had of late been exceedingly fluctuating. For many years of her life she had had two sons; but the crime and annihilation of Edward a few weeks ago, had robbed her of one; the similar annihilation of Robert had left her for a fortnight without any; and now, by the resuscitation of Edward, she had one again.

In spite of his being allowed once more to live, however, he did not feel the continuance of his existence secure, till he had revealed his present engagement; for the publication of that circumstance, he feared, might give a sudden turn to his constitution, and carry him off as rapidly as before. With apprehensive caution therefore it was revealed, and he was listened to with unexpected calmness. Mrs. Ferrars at first reasonably endeavoured to dissuade him from marrying Miss Dashwood, by every argument in her power;—told him, that in Miss Morton he would have a woman of higher rank and larger fortune;—and enforced the assertion, by observing that Miss Morton was the daughter of a nobleman with thirty thousand pounds, while Miss Dashwood was only the daughter of a private gentleman, with no more than *three*; but when she found that, though perfectly admitting the truth of her representation, he was by no means inclined to be guided by it, she judged it wisest, from the experience of the past, to submit—and therefore, after such an ungracious delay as she owed to her own dignity, and as served to prevent every suspicion of good-will, she issued her decree of consent to the marriage of Edward and Elinor.

What she would engage to do towards augmenting their income, was next to be considered; and here it plainly appeared, that though Edward was now her only son, he was by no means her eldest; for while Robert was inevitably endowed with a thousand pounds a-year, not the smallest objection was made against Edward's taking orders for the sake of two hundred and fifty at the utmost; nor was any thing promised either for the present or in future, beyond the ten thousand pounds, which had been given with Fanny.

It was as much, however, as was desired, and more than was expected by Edward and Elinor; and Mrs. Ferrars herself, by her shuffling excuses, seemed the only person surprised at her not giving more.

With an income quite sufficient to their wants thus secured to them, they had nothing to wait for after Edward was in possession of the living, but the readiness of the house, to which Colonel Brandon, with an eager desire for the accommodation of Elinor, was making considerable improvements; and after waiting some time for their completion, after experiencing, as usual, a thousand disappointments and delays, from the unaccountable dilatoriness[1] of the workmen, Elinor, as usual, broke through the first positive resolution of not marrying till every thing was ready, and the ceremony took place in Barton church early in the autumn.

The first month after their marriage was spent with their friend at the Mansion-house, from whence they could superintend the progress of the Parsonage, and direct every thing as they liked on the spot;—could chuse papers,[2] project shrubberies, and invent a sweep.[3] Mrs. Jennings's prophecies, though rather jumbled together, were chiefly fulfilled; for she was able to visit Edward and his wife in their Parsonage by Michaelmas, and she found in Elinor and her husband, as she really believed, one of the happiest couple in the world. They had in fact

[1] *dilatoriness*: tendency to work slowly (as in dillydallying).
[2] *papers*: i.e., wallpapers.
[3] *sweep*: drive leading to a noble house.

nothing to wish for, but the marriage of Colonel Brandon and Marianne, and rather better pasturage for their cows.

They were visited on their first settling by almost all their relations and friends. Mrs. Ferrars came to inspect the happiness which she was almost ashamed of having authorised; and even the Dashwoods were at the expense of a journey from Sussex to do them honour.

"I will not say that I am disappointed, my dear sister," said John, as they were walking together one morning before the gates of Delaford House, "*that* would be saying too much, for certainly you have been one of the most fortunate young women in the world, as it is. But, I confess, it would give me great pleasure to call Colonel Brandon brother. His property here, his place, his house, every thing in such respectable and excellent condition!—and his woods!—I have not seen such timber any where in Dorsetshire, as there is now standing in Delaford Hanger![4]—And though, perhaps, Marianne may not seem exactly the person to attract him—yet I think it would altogether be adviseable for you to have them now frequently staying with you, for as Colonel Brandon seems a great deal at home, nobody can tell what may happen—for, when people are much thrown together, and see little of anybody else—and it will always be in your power to set her off to advantage, and so forth;—in short, you may as well give her a chance—You understand me."—

But though Mrs. Ferrars *did* come to see them, and always treated them with the make-believe of decent affection, they were never insulted by her real favour and preference. *That* was due to the folly of Robert, and the cunning of his wife; and it was earned by them before many months had passed away. The selfish sagacity of the latter, which had at first drawn Robert into the scrape, was the principal instrument of his deliverance from it; for her respectful humility, assiduous attentions, and endless flatteries, as soon as the smallest opening was given for their exercise, reconciled Mrs. Ferrars to his choice, and re-established him completely in her favour.

[4] *Hanger*: woods on the side of a steep hill.

The whole of Lucy's behaviour in the affair, and the prosperity which crowned it, therefore, may be held forth as a most encouraging instance of what an earnest, an unceasing attention to self-interest, however its progress may be apparently obstructed, will do in securing every advantage of fortune, with no other sacrifice than that of time and conscience. When Robert first sought her acquaintance, and privately visited her in Bartlett's Buildings, it was only with the view imputed to him by his brother. He merely meant to persuade her to give up the engagement; and as there could be nothing to overcome but the affection of both, he naturally expected that one or two interviews would settle the matter. In that point, however, and that only, he erred;—for though Lucy soon gave him hopes that his eloquence would convince her in *time*, another visit, another conversation, was always wanted to produce this conviction. Some doubts always lingered in her mind when they parted, which could only be removed by another half hour's discourse with himself. His attendance was by this means secured, and the rest followed in course. Instead of talking of Edward, they came gradually to talk only of Robert,—a subject on which he had always more to say than on any other, and in which she soon betrayed an interest even equal to his own; and in short, it became speedily evident to both, that he had entirely supplanted his brother. He was proud of his conquest, proud of tricking Edward, and very proud of marrying privately without his mother's consent. What immediately followed is known. They passed some months in great happiness at Dawlish; for she had many relations and old acquaintance to cut—and he drew several plans for magnificent cottages;— and from thence returning to town, procured the forgiveness of Mrs. Ferrars, by the simple expedient of asking it, which, at Lucy's instigation, was adopted. The forgiveness at first, indeed, as was reasonable, comprehended only Robert; and Lucy, who had owed his mother no duty, and therefore could have transgressed none, still remained some weeks longer unpardoned. But perseverance in humility of conduct and messages, in self-condemnation for Robert's offence, and gratitude for the unkindness she was treated with, procured her in time the haughty notice which overcame her by its graciousness, and led soon afterwards, by rapid degrees, to the highest state of affection and influence. Lucy became as necessary to Mrs. Ferrars, as either Robert or Fanny; and while Edward was never cordially forgiven for having once intended to marry her, and Elinor, though superior to her in fortune and birth, was spoken of as an intruder, *she* was in every thing considered, and always openly acknowledged, to be a favourite child. They settled in town, received very liberal assistance from Mrs. Ferrars, were on the best terms imaginable with the Dashwoods; and setting aside the jealousies and ill-will continually subsisting between Fanny and Lucy, in which their husbands of course took a part, as well as the frequent domestic disagreements between Robert and Lucy themselves, nothing could exceed the harmony in which they all lived together.

What Edward had done to forfeit the right of eldest son, might have puzzled many people to find out; and what Robert had done to succeed to it, might have puzzled them still more. It was an arrangement, however, justified in its effects, if not in its cause; for nothing ever appeared in Robert's style of living or of talking, to give a suspicion of his regretting the extent of his income, as either leaving his brother too little, or bringing himself too much;—and if Edward might be judged from the ready discharge of his duties in every particular, from an increasing attachment to his wife and his home, and from the regular cheerfulness of his spirits, he might be supposed no less contented with his lot, no less free from every wish of an exchange.

Elinor's marriage divided her as little from her family as could well be contrived, without rendering the cottage at Barton entirely useless, for her mother and sisters spent much more than half their time with her. Mrs. Dashwood was acting on motives of policy as well as pleasure in the frequency of her visits at Delaford; for her wish of bringing Marianne and Colonel Brandon together was hardly less earnest, though rather more liberal than what John had expressed. It was now her darling object. Precious as was the company of her daughter to her, she desired nothing so much as to give up its constant enjoyment to her valued friend; and to see Marianne settled at the mansion-house was equally the wish of Edward and Elinor. They each felt his sorrows, and their own obligations, and Marianne, by general consent, was to be the reward of all.

With such a confederacy against her—with a knowledge so intimate of his goodness—with a conviction of his fond attachment to herself, which at last, though long after it was observable to everybody else—burst on her—what could she do?

Marianne Dashwood was born to an extraordinary fate. She was born to discover the falsehood of her own opinions, and to counteract, by her conduct, her most favourite maxims. She was born to overcome an affection formed so late in life as at seventeen, and with no sentiment superior to strong esteem and lively friendship, voluntarily to give her hand to another!— and *that* other, a man who had suffered no less than herself under the event of a former attachment, whom, two years before, she had considered too old to be married,—and who still sought the constitutional safeguard of a flannel waistcoat!

But so it was. Instead of falling a sacrifice to an irresistible passion, as once she had fondly flattered herself with expecting,— instead of remaining even for ever with her mother, and finding her only pleasures in retirement and study, as afterwards in her more calm and sober judgment she had determined on,—she found herself at nineteen, submitting to new attachments, entering on new duties, placed in a new home, a wife, the mistress of a family, and the patroness of a village.

Colonel Brandon was now as happy, as all those who best loved him, believed he deserved to be;—in Marianne he was consoled for every past affliction;—her regard and her society restored his mind to animation, and his spirits to cheerfulness; and that Marianne found her own happiness in forming his, was equally the persuasion and delight of each observing friend. Marianne could never love by halves; and her whole heart became, in time, as much devoted to her husband, as it had once been to Willoughby.

Willoughby could not hear of her marriage without a pang; and his punishment was soon afterwards complete in the voluntary forgiveness of Mrs. Smith, who, by stating his marriage with a woman of character, as the source of her clemency, gave him reason for believing that had he behaved with honour towards Marianne, he might at once have been happy and rich. That his repentance of misconduct, which thus brought its own punishment, was sincere, need not be doubted;—nor that he long thought of Colonel Brandon with envy, and of Marianne with regret. But that he was for ever inconsolable, that he fled from society, or contracted an habitual gloom of temper, or died of a broken heart, must not be depended on—for he did neither. He lived to exert, and frequently to enjoy himself. His wife was not always out of humour, nor his home always uncomfortable; and in his breed of horses and dogs, and in sporting of every kind, he found no inconsiderable degree of domestic felicity.

For Marianne, however—in spite of his incivility in surviving her loss—he always retained that decided regard which interested him in everything that befell her, and made her his secret standard of perfection in woman;—and many a rising beauty would be slighted by him in after-days as bearing no comparison with Mrs. Brandon.

Mrs. Dashwood was prudent enough to remain at the cottage, without attempting a removal to Delaford; and fortunately for Sir John and Mrs. Jennings, when Marianne was taken from them, Margaret had reached an age highly suitable for dancing, and not very ineligible for being supposed to have a lover.

Between Barton and Delaford, there was that constant communication which strong family affection would naturally dictate;—and among the merits and the happiness of Elinor and Marianne, let it not be ranked as the least considerable, that though sisters, and living almost within sight of each other, they could live without disagreement between themselves, or producing coolness between their husbands.

FINIS.

Contemporary Essays

"Everything in Such Suspense and Uncertainty"— Suspense in Jane Austen's *Sense and Sensibility*

Raimund Borgmeier

University of Giessen, Germany

> *The person, be it gentleman or lady, who has not pleasure in a good novel, must be intolerably stupid. I have read all Mrs. Radcliffe's works, and most of them with great pleasure. The Mysteries of Udolpho, when I had once begun it, I could not lay down again;—I remember finishing it in two days—my hair standing on end the whole time.*
>
> —Jane Austen, *Northanger Abbey*

The above quotation from Jane Austen's *Northanger Abbey* (1818) is what Henry Tilney says about the practice of reading fiction, as he describes his own experiences as a reader of novels. He does this to correct the assumption of Catherine, the protagonist, who presumes that "gentlemen read better books."[1] Henry's reaction makes it clear that Catherine, in her statement, does not primarily refer to the literary quality of the texts read. She rather thinks that educated people—and these were then primarily "gentlemen"—should read, instead of fictional works, expository texts deemed to be of higher quality ("the History of England" and "the Spectator" are mentioned at the beginning of the novel by the author in her emphatic declaration for her own genre[2]). Henry, however, stresses the potentially high value of novel reading as an affective experience. As the author did before, he declares himself personally and decidedly for the novel as a genre and emphasizes, in his

---

[1] Jane Austen, *Northanger Abbey* (London: Penguin, 1995), p. 95.
[2] Ibid., p. 34.

own encounter with an outstanding example of this kind of text, the experience of suspense: he was not able to interrupt his reading but had to read on and found himself in an obviously pleasant state of excitement.

Henry is one of the most positive male characters in Jane Austen's novels. He has the function of a mentor for Catherine by providing impulses for her moral development and by drawing her attention to basic aspects of the world and contemporary society. He stands, therefore, as we must assume—with his values and ideas, to a great extent—for the author herself. And in a novel in which not only the Gothic novel but the novel in general is an important theme, we must take his statements about the genre seriously. So we can assume that for Jane Austen suspense essentially belongs to the novel. She obviously thinks that for the reader of a novel, suspense very much determines the experience of reading and makes it attractive.

This is in marked contrast to the fact that suspense is hardly ever discussed in Jane Austen criticism. Could it be possible that Austen does not pay attention in her own novels to what she has recognized to be so essential for the reader? Or are there perhaps reasons why the critics have neglected this aspect so much?

An important reason must certainly be seen in the fact that criticism for a long time has become accustomed to discussing Jane Austen's novels preferably as paintings, thus considering them static. The author herself is not quite innocent in this matter. She started this when, in a letter to her nephew Edward written on December 16, 1816, she refers to her fictional art as a miniature painting, as "the little bit (two Inches wide) of Ivory, on which I work with so fine a Brush, as produces little effect after much labour".[3]

This kind of view is also dominant with the contemporaries. Richard Whately, in a detailed review of Austen's last novel

---

[3] R. W. Chapman, ed., *Jane Austen's Letters to Her Sister Cassandra and Others* (London: Oxford University Press, 1959), p. 469.

publication, talks of "this Flemish painting,... this accurate and unexaggerated delineation of events and characters".[4] Similarly, Sir Walter Scott, who recognized the importance of his writer colleague early on, writes in his journal on September 18, 1827, "There is a truth of painting in her writings which always delights me."[5] Likewise, the famous Shakespearean actor and theater manager William Charles Macready, in a diary entry, praises "her [Jane Austen's] power of *drawing* and sustaining character" and states, "She is successful in *painting* the ridiculous to the life."[6]

Victorian novelists view Austen's art much more reservedly but use the same descriptive model. After reading *Emma*, Charlotte Brontë, who is not very fond of Jane Austen, observes in 1850 in a letter, "There is a chinese fidelity, a miniature delicacy in the painting."[7] And her literary colleague Julia Kanavagh judges, in her study *English Women of Letters* (1862), that "Miss Austen,... though she adopted the pictorial method, is not an effective writer."[8]

Also when, toward the end of the nineteenth century, a clearly more positive assessment of the novelist evolves, the pictorial view is maintained. In a *Spectator* article of 1890, R.H. Hutton praises Jane Austen's "great charm" and mentions in this context "her exquisite pictures".[9] Even Virginia Woolf, who admires Austen very much, pays tribute to her and says, "More than every other novelist she fills every inch of her canvas with observation."[10]

A pictorial, static view of this kind, however, excludes suspense from the outset. As Eric S. Rabkin remarks in *Narrative Suspense*, one of the few books dealing with this subject,

[4] Brian C. Southam, ed., *Jane Austen: The Critical Heritage*, 2 vols. (London and New York: Routledge, 1968), vol. 1, p. 88.
[5] Ibid., p. 106.
[6] Ibid., p. 118 (emphasis added).
[7] Ibid., p. 128.
[8] Ibid., vol. 2, p. 176.
[9] Ibid., p. 195.
[10] Ibid., p. 244.

suspense is essentially connected with the procedural character of language and reading:

> Of course, our written language is linear. And of course, then, it must present progressions. But he [the reader] is into this progression because, having been interested by the title, he waits now to find out more. "And then?" He waits. And he reads while he waits. This is suspense.[11]

This is the point of view of the reader, who in the process of reading gets to know in a consecutive experience the world of the novel. While reading, he is more or less prompted to move on, becomes involved, and wants to see more and to know more details.

It seems to be hardly a coincidence when Virginia Woolf—in a different context, as she once discusses Austen's novels predominantly from the point of view of the reader—uses the keyword "suspense"—a rare phenomenon in Austen criticism. She states about the novelist's achievement as we experience it as readers,

> Jane Austen is thus a mistress of much deeper emotion than appears on the surface. She stimulates us to supply what is not there. What she offers is, apparently, a trifle, yet is composed of something that expands in the reader's mind and endows with the most enduring form of life scenes which are outwardly trivial. Always the stress is laid upon character.... The turns and twists of the dialogue keep us on the tenterhooks of *suspense*. Our attention is half upon the present moment, half upon the future.[12]

Indeed, we do not view an Austen novel like a painting, which we may study at our leisure from this side or that side, but we follow the narrative in a certain direction. And, in reading, we do not have to make a laborious effort to reach the information

---

[11] Eric S. Rabkin, *Narrative Suspense* (Ann Arbor, Mich.: University of Michigan Press, 1973), pp. 5–6.

[12] Quoted in John Odmark, *An Understanding of Jane Austen's Novels: Character, Value and Ironic Perspective* (Oxford: Blackwell, 1983), pp. xiii–xiv (emphasis added).

conveyed by the text, but we can observe how the reading stimulates us—we get interested and wish to know more and read on with commitment.

In the following, I will look at Jane Austen's *Sense and Sensibility* and find out how she builds up and uses suspense. As a working definition I will take up what a regular literary dictionary says about "suspense": "A state of uncertainty, anticipation and curiosity as to the outcome of a story or play, or any kind of narrative in verse or prose."[13] It seems advisable, however, to distinguish between two basic kinds of suspense. There is what one may call "final suspense", when the final result is important and the reader wants to know the answer to a certain question; as the colloquial term "whodunit" suggests, this kind of suspense is, above all, to be found in detective novels. Another kind of suspense may be termed "procedural suspense". This occurs when we know or can expect with some degree of certainty a specific outcome, but we wonder and are interested to learn in what way this comes about. In this case the details and the process are essential.

Procedural suspense (*how*) is, one might say, a milder form of suspense than final suspense (*what*), and we can assume that this is the more important kind in Jane Austen's novel. That she is not interested in making the reader's experience of reading *Sense and Sensibility* as thrilling as possible can be seen, at the outset, from the fact that the most dramatic event in the whole plot—the duel fought between Colonel Brandon and Willoughby—is not used to create suspense at all and is merely mentioned in a brief paragraph to demonstrate the colonel's decision and seriousness.[14] But nevertheless, suspense is important.

As Virginia Woolf suggests in the statement quoted above, in Jane Austen's novels the characters are of prime importance.

---

[13] J. A. Cudden, *A Dictionary of Literary Terms* (Harmondsworth, England: Penguin, 1982), s.v. "suspense".

[14] Jane Austen, *Sense and Sensibility*, ed. Eleanor Bourg Nicholson, Ignatius Critical Editions (San Francisco: Ignatius Press, 2014), p. 205. Subsequent quotations from this edition will be cited in the text.

The author conceives the various figures in the narrative so that we can expect interesting developments. In *Sense and Sensibility*, this concerns, above all, the two protagonists, Elinor and Marianne Dashwood, who are clearly related to the two qualities mentioned in the title.

Elinor, the eldest daughter, is introduced in the opening chapter in a decidedly positive manner:

> Elinor ... possessed a strength of understanding, and coolness of judgment, which qualified her, though only nineteen, to be the counsellor of her mother.... She had an excellent heart;— her disposition was affectionate, and her feelings were strong; but she knew how to govern them: it was a knowledge which her mother had yet to learn, and which one of her sisters had resolved never to be taught. (See pp. 6–7.)

Though the narrator emphasizes that Elinor also has strong feelings, she mainly stands for sense and reason. Because of her "coolness of judgment" she is able to control herself and advise others. She is the most important character, and Stuart M. Tave rightly observes, "The whole of the story comes to us through Elinor."[15] Elinor represents Jane Austen's positive norms. She is viewed in a strong contrast to her sister Marianne; when the narrator, in the last sentence of the above-quoted paragraph, makes us aware that Marianne not only lacks the knowledge her sister has but vehemently refuses to acquire it, we become curious and wonder what harmful consequences this will have.

This essential source of suspense is further enhanced when Marianne is specifically introduced and, again, contrasted with her prudent sister:

> Marianne's abilities were, in many respects, quite equal to Elinor's. She was sensible and clever; but eager in every thing; her sorrows, her joys, could have no moderation. She was generous, amiable, interesting: she was every thing but prudent. (See p. 7.)

---

[15] Stuart M. Tave, *Some Words of Jane Austen* (Chicago: University of Chicago Press, 1973), p. 96.

Marianne's definite lack of moderation and control makes the reader apprehensive that this will lead to serious and unhappy developments, and, indeed, this is what much of the narrative is about.

The same apprehensions that the reader has are also felt by the prudent sister: "Elinor saw, with concern, the excess of her sister's sensibility" (see p. 7). So Marianne stands for the second quality mentioned in the novel's title, which means "delicate, sensitive awareness or responsiveness".[16] The fact that both Mrs. Dashwood, the mother, and Margaret, the younger sister, have similar personalities to Marianne and also lack restraint and moderation—"[t]hey gave themselves up wholly to their sorrow", we learn (see p. 7)—intensifies the apprehension and doubtful expectation we feel early on.

The two qualities of the title are not only mentioned at the beginning when the two protagonists are introduced, but they are taken up later in the course of the narrative also with reference to other characters. When Edward Ferrars appears, in the following chapters, Marianne criticizes him that he can "read with so little sensibility" (see p. 18). A little later, however, when Elinor defends him, Marianne has to admit, "I have the highest opinion in the world of his goodness and sense" (see pp. 19–20). So we wonder how this will work out, and if we already expect him to turn out to be the right man for sensible Elinor, we are made curious in what way this may come about.

Similarly, Colonel Brandon is introduced by the narrator: "[T]hough his face was not handsome his countenance was sensible, and his address was particularly gentlemanlike" (see p. 34). Elinor also calls the colonel afterward "a sensible man" (see p. 51), which makes us sympathize with him and wait to see how he may succeed in his endeavors to win Marianne. Shortly before the end, the narrator confirms our positive appreciation of the two men who become happy bridegrooms:

16 *Webster's New World College Dictionary*, 4th ed., s.v. "sensibility".

> Their resemblance in good principles and good sense, in dispo-
> sition and manner of thinking, would probably have been suffi-
> cient to unite them in friendship, without any other attraction;
> but their being in love with two sisters, and two sisters fond of
> each other, made that mutual regard inevitable and immediate.
> (See pp. 355–56.)

Now the arch of suspense built up at the beginning is closed.

While the two positive male figures are linked with sense,
Willoughby—the antagonist, the source of most of the sufferings Marianne and, consequently, her family have to
undergo—is not only contrasted with Edward but brought in
connection with the second quality of the title when the narrator tells us early on, "[H]e read with all the sensibility and
spirit which Edward had unfortunately wanted" (see p. 49).
This contributes to make us skeptical whether this man will
really prove to be as good as he seems—and, of course, our
misgivings are very soon confirmed.

When the Miss Steeles are introduced, we learn that "Elinor
soon allowed them credit for some kind of sense" (see p. 117),
and later on Elinor acknowledges, "Lucy does not want sense"
(see p. 254). In both cases, this is only qualified approval, but
it serves to make us aware that Lucy, Elinor's rival, is not only
malicious but also intelligent and has to be taken seriously.
We pay greater attention to what she says and does, and we
become curious about what will happen.

So Jane Austen conceives the characters and their personalities with a potential for future problems and solutions,
which we partly understand, so that it becomes an important
source of suspense—a conception, of course, not only with
regard to the salient features mentioned in the title. This even
concerns the minor characters. Mrs. Jennings, for example, is
represented as "a great wonderer, as every one must be who
takes a very lively interest in all the comings and goings of all
their acquaintance" (see p. 70). And the reader, of course, is
meant to take part in her conjectures (which often prove to
be wrong). Sir John Middleton, who is extremely sociable and
always wants to bring people together, has a similar function.

In addition to the characters and their potential, Jane Austen also creates suspense by the way she devises her plot. Right at the beginning, we learn about the unstable condition in which Mrs. Dashwood and her three daughters find themselves after the death of the husband and father. The new owner's wife, Mrs. John Dashwood, immediately comes to take possession of the estate of Norland, "and her mother and sisters-in-law were degraded to the condition of visitors" (see p. 8), as the narrator tells us in unmistakable terms. That means, of course, that their future is insecure, and we ask ourselves what will happen to them and how and under what circumstances they will manage to live. Thus procedural suspense is generated.

There are also a number of actual puzzles in the plot of the novel. It is with good reason that in Tony Tanner's insightful book *Jane Austen*, he has a chapter entitled "Secrecy and Sickness: *Sense and Sensibility*".[17] He notices "just how much secrecy there is among the few, and closely related, characters in the book".[18] And it seems convincing when he interprets Elinor's talent for screen painting also figuratively, and he sees in the novel "a world of screens".[19] The word "secret" repeatedly occurs in the text, and we wonder, naturally, about circumstances and solutions.

A major puzzle occurs when Colonel Brandon receives a letter and decides to leave at once although that means that the intended excursion everybody has looked forward to cannot take place. His statement, "[I]t is not in my power to delay my journey for one day!" (see p. 64), and then even, "I cannot afford to lose *one* hour" (see p. 64), lends dramatic emphasis to the mysterious decision. We know, of course, that Willoughby's malicious explanation that the colonel has written the letter himself to have an excuse for not taking part in the planned excursion is wrong; but we are curious about the real reason.

---

[17] Tony Tanner, "Secrecy and Sickness: *Sense and Sensibility*", in *Jane Austen* (Basingstoke, England: Macmillan, 1986), pp. 75–102.
[18] Ibid., p. 79.
[19] Ibid., p. 89.

The explanation is not given until later in the novel when the colonel tells Elinor the story of his life and of his first love (see p. 199). Then we learn that his hasty departure had to do with Willoughby's villainy; characteristically, Colonel Brandon was called away to bring relief to Willoughby's victim (see p. 203).

The suspense created by the colonel's mysterious departure is heightened by the "great wonderer" (see p. 70) Mrs. Jennings, who develops several theories about what may be behind the sudden decision. Her favorite idea that it may have something to do with "Miss Williams" proves to be correct eventually—though, of course, her assumption that this young woman is Brandon's "natural daughter" (see p. 66) is completely unjustified.

We naturally share Mrs. Jennings' curiosity to some extent, but, unlike the writer of a detective novel, Jane Austen does not choose to uphold or even intensify that final suspense but rather appears to change it into procedural suspense, by turning our attention to something else. The way she achieves this has to do with Elinor, the focus character of the novel, of whom we read,

> Elinor, though she felt really interested in the welfare of Colonel Brandon, could not bestow all the wonder on his going so suddenly away, which Mrs. Jennings was desirous of her feeling; for besides that the circumstance did not in her opinion justify such lasting amazement or variety of speculation, her wonder was otherwise disposed of. (See p. 71.)

Together with Elinor, we, the readers, direct our curiosity to the important question of whether Willoughby and Marianne are really engaged or not. Elinor's mother is convinced that this is the case, but Elinor becomes more and more doubtful, and there are increasingly indications that corroborate her skepticism. It is not until much later in the novel, when the sisters are in London, that Marianne tells her sister that she is not, strictly speaking, engaged but feels "to be as solemnly engaged to him, as if the strictest legal covenant had bound us to each other" (see p. 183).

Yet first of all, Willoughby leaves as suddenly and as mysteriously for London as Colonel Brandon did before. Elinor voices our own uncertainty when she calls this "very strange" and says, "[S]uspicion of something unpleasant is the inevitable consequence of such an alteration as we have just witnessed in him [Willoughby]" (see pp. 77–79). This puzzle remains for some time and is even aggravated by Willoughby's strange and reserved behavior toward Marianne in London and, worst of all, by the cruel letter he sends her, in order to return her letters and the lock of hair she has given him (see pp. 177–78). The mystery is partly solved when we hear about Willoughby's imminent marriage to a rich heiress. It is completely explained toward the end of the novel when Willoughby surprisingly turns up at Cleveland and tells Elinor the story of his life and his love for Marianne (see pp. 309–20).

In this case as well, Austen does not continuously uphold the suspense we feel but directs our attention to other questions. She does this by a device she uses several times in *Sense and Sensibility*, as W. A. Craik observes:

> [T]he device where one character is expected and another arrives occurs three times: at Barton, Marianne expects Willoughby and we see Edward, in London she expects him again and Colonel Brandon calls, and at Cleveland, Elinor runs to meet her mother and finds Willoughby.[20]

When Elinor is worrying about her sister and wondering about her possible engagement, Edward Ferrars turns up and gives rise to new questions by his strange behavior. The sisters ask themselves why he "was confused, seemed scarcely sensible of pleasure in seeing them, looked neither rapturous nor gay, said little but what was forced from him by questions" (see p. 87), and Elinor comes to the conclusion that "[i]t was evident that he was unhappy" (see p. 94). This is, of course, only a partial explanation, and we thereby want to know the reason for his unhappiness.

[20] W. A. Craik, *Jane Austen: The Six Novels* (London & New York: Methuen, 1968, first 1965), p. 57.

We get more and more informed about Edward's situation after the Miss Steeles have arrived at Barton. At first the elder Miss Steele mentions that she knows Edward as "a very agreeable young man ... very well" (see p. 122), and the narrator tells us,

> The manner in which Miss Steele had spoken of Edward, increased her [Elinor's] curiosity; for it struck her as being rather ill-natured, and suggested the suspicion of that lady's knowing, or fancying herself to know something to his disadvantage. (See pp. 122–23.)

So there are new uncertainties. Yet shortly afterward, Lucy tells Elinor as "a great secret" (see p. 126) that she has been engaged to Edward "these four years" (see p. 127) and proves this by showing Elinor a picture of him and a letter he has written.

She also brings up that she has given Edward a lock of hair that he wears in a ring. This solves a particular puzzle introduced some chapters earlier when Marianne discovers that Edward is wearing a ring she has not noticed before "with a plait of hair in the centre, very conspicuous". She asks whether it is his sister's hair, which he answers in the affirmative. Since the narrator tells us, however, "He coloured very deeply" (see p. 96) and that he hesitates before he answers, we have some doubts, and Lucy's disclosure confirms such misgivings and purveys an explanation.

Lucy presents her engagement to Edward in dramatic terms and suggests, "Every thing [was] in such suspense and uncertainty" (see p. 129). Though her disclosure offers an explanation why Edward behaved so strangely when he came to visit at Barton, it brings new questions for Elinor (and the reader) that concern both the past and the future. With regard to the past Elinor asks, "Had Edward been intentionally deceiving her? Had he feigned a regard for her which he did not feel? Was his engagement to Lucy, an engagement of the heart?" She is confident that "[h]is affection was all her own.... He certainly loved her" (see p. 135). We naturally share her reassurance, and the suspense we feel to know why Edward behaved as he did is consequently rather mild, but still we are curious—only in the penultimate chapter of the novel do we find an answer why Edward became engaged to Lucy at all (see p. 348).

The questions concerning the future are probably more serious, and Elinor reflects,

> She [Elinor] might in time regain tranquility; but *he*, what had he to look forward to? Could he ever be tolerably happy with Lucy Steele; could he, were his affection for herself out of the question, with his integrity, his delicacy, and well-informed mind, be satisfied with a wife like her—illiterate, artful, and selfish? (See p. 136.)

Such considerations provide procedural suspense, and with such a basis, we continue reading the story involving the characters we have become interested in and sympathize with.

In this way, we undoubtedly feel relief and joy about the happy ending. It is brought about by the final discovery that it was not Edward but his brother, Robert, who married Lucy Steele, so that Edward is free and Elinor can become joined in marriage to the man she loves. Although there seemed to be no hope for Elinor anymore, experienced readers are probably led by the predominantly light and serene nature of the narrative and the prevalence of Jane Austen's famous irony to assume that *Sense and Sensibility* rather belongs to the genre of comedy than tragedy. Thus they can go on reading with some hope for the happiness of their favorite (focus) character. The generic quality of Jane Austen's novel in this manner also creates suspense.

The puzzles, like Colonel Brandon's sudden departure, which primarily bring about final suspense, appear to occur mostly in the early parts of the novel. Afterward we are sufficiently involved with the characters, in particular with the focus character, to make us highly interested in what happens to them. It is, above all, partial knowledge that renders us curious to get to know more and to learn in what way our expectations come true.

At any rate, the preceding analysis of *Sense and Sensibility* has corroborated that it is at best one-sided to regard Jane Austen's novel in pictorial terms and that suspense is clearly a vital part of the reader's experience. Even if the author rather avoids the highly developed form of final suspense one finds in detective novels and works like Radcliffe's Gothic novels, suspense, mostly in the form of procedural suspense, is very important. It motivates us and makes us wonder what will happen and essentially influences our reading experience.

The Indulgence of *Sense and Sensibility*:
A Human Comedy

Crystal Downing
Messiah College

In a 1947 letter to C. S. Lewis, Anglo-Catholic writer Dorothy L. Sayers refers to the Jubilee Indulgence instituted by Pope Boniface VIII in 1300, discussing how Dante alludes to the event in his *Divine Comedy*. After four paragraphs of intricate analysis, she ends the letter on an entirely different note:

> I have purchased two Hens. In their habits they display, respectively Sense and Sensibility, and I have therefore named them Elinor and Marianne. Elinor is a round, comfortable, motherly-looking little body, who lays one steady, regular, undistinguished egg per day, and allows nothing to disturb her equanimity.... Marianne is leggier, timid, and liable to hysterics.... On the days when she lays no egg she nevertheless goes and sits in the nest for the usual time, and seems to imagine that nothing more is required.... Too much imagination—in fact, Sensibility. But when she does lay an egg it is larger than Elinor's.[1]

Sayers thus wittily encapsulates a common reading of Jane Austen's first published novel, *Sense and Sensibility*. According to this conventional reading, *Sense and Sensibility* is about two sisters with contrasting personalities: one who is steady and practical, the other who exercises an "indulgence of feeling".[2] Both must discover and surmount their character flaws in order to attain a "stable middle ground represented by matrimony".[3]

---

[1] Barbara Reynolds, ed., *The Letters of Dorothy L. Sayers*, vol. 3, *1944–1950: A Noble Daring* (Cambridge, UK: Carole Green, 1998), p. 305.

[2] Jane Austen, *Sense and Sensibility*, ed. Eleanor Bourg Nicholson, Ignatius Critical Editions (San Francisco: Ignatius Press, 2014), p. 83. Subsequent quotations from this edition will be cited in the text.

[3] Candace Ward, ed., Note to Jane Austen, *Sense and Sensibility* (Toronto: Dover, 1996), p. v.

Sense and Sensibility is much more than an intriguing character study, however. Just as Dante's *Divine Comedy* reflects theological and political issues of late thirteenth-century and early fourteenth-century Italy, so Austen's *Sense and Sensibility* reflects cultural issues of late eighteenth-century and early nineteenth-century England. I will argue that the novel illuminates tensions between Neoclassical and Romantic literary theories that dominated the 1790s, when Austen wrote its initial draft.

We know that Austen put a great deal of thought into the literary styles of her day. The first novel she completed— *Northanger Abbey* (not published until after her death)— explicitly addresses eighteenth-century reading practices. Its heroine, Catherine Morland, immerses herself in contemporary Gothic novels, especially those of Ann Radcliffe, who was born only eleven years before Austen. Because Radcliffe's novels focus on terrifying events and morally depraved individuals within medieval settings, Catherine starts to read the home of a friend as terrifying and her friend's father as morally depraved simply because the home was once a medieval abbey. Later, Catherine realizes that her interpretation of Northanger Abbey and its owner "had been all a voluntary self-created delusion" generated by her "craving to be frightened"; "it seemed as if the whole might be traced to the influence of that sort of reading which she had there indulged."[4] The indulgence of a certain kind of reading distorts her perception.

Immediately after this realization, Catherine becomes "impatient to know how the Bath world went on".[5] For Austen, who spent time there, Bath exemplifies the order and control of a different kind of reading, what literary critic Geoffrey Tillotson calls "the preeminence of public truth over private speculation", reflective of eighteenth-century Neoclassicism.[6]

---

[4] Jane Austen, *Northanger Abbey* (New York: Dover, 2000), pp. 140–41.
[5] Ibid., p. 142.
[6] Geoffrey Tillotson, ed., introduction to *Eighteenth-Century English Literature* (New York: Harcourt, Brace and World, 1969), p. 4.

Bath's decorously symmetrical "Royal Crescent", an arc of thirty identical attached townhouses in the Neoclassical style, celebrates what Thomas Paine called, in 1794, "The Age of Reason". Significantly, the Royal Crescent was built between 1767 and 1774—just as Gothic fiction was becoming popular. The first Gothic novel, Horace Walpole's *Castle of Otranto*, was published in 1764, and by 1773 the first apologetic for Gothic fiction had been produced: "On the Pleasure Derived from Objects of Terror".[7]

In *Northanger Abbey*, then, Austen juxtaposes Neoclassical architecture (the Royal Crescent) with Gothic architecture (the medieval abbey) as a way to explore the tension between reason and imagination—what we might call the tension between sense and sensibility. Indeed, many literary critics describe Gothic fiction as a subset of "the novel of sensibility", which emerged in the latter half of the eighteenth century as a reaction to Neoclassical strictures about literary decorum. Early in the century Neoclassicist Alexander Pope had advocated "a new attention to precision, control, and 'correctness' in poetry".[8] By 1798—the year that Austen was writing *Northanger Abbey*—William Wordsworth was defying Pope's rules about proper poetic diction, energizing the Romantic movement through his emphasis on individual imagination and private perception.[9] The Gothic novel, then, greased the hinges of the door between Neoclassicism and Romanticism. As M.H. Abrams summarizes, "the literature of sensibility" can be defined as "a turn from neoclassic 'correctness' and its emphasis on judgment and restraint to an emphasis on instinct and feeling".[10] The relevance to *Sense and Sensibility* is obvious.

---

[7] The essay was written by siblings Anna Letitia Aikin and John Aikin.

[8] Quoted in Tillotson, *Eighteenth-Century English Literature*, p. 2.

[9] 1798, of course, is the year that Wordsworth and Coleridge published their groundbreaking *Lyrical Ballads*. For the 1800 edition, Wordsworth wrote a preface, explaining how *Lyrical Ballads* defied the "correctness" touted by Pope and other Neoclassicists.

[10] M.H. Abrams, *A Glossary of Literary Terms*, 8th ed. (Boston: Thomson Wadsworth, 2005), p. 223.

Marianne values instinct and feeling: "eager in every thing; her sorrows, her joy, could have no moderation.... [S]he was every thing but prudent" (see p. 7). In contrast, Elinor is repeatedly aligned with judgment and restraint, exercising more "prudence" and "steadier judgment" than both her mother and her sister (see p. 14). Together, Elinor and Marianne embody the literary tensions of Austen's day.

Indeed, Marianne responds to nature in ways that anticipate Wordsworth's "powerful feelings ... recollected in tranquility".[11] When she tranquilly recollects the grounds of Norland, their former home, Marianne effusively recalls the fallen leaves of autumn: "How have I delighted, as I walked, to see them driven in showers about me by the wind! What feelings have they, the season, the air altogether inspired!" Elinor responds with cool rationality: "It is not every one ... who has your passion for dead leaves" (see p. 87). A similar rationality marks the thought of Edward Ferrars, Elinor's love interest. While discussing "admiration of landscape scenery" with Marianne, Edward repudiates a Romantic view of nature. When he says, "I do not like crooked, twisted, blasted trees", and, "I do not like ruined, tattered cottages" (see pp. 95–96), he seems to reject, in advance, Wordsworth's poems "The Thorn" and "The Ruined Cottage".[12]

Readers of both *Sense and Sensibility* and *Northanger Abbey* cannot help feeling that Austen tips the scales in favor of rationality and restraint; Neoclassicism seems to win out over Romanticism. Indeed, both Marianne Dashwood and Catherine Morland make horrible mistakes due to their Romantic readings. While Catherine imagines the owner of Northanger Abbey to be a wife abuser worthy of the most gruesome Gothic novel, Marianne interprets the duplicitous

[11] William Wordsworth, preface to "Lyrical Ballads", in *The Norton Anthology of English Literature: The Romantic Period*, 8th ed., ed. Stephen Greenblatt (New York: Norton: 2006), p. 273.

[12] Edward refers to motifs found in poets that functioned as stepping-stones in the transition from Pope's Neoclassicism to Wordsworth's Romanticism: "Thomson, Cowper, Scott" (see p. 91).

Willoughby according to the novel of sensibility: "His person and air were equal to what her fancy had ever drawn for the hero of a favourite story.... Her imagination was busy" (see pp. 42–43). And she judges him according to the way he reads. While it distresses her to hear Edward "read with so little *sensibility*" (see p. 18), she delights in the fact that Willoughby "read with all the *sensibility* and spirit which Edward had unfortunately wanted" (see p. 49).[13] She therefore believes Willoughby to be her soul mate because of their shared passion for the literature of sensibility: "Their taste was strikingly alike. The same books, the same passages were idolized by each" (see p. 47). Drowning out "sense", Marianne's Romantic sensibilities cause intense misery when Willoughby abandons her.

According to Tillotson, those who privileged "sense" over "sensibility" in the eighteenth century were influenced by John Locke's extremely popular *Essay Concerning Human Understanding* (1690): "Locke had concluded that the experience of the senses is the sole avenue of knowledge and that new ideas are the result not of private 'inspiration' but rather of new combinations and arrangement of public materials lodged in the memory."[14] The senses, in other words, lead to common sense, while individualized inspiration leads to trouble. In *Northanger Abbey*, Catherine Morland's love interest, Henry Tilney, makes this very point when he learns of Catherine's Gothic fantasies: "Consider the dreadful nature of the suspicions you have entertained. What have you been *judging* from? ... Consult your own *understanding*, your own *sense* of the probable, your own *observation* of what is passing around you".[15] Note Henry's appeal to empirical observation, which was fundamental to Locke's philosophy of human understanding.

Locke's views dominated British thought for most of the eighteenth century, affecting politics as well as art. In 1776,

---

[13] Unless otherwise noted, all italics in quotations from the novel indicate my emphasis, not Austen's.

[14] Tillotson, *Eighteenth-Century English Literature*, p. 3.

[15] Austen, *Northanger Abbey*, p. 139.

the year after Austen's birth, not only did Thomas Paine pub-
lish his famous pamphlet *Common Sense*, but painter and Royal
Academy president Sir Joshua Reynolds pronounced,

> As the imagination is incapable of producing any thing origi-
> nally of itself, and can only vary and combine those ideas with
> which it is furnished by means of the senses, there will be nec-
> essarily an agreement in the imaginations as in the senses of
> men. There being this agreement, it follows, that … we must
> regulate our affections of every kind by that of others.[16]

Elinor Dashwood seems to live by these words. While the
abandoned Marianne seeks solitude, caring nothing about
what others think of her, Elinor repeatedly regulates her affections and behavior out of concern for others. Marianne mar-
vels over the way her sister controls her feelings: "When is she
dejected or melancholy? When does she try to avoid society,
or appear restless and dissatisfied in it?" (see p. 39). Elinor thus
fulfills Tillotson's description of the Neoclassical individual
who self-consciously functions "as a member of society, not
a special creature withdrawn from it".[17] Even when Edward
Ferrars starts acting strangely distant from her, "she did not
adopt the method so judiciously employed by Marianne, on
a similar occasion, to augment and fix her sorrow, by seeking
silence, solitude, and idleness." Instead, she "appeared to interest herself almost as much as ever in the general concerns of
the family", despite "her own grief" (see p. 102). And when
she later discovers that the man she loves is secretly engaged to
another woman, she conceals the news in order to avoid caus-
ing "affliction" to her family (see p. 137). Out of consideration
for others, Elinor's "own good sense" enables her to maintain
the "appearance of cheerfulness" (see p. 137): she was "the
comforter of others in her own distresses" (see p. 253).

We have excellent reason, then, to admire Elinor as the
respected protagonist of *Sense and Sensibility*. Nevertheless,

[16] Quoted in Tillotson, *Eighteenth-Century English Literature*, p. 4.
[17] Ibid., p. 5.

Austen is doing something far more subtle than the endorsement of Neoclassical sense over Romantic sensibility, or even
a "golden mean" between two egg-laying hens. While she
makes painfully obvious the fallacies and failures of fiction-fed
sensibilities, Austen's most searing indictment is for the self-
serving manipulations of common sense. As Tillotson notes,
advocates of sense believe that "what is real and important is
what is public and 'normal' rather than private and singular."
Problematically, however, endorsement of the "normal" easily
transitions into advocacy of the status quo, "subsum[ing] individuality within a large paradigm of uniformity". After all, "if
ideas enter the mind only through external experience, then
truth must be both simple and ultimately apparent to all."[18] As
a result, the way things are is the way they were meant to be and
always should be; the status quo is simply a matter of common
sense. Or, as the Neoclassical Alexander Pope tersely put it,
"Whatever is, is right."[19] Pope's eighteenth-century truism, in
fact, directs the way Sir Joshua Reynolds closes his discussion
about the superiority of sense to imagination indented above.
Immediately after he invokes the Elinor-like need to "regulate
our affections of every kind by that of others", Reynolds writes,
"The well-disciplined mind acknowledges this authority, and
submits its own opinion to the public voice."[20]

Significantly, Austen begins *Sense and Sensibility* with disturbing consequences of submission to common sense. The
Dashwood females are forced out of their home by the public voice that endorses primogeniture, a convention by which
eldest sons inherit all the property when a father dies. Though
John Dashwood and his wife are already very wealthy, they
assume "whatever is, is right" and take over the house that
Elinor and Marianne have called home for their entire lives.
Austen, in fact, parodies the submission of "opinion to the
public voice" through John Dashwood's submission to the

---

[18] Ibid., p. 4.
[19] This famous line is from Epistle 1 of Pope's long poem "An Essay on Man".
[20] Quoted in Tillotson, *Eighteenth-Century English Literature*, p. 4.

opinion of his wife, Fanny. Originally planning to provide his father's second wife (mother to Elinor and Marianne) with a substantial annuity, John submits to Fanny's argument that common sense dictates otherwise. After all, Fanny asserts, when the dying Mr. Dashwood asked John to look out for his stepsisters, "he was light-headed at the time. Had he been *in his right senses*, he could not have thought of such a thing as begging you to give away half your fortune from your own child" (see p. 9). Using a logic admirable in its manipulative rationality, Fanny convinces John to give his father's second family no allowance at all. He submits to the opinion of her voice, saying, "My father certainly could mean nothing more by his request to me than what you say. I clearly understand it now" (see p. 12). Such is his essay concerning human understanding.

In contrast to John's submission to the public voice of common sense, Marianne's repudiation of common sense feels like a breath of fresh air. Not only does she "abhor every *common*-place phrase" (see p. 45), but she refuses to make commonsense statements if she does not believe them: "[I]t was impossible for her to say what she did not feel" (see p. 119). Marianne therefore indulges her uncommon passion for Willoughby, stating, "I have erred against every *common*-place notion of decorum; I have been open and sincere where I ought to have been reserved, spiritless, dull, and deceitful" (see p. 48). As Austen's narrator comments, "[T]o aim at the restraint of sentiments which were not in themselves illaudable, appeared to her ... a disgraceful subjection of reason to *common*-place and mistaken notions" (see p. 53).

Willoughby, of course, proves to be a cad, but I would argue that the misery he causes results not from his indulgence of sensibility but from his submission to the public voice of common sense. He may captivate innocent girls through an excess of Romantic sensibility, but he abandons them because of public opinion. His culture has made clear that it is not "normal" for a man of his class to lower himself to the status of wage earner. He therefore must marry a rich woman to submit to approved notions about respectability. Though Willoughby turns his back on the Dashwoods to marry the wealthy Miss Grey, it is clear by the end of the novel that he still loves the innocently passionate, if misguided, Marianne. His sensibility—in the form of genuine affection—is more humane than is his commonsense understanding that marriage is a form of "commercial exchange" (see p. 38).

Willoughby's mirror opposites in the novel, Colonel Brandon and Edward Ferrars, also cause pain due to common sense. Hence, like mirrors, both men reflect aspects of Willoughby while also standing in opposition to him. Brandon mirrors Willoughby's attraction to Marianne, but responds to that attraction with sense rather than sensibility. When Elinor tells him that her sister's "opinions are all romantic", Brandon responds, "A few years ... will settle her opinions on the *reasonable* basis of *common sense* and *observation*" (see pp. 55–56); in other words, Marianne will someday submit her "opinion to the public voice". Brandon's commitment to Neoclassical "common sense", however, contributes to Marianne's emotional breakdown. Believing that truth is a function of "observation" rather than "revelation", Brandon refuses to warn the Dashwoods by informing them of Willoughby's impregnation and abandonment of a young girl. Marianne must therefore, like a good student of Locke, learn of Willoughby's deceptions through experience.

Edward mirrors both Brandon and Willoughby. As a young man he indulged Willoughby-like sensibilities when he proposed to the enticing Lucy Steele. Unlike Willoughby, however, he holds fast to his word, maintaining his engagement even after he falls out of love with the shallow and manipulative girl. Fulfilling a "norm" of integrity in his day, he keeps his word to Lucy. However, he continues to hide the engagement from the world. Why? Because it does not match the opinion of public voice about his status as well-born gentleman. Hence, just as Brandon's secrecy contributes to Marianne's breakdown, Edward's secrecy, born of common sense, misleads Elinor, who experiences intense pain when the wily Lucy makes known her secret engagement. Edward and Brandon therefore exercise

commonsense secrecy very similar to that of Willoughby.
When the latter inexplicably leaves Marianne to head toward
London, Elinor justifies Willoughby's secrecy: "Secrecy may be
advisable; but still I cannot help wondering at its being practised by him" (see p. 79). In other words, secrecy is a sign of
commonsense people, like Edward and Brandon—rather than
of a man of sensibility like Willoughby. It would seem that
Willoughby has more common sense than Elinor realized!
After all, to maintain the Neoclassical decorum endorsed by
public opinion, distortions of the truth are often appropriate.
Indeed, when Marianne refuses to lie, "upon Elinor ... the
whole task of telling lies when politeness required it, always
fell" (see p. 119).

Nevertheless, Austen quite obviously means us to value the
commonsense secrecy of Edward and Brandon while disdain-
ing the commonsense secrecy of Willoughby. Understanding
why is key to understanding her novel. Austen makes quite
clear that Willoughby's secrecy, like his love, is self-serving. As
Elinor notes, "The whole of his behaviour, ... from the beginning to the end of the affair, has been grounded on selfishness"
(see p. 338).[21] In contrast, Edward and Brandon cover up truth
in consideration of others: Edward puts Lucy's desires above
his own, and Brandon puts Marianne's desires above his own.
Both men experience sorrow in order to make others happy.
Even Marianne, who despairs over the commonsense attitudes of Brandon and Edward, recognizes their self-sacrificial
natures. She honors Edward with genuine praise: "He is the
most fearful of giving pain, of wounding expectation, and the
most incapable of being selfish, of any body I ever saw" (see
p. 236). And she honors Brandon with eventual marriage.
Austen thus implies that *Sense and Sensibility* is not about

[21] Austen employs similar language later to describe the common sense of Lucy
Steele: "The whole of Lucy's behaviour in the affair, and the prosperity which
crowned it, therefore, may be held forth as a most encouraging instance of what
an earnest, an unceasing attention to self-interest ... will do in securing every
advantage of fortune, with no other sacrifice than that of time and conscience"
(see p. 362).

achieving a balance between restraint and passion; it is about sacrificing one's own interests—whether motivated by sense or sensibility—for the benefit of others.

Significantly, Edward and Brandon, though advocates of good sense, value sensibility when it comes to one sacred arena: marriage. Rather than submit to the cultural endorsement of marriage as a form of "commercial exchange" (see p. 38), they both marry for love. And both are able to do so when other self-serving characters manipulate common sense to their own best interests. In Brandon's case, Willoughby's submission to the marriage market forces Marianne to release her infatuation with his Romantic sensibilities, preparing her for the more stable and enduring embrace of an older man. In Edward's case, Lucy Steele, like Willoughby, recognizes that the acquisition of money makes more sense in her culture than the acquisition of love. (Note that when Elinor first meets the Steele sisters she "allowed them credit for some kind of *sense*" [see p. 117], and she later admits that "Lucy does not want *sense*, and that is the foundation on which every thing good may be built" [see p. 254].) Hence, not long after Lucy discovers Edward has been disinherited due to his secret engagement to her, she takes up with his monetarily endowed younger brother instead.

Austen thus indicts a culture in which marrying for money and status makes more "sense" than marrying for the "sensibility" of love. This is confirmed through her depictions of mothers in the novel: those who communicate the "public voice" to their children. Like Fanny Dashwood, who elevates her son's financial interests above her husband's stepsisters' needs, most mothers in *Sense and Sensibility* have done the commonsense thing by marrying for money and status rather than compatibility. Lady Middleton, whose husband provides the cottage to which the Dashwoods move after leaving Norland, quite clearly has nothing in common with her husband: "Sir John was a sportsman, Lady Middleton a mother. He hunted and shot, and she humoured her children; and these were their only resources" (see p. 32), owing, in part, to her "cold insipidity" (see p. 34). Furthermore, because Elinor and Marianne "neither flattered herself nor her children, she could not believe them good-natured". Tellingly, Austen comments, "It was censure in *common* use, and easily given" (see p. 238).

Lady Middleton's mother, Mrs. Jennings, is a good-hearted gossip devoted to making matches that fulfill her "*common* prudence" (see p. 313). She tells Elinor and Marianne, "[I]f I don't get one of you at least well married before I have done with you, it shall not be my fault" (see p. 149). And, of course, by "well married" she means wedded to well-off men. As Mrs. Jennings' other daughter, Charlotte, notes of a possible marriage proposal, "[M]ama did not think the match good enough for me" (see p. 114). Whether or not Charlotte is correct to think that a proposal was imminent, her statement expresses the commonsense notion that a "good" match is a financially beneficial match—which Charlotte does make. Her husband, Mr. Palmer, exudes "fashion and *sense*"—along with contempt for his wife (see p. 104). When Charlotte simply laughs off Mr. Palmer's rude disdain, Austen singles out Mrs. Dashwood as the one most disturbed: "Mrs. Dashwood ... had never been used to find wit in the inattention of any one" (see p. 105).

Indeed, the mother of Elinor and Marianne contrasts sharply with all the other mothers in the novel: "[C]ommon sense, common care, common prudence, were all sunk in Mrs. Dashwood's romantic delicacy" (see p. 85). Austen's repetition of "common" is telling: Mrs. Dashwood's "romantic" sensibility is uncommon, leading her to value love over money. Indeed, the phrase "common prudence" is the phrase used to praise Mrs. Jennings' commitment to "materially advantageous" marriages (see p. 220), and also the phrase Willoughby uses to describe his abandonment of Marianne: "I persuaded myself to think that nothing else in common prudence remained for me to do" (see p. 313). We should pay attention, then, when the person without common prudence, Mrs. Dashwood, anticipates the happy ending of the novel whereby Edward Ferrars marries Elinor for love. As early as the third chapter Austen writes,

Some mothers might have encouraged the intimacy from motives of interest, for Edward Ferrars was the eldest son of a man who had died very rich; and some might have repressed it from motives of *prudence*, for, except a trifling sum, the whole of his fortune depended on the will of his mother. But Mrs. Dashwood was alike uninfluenced by either consideration.... It was contrary to every doctrine of her's that difference of fortune should keep any couple asunder who were attracted by resemblance of disposition. (See p. 15.)

The sensibility of Mrs. Dashwood, then, fulfills Austen's purposes more than the sense of Mrs. Ferrars, who pressures Edward, her oldest son, to fulfill common notions of "wealth" and "grandeur" (see p. 90). Even though Edward desires to become a clergyman, he notes that such a choice "was not smart enough for my family.... I was therefore entered at Oxford and have been properly idle ever since" (see pp. 100–101). And Mrs. Ferrars plans to keep him *properly* idle, offering him a tremendous sum of money if he will marry Miss Morton, the wealthy heiress of her choice: a sign, says the public voice, of the mother's "noble spirit" (see p. 218). Her "conduct", notes John Dashwood, "has been such as every conscientious, good mother, in like circumstances, would adopt" (see p. 259). And public opinion endorses him: "[N]obody in their *senses* could expect Mr. Ferrars to give up a woman like Miss Morton" (see p. 263). Significantly, while Mrs. Dashwood's sensibilities are confirmed by Austen's plot structure, the good sense of Edward's mother, who disinherits Edward when she hears of the Lucy engagement, is made mockery of when Lucy abandons the disinherited son in order to marry the one that gets the estate. Mrs. Ferrars has met her match when it comes to common sense!

Austen's subversion of common sense reflects, I would argue, a fundamentally Christian view of the universe. The men who defy commonsense attitudes about marriage are gifted not only with love but also through Christian vocation: Brandon gains a best friend as a result of giving Edward the position of clergyman funded by his estate. Of course, public opinion, as represented by John Dashwood, considers Brandon's offer to Edward to be nonsensical: "a man of Colonel Brandon's *sense!*—I wonder he should be so improvident in a point of such *common*, such natural, concern!" (see p. 286). However, as daughter to and sister of clergymen, Austen well knew that church doctrine does not depend on commonsense ideas bred of empirical observation. It does not make sense that God would enter our world in the form of a baby. It does not make sense that Jesus could be both fully God and fully human. It does not make sense that the dead can rise again. It does not make sense that the last shall be first. It does not make sense that self-sacrifice leads to fullness of life. Hence, when Austen repeatedly makes mockery of those who, out of common sense, marry for financial reward rather than for love, she echoes what great Christian writers like Dante and Dorothy Sayers have long known: salvation is not a commonsense reward for good behavior; rather, it is God's indulgence of love for those who exercise the sensibility of faith. Only with this recognition, and only then, does life make sense.

"Esteem": The Enduring Foundation of Marriage in *Sense and Sensibility*

Mitchell Kalpakgian
The College of Saint Mary Magdalen

Man by nature is a rational animal who, according to Aristotle's famous definition, both thinks and feels as Jane Austen's terms "sense" and "sensibility" indicate. Reason can be reduced to mere "reckoning", the calculation of profit and loss in regard to self-interest, or it can exemplify the cardinal virtues of prudence, temperance, justice, and fortitude. It functions as a scientific instrument that draws conclusions from empirical evidence and also operates as a moral power that determines matters of right and wrong. While the classical image of the relationship between reason and will, to use Plato's image, compares reason to a charioteer and the passions to the horses—the lower appetites subject to the authority of the highest part of man—this hierarchy suffers reversal when, to use Shakespeare's phrase, "reason panders will" (*Hamlet*, 3.4.88), that is, reason rationalizes or justifies evil by making the weaker argument appear the stronger. *Sense and Sensibility* portrays this wide range of thinking and feeling that governs a person and that especially influences personal decisions about love and marriage. For Jane Austen, thinking without feeling easily develops into hard-heartedness, selfishness, and insensitivity, and feeling without thinking quickly leads to prejudice, sentimentality, and imprudence.

Fanny Dashwood's appearance of great common sense and practical wisdom disguises a cunning mind that thinks only in terms of narrow self-interest. Objecting to her husband's (John's) desire to respect his dying father's last wishes on behalf of his widow and three daughters "to do every thing in his power to make them comfortable",[1] Fanny regards her

[1] Jane Austen, *Sense and Sensibility*, ed. Eleanor Bourg Nicholson, Ignatius Critical Editions (San Francisco: Ignatius Press, 2014), p. 5. Subsequent quotations from this edition will be cited in the text.

husband's proposals of generous gifts of money to his half sisters as foolish and impractical: "To take three thousand pounds from the fortune of their dear little boy, would be impoverishing him to the most dreadful degree" (see p. 8). Because Elinor and Marianne are John's half sisters, she argues, the large sum is unwarranted because "no affection was ever supposed to exist between the children of any man by different marriages" (see p. 8). Fanny agrees that "*something* be done for them" (see p. 9; italics added) but not to the amount of three thousand pounds. When John reconsiders and suggests the idea of an annuity for the mother of his half sisters, again the calculating Fanny protests because "people always live for ever when there is any annuity to be paid them; and she is very stout and healthy, and hardly forty" (see p. 11). When John changes his idea of assistance to occasional annual gifts of money, "a present of fifty pounds, now and then", Fanny once again complains of the unreasonableness of monetary gifts that were not exactly stipulated in the will: "I am convinced within myself that your father had no idea of your giving them any money at all. The assistance he thought of, I dare say, was only as might be reasonably expected of you; for instance, such as looking out for a comfortable small house for them, helping them to move their things, and sending them presents of fish and game, and so forth, whenever they are in season" (see p. 12).

While the deceased Mr. Dashwood's final wishes for his family demonstrate the cardinal virtue of prudence—provident foresight on behalf of the happiness of others—Fanny's thinking amounts to no more than what Thomas Hobbes calls "reckoning", or shrewd calculation for the sake of one's worldly advantage—foresight only on behalf of one's own gain even at the expense of others. Of course this use of the mind does not correspond to Jane Austen's idea of "sense", because it lacks moral reasoning based on the ideals of justice and charity. In Austen's novels the best moral decisions, especially choices about marriage, integrate both sense and sensibility and combine the virtues of the head and the heart, and the most noble heroes and heroines in Austen's novels, admired for their "esteem" and "amiability", never act like cold rationalists or irrational sentimentalists.

Unlike Fanny, who calls selfishness prudence, Elinor Dashwood epitomizes the virtue of *sense* that Jane Austen celebrates in her novel—the exercise of reason that governs passions, exerts patience, and exercises the restraint that forms the ideal of propriety. This virtue encompasses economic matters, moral judgments, and good manners. It combines common sense, prudence, and self-possession in dealing with the nature of things as they are rather than losing contact with reality by imaginary fantasies that result from unrealistic wishes. While Mrs. Dashwood shows imprudence in her management of money and spends it lavishly, Elinor, "whose steadier judgment rejected several houses as too large for their income" (see p. 14), curbs her mother's expensive taste. In her judgment of moral character, Elinor also weighs and balances a person's virtues and flaws with reasonable objectivity free of prejudice and rash judgment. While Marianne sees no basis for courtship and romance between Elinor and Edward Ferrars because of his reserve and shyness, complaining of his lack of passion and vivacity and the absence of spirit, grace, taste, and sensibility in his demeanor, Elinor appreciates his integrity, civility, and kindness: "[B]ut I have the highest opinion in the world of his goodness and sense. I think him every thing that is worthy and amiable" (see pp. 19–20).

When Willoughby's courtship of Marianne abruptly ends with his sudden, unexplained departure, Elinor detects a moral flaw that escapes her sister and mother. Assuming Willoughby's romance with her sister as approaching an engagement, Elinor finds it unreasonable that he should unexpectedly depart "with such indifference, such carelessness of the future" (see p. 80) with regard to the continuation of their relationship. This secrecy troubles Elinor more than her unsuspecting mother: "In such a case, a plain and open avowal of his difficulties would have been more to his honour" (see p. 81).

Elinor's use of reason or sense also shows in her propriety and civility, the "self-command" (see p. 39) she demonstrates in all social situations. Even when Ferrars exasperates her by his halfhearted romantic interest and undeclared courtship, her forbearance and patience uphold the ideal of good manners: "His coldness and reserve mortified her severely; she was vexed and half angry; but resolving to regulate her behaviour to him by the past rather than the present, she avoided every appearance of resentment or displeasure" (see p. 88). Elinor's great good sense, then, reflects prudence in the use of money, good judgment in moral matters, and self-possession in social situations that require restraint. These qualities reflect the moral excellence of Austen's heroines—traits that Elizabeth Bennet in *Pride and Prejudice*, Anne Elliot in *Persuasion*, and Fanny Price in *Mansfield Park* also exemplify.

Whereas Fanny's idea of "sense" means worldly prudence in the form of miserly selfishness, and Elinor's virtue of "sense" as used by Jane Austen in the title of the novel signifies the power of reason to judge moral questions and the government of the passions, Marianne's abandonment of all sense in the name of the higher ideal of sensibility relegates reason to a lower status under the rule of the emotions. Whereas Fanny's calculating mind that hoards all the fortune from the family estate lacks all feelings of kindness and charity, Elinor's common sense and true prudence reveal both "strength of understanding, and coolness of judgment" (see p. 6) on the one hand and "an excellent heart" on the other ("her disposition was affectionate, and her feelings were strong") (see p. 7). Marianne's sensibility, however, finds all thought of money unromantic and all appeal to restraint a "disgraceful subjection of reason to common-place and mistaken notions" (see p. 53). She misrepresents Elinor's idea of sense by associating it with mere convention or conformity—"to be guided wholly by the opinion of other people" (see p. 92)—and therefore finds all the norms of sense unimaginative, confining, and commonplace.

When Elinor praises the shy Edward Ferrars for his sense of propriety, good taste, and sound understanding with the compliment "I do not attempt to deny … that I think very highly of him—that I greatly esteem, that I like him", Marianne finds the relationship most unromantic: "Esteem him! Like him! Cold-hearted Elinor! Oh! worse than cold-hearted!" (see p. 21). When Marianne recalls the farewells between Elinor and Edward before the Dashwoods moved from Sussex to Barton, she detects no sentiments of a man and woman falling in love: "How cold, how composed were their last adieus! How languid their conversation the last evening of their being together! In Edward's farewell there was no distinction between Elinor and me: it was the good wishes of an affectionate brother to both" (see p. 39).

On the other hand, when Marianne and Willoughby feel the attraction of love at first sight, she rhapsodizes about their ecstatic happiness, praising Willoughby for his animated reactions, expressive emotions, lively nature, and forthright opinions. Everything that Marianne values as proof of manly attractiveness—spirit, genius, taste, ardor, and sensibility—she identifies in Willoughby, who talks, reads, and sings with enthusiasm. These are all the qualities that she finds missing in Edward Ferrars and Colonel Brandon, whose virtues of prudence, propriety, and self-possession—all aspects of *sense*—Elinor admires. Whereas Edward's lukewarm interest in Elinor lacks fervor, and Brandon's unrequited love for Marianne lacks the éclat of love at first sight (it is a "second attachment" [see p. 55]), the dashing Willoughby as chivalrous knight rescues Marianne from her walking accident: "The gentleman ... took her up in his arms without farther delay, and carried her down the hill" (see pp. 41–42). Because Marianne and Willoughby spend every available moment in each other's delightful company during the next few weeks, she assumes that she has found true love, discovered "her ideas of perfection" (see p. 49) in a man of exquisite sensibility who complements her perfectly by his taste in music, books, and art. Since Marianne does not approve of love and marriage by way of "second attachments" (see p. 55), she identifies her first love as a romantic dream come true that transcends mere convention and proper matches based on social rank and family fortune: "Willoughby was all that her fancy had delineated" (see p. 49). Sensibility, then, values self-expression more than self-restraint and displays the emotions freely, equating restraint with unimaginative dullness and stifling rigidity.

Responding impetuously to the impression of love at first sight, sensibility overreacts and sentimentalizes, exaggerating both sorrow and joy as agony or ecstasy. Sensibility idealizes the perfect and regards "second attachments" as inferior relationships that rob love of its exhilaration. Sensibility responds instantly, rushes the experience of falling in love, and eliminates the necessary time or intermediate stages required for falling in love and making wise decisions. In its uncompromising attachment to the perfect or ideal, sensibility depreciates the normal, the moderate, and the natural—the ordinary experiences of common life that escape the extremes of feeling. Sensibility easily alters reality to correspond to preconceptions and prejudices in the way Marianne imagines the gallant Willoughby to be the paragon of manhood: "That is what I like; that is what a young man ought to be. Whatever be his pursuits, his eagerness in them should know no moderation, and leave him no sense of fatigue" (see p. 44). Marianne's brief romance that proceeds on the basis of "eagerness" rushes from wishes to hopes to expectations in quick succession so that no one doubts her eventual marriage to Willoughby in a matter of a few weeks. Sensibility, then, ignores the role of *sense* both in social life, in moral matters, and in romantic relationships. It does not allow love, romance, and marriage to follow their natural course.

While Marianne's romance appears glamorous and thrilling compared to Elinor's tepid, lackluster relationship with Edward, the folly of sensibility without sense soon exposes its superficiality. When Willoughby suddenly bids farewell to all his friends with the excuse of an urgent need to travel to London and explains, "I have no idea of returning into Devonshire immediately" (see p. 76), everyone finds his behavior strange and tactless. Elinor reflects, "So suddenly to be gone! It seems but the work of a moment. And last night he was with us so happy, so cheerful, so affectionate? And now after only ten minutes' notice—Gone too without intending to return!—Something more than what he owned to us must have happened" (see p. 77). All of Willoughby's spectacular display of spirit, enthusiasm, eagerness, and ardor dissolves into nothing. Marianne's ideal man seems all too imperfect.

All the violations of propriety and sense that Elinor observed prove to be telltale signs that Marianne conveniently ignored because of Willoughby's aura of romantic chivalry. Elinor noticed Willoughby's glib, thoughtless remarks, "saying too much what he thought on every occasion, without attention to persons or circumstances." She also observed his lack of graciousness and failure in civility by only keeping company with Marianne, "sacrificing general politeness to the enjoyment of undivided attention where his heart was engaged" (see p. 49). On several occasions Elinor noted a carelessness in matters of propriety. For example, when Willoughby surprises Marianne with the gift of a horse as a token of love, Elinor regards the gesture as inappropriate and excessive, troubled about "the propriety of her receiving such a present from a man so little, or at least so lately known to her" (see p. 58).

During the excursion to Whitewell, Willoughby and Marianne leave the entire company of fellow travelers to go on a private tour of the home that he will inherit. Without the permission of the occupant Mrs. Smith and without the thoughtfulness of inviting their friends to accompany them, Willoughby and Marianne put their private pleasure above the happiness of others. When corrected by Elinor who cautions, "Yes, Marianne, but I would not go while Mrs. Smith was there, and with no other companion than Mr. Willoughby", Marianne can only reply that the sheer spontaneous enjoyment of the drive and the grand views made it an innocent pleasure. Nevertheless, Elinor insists that the couple's conduct was in poor taste and violated good manners: "I am afraid ... that the pleasantness of an employment does not always evince its propriety" (see p. 68). Elinor's remarks reveal the subtle form of narcissism that sensibility assumes in justifying its rude behavior in the name of ardent love and spontaneous feelings—a flaw that assumes grave seriousness later in the novel when Elinor summarizes the essence of Willoughby's character: "The whole of his behaviour ... from the beginning to the end of the affair, has been grounded on selfishness.... His own enjoyment, or his own ease, was, in every particular, his ruling principle" (see p. 338).

Likewise, Marianne's sensibility also proves to be as insubstantial and empty as Willoughby's profession of love. After Willoughby's unexplained departure, she suffers inconsolable grief, broods in profound melancholy, and sheds her tears day and night. Austen writes, "Her sensibility was potent enough!" In this case Marianne's "indulgence of feeling", "nourishment of grief", and "violence of affliction" (see p. 83) also show a self-centeredness that exaggerates sadness and develops self-pity as it disregards all consideration of others, imagining that one's own sufferings supersede all obligations of civility or thoughtfulness for others. On the other hand, Elinor's *sense* provides moral strength, self-control, and poise even in the midst of her greatest sorrows and in the most exasperating social situations. Attracted to Edward and pleased by his attachment to her, Elinor incredulously listens as Lucy Steele privately reveals her secret engagement to him these past four years. Shocked, Elinor can barely control her disbelief: "Engaged to Mr. Edward Ferrars!—I confess myself so totally surprised at what you tell me, that really—I beg your pardon; but surely there must be some mistake of person or name. We cannot mean the same Mr. Ferrars." When Lucy offers more information about the need to conceal the engagement from the disapproving Mrs. Ferrars, reveals a picture of Edward in her possession, and mentions a lock of her hair set in a ring that Elinor has seen him wearing, Elinor feels heartbroken and depressed at the cruelty of betrayal she suffers. Under the circumstances, however, she conducts herself with the self-possession that sense exercises even in the most distressing circumstances: "She was silent.— Elinor's security sunk; but her self-command did not sink with it" (see pp. 127–28). Motivated by jealousy for a rival, Lucy slyly contrives to unsettle Elinor by dispelling all thoughts of

a possible romance with Edward, but Elinor recovers her composure during the entire conversation despite the fact that she
sensed Lucy's designs and that "[s]he was mortified, shocked,
confounded" (see p. 131). The contrast between the two sisters'
reactions to their sudden disappointments in love distinguishes
the moral strength of sense and the emotional weakness of sensibility, illuminating the disinterested goodness of Elinor and
the narrow egoism of Marianne.

When Marianne learns of Willoughby's engagement to Miss
Grey and realizes his duplicity in giving every impression of
falling in love and even begging for a lock of her hair as a keep-
sake, she not only feels betrayed, heartbroken, and insulted
but also lets her sensibility lead to outbursts of uncontrollable
tears and wailing. Almost fainting, not eating for many days,
and losing sleep for several nights, Marianne's sorrow turns to
anguish that causes grave concern for everyone. Wretched and
sobbing uncontrollably, Marianne's state of exhaustion threat-
ens her health and leads to a critical illness after she contracts
a cold from staying in wet clothes: Elinor "fancied that all
relief might soon be in vain, that every thing had been delayed
too long, and pictured to herself her suffering mother arriving
too late to see this darling child, or to see her rational" (see
p. 302). When Elinor appeals to her sister, "Exert yourself ... if
you would not kill yourself and all who love you", and implores
Marianne to think of the misery of their mother, Marianne
pleads weakness: "I cannot, I cannot ... leave me, leave me, if I
distress you; leave me, hate me, forget me!" (see p. 180).

This episode and the earlier scene of Willoughby's farewell
from Barton expose the moral indolence that accompanies the
indulgence of sensibility. Marianne claims it is impossible for
her reason and will to master her sorrow: "But to appear happy
when I am so miserable—Oh! who can require it?" (see p. 184).
Releasing all her anger, grief, and resentment at Willoughby's
insensitive exploitation of her feelings, Marianne, without any sensitivity for the feelings of others, burdens Mrs.
Jennings, Elinor, and her mother with the weight of her sorrows. Sensibility, then, breeds a preoccupation with one's

own grievances at the neglect of the suffering of others and assumes that no one else knows the depths of love's sorrows. Marianne excludes her sufferings from the universal experience of the human race. Unaware of Elinor's state of sadness at Lucy Steele's news of her engagement to Edward, Marianne dismisses her sister's plea for composure with the suggestion that no one can relate to the depths of her grief: "Oh! how easy for those who have no sorrow of their own to talk of exertion! Happy, happy Elinor, *you* cannot have an idea of what I suffer" (see p. 180). Because Elinor exerts self-command and does not indulge grief in the form of self-pity, she consoles Marianne, practices civility in the home of Mrs. Jennings, and grasps the larger truth that escapes Marianne's emotional overreaction: Marianne has been delivered from an imprudent marriage to a dishonorable, unprincipled man who marries Miss Grey for the sake of her wealth.

Just as the novel exposes the moral defects of undisciplined sensibility in Marianne's convulsions of grief that ignore the sensitivities of others and that evince a lack of propriety, the story also shows the moral vices that proceed from ungoverned sensibility in the form of uncontrolled passions in the case of Willoughby. The gentleman who gave every appearance of being in love at first sight and on the verge of engagement to Marianne not only suddenly ends the romance with the cavalier excuse that "my affections have been long engaged elsewhere, and it will not be many weeks, I believe, before this engagement is fulfilled" (see p. 178), but he also commits the sins of avarice and lust—his match with Miss Grey and his seduction of Eliza Williams. As Colonel Brandon relates his family history to Elinor to comfort Marianne in her sorrow, he refers to Eliza, the woman he once loved who lived a tragic life, divorced, and died in debtors' prison because of her marriage to an unworthy man. He recites the episode as a moral warning: Marianne has been spared the tragic fate of Eliza, who married Brandon's brother, a scoundrel similar to Willoughby in his lack of integrity and honor. Brandon informs Elinor of this sordid incident to persuade Marianne of her good fortune in the loss of Willoughby, "an escape from the worst and most irremediable of evils, a connection, for life, with an unprincipled man, as a deliverance the most real, a blessing the most important" (see p. 179).

As Brandon continues his account of the past, he explains that he assumed the responsibility of guardian to Eliza's child (little Eliza) out of affection for both Eliza and his orphaned niece. Shocked at little Eliza's mysterious disappearance at the time of her adolescence, Brandon learns that she has given birth to an illegitimate child fathered by Willoughby: "He had left the girl whose youth and innocence he had seduced, in a situation of the utmost distress, with no creditable home, no help, no friends, ignorant of his address!" (see p. 203). While Marianne's sensibility in the form of uncontrollable sorrow epitomizes self-centeredness that ignores the feelings of others and the obligations of civility, Willoughby's sensibility in the form of an uncontrollable pursuit of pleasure and money signifies the self-indulgence that uses others for its selfish desires.

As the novel shows, the corruption of sense in the form of prudent self-interest leads to marriages based solely on money, and the corruption of sensibility in the form of license leads to elopement, seduction, and children out of wedlock. Both attitudes destroy the ideal of marriage that forms the basis of civilization in Austen's novels. Mrs. Ferrars' demand that Edward marry the wealthy Miss Morton and also receive his inheritance as heir and favored son prompts his defiance of his mother's wishes—even at the loss of his entire family fortune.

The romances that mature and culminate in marriages at the end of the novel do not begin on the note of sensibility that precipitated Marianne's falling in love at first sight, and they do not conform to the romantic model of exclusively first attachments. Edwards' four-year engagement with Lucy Steele, his first attachment, neither meets the approval of his mother nor expresses the deepest sentiments of his own heart. Colonel Brandon's first attachment to Eliza never blossomed into the true love or the marriage he envisioned. The engagements of Marianne to Brandon and Elinor to Edward have the elements of true romances, the natural surprises of love rather than the exaggerated overreactions of "violent agitation" and "impetuous grief" (see p. 253). They escape the worldly motives of Willoughby's match to Miss Grey and Mrs. Ferrars' idea of marriage based on family fortunes, and they do not begin as single attachments, love at first sight, or premature ideas about marriage without courtship. While both sisters suffer rejection, experience broken hearts, and feel betrayed, their sorrows lead them to true love based on both reason and feeling as they both eventually marry men who prove themselves worthy of their esteem and affection—men whose constant devotion to their beloved transcends the momentary sensations of sensibility and disregards the cold calculation of fortune as the foundation of marriage.

When Marianne hears the news of Edward's engagement to Lucy Steele and discovers that Elinor has kept this secret to herself for the past four months, she learns the wisdom of sense over sensibility. Whereas Marianne's sensibility refused all comfort and luxuriated in self-pity, Elinor's sense never mentioned her grief to a single person: "[A]nd I owed it to my family and friends, not to create in them a solicitude about me, which it could not be in my power to satisfy." Whereas Marianne's broken heart rendered her moody, weakened, and rude, Elinor's dejection at the news of Edward's engagement does not rob her of composure, courtesy, or kindness to others. Marianne is moved by Elinor's compassion for the grief of others while burdened by her own sorrow: "What!—while attending me in all my misery, has this been on your heart?—and I have reproached you for being happy!" Because Marianne felt powerless when abandoned by Willoughby, she wonders at the source of her sister's strength: "Four months! ... So calm—so cheerful!—how have you been supported?" Elinor's simple answers explain the moral resources that exalt sense above sensibility. Elinor hid her despondent heart from others because she honored her promise to Lucy to keep the engagement a secret ("I was doing my duty"). She kept her sadness private because of special thoughtfulness for others ("I would not have you suffer on my account") (see p. 254). And Elinor governed her feelings, moods, and melancholy by reason and will power: "The composure of mind with which I have brought myself at present to consider the matter, the consolation that I have been willingly to admit, have been the effect of constant and painful exertion;—they did not spring up of themselves;—they did not occur to relieve my spirits at first" (see pp. 255–56).

At this moment in the novel Marianne admires the self-command of her sister, not as stoic apathy or insensibility, but as tender kindness and sensitive delicacy for the feelings of others. Acknowledging Elinor's virtue of *sense* that embraces good judgment, moral firmness, and refined feeling, Marianne now also exerts herself as she promises Elinor never to speak "with the least appearance of bitterness" about Edward's change of heart, never to show the smallest increase of dislike to Lucy, and never to express "any diminution of her usual cordiality" to Edward (see p. 256). Once Marianne gains sense, her whole idea of romance, love, and marriage begins to conform to reason and to know the true state of her heart.

After recovering from her life-threatening illness and hearing of Willoughby's apology from Elinor, Marianne acknowledges the unreasonableness of a marriage to Willoughby: "I never could have been happy with him, after knowing, as sooner or later I must have known, all this.—I should have had no confidence, no esteem" (see p. 337). She instead offers her hand to Colonel Brandon "with no sentiment superior to strong esteem" (see p. 364). While romances in Jane Austen's novels require economic and social considerations and consider manners, temperament, and mutual attraction, the sure foundation of a happy marriage depends on this virtue Austen refers to as "esteem"—an admiration and respect for the moral character of the beloved. Colonel Brandon and Edward as friends and brothers-in-law (both praised for "good principles and good sense" [see p. 355]) share the same ideals of integrity, honor, magnanimity, duty, and charity that inspire the "esteem" of the two sisters whom they marry.

In his kind, fatherly care for his niece little Eliza, in his generous offer of the living at Delaford to Edward upon the suggestion of Elinor, in his kind offer to travel a long distance to accompany Mrs. Dashwood during the crisis of Marianne's illness, in his kind, gentle manners and "genuine attention to other people", and in his constant, devoted attachment to Marianne throughout her romance with Willoughby, Brandon proves, as Elinor observes, that "his character and principles [are] fixed" (see p. 326). His virtue is a habit, not a mood, a habit that has proven itself over the course of a lifetime in his relations with all people. Likewise, Edward also demonstrates a similar character of integrity and honor that earns him the esteem of Elinor. Unwilling to marry his mother's choice of Miss Morton because of wealth and social status, true to his engagement with Lucy Steele rather than reneging on his word because of his mother's disapproval, Edward only proposes to Elinor after Lucy ends the engagement and marries Robert Ferrars: "I thought it my duty, ... independent of my feelings, to give her the option of continuing the engagement or not, when I was renounced by my mother" (see p. 353). Unlike Willoughby, who was courting Marianne while engaged to Miss Grey, Edward honorably disentangles himself from his relationship with Lucy, his "foolish" engagement (see p. 348), before declaring his love for Elinor.

Thus the role of *sense* in marriage acknowledges and cherishes this moral dimension of marriage more than the worldly considerations of money and status that rule Mrs. Ferrars, Willoughby, Lucy, and Mr. and Mrs. John Dashwood. Austen's virtue of *sense* discerns and values this inestimable quality of "esteem" in the moral character of the beloved because it endures in the course of a lifetime of marriage and does not come and go like Willoughby's sudden appearance and disappearance in Marianne's life, which promises much but leaves nothing.

Why Edward Ferrars Doesn't Dance[1]

Theresa Kenney
University of Dallas

Edward Ferrars alone among Austen's heroes does not dance, Penelope Fritzer observed in *Jane Austen and Eighteenth-Century Courtesy Books*.[2] This observation may not be entirely true, as we shall see below, but we as the readers of *Sense and Sensibility* certainly never see Edward (or Elinor) trip the light fantastic. By all accounts, this is a great deficiency in the novel. Though abler pens have detailed the meaning and uses of dancing in Austen's novels and have even observed the relative lack thereof in *Sense and Sensibility*, critics have been content to heave a sigh of regret rather than to ask why, in this novel, Austen chose to eschew dance-floor scenes, whereas they are important features in the two other early novels, *Pride and Prejudice* and *Northanger Abbey*. I would argue that she does so quite deliberately. Three motives seem to drive Austen's artistic choices for this novel: a desire to frustrate mythic expectations as she replaces symbolic actions with realistic ones; a desire to disconnect the spirit of play from the development of mature, long-lasting love; and a desire to create plain, old-fashioned suspense. Austen creates a novel with a designedly somber tone through this and other artistic choices, a novel dominated by the anxieties and difficulties of the cast of this problem comedy.

Edward's Character

Cynthia Griffin has said that "[t]he reader is hard-put to respond to Edward. We know he is supposed to attract us, but

[1] This essay originally appeared in and is reprinted by the kind permission of *Persuasions: The Jane Austen Journal*, no. 25, 2013, pp. 153–68, http://www.jasna.org/persuasions/printed/pers35.html.

[2] Penelope Fritzer, *Jane Austen and Eighteenth-Century Courtesy Books* (Westport, Conn.: Greenwood Press, 1997), p. 36.

his backward behavior and seeming distaste for action do not recommend him in our eyes."[3] Langdon Elsbree even more damningly remarks that the dull Elinor, Colonel Brandon, and Edward sit out dances or never engage in them. For him, this is part of a general "subtle deficiency of energies" in the three.[4] Elsbree is, however, wrong to think that Austen considers this "deficiency of energies" as evidence of a natural phlegmatic disposition in any of the three characters he targets. First of all, it is important to note that Austen, in spite of her admiration for both energy and, more especially, exertion, distinguishes the charms of physical vitality from virtue, kindness, and fidelity, even in *Pride and Prejudice*. Still, mere sobriety of spirits does not fully account for Edward's characteristics if we see him in the context of Austen's other novels. The character Edward most resembles is, oddly, one who is very much associated with music and dance: *Emma*'s Jane Fairfax. Austen paints him with the same moodiness, stiffness in conversation, and reticence that she later sketches in her picture of Jane. Like her, he is in a chafing secret engagement, which oppresses the candor of his spirit. As Tony Tanner notes, "secrecy and sickness" are linked in this novel, though regrettably he did not turn that observation to the task of explaining Edward's manner.[5] Later in the London scenes of the novel, Austen imagines Edward avoiding social events no doubt because he is engaged to Lucy Steele and wishes to avoid meeting either her or Elinor in public. There can be no dancing if the gentleman is not on the scene, and he most assuredly wishes to absent himself from it given his uncomfortable situation. Austen nowhere says that Edward does not dance because he cannot or does not wish to. The issue never comes up, and as we know, it certainly does in regard to Mr. Darcy and Mr. Knightley.

[3] Cynthia Griffin, "The Development of Realism in Jane Austen's Early Novels", *English Literary History* 30, no. 1 (March 1963): 46.

[4] Langdon Elsbree, *Ritual Passages and Narrative Structures* (New York: Peter Lang, 1991), p. 118.

[5] Tony Tanner, "Secrecy and Sickness: *Sense and Sensibility*", in *Jane Austen* (Cambridge: Harvard University Press, 1986), p. 75.

Edward's natural disposition is not on display until the end of the novel, when the narrator has a little laugh at Edward's discomfiture about proposing to Elinor as "he was not altogether inexperienced in such a question".[6] She is about to describe his transformation into "genuine, flowing, grateful cheerfulness" (see p. 348), and she devotes more time to their discussion after their engagement than to any other dialogue between the two in the novel. Thus we see that her withholding of such scenes to this point is also a form of suspense: the reader wants to see the two together in private, and we finally do. They can now speak as openly to one another as Emma and Mr. Knightley claim they do in *Emma*. Most importantly, here, as in other scenes in the novel, Austen shows us there is a real difference between Edward under constraint and Edward at liberty. From the very first, what we understand about Edward is that the warmth of others draws him out.

Austen introduces him thrice over in volume 1, chapter 3, always from the point of view of Mrs. Dashwood, who finds a reason to continue living at Norland in the arrival of "the brother of Mrs. John Dashwood, a gentlemanlike and pleasing young man" (see p. 15). This apparently strange artistic choice makes sense when we consider that both Edward and Willoughby grow sincerely attached to Mrs. Dashwood, enjoy her trust, and refer themselves to her judgment (especially Willoughby, unexpectedly). Later in the aforesaid chapter, we see her point of view mixed with narrative objectivity and irony (some of it directed against herself):

> Edward Ferrars was not recommended to their good opinion by any peculiar graces of person or address. He was not handsome, and his manners required intimacy to make them pleasing. He was too diffident to do justice to himself; but when his natural shyness was overcome, his behaviour gave every indication of an open affectionate heart. His understanding was good, and

[6] Jane Austen, *Sense and Sensibility*, ed. Eleanor Bourg Nicholson, Ignatius Critical Editions (San Francisco: Ignatius Press, 2014), p. 347. Subsequent quotations from this edition will be cited in the text.

his education had given it solid improvement. But he was neither fitted by abilities nor disposition to answer the wishes of his mother and sister, who longed to see him distinguished—as—they hardly knew what. (See p. 15.)

This description tells us that Edward's appearance and ways are not to the taste of Fanny Dashwood and Mrs. Ferrars, who only value money and power. What is not attractive immediately becomes so in the view of our Dashwoods because of the behavior Edward exhibits, which "gave every indication of an open affectionate heart". Lastly, again from Mrs. Dashwood's perspective:

Mrs. Dashwood now took pains to get acquainted with him. Her manners were attaching and soon banished his reserve. She speedily comprehended all his merits; the persuasion of his regard for Elinor perhaps assisted her penetration; but she really felt assured of his worth: and even that quietness of manner which militated against all her established ideas of what a young man's address ought to be, was no longer uninteresting when she knew his heart to be warm and his temper affectionate. (See pp. 16–17.)

Mrs. Dashwood is not a fully reliable touchstone for the reader, and it is interesting that Austen chooses to introduce Edward to us mainly through her estimation of him. She, of course, also will approve of Willoughby and judge him to be open and affectionate, wrongly. Austen gives us a few careful hints in this paragraph that Mrs. Dashwood may overestimate Edward because he has the good taste to admire her daughter, but she also tells us that Mrs. Dashwood's warmth "soon banished his reserve" (see p. 16). Edward becomes more open precisely because of the affectionate welcome he receives from Elinor's mother, so unlike his own. Edward's potential begins to be revealed in his private, familial interactions with the Dashwoods, not in communal celebrations or traditional patterns of wooing. That is our narrator's choice. He overcomes Mrs. Dashwood's romantic prejudices not by dint of effort but by the gradual revelation of what lies behind the exterior: an "affectionate" temper and a "warm" heart.

Yet the reader is strongly compelled to estimate the romance between Edward and Elinor at a lower rate than that between Darcy and Elizabeth Bennet, partly because Austen gives him some of the unsociable characteristics we traditionally associate with the discordant characters in a comedy—reticence, melancholy, disingenuousness, irony, and so on. However, the plot Austen constructs would hardly be served by Edward's entering into any festive behavior. Given his situation, it would mark him as heedless and pleasure-seeking, which he clearly is not. I suggested above an analog for him in the character of Jane Fairfax; the difference between them, then, is worth noting. Jane sings and dances when her fiancé is near, a fiancé she still desires and wishes to marry. Both these behaviors associated with courting and romance acquire a tinge of clandestineness from her situation, and for that reason we may deduce that even friendly critics such as Emma and Mr. Knightley might find something to fault in her enjoyment of Frank's presence. Though, as I will show below, we cannot assume that Edward and Elinor never dance, Austen clearly does not want to show Edward enjoying Elinor's company in this way. It would make his love for her more guilty, and his conduct while engaged to Lucy less excusable.

If his character is a youthful miscalculation of Austen's, it is a miscalculation she intended to miscalculate. Late in her life, we see exactly how Austen thinks about overly perfect heroes in her own letter of advice on writing to her niece Anna: "Henry Mellish I am afraid will be too much in the common Novel style—a handsome, amiable, unexceptionable Young Man (such as do not much abound in real Life)."[7] Austen goes out of her way to take the myth out of the hero in this novel, to make him more like the type of young man that does abound

[7] Jane Austen to Anna Austen Lefroy, September 28, 1814, in *Letters of Jane Austen*, 3rd ed., ed. Deirdre Le Faye (Oxford: Oxford University Press, 1995), p. 277.

in real life. Peter Graham counts him among Austen's "Beta male" heroes, which is not a dismissal.[8] For readers who admire Austen's alpha males—Darcy, Wentworth, and Knightley—there will never be a chance for Ferrars, Bertram, and Tilney to compete. Yet I believe Graham is right in drawing the reader's attention to this modern classification based on animal behavior, but now meaning something quite different than the wolf who doesn't get to lead the pack—it can even mean the man who is not attracted to traditional markers of success, but who values the more important things in life. Therefore he will not be drawn to the following: big cars (unlike John Thorpe), big houses (unlike Robert Ferrars), titles (unlike Mr. Elliot), and big money (unlike Willoughby). Interestingly, all of the "Beta male heroes" are clergymen, not an attraction for the Mary Crawfords of the world, but certainly not a disqualifier for Austen herself. The rewards of myth and fairy tale, station, wealth, and possessions are not always her stamp of approval.

The Spirit of Play and the Spirit of Love

We should consider the risks Austen takes with potential disaffection of her reader. She disconnects the spirit of play from the development of romantic love in both major romantic relationships in *Sense and Sensibility*. This choice is key to the novel's character. Edward is playful in his own way, of course—in a way Colonel Brandon never is—an aspect of his personality Austen chooses to reveal in his teasing relationship with Marianne, whom he sees as too serious, too committed to her romantic ideology. But this playfulness does not appear in his relationship with Elinor, who nonetheless understands that it is there. Edward's ribbing of Marianne indicates the opposite of romantic interest; there is a freedom from the restraint, confusion, and silence that attend deep feeling. Austen intimates, like Shakespeare's Cordelia—but Cordelia in a comic universe—that to "love, and be silent" is a greater indication

---

[8] Peter W. Graham, "Henry Tilney: Portrait of the Hero as Beta Male", *Persuasions On-Line* 31, no.1 (Winter 2010).

of sincerity than to be able to "heave [one's] heart into [one's] mouth" (*King Lear* 1.1.93–94).[9]

There are practical reasons *Sense and Sensibility* lacks dancing scenes. For the first portion of the novel, the heroines are in mourning and, according to custom, so is anyone related to them, though for a shorter time. Whether there are sufficient couples to dance at Norland or not we will never know, for there would be no dancing there the entire time Mrs. Dashwood and her daughters remain in residence, from the death of Henry Dashwood in early February to their removal to Barton Cottage in August. A year of mourning was incumbent on a widow, and at least six months for the children of the deceased, though the Regency period was less systematic and rigid about these norms than the later Victorian period would be.[10] The number of weeks the Ferrars family would have been expected to be in mourning was much less—three weeks only were expected of step relatives and in-laws.[11] Since Fanny Dashwood is the daughter-in-law of the deceased, however, she too would have an obligation to mourn with her husband.

Then when the family is at Barton Cottage, Mrs. Dashwood's pride prevents her from accepting Sir John's invitations to mix more in society:

Their visitors, except those from Barton Park, were not many; for, in spite of Sir John's urgent entreaties that they would mix more in the neighbourhood, and repeated assurances of his carriage being always at their service, the independence of Mrs. Dashwood's spirit overcame the wish of society for her children; and she was resolute in declining to visit any family beyond the distance of a walk. There were but few who could

[9] William Shakespeare, *King Lear*, Ignatius Critical Editions, ed. Joseph Pearce (San Francisco: Ignatius Press, 2008).

[10] Deirdre Le Faye, for instance, says Frank and Jane (in *Emma*) can marry three months after the death of Mrs. Churchill (Le Faye, *Letters*, p. 274).

[11] Randolph Trumbach, *The Rise of the Egalitarian Family: Aristocratic Kinship and Domestic Relations in Eighteenth-Century England* (New York: Academic Press, 1978), p. 37.

be so classed; and it was not all of them that were attainable. (See p. 40.)

Here Austen makes it clear there is a kind of self-imposed isolation that the Dashwoods endure as a result of their poverty and their fear of appearing to accept charity from the generous-hearted Sir John. The Dashwoods' poverty is yet another reason why the novel does not feature parties and dances as primary scenes.

However, by volume 1, chapter 11, Mrs. Dashwood's scruples have been overcome:

> Little had Mrs. Dashwood or her daughters imagined, when they first came into Devonshire, that so many engagements would arise to occupy their time as shortly presented themselves, or that they should have such frequent invitations and such constant visitors as to leave them little leisure for serious employment. Yet such was the case. When Marianne was recovered, the schemes of amusement at home and abroad, which Sir John had been previously forming, were put into execution. The private balls at the park then began; and parties on the water were made and accomplished as often as a showery October would allow. (See p. 53.)

These private balls are the first dances for Elinor and Marianne since the novel has begun, and they very pointedly occur after the introduction of Willoughby to the plot. The reader is enticed to feel that the atmosphere of romance is intensifying; however, Austen knows these dances do not presage the unity of the couple, and she does not provide them with a narrated dance scene.

Importantly, in this novel Willoughby and Robert Ferrars are both dancers (see pp. 44, 242 [Robert's visit to Dartford]). One great attraction for Marianne in Sir John's initial description of Willoughby lies in his ability to dance all night, as he did the Christmas before the girls' arrival in Barton. Robert Ferrars (who, to the delight of the hero, heroine, and reader, will purloin Lucy Steele from his brother) quite handily resolves his friend Lady Elliott's concerns about giving a dance in her cottage near Dartford, and, as he tells Elinor, he attends the dance given thereafter. Since especially the latter description is an example of Robert's self-satisfaction and arrogance, neither of these men can be construed as gentlemen because of their devotion to the dance. We cannot deduce from the lack in this novel that participation in dance, à la Shakespeare, indicates sociability and marriageability and that sitting out indicates antisocial tendencies.[12] Austen certainly knew Shakespeare's comedies, but she practically reverses the conventional, mythic relationship between dancing and unity. The nondancers, unlike Jaques in *As You Like It* or Don John in *Much Ado about Nothing*, cannot be construed as being "compact of jars", whose entry into the orderly patterns of music formed by the engaged couples would "shortly cause discord in the spheres" (*As You Like It*, 2.7.5–7).

Henry Tilney's famous extended metaphor in *Northanger Abbey* comparing dancing and marriage is proof enough that Austen is conversant with this tradition of dance as image of marriage and unity and that she is able to employ it for her fictive ends. It stands as a quasi-marriage proposal at the beginning of his relationship with Catherine Morland and is the most outrageous piece of flirting in all of Austen. In *Pride and Prejudice*, the heroine's first dance with Darcy showcases an argument; unlike the reader, Elizabeth Bennet does not feel something romantic has passed between her and Darcy. The reader, however, contrasts Darcy's elegance with Mr. Collins' awkwardness and begins to deduce without much difficulty that Darcy's fine dancing presages romance. Austen uses this dance for many different purposes, and we would do well to recall the novel starts with Darcy's refusal to dance with Elizabeth at all.[13] Though Elizabeth and Darcy's dance scene in *Pride*

---

[12] See *As You Like It*, 5.4, and *Much Ado about Nothing*, 5.4. All quotations for these plays are from William Shakespeare, *The Riverside Shakespeare*, ed. G. Blakemore Evans and J. J. M. Tobin (Boston: Houghton Mifflin, 1973).

[13] Pat Rogers suggests that the interchange between Bingley and Darcy comes from Romeo's response to Mercutio in *Romeo and Juliet*: "Nay, gentle Romeo, we must have you dance." Romeo is as obdurate as Darcy: "Not I, believe me. You

and Prejudice is world famous, it pays to notice the details that
surround it. One comment that precedes their partnership represents an important observation of the youthful author, issu-
ing as it does from the hero's mouth.

Darcy tells Sir William Lucas that dancing, after all, is one
of the first accomplishments of any savage.

> "What a charming amusement for young people this is, Mr.
> Darcy!—There is nothing like dancing after all.—I consider it
> as one of the first refinements of polished societies."
>
> "Certainly, Sir;—and it has the advantage also of being in
> vogue amongst the less polished societies of the world.—Every
> savage can dance."[14]

In other words, to his mind, dancing is not a refinement or
symptom of elegant behavior, as Sir William proposes to him
and as everyone else in the room probably believes, but a prim-
itive expression of energy, something that any person can do
without the least advantage of education or refinement. *Pride
and Prejudice* being closest in time of composition to *Sense and
Sensibility*, its statements on dancing probably mirror most
accurately the musings of the young Jane Austen on the matter. I don't say beliefs, for Darcy's observation here is a double-
edged sword—it is meant to cut the flow of Sir William's spirits
as they run on in clichés, and it is also meant to make the
reader laugh at Darcy's rudeness as much as at his bon mot.[15]
The novel, of course, has it both ways; as Allison Thompson
points out, "a clearly traceable precept from Renaissance times
through the Regency was this concept that one measure of
determining whether a man was truly a gentleman was by his
ability to dance with confidence, to stand well, to move easily
without calling attention to himself, to enter a room grace-
fully. Clumsiness, haughtiness, and ostentatious display were

---

have dancing shoes/With nimble soles. I have a soul of lead/So stakes me to the
ground I cannot move" (1.4.13–16). See Jane Austen, *Pride and Prejudice*, ed. Pat
Rogers (Cambridge: Cambridge University Press, 2006), p. 466.

[14] Ibid., p. 25.

[15] Ibid.

to be avoided".[16] Austen herself made the same associations, and she knew well enough as an author what signals were sent by a dance between hero and heroine, however much verbal sparring accompanied it. Nonetheless, the young Austen wrote this line for Mr. Darcy, and so she thought it—dancing in *Pride and Prejudice* may be two things, at least: the symbol that satisfies the reader who responds to cultural myths or "plots" (which is what a mythos is in Greek, after all), and a thing the Netherfield assembly shares with the most uncultured savages. The stab is at a fiction of what constitutes civilized behavior— Sir William even calls dancing a "science"—and also at what creates love. Elizabeth does not fall in love with Darcy at this dance, though the dance signals to readers that she will fall in love with him. In the first half of the novel, the hero can dance as elegantly as he likes—he still does not deserve the heroine.

I focus on Darcy's quotation at length because it is proof that Austen can "think against the myth". The authorial use of dance as part of the structure and meaning of *Pride and Prejudice* and *Emma*—not to mention *Northanger Abbey*—is brilliant. Austen's timing of the first dances of Mr. Darcy and Mr. Knightley is very precise, and both heroes do eventually dance with the heroine, though both "dislike[] the amusement in general".[17] Austen very knowingly creates the fiction reader's response to the mythic qualities of dance.

Sir William has probably been reading Soame Jenyns' 1729 *The Art of Dancing*:

> Hence to mankind the Heav'n-born Science flew
> And one great Part of their Religion grew:
> The gracious Pow'rs above, they wisely thought,
> Must sure approve what first themselves had taught. . . .
> Nor did the Dancer's generous Science claim
> Inferiour Gains, or a less Share of Fame.[18]

---

[16] Allison Thompson, "The Felicities of Rapid Motion: Jane Austen in the Ballroom", *Persuasions On-Line* 21, no. 1 (Winter 2000).

[17] Austen, *Pride and Prejudice*, p. 29.

[18] Soame Jenyns, *The Art of Dancing: A Poem in Three Canto's* [sic] (London: W. P. and J. Roberts, 1729), canto 1, pp. 3–4.

Theresa Kenney

Since dance has these powerful cosmic and civic associations, connecting romantic love to the order of the universe, why is Austen so perverse as not to provide a dancing scene between Edward and Elinor (or Colonel Brandon and Marianne) in *Sense and Sensibility*? She does refer to dances and dancing several times throughout the novel; therefore, this notable omission cues us in to Austen's choices in constructing this story, which I would argue is not a festive comedy, celebrating young love's ability to overcome old suspicion and miserliness, but a problem comedy, to use terminology from Shakespearean criticism. The term "problem comedy" is of course a critical category Shakespeare never considered, but it is a convenient term to describe a drama that has the usual trajectory of a comedy from crises and obstacles to success in love and prosperity, but that poses unsettling questions, or creates doubt about the virtuousness of the protagonists, or does not ratify our hopes of happiness in the end for the main couple. Whatever kind of comedy that is (it certainly isn't tragedy), it is not just meant to be sunny and comforting. It is my contention that the spirit of play is for the most part absent from this novel, that it is compromised by its connection to sense, or pecuniary concerns, and to sensibility in its guise of ungoverned sexual passion.[19] Austen deliberately removes the development of marital love from the environs of play in *Sense and Sensibility*. My deduction is that she wants to purify it of unnecessary if not dangerous mythic trappings. Edward's character and behavior thus help create a subdued tone, a novel that walks rather than dances.

Austen has clearly taken care to deprive Edward of the standard characteristics of a hero. It is Willoughby who carries the injured damsel, it is Brandon who fights a duel with the villain, and it is Willoughby, notably, who can dance all night without tiring, only two months or so before abandoning the young girl he seduces, who was certainly not at that party. It is

Cf. Richard Jenkyns, *A Fine Brush on Ivory: An Appreciation of Jane Austen* (Oxford: Oxford University Press, 2004), p. 189.

Willoughby, so beloved by so many literary critics, who is most associated with the spirit of play in the novel. A sportsman, a flirt, a tireless dancer, Willoughby has energy and charisma. Yet he is a cad. Critics as great as Mary Poovey are confused and frustrated by the alliance of energy with immorality.[20] Austen is not.

Austen would have been familiar with an important and famous depiction of ungoverned youth from Shakespeare's *Henry IV, Part 2*. If nowhere else, Austen could have read it in *Elegant Extracts*, which she knew well.[21] The positive myth of dance always came along with a dark obverse, as this quotation from Shakespeare's play makes clear:

> The King: Down, royal state! All you sage counsellors,
>   hence!
> And to the English court assemble now,
> From every region apes of idleness;
> Now, neighbor-confines, purge you of your scum:
> Have you a ruffian that will swear, drink, dance,
> Revel the night; rob, murder, and commit
> The oldest sins the newest kind of ways? (*Henry IV,*
>   *Part 2*, 4.5.180)

The dying king imagines other countries sending to England under his son's misrule all their idle evildoers, among whose characteristics we find the ability to dance and party the night away. Shakespeare's Henry is surely not the only father Austen encountered in literature who connected staying up all night with "the oldest sins".

The connection of dance with the stereotype of gallant youth can be traced back at least to Chaucer's squire, who slept no more than a nightingale does:

[20] Mary Poovey, *The Proper Lady and the Woman Writer: Ideology as Style in Works of Mary Wollstonecraft, Mary Shelley, and Jane Austen* (Chicago: Chicago University Press, 1984), pp. 186, 193, 208 et passim.

[21] Vicesimus Knox, ed., *Elegant Extracts: Or Useful and Entertaining Pieces of Poetry, Selected for the Improvement of Young Persons: Being Similar in Design to Elegant Extracts in Prose*, vol. 2, part 3 (London: Charles Dilly, 1790), p. 63.

Wel koude he sitte on hors, and faire ryde.
(*He knew the way to sit a horse and ride,*)
He coude songes make and wel endyte,
(*He could make songs and poems and recite,*)
Iuste and eek daunce, and wel purtreye and wryte,
(*Knew how to joust and dance, to draw and write.*)
So hoote he lovede, that by nightertale.
(*He loved so hotly that till dawn grew pale*)
He sleep namoore than dooth a nyghtyngale.
(*He slept as little as a nightingale.*)[22]

Chaucer's squire is a prototype for the squires in Sir Walter
Scott's *Marmion*, which was published in 1810, a year before
the publication of *Sense and Sensibility*, so it is another possible source for Austen's connection of dancing all night
with all a young man should be—summed up in the deceitful
Willoughby. We could take Chaucer's description, in fact, and
reverse it and come up with a description of Edward Ferrars: he
doesn't sing or write well, he doesn't joust or dance, or draw,
or compose, and he doesn't strike us as a particularly hot lover.
Whether he sleeps or not, we do not hear.

Austen's own brothers had written of the connection
between adept dancing and scurrilous behavior in their college
publication, *The Loiterer*:

> To avoid, therefore, the possibility of such a relapse, it will be
> highly prudent to fix his affections on objects totally indepen-
> dent of thought and reflection; and to teach him to look on
> a Ball-room as the only theatre for merit, and dress the only
> criterion of taste. Let him recollect the following *truisms*, and
> model his conduct accordingly. "He who cannot dance is a
> *Dunce*; He who cannot swear a *Coward*; and, He who has not
> white teeth, a—*Scoundrel*."
>
> By following these directions, either in full or in part,
> as occasion presents itself whoever wishes to become *Loved*
> and *Respected*, will be certain of Success. Let him indulge in
> every species of Dissipation; let him riot in every Pleasure,

<hr>

[22] Geoffrey Chaucer, *The Canterbury Tales*, trans. Nevill Coghill (Harmondsworth, U.K.: Penguin, 1959), pp. 21–22.

and when merit is rewarded, He may *depend* upon an *exalted* situation.[23]

Here, the irony of the association between merit and dancing is intense: if swearing is courage and white teeth are a mark of virtue, well may a nondancer be a dunce. The young Jane Austen similarly challenges her readers to disconnect dancing from virtue.

Dance is often an indicator of vice, in fact, in an age that was much influenced by Calvinism and the religious enthusiasm of Low Church movements. In *The Way of the World* (1700) by English playwright William Congreve, Lady Wishfort tells Mrs. Marwood of her daughter's delusion that their priest is a woman, a delusion carefully nurtured by her family, who wish to keep her cloistered from the world:

> I warrant you, or she would never have borne to have been catechised by him, and have heard his long lectures against singing and dancing and such debaucheries, and going to filthy plays, and profane music meetings, where the lewd trebles squeak nothing but bawdy, and the basses roar blasphemy.[24]

Here even music is suspect.

Irish playwright Richard Brinsley Sheridan makes dancing the subject of a humorous scene in *The Rivals* (1775), as the melancholy and romantic Faulkland finds out that his beloved, Julia Melville, has actually sung and danced in his absence. This play Austen certainly knew well: her family put it on in their own home in 1784, when she was nine years old. For Faulkland, Julia's dancing country dances is absolute proof of her infidelity and callous heart (about which he is entirely mistaken):

> Faulkland: Nay, nay, nay—I'm not sorry that she has been happy—no, no, I am glad of that—I would not have had her sad or sick—yet surely a sympathetic heart would have shown itself even in the choice of a song—she might have been

[23] James Austen, *Loiterer* 1, no. 27 (August 1, 1779).
[24] Hartley Coleridge, ed., *The Dramatic Works of Wycherley, Congreve, Vanbrugh, and Farquhar* (London: E. Moxon, 1840), p. 283.

temperately healthy, and somehow, plaintively gay;—but she has been dancing too, I doubt not!

Bob Acres: What does the gentleman say about dancing?

Jack Absolute: He says the lady we speak of dances as well as she sings.

Acres: Ay, truly, does she—there was at our last race ball—

Faulk: Hell and the devil!—There!—there—I told you so! I told you so! Oh! she thrives in my absence!—Dancing! But her whole feelings have been in opposition with mine;—I have been anxious, silent, pensive, sedentary—my days have been hours of care, my nights of watchfulness.—She has been all health! spirit! laugh! song! dance!—Oh! damned, damned levity! … What, Mr. Acres, you were praising Miss Melville's manner of dancing a minuet—hey?

Acres: Oh, I dare insure her for that—but what I was going to speak of was her country dancing. Odds swimmings! she has such an air with her!

Faulk: Now disappointment on her!—Defend this, Absolute; why don't you defend this?—Country-dances! jigs and reels! am I to blame now? A minuet I could have forgiven—I should not have minded that—I say I should not have regarded a minuet—but country-dances!—Zounds! (2.1.207–20; 225–34)

Sheridan makes fun of the conventional lover's expectation of mutual languishing in each other's absence, but Faulkland's expectations in this scene are no more than Marianne Dashwood's. Sir John's ribbing of our younger heroine's refusal to dance in the absence of Willoughby is just such a gibe at the convention. Participation in the convention is a sign the society can read that indicates the young couple are in love. But as Sheridan points out through Faulkland, it is often no more than a fiction purposely engaged in. Nonetheless, if we look below at the disappointment that critic Langdon Elsbree expresses that dancing and music exit *Sense and Sensibility* after Willoughby's betrayal of Marianne, such knowledge of eighteenth-century models Austen may well have had in mind should act as a corrective. We cannot read an Austen novel as a twentieth-century psychoanalytical critic would; we would miss every purposeful subversion of convention.

Creating Suspense

Nonetheless, I would argue that Austen, aware of the deep associations between dancing, matrimony, and civic order, consciously employs the audience's expectations to create a gap, a sense of something missing. The proof is when Edward is finally visiting the Dashwoods in Barton long after his promised arrival (see pp. 86–102). At this point the Dashwood girls are no longer in mourning—it is fall—and there is talk of putting together a dance at Sir John's, as has clearly happened before. Marianne is teased by Sir John, who asks her if no one may dance just because Willoughby is not there. There is no indication that the dance happens, but there is no indication that it does not, and Austen leaves this tantalizing silence hanging over the event. It is going to be festive; Edward is there and would be in attendance. As one of the few men present, he would be expected to dance at the gathering *if* it turned into a dance. But Austen neither details Elinor's disappointment at not being able to join hands with her beloved, nor does she describe the witty and probing conversation they have as the music plays and they dance La Boulangère. If Elinor and Edward dance that evening—and they might—we are not to know of it.[25] This is Austen fashioning the development of the romance as well as setting a tone. Elsbree rightly points out that after the crisis of the disastrous party at which Willoughby snubs Marianne, dancing and music disappear from the novel.[26] For Elsbree, with his academic training in mythic and psychoanalytic approaches to literature, this is a turn for the worse and condemns the novel to classification as a failure. But I would argue two things: one, that we are meant to know nothing of the dancing and music in which Elinor professedly has little interest, for this is her story, and Austen fashions the setting, the plot, and the denouement with an eye toward consistency of tone and narrative attitude, not with a

[25] Most dramatizations have Edward begging off or departing much earlier than his full week with the Dashwoods, in order to avoid showing him at the party!

[26] Elsbree, *Ritual Passages*, p. 118.

concern for archetypal resonances; two, that we in fact cannot deduce that dancing is not on the docket, for Sir John is "for ever forming parties":

> Lady Middleton piqued herself upon the elegance of her table, and of all her domestic arrangements; and from this kind of vanity was her greatest enjoyment in any of their parties. But Sir John's satisfaction in society was much more real; he delighted in collecting about him more young people than his house would hold, and the noisier they were the better was he pleased. He was a blessing to all the juvenile part of the neighbourhood, for in summer he was for ever forming parties to eat cold ham and chicken out of doors, and in winter his private balls were numerous enough for any young lady who was not suffering under the insatiable appetite of fifteen. (See pp. 32–33.)

There must be no dearth of amusements for the Dashwood girls to engage in, but Austen does not portray them engaging in them.

There seems to be a kind of Austen criticism that consists of noting that the other five novels are not *Pride and Prejudice*. The question to ask is, why? If Austen herself, albeit in levity, remarked that *Pride and Prejudice* was "somewhat too light and bright and sparkling",[27] we need to inquire why the purveyor of such fine champagne would serve up something that seems rather more like a staid port or a rather tannic red wine, on purpose. I think the answer is a question of taste, or flavor. *Sense and Sensibility* is not meant to be festive and bubbly. It starts out with a death and ends with accommodations some readers find very off-putting. We never doubt that Edward loves Elinor throughout this novel, but Austen does make us doubt that he dances. His elegance, his bodily grace, are not the issue here; elegance, bodily grace, charm—in Willoughby these are all found to be deceitful, and to hide a callous heart and selfish purpose. Austen is interested in the problem of

---

[27] Jane Austen to Anna Austen Lefroy, Thursday, February 4, 1813, in *Letters of Jane Austen*, 3rd ed., ed. Deirdre Le Faye, p. 212.

surfaces and depths, of Shakespeare's seeming and being; and thus, dance, which is all physical, all seeming, all societal encoding, must not distract us. What she is writing is not just a tale of burgeoning love, for unlike Elizabeth Bennet and Emma Woodhouse, Elinor (like Fanny Price) knows whom she loves from the outset of the novel—*Sense and Sensibility* is, more than this, a novel of decipherment. Elinor and Marianne—yes, and Edward, too—are learning to read people, to understand their own motivations and the premises on which they judge themselves and others. They are discerning conscience and trying to make out whether reason, social convention, passion, or something else may indeed be the foremost guide to human behavior. And for that they need no dance floor.

Marriage in Jane Austen's England: Some Context for the Courtships in *Sense and Sensibility*

Jennifer Overkamp
St. Gregory the Great Seminary

Jane Austen explores marriage in *Sense and Sensibility* by walking readers through a portrait gallery of different late eighteenth-century and early nineteenth-century attitudes toward marriage. We see a whole range of viewpoints, from the utterly mercenary (Lucy Steele and eventually Willoughby) to the deeply romantic (Marianne and Mrs. Dashwood), with the quietly practical (Edward and Elinor) somewhere in the middle. Throughout the novel Austen offers her assessment of each perspective. What modern readers may not realize, however, is that the simple binary that good marriages are for love and bad ones are for money was not so simple for Austen and her readers. While Austen shares our disgust of marriages based on self-interest, she would not necessarily recommend marriages centered on passionate romance. The successful marriages in *Sense and Sensibility*, as in her other novels, are those wherein spouses were selected for their personal characteristics (liveliness, intelligence, pleasantness, etc.) and their virtues (constancy, sweetness, honesty, etc.).

Throughout the history of Western civilization there have always been marriages for love, of course, particularly in the lower classes. But the words "make an offer" for proposing and "alliance" for marriage, which continued to be used during the nineteenth century, remind us that marriage for political, social, and financial reasons was also common and perfectly acceptable throughout most of history. After all, love matches had the potential, among other things, to upset the class hierarchy that was seen as crucial to the well-ordered functioning of society. Austen writes during a fascinating time in social history when the idea that marrying for money was morally wrong had gained cultural acceptance, but contrary ideas and practices had not gone away.

In order to appreciate Austen's masterpiece in its cultural context, we will first look at the changing attitudes toward marriage in the centuries before Austen wrote her novel. This summary will be followed by a description of contemporary rules surrounding engagements, which will be used to explore Georgian ideas about marriage. Finally, we will get to the heart of the matter: analyzing Austen's stand on marriage by considering the many and varied marriages in the book, evaluating each by the criteria of parental involvement in spousal selection and motives for marriage.

Marriage 101: A Brief History

According to social historian Lawrence Stone, there are four basic methods by which a society can arrange marriages. The parents (or kin, or friends) can arrange a marriage without the consent of the groom or the bride. The parents can arrange the marriage while the children retain the right to veto their parents' choice. The children can select their own spouses with their parents able to overrule their decision. Finally, the children can choose for themselves and then merely inform their parents whom they have chosen. As in present times, there were also many reasons why parents (or their children) might choose a particular spouse, ranging from social, political, and economic motives to wanting an heir, conforming to social expectations, or escaping from a restrictive home environment. A bride or groom might be seeking help running an existing business or raising children from a previous marriage. They also might seek a relationship with an emotional component such as companionship, friendship, romance, passion, or some combination thereof.[1]

The history of marriage in Europe is usually summarized thus: marriages used to be arranged, this custom gradually changed,

[1] Lawrence Stone, *The Family, Sex and Marriage in England 1500–1800* (New York: Harper and Row, 1977), pp. 270–71.

and now people choose for themselves based on love. The historical reality is a bit more complex. Certainly marriages arranged by parents for political, social, and economic reasons were common from the earliest civilizations all through the seventeenth and early eighteenth centuries. Such marriages happen today in many places in the world. However, even far back in history there were exceptions. For example, from biblical times we have the Song of Songs, which is, among other things, clearly the story of a chaste yet passionate romance between a couple about to be married. In the Middle Ages the idea of courtly love, which was prevalent among the upper classes, insisted that love could never exist within marriage because marriages were involuntary and love should be freely given. But there are hints, such as Chrétien de Troyes' *Erec and Enide* (ca. 1170) and the occasional homily about companionship within married life, which suggest that such attitudes toward marriage were not monolithic.[2] In the Renaissance, Shakespeare

---

[2] A few quotations are offered below to support this point. They are taken from my article "'Great Pleasure in Their Play': Chrétien, Augustine, and Medieval Marriage", *St. Austin Review*, November/December 2008, pp. 4–7, where interested readers may find more information on this topic.

St. Augustine (A.D. 354–430) describes the mutual support the spouses ought to have for each other thus: "This [the goodness of marriage] does not seem to me to be a good solely because of the procreation of children, but also because of the natural companionship between the two sexes.... In a good marriage, although one of many years, even if the ardor of youth has cooled between man and woman, the order of charity still flourishes between husband and wife (*The Good of Marriage*, trans. Charles T. Wilcox [New York: Fathers of the Church, 1955], p. 20).

Jacques de Virty (ca. 1160/70–1240) argued in one of his sermons that husbands "ought not to despise or ill treat their wives, but should have them as partners, in bed, at the table, and with respect to money, food and clothing" (quoted in Erik Kooper, "Loving the Unequal Equal: Medieval Theologians and Marital Affection", *The Olde Daunce: Love, Friendship, Sex, and Marriage in the Medieval World*, ed. Robert Edwards and Stephen Spector [Albany: State University of New York Press, 1991], p. 53).

Guibert de Tournai (1210–1284?), a Franciscan friar, wrote in one sermon, "There is also a kind of love founded on partnership, and this is the love which husband and wife owe to each other, because they are equal and partners" (quoted in Michael Sheehan, "*Maritalis Affectio* Revisited", *Olde Daunce*, Edwards and Spector, p. 42).

mocks arranged upper-class marriages in *Midsummer's Night's Dream* when he has Lysander tell Demetrius, who is supposed to marry the woman Lysander loves in a match arranged by their parents, "You have her father's love, Demetrius: Let me have Hermia's: do you marry him."[3]

These are just a few examples of exceptions to the prevailing ideology. Yet in general the decades preceding Austen's life are considered by social scholars to be the time of the cultural shift between marriages arranged by families for practical reasons and marriages chosen by couples for companionship. As Stone puts it, "A major transformation occurred in the eighteenth century, with the results ... of a marked rise in more companionate relationships between husband and wife after marriage."[4] But cultural change is usually neither swift nor sweeping, and whether or not companionate marriages were a welcome idea depended primarily on class: "There was a very marked contrast between mid-seventeenth-century patriarchy and late eighteenth-century Romanticism, and the result among the upper classes was confusion and a wide diversity of ideal models of behavior. Lower down the social scale, the contrast and the confusion were far less severe."[5] This diversity of ideas is one topic of *Sense and Sensibility*; Austen presents and comments on a range of matchmaking attitudes and strategies in the novel because there was a range of ideas in her society even while there was an overall tendency toward companionate marriages. So while we can find evidence from advice books and letters supporting an increased emphasis on compatibility in marriage, we also find evidence, albeit less of it, showing that some people supported the idea of companionate marriage earlier than the 1700s, and some people insisted on marriages of alliance even when the culture at large was starting to oppose them.[6] Even long after Austen's lifetime, plenty

[3] *Midsummer's Night's Dream*, Act I, scene 1, lines 93–94.

[4] Stone, *Family, Sex and Marriage*, p. 273.

[5] Ibid., p. 367.

[6] For example, "in 1645, Lord North was the first in English history to publicly take the extreme radical position, urging 'parents to leave their children full

of Victorians made purely practical matches despite decades of reading Romantic poetry and novels like those written by Austen herself.

What this more complicated and realistic paradigm means for readers of *Sense and Sensibility* is that even though by the time of its publication, novels and plays had long championed

---

freedom with their consent in so important a case'" (ibid., p. 274, quoting Dudley Lord North, *A Forest of Varieties*, vol. 2 [London, 1645], p. 141). Yet when Alice Wandesford described her marriage negotiations, which took place only a few years later in 1651, she wrote, "The bargain was struck betwixt them before my dear mother or myself ever heard of syllable of the matter ... in a case on which all the comfort of my life, or misery, depends" (*The Autobiography of Mrs. Alice Thorton* [Edinburgh: Blackwood, 1875], p. 61). She goes on to write that she thought it "a duty in me to accept my friends' desires" even though she preferred to remain single (ibid., p. 77).

In the next century one young lady declined a match, declaring, "I cannot for my life think him agreeable ... and I think that man and woman must run a great hazard of living miserably all their lives where there is not mutual inclination beforehand.... My Papa has left me entirely to choose which way I please in this affair" (Mary Banks, *The Letters and Papers of the Banks Family of Revesby Abbey: 1704–1760* [Hereford: Lincolnshire Record Society, 1952], p. 15).

Yet in the same year (1710) another young woman, an aristocrat, remarked, "People in my way are sold like slaves, and I cannot tell what price my master will put upon me" (*The Letters and Works of Lady Mary Wortley Montagu*, Lord Wharncliffe, ed., vol. 1 [London: Swan Sonnenschein, 1893], p. 174.) When she was later told of her arranged marriage to a man she detested, her father was surprised at her resistance and her relatives were not all sympathetic: "They found no necessity of loving; if I lived well with him, that was all that was required of me; and if I considered this town [London], I should find very few women in love with their husbands, and yet many happy" (ibid., p. 190).

By the time we come to Austen's lifetime we find more comments like the following, in 1776 from Lady Sarah Lennox, who said of an unhappy marriage that "he had no more business to marry a girl he did not like than she had to accept a man she was totally indifferent to" (*The Life and Letters of Lady Sarah Lennox 1745–1826*, vol. 1 [London: John Murray, 1901], p. 251).

Yet we still find quotes like this one from the 1780s from a recently engaged niece to her aunt: "I wish I could have known him a little better first, but my dear papa & mamma say that it will make them the happiest of creatures, and what would I not do to see them happy?" (Lady Harriet Spencer, quoted in *Lady Bessborough and Her Family Circle* [London: John Murray, 1941], p. 31). Austen herself owned an advice manual by the Marquise de Lambert (1647–1733), a well-born Frenchwoman, "which insisted on the point that young ladies should never experience love, which might interfere with their parents' marital plans for them" (Claire Tomalin, *Jane Austen: A Life* [New York: Knopf/Random House, 1997], p. 307).

companionate marriage, the questions of how one should choose a spouse and how involved one's parents should be are not settled. I am not suggesting that Austen is in any way radical by being scornful of her characters who opt for mercenary marriages. But her satire worked because the behavior being satirized still existed. Among other reasons, however appealing the ideal of marrying for companionship may have been, marriage still remained a middle- or upper-class woman's sole means of improving her financial and social position. It was also an easy way for an impoverished gentleman to enrich his coffers without work. During an era when men's and women's different spheres meant that husbands and wives could arrange to spend very little time together, the temptation to marry for money must have been great for both men and women.

The issue is also complicated by the fact that class mattered enormously in the process of choosing a spouse, just as it mattered enormously in practically every other area of life. The amount of freedom someone would have in picking a spouse would be much less at the very bottom and the very top of the social and economic scale.[7] Those desperately scraping by had to make choices based on economics, as did the extremely wealthy who had estates to safeguard.

The ordinary working class had been choosing spouses based on affection for much longer than their supposed betters. A girl working in a shop or a mill, or a farmer's daughter, would likely have much more freedom during courtship to get to know potential husbands, and, if she was a country girl, would probably choose from among young men she had known for many years.

The children of the overlapping middle, professional, and gentry classes to which Austen belonged would also have had significant freedom to select a spouse, if their families were free

[7] Mary Wollstonecraft correctly noted in a January 15, 1787, letter to a friend that "in many respects the great and the little vulgar resemble, and in none more than the motives which induce them to marry" (quoted in Eleanor Flexner, *Mary Wollstonecraft: A Biography* [New York: Coward, McCann and Geoghegan, 1972], p. 76).

of social ambition or financial pressures.[8] However, middle-class daughters and sons were subject to some constraints. Because work would oust a woman from the middle or upper classes, such a daughter would not have any earnings of her own, and the size of her dowry would be determined by factors beyond her control. She would probably have the opportunity to accept the husband of her choice, though, if he offered for her. All but the most odious of parents would grant her the privilege of rejecting a suitor she found distasteful or permitting the courtship of any suitable young man whom she favored.[9] She might have known her potential husbands since childhood. The exception to the latter point would have been those families who were wealthy enough (Austen's was not) to go to London for the Season of, among other things, husband hunting. During the Season it was perfectly common for a teenager to bind herself for life to someone she had known only a couple of months.

The situation of a son was no less determined by economics. An eldest son could not necessarily marry whom he pleased, because of his responsibility for the family social standing and because of the financial needs of the estate he would inherit. A younger son would have less income.[10] He could either earn

[8] Jane Austen's class sometimes confuses modern readers. Scholars tell us she was considered middle-class or lower-gentry, but we do not equate living in a large, comfortable house with servants and no need to work as middle class. But having servants, for example, while it is now a sign of great wealth, was a sign of middle-class status until the early twentieth century. In fact, it was one definition of being middle-class, and if any family could not afford at least one teenage maid of all work, that family automatically dropped into the lower class. While Austen sometimes would have had to supervise the housework or perform light chores such as making tea or shopping, she would not have had a job or any onerous household duties. Austen's family was not wealthy (and their financial fortunes rose and fell during her lifetime), but they were comfortable, and she was part of what we would call a leisure class.

[9] There was, however, the occasional odious parent. One eighteenth-century admiral locked his daughter in her room for two months, allowing her neither visitors nor pen and paper until her unwelcome suitor's ship had sailed (see Stone, *Family, Sex and Marriage*, p. 288).

[10] Families almost invariably left the bulk of their wealth to the eldest son, thereby consolidating and continuing the family's financial standing and influence.

additional money in one of the few professions he could enter without losing his status as a gentleman, marry a woman of fortune, or find someone content to accept his smaller income.[11]

The Rules of Engagement

An engagement was a much more important event in Austen's day than in our own. First, it was one of the few significant choices that a woman would make in her lifetime. Social norms and her husband's situation would determine where she lived, with whom she socialized, how or if she ran her household, and the way in which she and her staff would raise her children. She would have endless small choices in life, but few big ones. Second, an engagement was much more difficult to end then than it is now, especially for men. For a woman to break an engagement was a serious matter, and she could not do so very often without being labeled a jilt. But for a man to break an engagement was highly reprehensible. A respectable man simply did not do such a thing.

This cultural taboo helps explain why Edward does not end his engagement to Lucy, even though he clearly dreads their marriage. A type of legal suit called a breach-of-promise case also helps explain Edward's bind. Breach-of-promise cases were lawsuits brought by one party of a broken engagement against the person who refused to honor the agreement to marry. Usually, these lawsuits were brought by women against men, and usually the women had an advantage in court because of contemporary ideas about gender. The judge and jury knew that women were at a disadvantage during courtship because they could only respond and not initiate. A woman was also thought to be more emotionally vulnerable and more likely to be deeply wounded by her fiancé's rejection. In addition, men

[11] When the upper-class Edward Ferrars discusses possible remedies to his idleness, Austen lists professions that he could follow without losing his status as a gentleman. He could be a clergyman, soldier, sailor, or lawyer. (See Jane Austen, *Sense and Sensibility*, ed. Eleanor Bourg Nicholson, Ignatius Critical Editions [San Francisco: Ignatius Press, 2014], pp. 100–101. Subsequent quotations from this edition will be cited in the text.)

had more choices on the marriage market and were considered marriageable longer, so a long engagement not followed by marriage could truly be a disaster for a woman. If she was engaged, for example, from age twenty to twenty-six, by the time the engagement ended she would be much less able to attract a second suitor. With marriage as the primary option for her livelihood, this was a serious matter. Of course, there was also the idea that a gentleman ought to keep his word, especially to those who were thought inferior to him.[12]

Even if the threat of a breach-of-promise lawsuit is not a possibility in Edward's case, the ideas and cultural values that such lawsuits existed to defend remain in the background, unspoken. One contemporary lawyer indignantly described the behavior of a breach-of-promise defendant as "the injury of fixing a young woman's affections, and then trifling and flying off",[13] and that is exactly how society would view Edward if he attempted to end the engagement. Interestingly, Austen's emphasis on the importance of the character of a prospective spouse becomes clear when we learn that Edward had falsely presumed Lucy to be a "good-hearted girl" who loved him, and "[n]othing but such a persuasion could have prevented his putting an end to an engagement, which ... had been a continual source of disquiet and regret to him" (see p. 352). The shocking assertion that Edward would have broken his engagement had he known Lucy's true values shows Austen's firm conviction of the importance of character in choosing a spouse. Edward then explains that, since he did not know Lucy to be deceitful, he felt honor-bound to marry her if she wished him for a husband.

Now about this point a modern reader is probably plaintively protesting, "But he doesn't love her!" Despite the cultural emphasis on companionate marriage by the end of the eighteenth and beginning of the nineteenth centuries, not

---

[12] Ginger S. Frost, *Promises Broken: Courtship, Class, and Gender in Victorian England* (Charlottesville: University of Virginia Press, 1995), p. 40. (Despite the word "Victorian" in the title, Frost's research extends back as early as 1750.)

[13] Quoted in ibid., p. 15.

being in love with someone at all or anymore was simply not an acceptable reason for a man breaking an engagement.[14] Edward himself does not consider his own lack of love a valid reason either. Even though courtships during this era could be notoriously brief, that did not excuse the gentleman from keeping his word and marrying the lady if she still wished it. After studying 875 breach-of-promise cases, the historian Ginger Frost notes, "What was surprising was how many women still wanted to marry men whom they apparently did not even like, much less love."[15]

If the most important rule about engagements was that they were nearly unbreakable, the second most important rule was that they must be public. The question of who is going to marry whom was an important one. It mattered very much to the family, since they contracted an alliance as well as the couple. Any concealment was scandalous, almost as scandalous as an elopement. Among other problems, secret engagements removed or postponed the possibility of parental influence or veto.[16]

Once a couple was engaged, they were granted specific privileges, the most significant of which was probably that of correspondence. In Austen's day, letters were written much more frequently and were much more important than in our own. Correspondence granted a significant measure of privacy, even intimacy, to the couple. Therefore Elinor is convinced that Marianne is engaged to Willoughby because she writes to him. Lucy proves her engagement to Edward by showing Elinor letters from him.

The Good, the Bad, the Ugly:
Some of the Many Marriages in *Sense and Sensibility*

The marriages in the novel fall in different places along two important continuums: motives for marriage and parental/familial influence or control. Austen favors parental guidance

---

[14] Frost notes, "Even if it meant alienating family or enduring an unhappy union, a man was expected to fulfill his contracts" (ibid., p. 55).

[15] Ibid., p. 96.

[16] Ibid., p. 42.

but not coercion, and marriages based on esteem and compatibility, not money, social standing, or attraction.

In Austen's portrait gallery of marriages in the novel, there are plenty of frowning couples. Of all of the odd or unhappy marriages in the book, Lucy and Robert will probably have the worst, with the former marrying for money and position, and the latter to spite his family in general and his brother in particular. They are likely doomed to a lifetime of shared spite and snobbery alternating with quarrels. To show that they are not marrying with each other's character in mind, Austen provides two parallel scenes prior to their engagement when Lucy and Robert both disparage each other. When Elinor asks Lucy if she knows Robert, Lucy replies, "I never saw him; but I fancy he is very unlike his brother—silly and a great coxcomb" (see p. 144). Robert in turn describes Lucy as "[t]he merest awkward country girl, without style, or elegance, and almost without beauty" (see p. 290). Since their assessments are shallow but correct, it seems unlikely that either of them improved upon acquaintance prior to their marriage. Their union originates in her manipulation of his vanity:

> When Robert first sought her acquaintance, ... [h]e merely meant to persuade her to give up the engagement; and as there could be nothing to overcome but the affection of both, he naturally expected that one or two interviews would settle the matter. In that point, however, and that only, he erred;—for though Lucy soon gave him hopes that his eloquence would convince her in *time*, another visit, another conversation, was always wanted to produce this conviction.... Instead of talking of Edward, they came gradually to talk only of Robert,—a subject on which he had always more to say than on any other, and in which she soon betrayed an interest even equal to his own; and in short, it became speedily evident to both, that he had entirely supplanted his brother. He was proud of his conquest, proud of tricking Edward, and very proud of marrying privately without his mother's consent. (See p. 362.)

The second factor under consideration—parental manipulation of marriage choice—is absent by irony. Mrs. Ferrars has already given Robert the inheritance that was supposed to be

Edward's and thus deprived herself of her usual means of coercion. Her pride, anger, and self-indulgent hysterics (and Fanny's echo of them) are treated with caustic humor by Austen.

Mrs. Ferrars' attempt to coerce Edward into ending his first engagement still leaves him a choice; he can and does opt to continue his engagement to Lucy and reject the proffered match with Miss Moron, thereby losing his financial security. The only marriage in the book where a child was not given another option and instead was successfully forced to marry against her will happens, significantly, in the previous generation. The unwilling Eliza marries Colonel Brandon's brother, who breaks her heart and whom she abandons for another man. While we only read a brief description of it via Colonel Brandon, it is arguably the most disastrous marriage in all of Austen's novels because not only does it involve adultery, but it also produces a daughter who is in turn vulnerable and disgraced. Thus we see the depth of Austen's horror at a young woman being unable to avoid a marriage she despises, a marriage arranged entirely for the financial benefit of the groom's family.

Austen decisively rejects the idea of mercenary marriages. So what about romance? What happens to the couple who fall madly in love? In the beginning of the novel, Marianne seeks a soul mate, convinced that her high standards doom her to spinsterhood (see p. 18). Her qualifications are in keeping with the budding cult of Romanticism. When they meet, Willoughby carries the soaked-to-the-skin Marianne back to the cottage. Thus they have already shared, due to absolute necessity, far more physical contact than was usually granted unmarried couples. Even though Marianne is abashed by this circumstance (and she is not abashed by much, so her blushes tell us how *very* unconventional the situation is), it is no wonder being in Willoughby's arms sparks a deep attachment on her part. Willoughby soon falls as madly in love with her as she with him. But from the very beginning she does not properly evaluate his character:

[S]he had seen enough of him to join in all the admiration of the others, and with an energy which always adorned her praise. His person and air were equal to what her fancy had ever drawn for the hero of a favourite story; and in his carrying her into the house with so little previous formality, there was a rapidity of thought which particularly recommended the action to her. Every circumstance belonging to him was interesting. His name was good, his residence was in their favourite village, and she soon found out that of all manly dresses a shooting-jacket was the most becoming. Her imagination was busy, her reflections were pleasant, and the pain of a sprained ankle was disregarded. (See pp. 42–43.)

Marianne has just met Willoughby, and that might excuse her facile portrait. But Marianne clearly is not preparing to make any careful analysis of her favorite in the future. Elinor tries with humor to suggest that her sister ought to be attuned to more than just Willoughby's Romantic sensibilities, stating,

[F]or *one* morning I think you have done pretty well. You have already ascertained Mr. Willoughby's opinion in almost every matter of importance. You know what he thinks of Cowper and Scott; you are certain of his estimating their beauties as he ought, and you have received every assurance of his admiring Pope no more than is proper.... Another meeting will suffice to explain his sentiments on picturesque beauty, and second marriages, and then you can have nothing farther to ask. (See pp. 47–48.)

Marianne later declares, "It is not time or opportunity that is to determine intimacy;—it is disposition alone.... [O]f Willoughby my judgment has long been formed" (see pp. 58–59). Most readers, like Elinor, are not reassured.

Intense, romantic, passionate love is not high on Austen's list of reasons to get married. In fact, as is usual in Austen's novels, physical attraction or chemistry outside of marriage leads to disgrace in *Sense and Sensibility*, first for Eliza (the daughter of the fallen woman Eliza Brandon), whom Willoughby seduces, and second, to a lesser degree, for Marianne, whose public demand that Willoughby explain himself places her in a laughable position.

In the case of Marianne and Willoughby, Austen shows us parental influence being improperly neglected. Mrs. Dashwood delicately declines to interfere in Marianne's situation, stating that she cannot force a confidence from her. However, Mrs. Dashwood is responsible for teaching Marianne to preserve her reputation and guiding her in wisely choosing a husband. She neglects both of these duties, leaving Marianne open to a potential scandal, since her teenage judgment is not good. Mrs. Dashwood does not oppose Marianne's wishes, but neither does she advise.

Willoughby suffers from the opposite type of familial influence. His relative uses the power of her money to deprive Willoughby of any expectations, and he decides he cannot marry Marianne without them. Mrs. Smith's decision to cut him out of her will results in his engagement to Miss Grey. The situation is different than Mrs. Ferrars' disapproval of Lucy Steele. Mrs. Smith probably does not know anything about Marianne—she knows about Eliza, which is enough. She is not seeking to punish him for marrying one whom she disapproves of, but the influence on marital choice of relatives who offer or withhold money is clear. In the end, Willoughby marries for money. Austen does not doom him to perpetual misery, though: "He lived to exert, and frequently to enjoy himself. His wife was not always out of humour, nor his home always uncomfortable; and in his breed of horses and dogs, and in sporting of every kind, he found no inconsiderable degree of domestic felicity" (see p. 365). Perhaps this authorial mercy is because there is no deception in this match; Miss Grey accepts him for reasons of her own, but she has no delusions that he loves her.

Many readers find the elder Dashwood sister's courtship a pale, passionless one compared to the evident physical attraction between Marianne and Willoughby. Yet the marriage of Edward and Elinor is probably the most satisfactory one in the book, even if we catch only a glimpse of it. Austen assures us in the novel's final pages of Edward's "increasing attachment to his wife and his home" (see p. 363). However, prior to the engagement, there is little talk of love. Elinor esteems Edward. When she and Marianne discuss him, Elinor provides a rational assessment of Edward's abilities. She doesn't even seem particularly attracted to him, stating, "At present, I know him so well, that I think him really handsome; or, at least, almost so" (see p. 20), and notes that she is waiting to be certain of his feelings before committing hers. Elinor tells Marianne, "I am by no means assured of his regard for me. There are moments when the extent of it seems doubtful; and till his sentiments are fully known, you cannot wonder at my wishing to avoid any encouragement of my own partiality, by believing or calling it more than it is" (see p. 21).

Elinor's hesitation turns out to be prudent since Edward is engaged and unable to court her. In fact, the couple falls in love entirely without courting—the first time Elinor meets Edward when he is not engaged to Lucy is the afternoon when he proposes to her. This dearth of romance is replaced by something Austen considers much more valuable: Elinor's perception of Edward's character. Elinor's summary of Edward's good qualities shows readers what Austen considers valuable in a husband:

> Of his sense and his goodness ... no one can, I think, be in doubt, who has seen him often enough to engage him in unreserved conversation. The excellence of his understanding and his principles can be concealed only by that shyness which too often keeps him silent. You know enough of him to do justice to his solid worth.... I have seen a great deal of him, have studied his sentiments and heard his opinion on subjects of literature and taste; and, upon the whole, I venture to pronounce that his mind is well-informed, his enjoyment of books exceedingly great, his imagination lively, his observation just and correct, and his taste delicate and pure. His abilities in every respect improve as much upon acquaintance as his manners and person. At first sight, his address is certainly not striking; and his person can hardly be called handsome, till the expression of

his eyes, which are uncommonly good, and the general sweetness of his countenance, is perceived. (See p. 20.)

This calm evaluation is like that of a careful teacher, not a potential wife. But this thoughtful analysis shows that Elinor values enduring and morally significant traits in Edward. Her motive for considering him someone she would marry is high regard, which later becomes love. Elinor's sedate appraisal contrasts vividly with Marianne's enthusiastic appreciation of Willoughby quoted earlier, but a comparison shows that Marianne lacks the sense to focus on Willoughby's crucial qualities, just as Elinor's sensibility to romance is conspicuously absent.

Parental involvement becomes a hurdle for the young couple. Edward and Elinor become and remain engaged without approval from his mother. However, they cannot marry without some parental funding. Lord David Cecil's oft-quoted summary of Austen's attitude toward marriage and money fits: "It was wrong to marry for money, but it was silly to marry without it."[17] This tendency is not terribly romantic, but it is practical, and Austen approvingly narrates both how they waited until they could afford marriage and how little money they needed.

The final marriage in the book is between Marianne and Colonel Brandon, but for Marianne it is not a love affair at all. In fact, close readers of Austen often find how the match is described to be rather disturbing. She is to be his "reward", a word usually given to objects, and rather than wanting marriage, she "found herself ... submitting to new attachments" (see p. 364). Plus, a significant aspect of Colonel Brandon's love for Marianne is tied up in his love for the lost Eliza. By modern standards the match, more or less arranged for the bride by her friends and family, does not seem very promising!

However, Austen uses Mr. and Mrs. Brandon to argue that romantic love before marriage is not a prerequisite for a loving,

---

[17]Lord David Cecil, *Jane Austen* (Cambridge: Cambridge University Press, 1936), p. 33, as quoted in C. S. Lewis' *Selected Literary Essays*, ed. Walter Hooper (Cambridge: Cambridge University Press, 1969), p. 179.

happy union. She is clear that Marianne marries without love but with knowledge of and respect for her husband's character: "She was ... with no sentiment superior to strong esteem and lively friendship, voluntarily to give her hand" (see p. 364). Both Marianne and Colonel Brandon are honest and honorable, and they have had heartbreak enough to cherish the companionship of the other. The family and friends who have arranged this match recognize the compatible, though different, personalities and situations. Austen makes it clear that the marriage is a success:

> Colonel Brandon was now as happy, as all those who best loved him, believed he deserved to be;—in Marianne he was consoled for every past affliction;—her regard and her society restored his mind to animation, and his spirits to cheerfulness; and that Marianne found her own happiness in forming his, was equally the persuasion and delight of each observing friend. Marianne could never love by halves; and her whole heart became, in time, as much devoted to her husband, as it had once been to Willoughby. (See p. 364.)

Of course, in some ways Austen does not make the happy union of Colonel Brandon and Marianne believable. Marianne's fate is neatly wrapped up in a couple of paragraphs, without the courtship being depicted or even any dialogue between the future spouses. Most readers find the marriage contrived. It requires too dramatic a change in Marianne's principles, those principles which she has clung to tenaciously throughout the book. Granted, they have cost her dearly, and she certainly does rethink her ideals during her illness. But to change from believing that marriage should be between emotional and aesthetic soul mates to being content to marry out of friendship and gratitude seems too drastic. Nonetheless, if Austen the novelist cannot quite pull it off, Austen the observer of society has clearly conveyed her message. Edward and Elinor marry based on an enduring affection and esteem for the other's reliable qualities, such as intelligence and sweetness, an affection which has matured into love by the time of their wedding. Marianne and Colonel Brandon marry based on her affection and gratitude, and his middle-aged love. The novelist rewards both unions with happiness even though there is no passion or desire or chemistry to be detected.[18]

The purpose of *Sense and Sensibility* was primarily to explore how Marianne learned sense and Elinor gained sensibility. But it also gives us insight into Austen's ideas about how marriages should be formed. The novel was drafted and revised in Austen's teens and twenties, when the questions of how one should choose a spouse would have been particularly relevant to her. About those years when Austen was first entering the world of courtships and proposals, the historian Stone writes that while affection was considered important, "[a]lmost everyone agreed, however, that both physical desire and romantic love were unsafe bases for an enduring marriage, since both were violent mental disturbances which would inevitably be of only short duration."[19] He notes that "the eighteenth century thus firmly rejected the popular image of the twin bases of modern marriage."[20] In *Sense and Sensibility* Austen depicts and rejects mercenary social climbing and parentally dictated matches. She does not permit the one passionate romance to end in marriage. Instead, Austen suggests a union based on esteem, respect, and compatibility, tested by time and trials, as the best plan for a happy marriage. However beloved Jane Austen is by our age, she is much more a child of her own.

---

[18] Some readers might object that Austen would not have been able to portray any connection between the couples hinting at sexual desire, but considering that the novel has not one, but two, children conceived out of wedlock in tempestuous romances, she certainly is not ignoring the existence of powerful physical desire. She is arguing, instead, that it is an inadequate basis for a marriage. For more on Austen's ability to portray sexual desire and tension, see Juliet McMaster's *Austen on Love* published by the University of Victoria's English Literary Studies Monograph Series in 1978. McMaster summaries her thesis on page 7, arguing that Austen is "far from deficient in feeling.... [S]he is acutely awake to sex, and quite able to convey sexual feeling even though she may not take us into bedrooms."

[19] Stone, *Family, Sex and Marriage*, p. 272.

[20] Ibid., p. 281.

Marianne's Folly and the Rule of Propriety in Jane Austen's *Sense and Sensibility*

Jack Trotter
Trident College

Contemporary readers, especially those not well acquainted with Jane Austen's Georgian social milieu, are often puzzled by Elinor Dashwood's unyielding adherence to a code of propriety that at times seems designed to perpetuate her own social isolation and unhappiness. When she learns of her beloved Edward Ferrars' secret engagement to Lucy Steele—a knowledge thrust upon her by Lucy herself—Elinor never once thinks of betraying Lucy's secret, though she knows that Lucy is unworthy of Edward, and that Edward cannot possibly love Lucy. Surrounded by friends and family who all assume that she and Edward will eventually announce an engagement that she now knows to be an impossibility, Elinor, in spite of her powerful feelings of shock and disappointment, must wear a mask of calm and amiability. Even with her mother and her sister, Marianne, she refrains from sharing Lucy's uninvited confidence, though to do so would relieve Elinor of an emotional burden that is all but intolerable. Similarly, Edward, having become engaged to Lucy under the spell of an infatuation that has long since dissipated, refuses to break with her, though he knows all too well that his impending marriage will be an unhappy one.

Both Elinor and Edward remain true to their promises because to break them would be morally repugnant. Their sense of propriety is far more than a conventional matter of "keeping up appearances", though for many of the characters in *Sense and Sensibility*, it is little more than that, or worse—a cover for self-aggrandizement. What Elinor and Edward understand is that promises cannot be broken for the sake of merely personal advantage. Whether the recipient of the promise is "worthy"

449

or "unworthy" is not at issue. Every broken promise has, sooner or later, wider social consequences, dissolving in some measure those bonds of trust that make genuine human community possible, that make it something more than a Hobbesian "war of all against all". Austen understood that propriety is not merely an arbitrary and class-bound code of manners, but a product of the moral imagination and a school of Christian virtue. In *Sense and Sensibility*, it is Elinor's sister, Marianne, who must learn the necessity of submission to propriety, or what the Irish political theorist and philosopher Edmund Burke called the "soft collar of social esteem".[1] Following a pattern that is deeply rooted in Christian moral allegory, Marianne moves from the folly of "sensibility", through humiliation and suffering, toward a recognition of her error, followed by penitence and reconciliation.

For all of Austen's most admirable characters, propriety is rooted in a tradition of moral wisdom that has its origin in the Classical age, but which was profoundly shaped and spiritualized by centuries of Christian influence. This tradition, though it does not begin with Aristotle, finds its clearest pre-Christian expression in his ethics. As Alasdair MacIntyre has noted, for Aristotle, "Every activity, every inquiry, every practice aims at some good."[2] Moreover, mankind possesses a "nature" and is moved by that nature toward a telos, an end or goal that is at once particular (conditioned by one's existence in a given social milieu) and universal. In Aristotle's schema, the highest good for man is *eudaimonia*, or happiness. Yet, crucially, happiness cannot be achieved through pleasure or mere accumulation of worldly goods. Thus, Aristotle parts ways with one of the most influential pre-Socratic visions of the good, the Epicurean, which equates the good with pleasure and reduces ethics to a utilitarian calculus of pleasure seeking (which, to be fair, is not necessarily to be identified with mere hedonism).

[1] Edmund Burke, *Reflections on the Revolution in France*, 5th ed. (London: J. Dodsley, 1790), p. 114.

[2] Alasdair MacIntyre, *After Virtue: A Study in Moral Theory*, 2nd ed. (Notre Dame: University of Notre Dame Press, 1984), p. 148.

On the contrary, Aristotle refuses to separate happiness from the practice of the virtues, which "are dispositions not only to act in particular ways but also to feel in particular ways". Note, then, that to behave virtuously is not to eradicate desire or even to act against desire, but to act from "an inclination formed by the cultivation of the virtues".[3]

But how is such an inclination to act virtuously to be cultivated? According to Cicero, whose *De Officiis* (On Duties) was enormously influential in the Middle Ages, the handmaiden of virtue is "propriety" (Latin, *proprietas*). For Cicero the term does not yet indicate a code of manners or obligations, but it refers to that which is "fitting" or "appropriate" to the practice of particular virtues. One part of propriety, then, is its aesthetic dimension: "For just as the beauty of the body in which the members are rightly proportioned delights our eyes and pleases us because all the parts are charmingly symmetrical, so propriety, when it illumines a human life, is universally admired because of the orderliness, stability, and restraint with which it clothes every word and act."[4] This aesthetic dimension is, of course, much closer to what Austen would call "decorum" (or, in some cases, "elegance"), but she would probably agree that true propriety is always also decorous (just as she would say that there can be a false decorum that is concerned merely with appearances). But, more importantly, for Cicero and for the Christian moral tradition of the high Middle Ages, the primary part of propriety involves managing the passions. Thus temperance is a cardinal virtue for both Cicero and Saint Thomas Aquinas. And for both, the practice of temperance involves the subjection of the passions to the rule of reason "in conformity to Nature's decrees".[5]

"Nature's decrees", or what Aquinas (following Cicero) calls "lex naturalis", the law of nature, is fundamental to understanding how propriety can be more than merely an

[3] Ibid., p. 149.
[4] Marcus Tullius Cicero, *On Duties*, trans. Hubert M. Poteat (Chicago: University of Chicago Press, 1950), p. 500.
[5] Ibid., p. 501.

arbitrary, culture-bound set of rules. It is nature, argues Cicero, that "instructs us to guard our conduct in relations with our fellows".[6] Nature is a *teacher*, but its decrees are not, in the Christian view, always so easy to discern. Both Cicero and Aquinas agree that natural law is inscribed upon the soul, so to speak, but for Aquinas the capacity of reason to discern the good and the capacity of the *will* to act virtuously are both impaired by the reality of original sin. As Etienne Gilson writes, following Aquinas, "If man were a pure spirit, or if the body to which his soul is united were completely docile, he would only have to see what he should do in order to do it."[7] If in our prelapsarian state we were predisposed to act virtuously, then in our postlapsarian condition our disposition to choose the good must be inculcated by habit and assisted by reason, as well as, of course, by prayer, participation in the sacraments, the Commandments, and the examples of moral righteousness exhibited in Holy Scripture. But the habit of virtue must also be shaped and reinforced by custom—that is, by moral conventions (the proprieties) that, because they have survived the test of time, function as a touchstone of collective moral wisdom.

The moral tradition of which we have been speaking reached Austen primarily by way of Anglican Christianity.[8] Modern literary critics have generally failed to do justice to the Anglican influence in Austen's life and work. Frequently, her personal piety is cast into doubt, or it is treated as something altogether separate from the world of her novels, whose concerns are thought to be altogether secular. This view has been challenged most effectively by Laura Mooneyham White, who argues forcefully that if Austen's sense of "religious decorum" persuaded her that explicit appeals to religion should not be

[6] Ibid., p. 500.

[7] Etienne Gilson, *The Christian Philosophy of Thomas Aquinas*, trans. L.K. Shook, C.S.B. (Notre Dame: University of Notre Dame Press, 1994), p. 261.

[8] The most recent and best treatment of Austen's religious and philosophical influences can be found in Laura Mooneyham White, *Jane Austen's Anglicanism* (Burlington, Vt.: Ashgate Publishing, 2011). See especially chap. 3, "Austen and the Anglican Worldview", pp. 75–127.

imposed upon her readers, her moral concerns are nonetheless closely tied to her faith and are deeply but subtly woven into the thematic fabric of her works, especially for readers properly versed in the diction of Georgian religiosity.[9] Most importantly, Austen's Anglican tradition was still permeated by an almost medieval understanding of natural law as a divinely appointed rational order guiding and controlling every aspect of God's creation. Still widely read and influential in the first decades of the nineteenth century, for example, was Bishop Joseph Butler's *Analogy of Religion* (1736), which emphasizes the capacity of the human conscience to discern the "moral rule of action interwoven in our nature".[10] Although Butler does not speak directly about the role of propriety, he would no doubt have agreed with Adam Smith, who was himself influenced by Butler's *Analogy*, that the formation of conscience depends in part upon our adherence to "general rules of conduct". When one lacks a "sacred regard to general rules", Smith argues in his *Theory of Moral Sentiments* (1759), "there is no man whose conduct can be much depended on." Indeed, "[U]pon the tolerable observance of these duties, depends the very existence of human society, which would crumble into nothing if mankind were not generally impressed with a reverence for those important rules of conduct." This universal reverence, he adds, is "first impressed by nature".[11]

One might almost claim that the *necessity* of propriety is the central theme of *Sense and Sensibility*. The terms "propriety" and "impropriety" appear more frequently there than in any of Austen's works, with the exception of *Mansfield Park*,[12] and

[9] Ibid., pp. 64–65.

[10] Joseph Butler, *Analogy of Religion, Natural and Revealed, to the Constitution and Course of Nature*, ed. G.R. Crooks (New York: Harper and Brothers, 1860), p. 336.

[11] Adam Smith, *The Theory of Moral Sentiments*, ed. D.D. Raphael and A.L. Macfie (Indianapolis: Liberty Fund, 1984), p. 163. While Smith was a Deist, his reflections on morality were deeply influenced by the natural law tradition, especially via Greek and Roman Stoicism.

[12] The terms appear seventeen times in *Sense and Sensibility* and eighteen times in *Mansfield Park*.

its heroine, Elinor, is a paragon of those virtues most lauded by Cicero as the essence of propriety: temperance and self-restraint. But it is Marianne Dashwood, the misguided devotee of "sensibility", whose story occupies the heart of the novel. While Austen does not altogether reject the claims of sensibility, which are the claims of the heart, of feeling and intuition, she clearly mounts an attack in this novel upon what has been termed the "cult of sensibility". This exaltation of the affective realm of human experience is often traced to J. J. Rousseau, but it was already in the first half of the eighteenth century an aspect of the philosophies of the third Earl of Shaftesbury (Anthony Ashley Cooper) and Scot Frances Hutcheson, and it was popularized by "sentimental" novelists such as Samuel Richardson and Lawrence Sterne and by many other novelists and poets with whom Austen was familiar. For an Anglican traditionalist like Austen, sensibility in its most doctrinaire form was objectionable because it was—as Edmund Burke had recognized—a thinly disguised, modern Epicureanism that idealized the subjective realm of the passions, while denigrating or minimizing the claims of reason and revelation. As Peter Stanlis has noted, "To Burke sensibility [promoted] a vile philosophy of pleasure, power and will" covered in a patina of "moral feeling".[13]

Early in *Sense and Sensibility* we learn that Marianne is not without "sense" but that she is dominated by her feelings. Like her mother, "her sorrows, her joys, could have no moderation". At the death of Mr. Henry Dashwood, Marianne and Mrs. Dashwood are overwhelmed with grief, a perfectly natural response to the death of a beloved husband and father. But "[t]he agony of grief which overpowered them at first, was voluntarily renewed, was sought for, was created again and again."[14] For the devotees of sensibility, profound emotional display is evidence of profundity of soul. For those who seem

---

[13] Peter Stanlis, *Edmund Burke and the Natural Law* (Ann Arbor, Mich.: University of Michigan Press, 1958), p. 193.

[14] Jane Austen, *Sense and Sensibility*, ed. Eleanor Bourg Nicholson, Ignatius Critical Editions (San Francisco: Ignatius Press, 2014), p. 7. Subsequent quotations from this edition will be cited in the text.

emotionally deficient, Marianne has a barely concealed contempt. Of Edward she laments that "there is a something wanting.... His eyes want all that spirit, that fire, which at once announce virtue and intelligence." Even his attempts at reading aloud fall short of Marianne's high expectations, for his manner is "spiritless" and "tame" and without "sensibility" (see pp. 17–18). Note that Marianne here assumes that virtue can be discerned in another's character by purely aesthetic manifestations. For her the possession of fine feelings and exquisite taste is of greater value than simple kindness. She excuses her own rudeness to people like the Middletons and Mrs. Jennings— all of them kind but deficient in sensibility—on the grounds that private judgment is superior to the good opinion of others (see pp. 92–93). When Marianne performs for the first time on the piano at Barton Park, she is appalled at her audience's pretense at enjoyment. Her passion for music is wasted on them and their "shameless want of taste", though she is willing to grant that Colonel Brandon was more respectfully attentive and sincere in his expressions of admiration for her skill—even though his pleasure fell short of that "extatic delight which alone could sympathize with her own" (see p. 35).

When Marianne meets John Willoughby, it is almost immediately apparent that she has found one whose capacity for "extatic delight" is a match for hers. But Marianne's thinly veiled disdain for the claims of propriety (at least when they impinge upon her own pleasure) leads her into emotionally dangerous territory. That Marianne should be so instantly captivated by Willoughby is understandable: he is possessed of uncommon "manly beauty" (see p. 42) and a grace of deportment that is universally admired. Indeed, "[h]is person and air were equal to what her fancy had ever drawn for the hero of a favourite story" (see p. 42). Though very little is known to the Dashwoods of Willoughby's background or habits, Marianne's imagination works overtime (with the collusion of her mother) in concocting assurances of his quality, largely woven out of fancy and wishful thinking. Elinor knows, however, that "what Marianne and her mother conjectured one moment, they believed the next—that with them, to wish was to hope, and to hope was to expect" (see p. 21). Yet Marianne's hastily assumed expectations of Willoughby are not wholly groundless. On the contrary, his attentions to her and to her family are those one would expect of a man whose intentions are to propose marriage. Even so, Elinor is wary, and her concern grows as she observes him socially. She notices that, like Marianne, Willoughby is too inclined to express his mind, regardless of occasion or circumstance: "In hastily forming and giving his opinion of other people, in sacrificing general politeness ... and in slighting too easily the forms of worldly propriety, he displayed a want of caution which Elinor could not approve" (see p. 49).

This disregard for propriety, shared by both Marianne and Willoughby, becomes an even greater cause for concern as their intimacy grows. While Elinor has as yet no grounds for supposing that the attachment between them is objectionable, she does wish that "it were less openly shewn; and once or twice did venture to suggest the propriety of some self-command to Marianne." The younger sister's response to such suggestions is revealing. To conceal her feelings where no "real disgrace" might result seems to her "a disgraceful subjection ... to common-place and mistaken notions" (see p. 53). To the contemporary reader Elinor's concern that Willoughby and her sister are too open in their displays of affection may seem unnecessarily censorious. But it should be remembered just how easily in Austen's day the reputation of an unmarried woman might be tarnished by casual gossip, and how profoundly her future happiness rested upon her marrying well. As to Marianne's response to her sister's advice, we see once again that for her the claims of sensibility trump all other claims. To conceal her feelings would be a form of self-betrayal, for one's individuality is authenticated not by conformity to social codes and conventions ("common-place and mistaken notions") but by the spontaneous expression of feeling, which is assumed by the devotees of sensibility to arise unmediated from the "heart", that *fons et origo* of the true self.

It is not surprising, then, that when the Middletons arrange an outing to Whitwell, Marianne, prompted by a heartfelt confidence in Willoughby's integrity, throws off the reins of propriety and, without a word of explanation to the party, disappears with him. When it is later revealed that she and Willoughby spent the day at his family estate at Allenham, touring the house unchaperoned, Marianne becomes the object of a good deal of merry insinuation at the Middleton's supper table. Though no one is scandalized by the incident, Elinor feels it her duty to remind her sister of the impropriety of exposing herself to further "impertinent" gossip. In reply Marianne asserts that "if there had been any real impropriety in what I did, I should have been sensible of it at the time, for we always know when we are acting wrong, and with such a conviction I could have had no pleasure" (see p. 68). While Austen makes no authorial comment on this scene, the underlying irony is palpable. Just before the Middleton party embarks upon their outing, Elinor and Marianne learn the story of Miss Williams, Colonel Brandon's "natural daughter" (see p. 66), the very same Miss Williams who, as we learn later in the novel, has recently been seduced and abandoned by Willoughby. Thus Marianne's confidence in her own unaided ability to distinguish "real impropriety" from what is merely false and repressive convention is exposed as a dangerous delusion. Austen clearly suggests that the feelings alone are no infallible source of moral discernment.

The attentive reader will have surmised that much of Marianne's contempt for the "common-place" forms of propriety is rooted in simple pride. After Willoughby's abrupt and mysterious departure from Barton cottage, she becomes inconsolable, increasingly isolating herself from her friends and family. Though her affliction is real enough, Elinor suspects her of "feeding and encouraging" (see p. 77) it, as if her passion were too sublime to be subjected to the ordinary obligations of self-control. Inwardly, Marianne compares her own "affections" (see p. 102) with those of Elinor's, to the detriment of the latter: "The business of self-command she settled

very easily;—with strong affections it was impossible, with
calm ones it could have no merit" (see p. 102). Later, when
it becomes public knowledge that Willoughby is engaged,
Marianne insists upon leaving London at the earliest possible
moment, for she will not "endure the questions and remarks of
all these people. The Middletons and Palmers—how am I to
bear their pity? The pity of such a woman as Lady Middleton!"
(see p. 185). But Austen's anatomy of sensibility probes deeper
still. Marianne's prideful rebellion against the claims of propriety allows her unregulated feelings for Willoughby to exercise, ironically, a sort of tyranny over her will. In London she
becomes "restless and dissatisfied", indifferent to everything
but the prospect of encountering Willoughby: "Wherever
they went, she was evidently always on the watch ... [and] her
mind was equally abstracted from every thing actually before
them, from all that interested and occupied the others" (see
p. 159). When Willoughby fails to respond to her letters, she
clings pathetically to the illusion that he may, after all, be out
of town. Then, after the dreadful encounter with him at Lady
Middleton's party, while she is still unaware of his engagement
to Lady Grey, she further humiliates herself by writing a letter demanding an explanation of his conduct. By nineteenth-
century standards of propriety, as Elinor is well aware, such
demands are unwarranted. No matter how many "unsolicited
proofs of tenderness" (see p. 183) Willoughby may have given,
no formal avowals (as Marianne admits) were ever exchanged.
Even after it has become painfully clear to everyone else that
Willoughby has acted unconscionably, Marianne continues
to find excuses for his behavior. To do otherwise would be
to admit that somehow her own feelings had betrayed her. "I
could rather believe every creature of my acquaintance leagued
together to ruin me", she asserts, "than believe his nature capable of such cruelty" (see p. 183). Even as she proclaims that
a misery like hers "has no pride", it is apparent that her self-
flagellating insistence upon the uniqueness of her suffering is
itself another manifestation of pride: "[T]hey who suffer little
may be proud and independent as they like—may resist insult,

or return mortification—but I cannot. I must feel—I must be wretched" (see p. 184).

Marianne's awakening from the folly of excessive sensibility is driven by several factors. The first of these is her gradual recognition that Willoughby *has* in fact treated her dishonorably, and that recognition perforce leads to an understanding that the possession of an acute sensibility is not in itself a warranty of virtue. Just as importantly, Marianne is shocked to learn that, despite her earlier assumption that her sister lacked strong feelings, Elinor has been all along suffering just as much as she, yet restraining her feelings for the sake of others. Learning this, Marianne seems genuinely humiliated by her own selfishness (see p. 256). A third factor is Marianne's life-threatening illness, which appears to function as a metaphor for the purging of the poison of excessive sensibility. In any event, her recovery is clearly a turning point in Marianne's awakening. Elinor notices in her sister a new "composure of mind, which, in being the result ... of serious reflection, must eventually lead her to contentment and cheerfulness" (see p. 329). Indeed, Marianne resolves upon what she calls "a course of serious study" (see p. 331). For modern readers, the term "serious" signifies little more than sober moral reflection, but within the context of Austen's Anglican spiritual tradition, the word "serious" strongly suggests not simply moral but *religious* reflection.[15] What Austen is suggesting is that Marianne's suffering has led at once to a dawning recognition of the nature of her folly and to a renewal of faith through penitential devotion. "Contentment" is another key term here, because it is a hallmark of sensibility that it is never content, but always drawn from desire to desire, forever seeking more intense emotional and aesthetic stimulation. To have achieved some degree of

---

[15] See White, *Jane Austen's Anglicanism*, pp. 62–63. See also C.S. Lewis, "A Note on Jane Austen", in *Selected Literary Essays*, ed. Walter Hooper (Cambridge: Cambridge University Press, 1969), pp. 175–86. One of the key texts here that would almost certainly have been familiar to Austen was Anglican theologian William Law's *A Serious Call to a Devout and Holy Life* (1729), a devotional work that deeply influenced Samuel Johnson, as well.

contentment is to have achieved a measure of detachment from the passions.

Marianne's progress from folly to moral wisdom, indicated by her hard-won capacity for self-examination, is strikingly illustrated when, several days after the sisters return to Barton cottage, she is able to gaze dispassionately upon the place near the cottage where she first met Willoughby. "I am thankful", she says, "that I can look with so little pain on the spot!" She is clearly ashamed of the "unguarded affection" that has exposed her to so much pain and which might very well have been her undoing (see pp. 332–35). In one of the most overtly religious passages in the Austen canon, Marianne confesses that "serious recollection" has revealed her relations with Willoughby to have been "nothing but a series of imprudence towards myself, and want of kindness to others." She admits that her sufferings have been the result of her own unregulated feelings, implying that however wicked Willoughby's actions may have been, it is she herself who must assume primary responsibility. Even her illness, she avers, was the result of self-neglect, and, had she died, "it would have been self-destruction" (see p. 333). Marianne's mood here is clearly penitential: "I wonder at my recovery," she exclaims, "wonder that the very eagerness of my desire to live, to have time for atonement to my God … did not kill me at once." As the passage continues, she accuses herself bitterly of having been unjust to her friends—the Middletons, Mrs. Jennings, the Palmers, and others—and, above all, to Elinor herself. Furthermore, she avows her readiness to adopt a "plan" of moral improvement: "[M]y feelings shall be governed and my temper improved." She concedes that while she cannot obliterate the memory of her love for Willoughby, "[h]is remembrance … shall be regulated, it shall be checked by religion, by reason, by constant employment" (see pp. 333–35).

Certainly, it might be argued that there is a degree of self-dramatization in Marianne's confession and in her somewhat overzealous promise to Elinor to "share my affections" with no one other than her family: "From you, from my home, I shall never again have the smallest incitement to move; and if I do mix in other society it will be only to show that my spirit is humbled, my heart amended, and that I can practise the civilities, the lesser duties of life, with gentleness, and forbearance" (see p. 334). One can easily imagine Austen smiling as she penned this passage, but the satire is gentle and forgiving. After all, Marianne is still quite young, and her zeal for a life of almost cloistered virtue is surely understandable in view of her still raw feelings of mortification at her own moral failings. But her sincerity is genuine. If as yet she does not quite grasp that her desire to "practise the civilities, the lesser duties of life" must be disciplined by a greater duty—the duty to marry—that realization is just around the corner.

Austen's critics have sometimes expressed their impatience at her almost invariable practice of hastily marrying off her heroines in the concluding pages of her novels. But, as we have noted, marriage is the telos, the good that her heroines seek. No other end would be fitting or proper. One might say that, given the options available to women in Austen's England, the *propriety* of Austen's comic vision demands that her heroines not only marry but marry happily. In this respect her novels bear a striking resemblance to Shakespeare's great early comedies, where marriage so often signifies the renunciation of folly and the beginning of wisdom.[16] Marianne's union with Colonel Brandon is especially fitting. Like Marianne, he too acted unwisely in love at a young age and subsequently suffered from his folly, though, unlike Willoughby, he never for a moment abandoned his moral responsibilities. Moreover, in marrying Colonel Brandon, Marianne effectively renounces her dreams of an "irresistible passion" and takes her nuptial vows on the grounds of "strong esteem and lively friendship"— surely a striking proof of her new maturity (see p. 364). That she has renounced the delusions of sensibility is apparent when she says to Elinor, not long before her marriage, "I have nothing to regret—nothing but my own folly" (see p. 338).

[16] The best examples are *A Midsummer Night's Dream*, *Much Ado About Nothing*, *As You Like It*, and *Twelfth Night*.

CONTRIBUTORS

Raimund Borgmeier is professor emeritus of English Literature at the University of Giessen, Germany. He has been visiting professor of English at the University of Wisconsin in both Madison and Milwaukee. His research fields are Shakespeare, eighteenth-century and Romantic poetry and culture, special genres (science fiction and crime fiction), nineteenth century fiction, and contemporary literature. In 2000, he was honored with a Festschrift, *Lineages of the Novel: Essays in Honour of R.B.*, eds. B. Reitz and E. Voigts-Virchow.

Crystal Downing received her Ph.D. from the University of California, Santa Barbara and is Distinguished Professor of English and Film Studies at Messiah College in Pennsylvania, where she teaches Austen in both her British Romanticism and Film Adaptation courses. Her three books explore the relationship between Christianity and poststructuralism: *Writing Performances* (2004); *How Postmodernism Serves* (My) Faith (2006); and *Changing Signs of Truth* (2012).

Mitchell Kalpakgian earned degrees from Bowdoin College (B.A.), the University of Kansas (M.A.), and the University of Iowa (Ph.D.). He has completed fifty years of teaching at a number of small liberal arts colleges including Simpson College (Iowa), Christendom College (Virginia), and Wyoming Catholic College. He currently teaches part-time at various schools and colleges in New Hampshire (Thomas More College, The College of Saint Mary Magdalen, Mount Royal Academy, and New England Classical Academy). He is a contributing editor of *New Oxford Review*, writes for *St. Austin*

Review and *Homiletic and Pastoral Review*, and reviews books for *The Wanderer*. He has published six books: *The Marvelous in Fielding's Novels*, *The Mysteries of Life in Children's Literature*, *The Lost Arts of Modern Civilization*, *An Armenian Family Reunion*, *Modern Manners: The Poetry of Conduct and The Virtue of Civility*, and *The Virtues We Need Again*. He has designed homeschooling literature courses for Seton Home School, and he also teaches online courses for Queen of Heaven Academy. He has written online columns for The Seton Magazine (www.setonmagazine.com), Truth and Charity Forum (www .truthandcharityforum.org), and The Civilized Reader (www .thecivilizedreader.com).

Theresa Kenney is the former chair of the English Department at the University of Dallas, editor and translator of *Women Are Not Human: A Renaissance Treatise and Responses*, co-editor of and contributor to *The Christ Child in Medieval Culture: Alpha es et O!* Her research is in three main fields: the Christ Child in Medieval and Early Modern culture, Seventeenth century poetry, especially that of John Donne, and the nineteenth century novelists, especially Jane Austen and Charles Dickens. She has published essays on these authors as well as Dante and Robert Southwell.

Eleanor Bourg Nicholson is the assistant executive editor for *Dappled Things* and assistant editor for the *Saint Austin Review* (StAR). She is editor of the Ignatius Critical Editions of *Mansfield Park* (2010), *Dracula* (2011), and *Sense and Sensibility* (2014), and has collaborated with other editors to provide footnotes for numerous other ICE volumes. Her epistolary novella, *The Letters of Magdalen Montague* (2011) is available through the kind patronage of Kaufmann Publishing. Her work has appeared in the *National Catholic Register* and *Touchstone*, as well as with *First Things* and *The Catholic Thing*. She and her husband, Professor Sam Nicholson, live in Charlottesville, Virginia, with their daughters, Beatrice and Veronica.

Jennifer R. Overkamp received her Ph.D. from the University of Nebraska and is an Instructor in the English Department at St. Gregory the Great Seminary in Seward, Nebraska. She wrote her dissertation on the fairy tales of George MacDonald, G. K. Chesterton, and C. S. Lewis. Her scholarly interests include nineteenth-century British novels, teaching Shakespeare through performance, and the epistemological claims of Christian fantasy.

Jack Trotter has a Ph.D. in medieval and Renaissance literature from Vanderbilt University (1995). He has published numerous essays on Shakespearean drama and, more recently, nineteenth-century literature. He also publishes frequently in *Chronicles: A Magazine of American Culture.*